FOREVER
SHIP

Francesca Haig grew up in Tasmania, gained her PhD from the University of Melbourne, and was a senior lecturer at the University of Chester. Her poetry has been published in literary journals and anthologies in both Australia and England, and her first collection of poetry, *Bodies of Water*, was published in 2006. In 2010 she was awarded a Hawthornden Fellowship. She lives in London with her husband and son.

www.francescahaig.com

@FrancescaHaig

Also by FRANCESCA HAIG

The Fire Sermon
The Map of Bones

The FOREVER SHIP

FRANCESCA HAIG

Harper*Voyager*
an imprint of HarperCollins*Publishers* Ltd
1 London Bridge Street
London SE1 9GF

www.harpercollins.co.uk

First published by HarperCollins*Publishers* 2017

This paperback edition 2018
1

A catalogue record for this book is available from the British Library

ISBN: 978-0-00-756316-6

Set in Janson Text
Typeset by Palimpsest Book Production Ltd, Falkirk, Stirlingshire

Printed and bound in Great Britain by
CPI Group (UK) Ltd, Croydon CR0 4YY

MIX
Paper from
responsible sources
FSC™ C007454

This book is produced from independently certified FSC™ paper
to ensure responsible forest management.

For more information visit: www.harpercollins.co.uk/green

This book is dedicated to Paul de Tores,
braver and funnier than any character from a book.

PROLOGUE

And so it did end in fire, after all: the flame bursting from its white centre. The blast opening like an eye. I'd seen that shape in my visions so many times that the explosion felt like coming home.

*

The water sealed over the boat's wake, erasing all trace of us. The sea had always been good at keeping secrets.

There was a song that bards used to sing, about ghosts. I'd heard it when Zach and I were children. Leonard and Eva had sung it, too, the night we met them. In the song, a man had strangled his lover and then been haunted by her ghost. He'd fled across the river to escape her, because ghosts can't travel over water.

As I sat in the prow of the boat, I knew better.

PART 1

CHAPTER 1

'Stop looking at me like that,' Paloma said.

'Like what?' I said.

I turned my face back to the fire, squinting against the smoke. I couldn't deny that I'd been staring. I watched her all the time. Sometimes I woke and half expected that she would be gone – that she had never come at all, or that she'd been nothing but a shape we had conjured out of our longing for Elsewhere.

But she had come: pale, like somebody seen through mist. Not the blondeness of Crispin, or of Elsa, who had hair with gold in it, and pink-flushed skin. Paloma's hair was so blonde it was nearly grey, like driftwood – as if she'd washed up on the beach instead of sailing here on *The Rosalind*. Her skin had a bleached-straw whiteness, and her eyes were light blue – barely a colour at all.

'Like I'm some kind of ghost,' Paloma said. She leaned forward to prod the fire.

I met her eyes. 'Sorry.'

She swept her hand in the air, brushing away my apology. 'It's not your fault. You all do it.'

She was right. After we'd found *The Rosalind*, in the few days I'd spent aboard I'd seen how even the sailors who'd travelled with Paloma for months still paused in their conversations when she passed them on the deck, and followed her movements from the corners of their eyes as they worked on the ship's repairs. Piper and Zoe stared at her too. And since we'd left the ship, and headed inland towards New Hobart, I found myself watching her all the time. She was a rumour made flesh. A person from Elsewhere. A person without a twin. Both of those ideas were so outlandish that it felt strange, sometimes, to see her picking out fish bones that had stuck between her teeth, or trimming her fingernails with her dagger. These were everyday things, and I wasn't prepared for her to be so real.

'We're just curious,' I said.

'I know,' she said, her accent making unfamiliar shapes from the familiar words.

She had her own curiosity, too. As we spoke she stared at Piper and Zoe. A short distance from the fire, they were patching a water flask, using a glue that Zoe had made by rendering pine resin over the fire until the whole clearing was sharp with the stink of pine pitch. Paloma watched as Zoe stretched the leather of the flask flat on the ground, while Piper applied the patch.

'When I see those two together—' she gestured to Piper and Zoe '—it's like something from a bard's song come to life. An old story, so old you can't be sure it was ever real.'

We were sitting together on the ground, close to the fire, looking at each other across a gulf that was wider than the miles of sea that lay between here and her homeland. Untwinned and twinned, each of us had stepped out of the other's myth.

The first days of our journey inland had been hard, the

snow thick on the mountain passes and turning to grey slush as we descended. Now the Spine Mountains were behind us, the snow had sunk into the ground. The days were starting earlier, and at night the sun refused to go down, lurking for hours on the horizon before sinking beyond the mountains in a red haze. Spring was coming.

When I was a child, I used to long for spring. It meant an end to the cold, and to the annual floods that swallowed the low-lying fields. It meant summer was nearly here: there would be swimming in the river with Zach, and long days out of the house, and away from the scrutiny of our parents.

Now, though, there were so many changes, so quickly. The tanks. The bomb. Elsewhere. Paloma. This spring's dawning – wildflowers returning colour to the land, thistles forcing their prickly stalks above the earth – brought with it only fear of what would follow.

Paloma was still watching Zoe and Piper.

'My grandmother claimed to have seen twins,' Paloma said.

'In Elsewhere?' I asked.

'It's not called Elsewhere,' she snapped. She'd already corrected me several times – I knew that in her homeland they called it the Scattered Islands – but it was hard to adjust a lifetime of habit. 'Anyway,' she went on, 'nobody's had a twin there for hundreds of years. Except for way off on some of the Northern Isles. Our expeditions only found them a century ago, so they didn't get the treatment until then. There are people from there who say they can remember twins. My grandmother was born up there. She said her mother had a twin. But I don't even know if that's true.' She gave a small shrug. 'My grandmother was always a bit of a storyteller.'

*

There were only the four of us now, heading south-east towards New Hobart: me, Piper, Zoe and Paloma. Thomas and his crew had remained on the coast with *The Rosalind*, to continue the repairs and to keep her away from the Council fleet's patrols.

Each night, around the fire, we brought our questions to Paloma, like offerings. She did her best to answer, but whenever we asked her about how they ended the twinning, she ran out of words.

'I don't know the details of how it works,' she said. 'The doctors are in charge of all of that stuff. Nobody else is allowed to deal with it. The doctors come around and give out the medicine: an injection for all new babies, and a booster at twelve for anyone on the outer islands, where the radiation's worse.'

'And here we are—' she looked down at her right leg, missing from just below the knee '—all of us, with something like this. No more twins. And nobody like you.' She gestured to Zoe. There was naked curiosity in her eyes as she stared at Zoe, and her unmarred body, Alpha. The end of the twinning came with a price, as the dwellers of Elsewhere and the Ark had discovered. Without the twins, every single person shared in the mutations brought about by the blast. No more of the intact bodies that the Alphas prized above all.

Paloma spoke of Elsewhere's doctors in the same way that many here spoke of the Council: with a mixture of awe and fear. 'There isn't a central government – just a loose confederacy of councils from the different islands. But all the islands get the medicine from the doctors on Blackwater. And I think even the Confederacy obeys the doctors, really. They're the ones who ended the plague of twins, and keep it from coming back.'

'And other machines?' Piper asked. 'The Electric?'

She shook her head. 'We had purges, too, like you did here.' We'd told her about the taboo: the fear that had grown out of the blast, as surely as the mutations of the survivors' bodies. We knew little about the blast, but we knew that it had been created by machines. Those few machines that survived the blast were destroyed in the purges. Even now, four hundred years later, people shuddered away from any remnants of machines from the Before.

'At home,' Paloma continued, 'they call it the Scouring. All the machines that couldn't heal us, or serve us – that was the law. Most of it was gone already, in the blast, or went to ruin without the power. They ran on fuel that we don't have. People used to dig it from the earth – a kind of oil. But in the blast . . .' She shrugged and raised both hands, empty. 'Everything that could burn, burned. The oilfields kept burning for more than eight years. And there's a coal seam north of Blackwater that they say burned underground for more than fifty. They say there was nothing they could do to stop it.'

'And now?' Piper said.

'There's not a lot of machines left. The comms machines stopped working a long time ago. Maybe the Confederacy didn't bother to keep them going – not after centuries of transmitting messages, and hearing nothing back. The only ones who have machines these days are the doctors. They work on things like this—' she looked again at her leg, the false limb neat in its socket. 'And they do what they can against the plagues that come most winters.'

'How many people are there, living in Elsewhere?' Zoe asked.

'Counting the Northern Isles? About a million. Hard to know exactly. Like I said, it's hundreds of islands, some of them days' sailing from Blackwater – and for the Northern Isles or the Southern Archipelago it's a voyage lasting weeks.'

She tugged the blanket that we were sharing a little closer to her side, and leaned forward to take off her false leg. It unfastened just below her knee with a firm click. Her trousers were rolled to her knees, and the tip of a pole protruded through the skin, like a steel bone emerging from the flesh, onto which the false leg fitted. There was scarring around the pole, but not the thick battle-scarring of Piper's arm and hand; instead, it was a neat line, pink on her white flesh. The scar wasn't raised; so smooth that if you ran a finger over it, I doubted that you would be able to feel it. It made me think of Kip, and how cunningly his scar had been hidden, so that even my curious hands had never discovered it.

The first few times Paloma had taken her leg off, and laid it near her on the ground, I'd found it disconcerting. I'd seen limbs severed before, and the sight of the leg tossed onto the ground made me wince at memories of the battle on the island, or of the wreckage of bodies in the snow outside New Hobart. But there was a sterile neatness to her false leg: no blood, no hair, no toenails. Just the precisely contoured surface.

She saw me looking at it. 'You can touch it. I don't mind.'

I leaned forward and picked it up. It looked like flesh but was hard and cold to the touch. It was lighter, too, than flesh would be.

'Does it hurt?' I asked, looking at the steel pole below her knee.

'No,' she said. 'It did when they fitted it. It was a big operation. My parents took me to Blackwater, where the doctors are. We knew there were risks. But it's been worth it. I can walk more easily. The old false leg, the one I used to strap on, used to hurt me. I'd get ulcers here—' she touched the end of her stump.

It felt strange holding her limb. If I were to toss it on the fire she would feel nothing. It was less a part of her than Zach's body was a part of mine.

*

That night I dreamed of him. Zach stood facing me. It was dark, barely light enough to see, so I reached out a hand to his face. When I trailed my thumb across his forehead, I felt a burn: a blistered shape, hot and fat with fluid, precisely where my own brand sat. I could smell the cooked flesh.

'It hurts,' he said, flinching from my touch.

'I know,' I said.

I woke, my hand on my forehead, where the Omega brand had left its mark, a puckered, pinking scar. I could still remember how it had felt, the day that Zach had finally exposed me as the Omega twin, and watched me being branded. In the twenty-something years of my life, I'd learned a little of the vocabulary of pain. The pain of a burn has a unique urgency, the whole body recoiling against it, the same way a finger jerks back from a hot skillet. When I remembered the branding, I could still feel the Councilman's hand on my neck, holding me in place as he forced the brand against my forehead.

All through that day's travelling, I thought of Zach, and the brand he had worn in my dream. It had felt so real – I could feel the blister's texture under my fingertips.

'Better than your usual nightmares, at least,' Zoe said, when I told her what I'd dreamed. 'Zach being branded makes a nice change from the end of the world.'

I laughed, but I knew that the two were connected: Zach's branded face, and the blast he was trying to unleash.

*

When Paloma talked of Elsewhere, there was so much that I couldn't recognise. The twinless people. The scattering of islands, spread over hundreds of miles. The mysterious doctors, and their medicines. But there was one thing that was all too familiar: the blast.

She didn't call it that – instead, she called it *the bomb.* But she spoke of it in the same way that it was spoken of here: the same silences, and the same gaps, where words faltered on the brink of the flames.

'It wasn't just the fire,' she said. 'It was the force of the explosion – that's what they say. Entire islands just disappeared: the bomb shattered them. My mum showed me an old map – there are whole islands on it that just aren't there now.'

The bomb had made the map into nothing but a story: a careful rendering of islands that didn't exist any more. Merely outlines on paper, meaning nothing in our scorched world.

'They say that there was a wave, afterwards,' she said. 'So high that any low-lying islands that had survived the bomb were swept clean. Nothing left at all.' She exhaled slowly. 'Imagine that: surviving the bomb somehow, and thinking that you might be OK, and then seeing the sea coming for you.'

She was quiet for a few moments.

'Some survived both, though – the fire and the water. Not many, and for years it was nearly impossible to keep going. Not just the darkness, and the lack of food – all the babies were horribly sick. Even if they managed to live, they could barely walk when they grew up, let alone farm, or fish. And all the fish were dead, anyway. For months after the bomb, and after the wave, the dead fish were washing up. Piles of them, rotting on the beaches, and floating in the shallows.' She gave a short laugh. 'It's funny – in all the stories that come down to us, that's one of the things they always mention: the stink of all those fish. You'd think, after the bomb and the wave and everything that had happened, that somehow it wouldn't matter – but so many of the stories mention it. How the world stank of dead fish, for months.'

Paloma told us stories of how, when the fish finally came back, they'd changed. They had bulbous growths on them, or more fins, more eyes. Some that had been striped or silver were pure white after the blast, as if even underwater they'd been bleached by the flash of the bomb.

And on land, too, the children were born into new bodies, in shapes that their parents didn't recognise. Babies who looked half-formed, and refused to live. Then came what Paloma called the plague of twins: the doubling, the flawless babies paired with those who carried the burden of the mutations. The ones who were born together, and died together.

'Nobody could believe it, at first,' she said. 'Even when they knew it was real, nobody fully understood how it worked, despite all the doctors' research. But it only lasted a few generations. Then the doctors found a way to treat it, eventually, and it was over: no more twins.' She spread her hands wide. 'Finished.' It seemed such a casual thing – a single word, to describe the end of everything that we knew.

Late into each night, we swapped stories; we told her about the deadlands, the stretch of land to the east, where nothing grows, and nothing moves but lizards and the drifts of ash. She told us about a place called the strike zone, an area to the south-east of Blackwater, where most of the islands had disappeared altogether. 'And not even the birds will land on the few islands that are still there,' she said. 'On the Southern Archipelago, closest to the strike zone, the mutations are worse than anywhere else. Some of them can't have children, even after the injections.'

'Have you ever been there?' Zoe said. 'To the strike zone?'

Paloma shook her head. 'But my father anchored off there once, when he went out that way, crewing on a seadoghunting ship. There were no fish in the water around it, and an oily sheen to the surface. Dad and the others rowed ashore for a few hours, just to look. In the south of the island there was a crater, miles and miles wide. He said it might have been a dried-up lake, or it might be from where a bomb hit. The ground was covered with grey sand.

'He brought back a handful of it, in a jar, to show us. Mum said it was disgusting, made him throw it out before it frightened me and my sisters. But I went through the bin, that night, and found the jar. There was a tooth in it, and tiny pieces that might have been stone, or bone.'

*

Despite the hush in her voice when she told us stories of the strike zone, of the wave and the fire, Paloma nonetheless spoke of the blast as something long gone. It had been six days since we'd left the coast to head towards New Hobart, but our warnings about the Council, and the blast machine that they had dug up from the Ark, didn't seem to have penetrated.

'She still doesn't understand,' I said to Zoe and Piper. We were whispering, drawn apart from the fire where Paloma was resting. 'She asked again, yesterday. She still wants to try to set up a meeting with the Council.'

Zoe rolled her eyes. 'Might as well tie a bow around herself, if she wants to hand them Elsewhere like a gift.'

There was a sound in the scrub behind Zoe. She jumped, spinning away from me, a knife already drawn. Piper had echoed her movement, pushing me behind a tree as he crouched next to Zoe, knife raised.

Paloma gave a yelp, raising her hands as she stepped out of the cover of the trees.

Zoe stepped back, slipping her knife back into her belt.

'Be careful creeping around like that,' she said quietly. 'You didn't come all the way across the sea just to get yourself skewered.'

'I heard what you were saying,' Paloma said. Her chin was tilted at a bold angle, but her hands were clenched to stop their shaking. 'I'm not an idiot.'

'Nobody said you were,' said Zoe. 'But you need to understand what you're dealing with.'

'I'm not afraid of your Council,' she insisted.

'You should be,' Piper said.

'Let me meet with them,' Paloma said. 'If I explain the trade terms that the Confederacy's willing to negotiate, they'll see the benefits.'

'You're not listening,' Zoe said. 'The Council will—'

'I'm an emissary,' interrupted Paloma. 'Empowered by the Confederacy to make contact, establish terms for trading negotiations and mutual cooperation.' Her voice grew faster and higher, as she repeated herself. 'I'm an emissary, on a peaceful expedition.'

'Not here, you're not,' I said. 'Here, you're the enemy.

They'll hunt you down.' I had known Zach since birth, but even I was afraid of what he had become. And I had seen how much he feared The General, who ruled the Council. Together, with the blast in their power, they would have no mercy towards Elsewhere. There was no *if* or *perhaps* or *maybe* about the flames that I'd seen in my visions. They were real, and they were coming.

I hadn't thought it possible for Paloma to grow more pale, but now her lips seemed blue-tinged, the freckles standing out more conspicuously on her white face.

Piper threw down his dagger. He lifted his shirt, pulling it over his head and tossing it to the ground beside the knife.

'Look,' he said, turning his back on Paloma. He reached his single arm across his body to point over his left shoulder. There, on the brown skin below his shoulder blade, was a cluster of horizontal scars, white and raised. I had seen them before, during the months of travelling together, hunching together over streams to wash, but Piper wore so many scars that I hadn't noted these ones in particular. I stared along with Paloma: these scars weren't like the skirmish of scars on his hand and arm, or the nicks and scratches on his face. They were faded, and unlike the jagged slash that striped his shoulder, they had a uniformity to them, all of them parallel, perfectly straight.

'That was a whipping I got when I was eight,' he said. 'A patrol came through our village, and Zoe and I had been playing a game with a few of the other kids. There was a song we used to sing: *Jack was strong and Jack was brave—*'

Zoe joined in, speaking the next words with him:

'*He sailed away to Elsewhere, across the mighty waves.*'

'It was just a kids' song,' Piper said. 'But the soldiers heard it, and made an example of me. Of course it was me they chose. Even out east, back then, when it wasn't so unusual to be split late, they were always going to pick the Omega for the whipping. I got ten strokes.'

I saw Zoe's jaw tighten at the memory of their shared pain.

'That was just for a mention of Elsewhere in a kids' song,' Piper said again. He picked up and pulled on his shirt, eyes fixed on Paloma. 'If they find Elsewhere, they will have no mercy. Do you really think they'll leave Elsewhere in peace, when they know what your medicines can do?'

'You don't know what the Council is like,' said Zoe, stepping closer to Paloma and speaking in a voice that was gentler than I was used to hearing from her. 'No matter what you do, or what you offer them, they'll see Elsewhere's very existence as a threat.'

Zoe was right. Elsewhere was everything that the Alphas feared. I had seen how our mutations repulsed them – heard the cries of *freak* and felt their spittle on my skin. I knew how hard they would fight to defend their own unmarred bodies. They ruled because they thought they were better than us. They were perfect, and we were broken, reflections in a warped mirror. That was how they saw it. To take away that difference, and their perfection, undermined everything they stood for. Especially now that they'd discovered how to eliminate the risks of the fatal bond: Omegas preserved in the Council's tanks, trapped indefinitely in a hellish half-life, until each Alpha's own life had run its course.

'Even if we could put you on a boat tomorrow, and if Elsewhere never helped us – never shared the cure, or sought us out again,' Zoe said, 'the Council will keep seeking. They found the message from Elsewhere in the Ark. They know Elsewhere exists, and that it has the technology to end the twinning. We found you. Sooner or later, they will too. And they'll destroy you all.'

Paloma had expected to return home at some point with news, a message. What message could she carry now, even if we could get her safely home? The only message that counted now was Xander's warning: *Forever fire*.

'Even if we had a ship fit for the journey,' Piper said, 'we can't take you back, or warn Elsewhere, until the weather clears – you've seen for yourself what the storms are like.'

I saw Paloma's lips tighten. She'd never discussed the storm that had almost sunk *The Rosalind*. But I'd seen the chunks hewn from the ship's hull, and I knew that Paloma's fellow emissary from Elsewhere had died, as well as two of Thomas's sailors. There was a reason it had taken this long for contact to be made with Elsewhere: the sea didn't deal in mercy. Zoe's partner Lucia, too, had been lost to a storm, years earlier.

Piper went on, relentless. 'Not to mention the ice sheets further north. And the spring northerlies would mean slow progress, battling the winds the whole way. Early summer will give us the best chance.'

'We can't force you to stay,' I said to her. 'Nor to try to help us. If you want to go, we'll do our best to protect you until we can get a ship ready. Nobody would blame you, if you wanted just to go back, and forget everything you've learned here.'

'Even if I wanted to run away,' Paloma said, 'it won't make a difference.' Her voice cracked. 'There were forty of us on our ship when we spotted *The Rosalind* in the spit. Caleb and I were the ones chosen to come aboard as emissaries, but our captain and all the crew know where you are. Thomas gave them the coordinates. The Confederacy will send ships.'

She swallowed before she went on. 'We spent two days moored alongside *The Rosalind* while her crew refilled their water barrels at a lake on the largest outcrop, and Thomas told us about the situation here: the twins; the Council; the Omegas. My captain, Rue, and her ship will have brought the news back to the Confederacy.'

The Rosalind's mast, spotted in the distance amongst the uninhabited and bleak islands of a spit. Maps and words exchanged on a stony shore. Such a small thing, to change the shape of the world. But it couldn't be undone.

'They'll have to wait until the ice sheets melt,' Paloma said, 'before they can send ships south. But they will come, and the spring winds will be with them, not against them. They're coming. A ship, or a fleet. Maybe forty people, maybe hundreds. They might not all make it, but they won't let it go, now that they know what's here.'

For so long, that had been a fantasy: that ships from some distant place might reach our shores. Now it was the nightmare. They would come to us, and their world would burn.

'Why will they be so keen to come?' I asked.

She looked down, shaking her head.

'You assumed we could help you. Maybe you were right – we can do some things that you can't. But we're not some magical haven. We have our own problems. Plagues that pass through, most summers. Bandits raiding villages in the outer islands, pirates picking off ships. Failing harvests, especially closer to the strike zone.'

She looked up at me. 'Do you really think we've sent ships out, year after year, because we want to help you?' She paused, and spoke more quietly. 'You were meant to have all the answers that we don't have. We're looking for help ourselves.'

CHAPTER 2

Zoe gave a snort. 'You could've saved yourself a long journey. There's nothing here for Elsewhere but trouble.'

'Stop calling it *Elsewhere*,' Paloma yelled. 'That's not its name. And it's not the place that you imagine. These are real people you're talking about – my parents, my little sisters. My friends – everyone I've ever known. A million people. And you tell me they're all going to burn, because of what we can offer you. Instead of finding friendship, cooperation, we'll be turned into a new strike zone.' She inhaled sharply. 'It's not your *Elsewhere*, some magical solution.' She took a shuddering breath. 'It's real. Real people live there.'

What she said was true: after all our hoping, Elsewhere didn't exist. Not the place we'd imagined, where things would be easy, and all the answers would be waiting for us, like ripe figs begging to be plucked. That place didn't exist. Instead we'd found the Scattered Islands, real places, infinitely more complex than our imaginings – and they could be destroyed before any of us had even seen them.

I looked across at Paloma. She was squinting against the wind, which had blown her hair across her eyes. Her eyelashes were pale, as if dusted with snow. Her arms were crossed, her hands clutching the fabric of her sleeves.

I had been thinking of her as a whole country. As the thing that changed everything. But as she stood there in the wind, shivering slightly, I saw that she was just a young woman, a long way from home, and very frightened.

Around the fire that night, when all of us had calmed down, the stories of Elsewhere spilled out of her. She described animals that I had never heard of, let alone seen: seadogs, huge swimming beasts, hunted for their rich layers of oily fat. Sleek in the water and cumbersome on land. Paloma took up a stick and drew a sketch in the sandy ground, though she ended up laughing at her own rendition: the beast was an elongated lump, whiskers at one end, fins splayed at the other.

'They look ridiculous enough in real life,' she said, 'without my bad drawing.' She scuffed the picture away with a sweep of her false leg.

There were other animals that she described: alks, beasts like huge cows but with tall, branching horns splaying from their heads. Snowfoxes, purest white. And trusses, birds so huge that if they spread their wings they would cast a shadow the length of a dinghy.

'They're supposed to be bad luck,' she said, 'but I don't know why. I love seeing them, when they come back from the Southern Archipelago after winter.'

I looked at the empty night sky, smeared with grey clouds. Since we'd left the screeching gulls of the coast, the only birds we'd seen were ravens, with their black hooked beaks and indifferent stares. Perhaps, before the blast, trusses had flown here as well.

Paloma's words offered us a new world, waiting to be seen. But there was an urgency to the way she spoke, leaning towards the fire and almost gabbling as she rushed to tell it all. There was an urgency in our listening, too. I wanted to clutch at every word, hold them in my hands. I longed for paper and ink to write it all down. I couldn't help feeling that every word she spoke about Elsewhere was a last testament, a record of all that she was about to lose.

*

I had thought the annihilating fire of the visions, of all the seers' visions, could get no worse. But through Paloma I was learning a little of the reality of the Scattered Islands, and that knowledge polished the agony of the visions to a new, fierce gleam.

Paloma knew what I was. She had known by the time we met: Zoe must have told her already that I was a seer, and what that meant. It was different, though, for her to see what really happened when I had a vision. She'd witnessed this the first night after we found her. We'd been gathered around the fire on the beach, maps and charts laid out on the sand as Paloma showed us a map of the Scattered Islands, describing how the archipelago speckled the sea, so far to the north-west of us that our own maps became useless. She had placed her maps next to Thomas's; to approximate the distance, she'd laid them several feet apart. In the gap between them, deadly sea. To comprehend the Scattered Islands, we were going to need new maps; a new scale.

Paloma had been speaking when the blast came: flames tearing through my head, and a white heat that stopped time. A fire so vast that it made everything impossible except fire.

When I'd stopped shaking, and could see again, Zoe was swearing as she patted at the smouldering edge of the map that I'd dropped in the coals of the campfire. Paloma was silent, her eyebrows drawn together as she stared.

Over the next few days, I'd tried to explain to her how the visions worked, and that I couldn't read the future the way we could read a book. That, like the uncharted spaces between our maps and Paloma's, the future was beyond my reach. All I got were flashes: glimpses of things that hadn't happened yet. Awake or asleep, I had no control over when the visions came, ripping me out of the present and throwing me briefly into a future where I could not navigate. If the visions came when I was sleeping, it was hard to distinguish between them and ordinary dreams – no way of knowing whether what I had seen really was a foretelling of something to come, or just a nightmare.

The visions had sometimes been useful: warnings or clues, though rarely clear. Most, though, were nothing but a terror that ambushed me with flashes of fire. It had become worse since the Ark, and what we had found there. Now that we knew the Council had found the blast machines and was readying them to use against Elsewhere, the flames burned with an added urgency.

I didn't tell Paloma what the visions did to seers, eventually. Lucia had been driven to the edge of madness, even before she drowned; Xander's mind had been left a darkened room, lit only by flashes of fire.

I told Paloma none of that. But she saw, soon enough, how the blast visions burned language from my lips. How the flames left me shaking, my eyes rolled back in my head as if searching the sky for fire. I felt Paloma watching me, from behind the strands of white hair that blew across her face.

I watched myself just as carefully. Sometimes I felt there

were only two certainties: the blast, and my own madness. I didn't know which would come first.

'Have you seen it?' she said to me, sidling up to me at the campfire, a few days into our journey. 'Have you seen them bombing my home?'

I couldn't lie to her. I had seen the fire, and the crumbling of the world.

After that, she was never quite the same around me. We had all told her what would happen if the Council found Elsewhere, but I was the one who had seen her homeland burn, and when she chose to share a blanket with Zoe the next day, instead of me, and to look down hurriedly if our eyes should meet across the campfire, I didn't blame her.

The first time I noticed what was happening between Zoe and Paloma was the morning when Zoe, without being asked, picked up the detached leg from where it lay beside Paloma's blanket, and held it for a moment, in both hands, before handing it to Paloma. I almost missed it – it lasted only a second or two. Zoe's hands, usually decisive, lingered for a moment, and those fingers, so quick to dispatch death with a knife, were soft against the false flesh.

After that, I watched more carefully. I came to understand that when Paloma stared at Zoe and Piper, it wasn't the unspoken unison of their movements that she was staring at, any more – or Piper at all.

It was as natural and as unhurried as moss claiming a rock. They were both the moss; they were both the rock. We'd all seen it happening, but hardly realised it: Paloma's blanket edging closer to Zoe's at night. Zoe reaching to free a twig snared in Paloma's hair.

No one spoke of it. Once or twice Piper and I exchanged a glance, or a smile, when we saw Paloma lean in towards Zoe, or when the two of them walked or rode together and

Zoe's laugh burst from her, louder than caution would usually allow.

There were many things Piper and I didn't talk about, during those long nights and days of travelling. We didn't mention the blast machine, Leonard's broken neck, the drowned children. All the things that we didn't want to conjure with language. But this, between Zoe and Paloma, was different: it was a bright bird that had come to land near us, and neither of us wanted to startle it away with words.

*

We seers are not all the same. Zoe had told me that Lucia had been good at predicting weather. The Confessor had had an aptitude for machines, allowing her to find her way through the wreckage of the taboo machines, and to create new and terrible ones. Xander, Piper had told me, used to have an instinct for whether somebody was lying or telling the truth. But whatever our particular aptitudes, all of us woke screaming from visions; all of us were busy patting down the fires that the blast ignited in our minds.

With me, it was an instinct for places. I could feel them, even if I wasn't there. It was all part of the same thing: the unreliability of time. Just as I could sometimes see things that hadn't happened yet, I could sometimes sense places I hadn't yet been. I'd found the tunnels that had led me from the Keeping Rooms, where Zach had imprisoned me; I'd found my way to the island; with Piper's help, I'd found the Ark.

So I turned my mind, now, with all the concentration I could muster, to the blast machine. In the Ark, Piper and I had seen how the machinery had been painstakingly disassembled and taken away. One of the soldiers had referred to about *the new bunker*. So I searched. It felt strange to want to find this thing – to seek it out, when every sense in my body jarred at the thought of it. The residue alone, four hundred years later, was enough to keep the deadlands barren, and to make the Alphas shy in disgust from Omega bodies.

I sat up, while the others slept, and forced myself to seek the connections, follow where they led. I strained to trace the source of the visions that blazed in the night, the blast machine in its bunker. But I would instead find myself with eyes scrunched closed and teeth clenched, unable to get a steady trace of its location.

One morning, halfway between the coast and New Hobart, I woke with a certainty that the blast machine was to the north. I felt its pull, drawing me. I ran to Piper, breathless with the news. But by the next day, my sureness was gone: the tug that I had felt was shifting. I felt like a sail, snatched by capricious winds. By that night, I could have sworn that the blast machine was to the west. The next day, I had no sense of it at all. When Piper asked me, I muttered about time, and distance, and that the machine might still be in transit, in many parts.

'Cass – stop.' Piper cut me off mid-excuse. 'I know all that. But I also know that you'll find it eventually.'

'*Eventually*'s too late,' I said, looking ahead to where Paloma rode, Zoe walking beside her horse, her hand resting on Paloma's foot. 'We need to seek it out. It's too important for us to just wait.'

Piper threw his arm wide. 'Seek it where?' he said. Behind us, the Spine Mountains, still snow-covered, cut off the horizon to the west. Ahead of us, plains and forests spread out to the east, until the morning haze blurred them with the sky. Where to begin?

'We have Paloma to protect now,' he said. 'We can't just run off on a whim. Once we're back at New Hobart, we can give orders to our scouts – The Ringmaster's network, too. We can put out word to report on any sign of unusual activity – any bunkers, any new installations. But without something to go on, we can't just wander in search of the blast machine.'

I tried not to hear a criticism in his words: *without something to go on*. What did I offer, if I couldn't even be relied on to harness my talent for locations? Many times I had felt useless compared to Piper and Zoe, as they fought and hunted and planned. My sense of places was one of the few things I'd been able to offer. Without it, was I still useful to the resistance? Useful enough that my life was worth more than the chance to kill Zach by killing me?

*

It was a hard journey. We'd started with only three horses for the four of us, and then lost one on Gallows Pass, where patches of ice still clung to the shale. Even though we'd dismounted and led the horses slowly, the grey horse had slipped and gone down thrashing, one of its front legs broken. Zoe was the only one who could get close enough to put it out of its misery. I watched how she spoke soothingly to it, right up to the moment that she slit its throat. We ate horse meat for five days, but our pace was slower with two of us walking. We had to travel at night whenever we were in Alpha territory, and Paloma's false leg pained her if she walked for too long, so she rode one horse while the rest of us took turns on the other.

I was grateful whenever it was my turn to ride – I felt

sluggish under the increasing onslaught of blast visions, each one an outburst of flame behind my eyes. One morning, a few days before we reached New Hobart, I woke from a vision with my whole head shrieking, a soreness in my temples and jaw that didn't dissipate even as the vision dispersed. All day I found myself touching the tender spots on my face, wondering if my visions had somehow spread to my body now, as well as my mind.

We came within sight of New Hobart, two weeks after we'd left the coast and *The Rosalind*. We finally crested the western ridge at dawn, and there was the ring of torches around the town, and the troops massed at the gates and sentry posts. I didn't know if I should feel relieved or afraid.

We were leading Paloma into a town held by The Ringmaster, until recently on the Council himself. I didn't know how long our uneasy alliance with him would hold, or how he would respond to Paloma, and her news of the Scattered Islands. With The Ringmaster's help, the resistance army had freed New Hobart from the Council occupation. But although Simon and what was left of our army were waiting for us in New Hobart, The Ringmaster had greater troop numbers, and the town was under his control.

Sally, Xander and Elsa were in there, too, at The Ringmaster's mercy. He knew exactly what they meant to me – he'd made that clear before Piper and I left, when he'd threatened me not to betray him.

But we needed him. It wouldn't be enough just to run, and hide, and keep Paloma away from the Council. We needed to outfit a fleet of ships; we needed money, and soldiers. We needed to strike back at the Council. Descending from the western ridge towards New Hobart with

Piper, Zoe and Paloma, I knew that this thing was bigger than the four of us.

Despite the fortifications around the town, I was surprised to see signs of ordinary life continuing. Farmers were tilling the earth in fields to the city's north and east, breaking the soil for planting when it was warm enough. Some of the houses beyond the town walls, on the open plains, had smoke coming from their chimneys. At intervals a mile or two beyond the walls, sentry posts encircled the town, and we saw two patrols making a slow lap of the perimeter, but New Hobart had once again spilled beyond its walls, and people were coming and going. I saw a hunchbacked silhouette in the driver's seat of a wagon, heading for the western gate, and couldn't help but smile. The Council's laws prohibited Omegas from owning animals, so even that wagon, hitched to an ageing donkey, was a small act of defiance.

Nonetheless, for an hour or more we laid low and watched the sentry post on the western road. The soldiers wore red Council uniforms, but we could see the black armband that distinguished The Ringmaster's men. Even then, we held back; only stepping out of cover after we'd watched a passing patrol of Omega troops, in their blue tunics, conferring with The Ringmaster's soldiers.

When we rode up to the watch post, we were greeted calmly enough, though they didn't conceal their stares as they took in Paloma. The Omega troops saluted Piper, while the Alphas gave grudging nods. Their matter-of-fact greeting felt strange. To them, we were just returning, as expected, after a few weeks, albeit with a pale stranger. They could not possibly know all that we had seen and learned in that time: the Ark. The blast. Elsewhere. They could not know that the whole world had changed in those weeks.

Word of our return had straight away been sent to The

Ringmaster, and when the western gate was dragged open he was there to meet us, arms crossed over his chest, curly hair pulled back from his face. It had only been a month since we'd left this place, but he'd grown thinner, and older, in that time.

He was staring at Paloma. We waited what felt like a long time for him to speak. Then he turned away, dragging his eyes from Paloma to me.

'Looks like you have a lot to tell me,' he said.

CHAPTER 3

Debriefing would be intense, I knew. The Ringmaster had set up his command in the former Tithe Collector's office, and that was where he took us, straight into the main hall. Simon, Piper's long-standing adviser, was waiting for us there, and Sally too – as soon as we entered, she hobbled to Piper and Zoe and embraced each of them fiercely. Even I received a smile, though her eyes seized quickly on Paloma. Xander was there too, though he didn't move, or even look at us when we entered. I moved closer to him, looking for some sign of recognition.

'Don't waste your time,' said The Ringmaster, shutting the door and jerking his head towards the corner where Xander sat. 'He's quiet, these days, at least. He's settled down a lot.' The Ringmaster looked back at me, and added meaningfully, 'Since you've been gone.' He gestured to the seats around the big table. 'Sit. Leave the boy where he is.'

For hours we were cloistered in that room, describing all that had happened since we'd left. Xander remained silent, never even glancing at Paloma. But The Ringmaster,

Simon and Sally looked hard at Paloma and interrupted all of us, including Paloma, at every stage of our story, hurling questions, prodding and prompting for more and more details. Paloma was tired, and I could see her bristling at The Ringmaster's repeated questions about the doctors and the untwinning. I was exhausted too, and longing to get to the holding house and see Elsa, but we answered their questions until I felt wrung out of words.

At first, I thought The Ringmaster had been right about Xander. I watched the younger seer in the corner: he sat unmoving where he was placed, mouth slightly open, a thread of drool dangling from his lip. No more muttering and yelling, rocking back and forth, moving his hands endlessly. But several times, during the hours that we were around that table, his whole body jerked, like somebody waking suddenly from a dream of falling. I was sure that he was still having visions, though he never cried out. He didn't make a noise. Even Sally could raise no response from him, other than persuading him to open his mouth when she raised a mug of water to it.

I'd hoped that our news – about the Ark, and *The Rosalind*'s return, might reassure Xander. That he might feel bolstered by the knowledge that he'd been right about both, and that he'd been listened to. Paloma was here to prove it. But he grew ever more distant, even as we spoke directly to him, or tried to. He sat slumped, eyes closed most of the time. When he opened his eyes, they stared, but not at us.

And I understood that our news, confirming the truth of his visions, was the worst thing we could have brought him.

I looked again at Xander. His head lolled awkwardly, as if he hadn't even the energy to hold up his own neck. How long could he have been expected to stand in the face of the blast, its certain approach, and not disintegrate?

*

When the questions finally subsided and we were readying to leave, I hung back for a second, watching The Ringmaster's guards lay out his meal on the table while Piper and the others were talking in the doorway. It was a grey afternoon, and The Ringmaster lit a lamp, changing the colour of the room to a sickly orange. I was gratified to see that despite the silver plate, the food laid out for him was no better than what the soldiers would be eating: a piece of flatbread no bigger than my hand, a handful of nuts, and some jerky.

He turned, the lamp still in his hand, and saw me watching him.

'I wanted to ask you something,' I said.

'Surely you should know the answers to most questions?' he said.

I shook my head, irritated. 'You know better than that. You know that's not how it works.'

'Go ahead then,' he said. He picked up his fork, poked ruefully at his half-bare plate.

I took a deep breath. 'You told me, when we first met, that you had your twin locked up. I want to know where she is.'

His face hardened. 'She has nothing to do with any of this.'

'Where is she?' I repeated.

'I told you all that you need to know, when we first met. She's not tanked,' he said. 'I've never broken the taboo. I'm not a hypocrite.'

'Aren't you?' I said. 'You're here, fighting alongside us, talking with us while we talk of freedom for Omegas. Where is she?'

'She's safe,' he said. 'Nowhere near here. You forget that I have my own garrisons, my own guards.'

I tried to form words, but I could almost feel the walls of the Keeping Rooms sealing around me again. Those days and days and years and years of darkness, when Zach had kept me in that cell. Wherever she was, The Ringmaster's twin must be feeling the same airless despair. The same panic that crept in when time became stripped of meaning, and days and months were no longer anything but a burden.

'How can you fight alongside us, and against the Council, when you think it's fair to keep her locked up?'

He looked at me coolly. 'I never said I think it's fair,' he said. 'I think it's necessary. If Zach or The General got their hands on my twin, I'd be dead. If she's not secure, I'm not secure. Nor is New Hobart. Do you think, for a minute, that my troops would stay here to protect this town if I weren't here?'

'I don't understand you,' I said.

'You don't need to understand me,' he said. His voice was a door shutting. 'We want the same thing: an end to the tanks.'

'Is that all you want?' I said. 'Is that really it? What are you doing here?'

My question sat between us for a long time, before he spoke.

'I don't know,' he replied. His voice sounded exhausted. I thought that for the first time he was telling me the truth.

*

It had been many years since I'd felt that I had a home, if ever. My parents' house, before they sent me away, was too full of scrutiny and suspicion to be a home. After my exile I'd found a kind of stability at the settlement, but my neighbours had kept their distance, and whispered about my visions. Then there had been the hell of the Keeping Rooms, and the breathless months on the run with Kip.

But that afternoon, when Elsa threw open the door of the holding house, being back with her felt as close to home as I had ever known. She rushed to greet me, almost toppling me, and my face was squashed into her shirt as she hugged me. For a few moments everything else receded.

'I heard you got back into town this morning,' she said, holding both my arms as she stepped back to look at me, then glancing pointedly at the sun behind me; it was already sinking towards the horizon.

'I wanted to come here sooner,' I said.

Elsa greeted Piper and Zoe; she welcomed Paloma too, though Elsa couldn't hide her stares. She grumbled about rations as she bustled around the kitchen, but I saw how she touched Piper's arm as she thrust a bundle of sheets at him, and how she pushed a hunk of bread into Paloma's hands and made her sit down and take the weight off her false leg.

There were more comfortable accommodations at the Tithe Collector's office, but none of us wanted to be there, close to The Ringmaster. I kept thinking about his words: *I never said I think it's fair. I think it's necessary.* What would happen when killing Zach became necessary? Would The Ringmaster even hesitate to kill me?

I was grateful when the others retreated to the front room, leaving me alone in the kitchen with Elsa. When I tried to explain to her everything that had happened, she didn't interrupt me like The Ringmaster, Sally and Simon had. She just busied herself around me, chopping the carrots and stirring the pot over the fire, and not staring at me as I tried to find the words. I told the story backwards, starting with Paloma, and Elsewhere, and all that we'd learned about the end of twinning. When I came to describing the earlier part of my journey, and the Ark, the words came even more slowly. The meal of watery soup was ready, but Elsa didn't hurry me; she hoisted the pot from the fire and placed it to the side. She sat quietly and waited, and I felt silence rising over me, like the water in the black corridors of the Ark.

I described finding Kip again, in the double prison of his smashed body and the tank. I told her how I had flooded the Ark, nearly killing myself and Zach and Piper, and burying Kip and The Confessor once and for all.

Elsa said nothing still, as she dished up the soup, but before she called the others in to eat, she squeezed my arm.

'You found Kip,' she said.

I nodded. It seemed a strange thing to be grateful for – those minutes in the Ark, with Kip's dead body laid on the gangway in front of me. But Elsa, who had never been given back her husband's body after the Council killed him, understood what those minutes had meant to me.

*

Later, Sally and Xander came to the kitchen as well. In the weeks we'd been away, they'd moved into the holding house, taking over the room next to Elsa's at the front of the house, where Nina had lived before the Council killed her.

Sitting close to the fire, Xander was still silent. There were leaves in his hair, and the knees of his trousers were browned with dirt.

'Where's he been this afternoon?' I asked Sally.

'The Kissing Tree,' Sally said.

I raised an eyebrow. The huge, hollowed-out stump in the burnt-out forest was all that remained of the hiding place where Elsa and her husband used to go when they were young. It was there that we'd found the documents for which he'd been tortured and killed: the papers that had helped to lead us to the Ark.

'He just took off one day,' Sally said, 'when we were out setting snares. He went straight to it, like he knew what he was looking for. Crawled in without a word, and stayed there for hours. Since then, he goes most days.' She shrugged. 'It keeps him calm. I go with him if my legs are up to it, otherwise we send a guard.'

Of all the places in and around New Hobart, the Kissing Tree had the strongest link to the Ark, and to the blast machine. I wondered why the flames in Xander's head weren't enough, and why he made his daily pilgrimage to that place.

He wasn't going to answer my questions. He sat without speaking, on the low stool by the fire. Beside him, Sally sat in Elsa's chair by the window overlooking the courtyard. If anyone else had tried to claim that chair, Elsa would have jabbed at them with the broom handle, but it seemed that in the weeks we'd been away she and Sally had become friends. There was at least thirty years between them, and their lives could hardly have been more different. Elsa had spent her life caring for the children in the holding house; Sally had been a pioneer of the resistance, an infiltrator and an assassin. But I watched how Elsa filled her pipe and passed it to Sally without even looking – Sally took it without a word – and how the two of them settled into an easy silence.

I saw, too, how Elsa bent to prop a cushion behind Xander's

head, where it slumped against the wall. Again and again she wiped the drool that unspooled from his open mouth. Now that the holding house was empty, and its children dead, Elsa was always looking for something to do with her hands, and I knew that she was glad of Xander's presence.

I wished that I could say the same – but being in the same room as Xander filled my nostrils with the scent of smoke. He was all fire now, all the time. I thought I understood, perhaps, why he went each day to the Kissing Tree. The flames had been calling him for so long that he had no choice but to answer.

Elsa was mixing some herbs to help Xander sleep through the night. She showed me how, and I ground the dried valerian myself, felt the satisfying grate of the pestle against the mortar.

When Elsa poured in some poppy tincture, she raised the glass bottle to the window light, squinting to look closely while she poured. 'Careful,' she said. 'Four drops only. No more.'

'Two spoons of that stuff,' Sally said, 'with a little henbane thrown in, and you can knock someone out entirely. A little more, and you can kill them.'

The way she phrased it, it didn't sound like a warning. It sounded like advice.

'Shut up and help,' said Elsa, manoeuvring around Sally with the bottle. 'We're not in the business of killing, in this house.'

I wished she were right. Perhaps it was true for her, and for Xander and Paloma. But I looked from Zoe, to Piper, to Sally, and down at my own hands. There was not one of us who was not in the business of killing.

*

That night we all slept together in the dormitory of the holding house: me, Piper, Paloma and Zoe. Zoe and Paloma had pushed two of the small beds together; it was as close to a declaration as we were going to get.

Both Piper and Zoe were too tall for the children's beds, and seeing Piper's calves and feet hanging over the edge of the bed made me laugh. But then Paloma said: 'Why are all the beds in here so small?' and my laugh halted, and we fell silent, until Zoe explained about the children that Zach and The General had tanked and then left to drown. Paloma sat on her bed and listened, knees drawn up and arms wrapped around her shins. Every day with us a new lesson in cruelty.

'It doesn't make sense,' Paloma said to me. 'When they kill the children, they're killing their own as well.'

There had been a time when the twinning had stopped Alphas and Omegas from killing one another. That time was long gone. It wasn't the first time that humans had turned on each other, and themselves, like this. Whoever had unleashed the blast, four hundred years ago, must have known that they would destroy more than just their enemies. The risk of obliterating themselves, and the world, hadn't been enough to stop the killing then. The twinning was never going to be enough to stop it now.

*

The Ringmaster came at dawn. He led me and Piper around the outskirts of the town, so that Piper could inspect the new fortifications. The encircling wall was topped with wire, and a walkway now ran along it, with slits for archers. The watchtowers were higher, and had been strengthened, squatting solidly against thick wooden buttresses. Beyond the wall, wide ditches ringed the town, and in each ditch sat rows of logs pierced with metal spikes, offering their metal barbs to the sky. There was an orderliness about them that belied their sole purpose: to impale and to kill. I thought of the horses I'd ridden, the soft skin of their underbellies, and turned away.

The Ringmaster had noticed my expression.

'It's not supposed to be pretty,' he said. 'The Council built the wall to keep the townsfolk in, not to repel an attack. We'd never have taken the town if it had been built to keep an attacking force out.'

'And now?'

He pressed his lips together. 'If we have to draw back behind the walls, the fortifications will buy us some time. If they throw everything at us, we'll still struggle. We don't have the supplies to withstand a long siege – rations are tight enough as it is. But the Council won't leave Wyndham undefended. Anyway,' he said, with the beginnings of a smile, 'the new defences have kept the troops busy. Idle troops make trouble.'

He was right. And he was right about the fortifications, too. They were impressive. Even Piper had no criticisms to make, and nodded when The Ringmaster pointed out various features.

'When will the Council attack, do you think?' I said.

'I don't know.' The Ringmaster glanced back up the hill towards the holding house, where we'd left Zoe and Paloma. 'We struck some major blows – the defection of my army; freeing this town; the destruction of the Ark. But they'll strike back eventually. Sooner rather than later, if they find out we've got somebody from Elsewhere here.'

There was such audacity in those words: *somebody from Elsewhere here*. Only weeks earlier, that phrase would have been unimaginable. 'Paloma changes everything,' I said.

'She'll change everything all right,' he grunted. 'Bring the Council down on us like never before. All for what?'

'For a chance to end all of this,' said Piper, waving his arm to include the walls and the trenches below us, and the ruthless metal spikes – all the careful architecture of death. 'Once and for all.'

The Ringmaster shook his head. 'Someone, a few hundred years ago, thought they'd come up with a clever way to end all of this too, with the blast. Your brother—' he turned to me, his movement so sudden that Piper stepped forward, putting his body between us '—he and The General think the tanks are a great way to end it all. When are you going to stop thinking that machines are the answer?'

I was about to speak when a whistle came from the wall below us, and a flurry of shouts from the watchtower. The Ringmaster yanked his gaze from me, and he and Piper moved quickly, running through the narrow streets towards the eastern gate. I ran too; by the time we reached the gate, my breath was fast and jerky from keeping up with them.

The gate was open; I recognised the dwarf sentry whose arrival had been signalled, and who now rode up from the gate to meet us. Crispin, one of Piper's soldiers from the island.

'It's an Alpha,' he said as he dismounted. 'They're bringing him in now.' Crispin was out of breath, and we all had to bend to hear him speak. 'He came to the sentry post on the eastern road, wouldn't give his name. Handed over his knife, willingly. We've searched him – no other weapons. But he says he'll only speak to Cass.'

Behind him, three more Omega soldiers rode through the gate. Hemmed between them was a tall man, hooded.

The gate was heaved shut, the crossbar dropped into

place with a weighty thud. The soldiers dismounted and dragged the hooded man to where we stood.

I knew it was him, even before one of the soldiers wrenched back his hood. He kept his head low, face all but buried in the scarf bundled around his neck. There was a bruise on his cheek, a cut on his temple, and his bottom lip was swollen and split.

I stared at Zach, and he stared back.

'I had nowhere else to go,' he said.

PART 2

CHAPTER 4

Piper charged at him – for a moment I thought he would punch him. But he just grabbed hold of Zach and, under the gaze of the soldiers, dragged him off the street and into the shadow of a narrow alley nearby. I followed with The Ringmaster and Crispin.

'And put that hood back up, for crying out loud,' Piper said, pushing Zach back against the wall. 'You think there's a soldier in this town who wouldn't knife you if they knew who you are?'

Zach pulled his hood forward, but kept his eyes on me.

'You need to take me in,' he said. His words were slightly blurred by his swollen lip. I ran my tongue across my own lip, expecting to taste blood.

'Did your men do this to him?' I asked Crispin.

'We weren't overly gentle when we searched him,' said Crispin. 'But someone else had got to him first.'

Mixed with my shock at seeing Zach was an element of relief: the pains I'd felt a few nights earlier, in the thick of my visions, had been Zach's pains, and not another step in my mind's disintegration.

The Ringmaster dismissed Crispin with a jerk of his head, but before Crispin had reached the end of the alley, Piper called him back.

'Not a word, do you understand? Not a word to anybody, if you value your life. You've seen nothing, heard nothing, and you don't know who this man is. Clear?'

Crispin nodded.

'And wake the second watch early,' The Ringmaster added. 'I want an extra squadron on the perimeter, and three more mounted patrols out, now.'

Crispin left at a trot.

Piper let go of Zach's arm. There was nowhere for Zach to run, backed against the wall in the cramped alley, with me, Piper and The Ringmaster facing him.

'Do you have any idea what you've done?' Zach said to me, his voice a hiss.

'What *I've* done?' I said. 'What are you talking about? Why are you here?'

'The General's trying to kill me, to get rid of you.'

'And you've come to me for help?' I said, incredulous.

'Where else am I supposed to go?'

He looked from me to Piper and The Ringmaster and back again. I thought of the half-strangled rabbit I'd found once, thrashing around in one of Piper's snares – the wire noose had snagged and failed to kill it. Zoe had leaned past me and swiftly broken its neck, but I'd seen the trapped animal's eyes. Zach's eyes were like that now.

'Say it,' I said.

'What?' Zach said. His eyes were still flicking from me to the others. 'Say what?'

'Admit it,' I said. 'Say that you need our help.'

'You want to play games?' Zach said. 'There's no time.

They're coming for me, and if you let them catch me, you'll die.'

'But so will you,' I said, keeping my voice even. 'And there are times I think that might be worth it.'

He stared at me for a long time. I felt the warmth of Piper, who stood close beside me; I heard the impatient breathing of The Ringmaster on my other side.

'Fine,' Zach said, his voice cracking. 'Help me.'

*

On the way to the Tithe Collector's office Piper gripped Zach's arm and The Ringmaster flanked him. The hood was pulled so low over his face he could barely see, and once or twice he stumbled, but Piper hauled him onwards. The streets were getting busier: a woman was beating a mat out of an upstairs window; three soldiers were chatting in a doorway, scrambling to attention as they saw Piper and The Ringmaster approach. Outside the bakery a man was unloading flour from a barrel, and flour dust settled on the shoulders of Zach's dark cloak as we passed. I couldn't reconcile it: such an ordinary, everyday thing, when I felt as though Zach's arrival had brought the whole world to a stop.

When we reached the partly-burnt building where the children had been tanked and then drowned, I looked back at Zach, and saw Piper's knuckles standing out white, his fingers crushing Zach's arm. If it hurt, Zach made no noise.

At the Tithe Collector's office, The Ringmaster dismissed the guards with a sweep of his hand, and pulled the door of the main chamber shut behind us.

In that large room, I was no closer to Zach than I had

been outside, but it somehow felt worse, and more intimate, to be sharing a room with him, away from the noise of the soldiers and the streets. I already shared too much with Zach. I didn't want to share the same air, the same enclosed space.

'Who knows you're here?' demanded Piper.

'Nobody,' Zach said. He pushed the hood back.

The last time I'd seen him had been in the Ark, but the space had been barely lit, and I'd never got close to him. Now I stared at his changed face. It wasn't only the bruises and scabs that made it different. There were new lines under his eyes, and between his eyebrows, and a long-healed scar on his jaw. So much of his life was unknown to me, now. How far our stories had diverged since the days of our childhood, when I could have drawn a map of every freckle on his cheekbones.

The Ringmaster moved closer to Zach. They were the same height, but The Ringmaster was broader, stronger. Once, these two had sat together on the Council, living and working in luxury that I could barely imagine. Now they faced off across the bare room. It had once been the Council's Tithe Collector's office, so it was plusher than anything else in the Omega town, but it wore the marks of the last few months. One wall was patched where it had burned during the battle. A broken window had not been mended – just nailed shut with slats. The planks of the balcony outside, where the townspeople used to line up to pay their tithes, had been ripped up for firewood during the coldest weeks of winter. In the next room, where the Tithe Collector used to dine, the floor was covered with sleeping rolls for The Ringmaster's personal guards.

'You should never have come here,' The Ringmaster said to Zach.

'I don't want this any more than you do,' Zach replied. 'You think I'd be here—' he waved a hand at the shabby room '—if I had a choice?'

His shoulders slumped. 'The General's turned on me. She's trying to kill me.' He turned back to me. 'You've gone too far now, done too much. Destroying the database. Warning the island that we were coming. Freeing New Hobart. Then trashing the Ark. You did too much,' he said again, his voice rising, 'and you found out too much. Until getting rid of you was worth the cost of getting rid of me.'

This was the kind of calculation that should have been familiar to him: he'd spent years weighing up the value of lives, and making choices he had no right to make. But he looked frantic, his voice swerving between rage and disbelief.

'Didn't you have anyone else you could turn to?' I said. 'You must have your own soldiers. Won't they protect you?'

'Against The General?' he said.

I remembered her: the way she kept her head still while her eyes roamed indifferently over us. How even Zach had obeyed her every command.

Zach continued. 'Ever since you took New Hobart, The General's been trying to push me out. She tried to hide it at first, but I knew. She was manoeuvring in the Council, making sure she had the support she needed. Talking more and more about the threat posed by the resistance. By you, especially. Then you drowned the Ark, and I knew it wouldn't be long. Six nights ago she came for me – sent her soldiers to my chambers before dawn. I wasn't there – I had a source who tipped me off. I got out through the kitchens, a few hours before the raid, but even then I had to fight my way past a sentry. One of my own soldiers – he said he had orders not to let me leave the fort. *Me*.' He closed his eyes and took two breaths. I didn't know who the anger on his face was aimed at: his soldiers; The General; me.

'You should have known this was coming,' The Ringmaster said. 'You should have known better than to trust her.'

'And I should have trusted you instead?' Zach shot back. 'You, who proved yourself so loyal, so trustworthy?'

'I've been loyal to the principles the Council was supposed to uphold. The taboo. Protecting our people from the machines.'

Zach shrugged impatiently. 'Everything I've done has been for the protection of our people. You're clinging to superstition, harping on about the taboo. Machines aren't the real threat – the Omegas are.'

'The taboo exists for a reason,' The Ringmaster said. 'The machines ended the world. They caused the Omegas.'

'We can harness the machines to help us,' Zach said. 'Everything I've done – the machines, the tanks – it's all to protect us from the burden of the Omegas.'

'And the blast?' I asked. 'Are you really stupid enough to think that can be harnessed? That the blast will protect you as well?'

'If need be,' Zach said. 'If that's what it takes, against the threat of Elsewhere.'

'You disgust me,' I said, each word a hiss.

I could not look at him without thinking of the tanks. The blast. The stink of death that came off him, like a rabbit carcass claimed by flies.

'Then at last you might begin to understand how I've always felt about you,' he said.

I pulled back my fist and swung at him. It wasn't an impulsive jab; I thought carefully about everything Zoe had taught me. I focused on his right cheekbone, and when I punched I made sure I punched through rather than at it, and I threw my whole weight behind the blow.

He saw me draw my fist back, but he didn't believe I would really do it. When my knuckles connected with his face, his whole head snapped backwards. Mine did too, the jerk of pain sharp enough that my teeth clashed together as my head recoiled.

I was still staggering slightly as I tried to punch him again, but Piper held me back, his arm tight around my waist, lifting me off my feet. My knuckles were red, but the ache in them was nothing compared to the pain beneath my eye.

Zach had one hand pressed to his face, his other hand raised at me, palm first.

'You're insane,' he said. 'If you attack me, you're attacking yourself.'

Piper released me, and I stood close to Zach.

'You're the mad one,' I said. 'You're disgusting. You look down on us, think that we're less than you. But the things that you've done—' I spat at the ground beside him. 'You're a monster. A freak.'

He lowered his hand. The skin was already purpling, his eye clenched shut against the hurt.

'It doesn't matter what you think of me,' he said. 'I'm not here to win you over. It doesn't make any difference that you hate me.' He had regained control of his breath now. His voice was measured, his gaze cool. 'If you don't take me in, I'm dead. You too. Do you want that?' He paused. 'You want it all to be over?'

If he'd asked me that question a few months ago, my answer might have been different. They had been the bleak days, when I'd wandered through the world like a half-dead thing, lost without Kip. But I had found my way back. I had found Kip's body and set it free, and I had chosen to live. I knew that I would choose it again, now, even if it meant protecting Zach.

I kept my gaze on Zach as I spoke to Piper. 'I want him shackled, and locked up,' I said.

The Ringmaster called for the shackles. When his soldiers brought them, I helped Piper with the chain myself, looping it tight around both Zach's wrists. When my skin touched his, I forced myself not to flinch.

*

Piper sent for Sally. I heard him explaining Zach's arrival in the corridor. I couldn't make out her words, but her tone was clear enough. When she came in she looked at Zach, and it was as though winter had come again, settling over her features.

'I should see to his face,' she said, her voice cold. 'If he gets an infection, it's bad news for Cass.'

His injuries didn't look dangerous – I'd seen far worse – but he'd taken a beating. Sally pushed him into a chair and stood over him. The tenderness with which I'd seen her care for Xander was completely absent in the way she examined Zach's face. She touched him only with the tip of her thumb and forefinger, pinching under his chin, pulling his head first one way and then the other to inspect the cuts on his temple and lip. She called for water and cloths, swiping firmly at the swollen flesh until the cloth was a rusted red. 'Hold this on,' she said to him, pressing another cloth onto the graze above his eye. Fishing a miniature bone-handled dagger from her boot, she leaned over Zach – he flinched – to flick out gravel embedded in the wound, using the very tip of the knife.

Zach gave a small grunt of pain.

'You want something to complain about?' Sally said, keeping her voice low and pressing the knife against the open wound. It was a tiny blade – the same one she used for chopping tobacco, and getting splinters from Xander's knees. But in Zach's grated flesh, it was big enough. He winced his eyes shut, and I jerked my head away from my own jab of raw-flesh pain.

'Get this mad old bitch off me,' grunted Zach, raising his bound arms to swipe at her.

'Sally,' Piper said, his hand on her arm. But she'd already stopped, turning away from Zach.

'I'm done,' she said, wiping the tip of the blade and slipping the dagger back into her boot. I watched her, and envied her those words: *I'm done.* When would I be done with Zach?

The Ringmaster stepped closer to Zach, peering at his face. Sally had cleaned the skin around his wounds, but the rest of his face was still smeared with grime.

'How far you've come,' The Ringmaster said quietly.

'Not only me,' said Zach. 'You too. It's a long way from the Council rooms at Wyndham. All those pretty serving girls. Yet here we both are.'

'There's a difference between us,' The Ringmaster said. 'I had a choice. I came here because I chose to – because I wanted to stand against you and The General, and your obsession with the machines. But you have no choice. You're here because you need help.' He gestured around at the rest of us, and the guards at the door. 'Without their protection – my protection – you're dead.'

Zach leaned forward, holding out his shackled arms towards The Ringmaster. 'I might be in chains,' he said, 'but we're both here because we have no choice. The only difference is that I've been honest about it. You wouldn't be here, helping them, if you didn't need them just as much as I do. You've never given something for nothing. Not ever. You've been trying to make out that you're here as the saviour of the Omegas? Here to help the oppressed?' Zach laughed, a hollow sound, like the clanking of his chains. 'You're only here because you were getting sidelined at the Council. You saw that The General and I were gaining power, and that you were being left behind because you refused to be reasonable about the potential of the machines.' Zach sat back, his chained arms crossed over his chest. 'You didn't leave the Council to help the Omegas,' he said to The Ringmaster. 'You left because you figured you could capitalise on their uprising as your best chance at overthrowing us, taking back the power for yourself.'

None of us came to The Ringmaster's defence. Zach was only saying what we'd all thought, at times. What we'd all feared.

For a few seconds nobody spoke. Piper's eyes narrowed as he surveyed Zach; beside me, The Ringmaster was standing stiffly, and I could hear the careful evenness of his breath. *Honest*, Zach had said. How many of us, in this room, were really being honest with one another?

'Take him to the storage room out the back,' The Ringmaster said. 'I want Simon at the door. Two of my men too.'

It didn't escape me that he chose Simon first. When I'd first met The Ringmaster, a few months earlier, he never would have trusted an Omega, let alone valued his skills. But whatever else The Ringmaster might have been, he wasn't stupid. He'd seen Simon fighting in the battle for New Hobart, and in the sparring ring where the soldiers trained. It wasn't only his three arms that made him a valuable fighter: Simon was fast, experienced, and strong. In the battle, I'd seen him stand, legs planted wide, hefting his swords as though he were the only solid thing in a flimsy world.

Piper nodded, grabbing Zach roughly by the elbow.

'And when he's locked up, send for Zoe from Elsa's,' I said. Piper hesitated for a moment before he nodded. We both knew that when I said Zoe, I meant Zoe and Paloma. I hated the thought of bringing Paloma into the same building as Zach – but Paloma needed to be part of this discussion.

In the doorway, Zach turned back.

'I will remember every detail of how you treat me,' he said.

'You're not the only one with a memory,' I said. I stared at him, and I wondered if I would ever be able to remember swimming with him in the river as children, without remembering the sodden bodies of the drowned children from the tanks. I remembered how the two of us used to clamber up the trees above the riverbank, and all I could think of was Leonard's distended neck as he hung from the tree.

'Take him away,' I said.

*

Zoe threw the door open so hard that it bounced back off the wall, almost hitting Paloma as she followed Zoe through.

'He has the hide to come to us?' she spat. 'After what he's done? And we're supposed to protect him now?'

'No,' Piper said. 'We're not protecting him. We're protecting Cass.'

'He's using us,' Zoe said.

The Ringmaster exhaled. 'Probably. He's always operated that way. But I don't see that we have any choice.'

Zoe turned to me. 'How do you even know he's telling the truth about The General turning on him?'

'He's telling the truth,' I said. It wasn't that I trusted him. It wasn't even the cuts and bruises on his face that convinced me. It was my certainty that he would never come to me unless he had no choice.

The Ringmaster spoke up. 'It was always a matter of when The General would turn on him, not if. You don't know The General like I do.' He paused, then continued slowly, each word slithering through gritted teeth. 'She's not somebody who likes to share.' I remembered how casually The General had told us about her capture and torture of the crew of one of our ships.

The Ringmaster went on. 'But it doesn't follow that Zach will be safe here, with us. If we keep him here, our own soldiers might kill him. Every soldier in this town, Alpha or Omega, would kill him with pleasure.'

'If that was true,' I said, 'they'd have killed me, months ago.'

'Do you think we haven't been protecting you?' Piper said. He threw the words out as though it were just an ordinary observation, but it knocked the air from my lungs. He went on. 'I always have guards that I trusted watching the holding house. Zoe and I have been with you ourselves whenever we could.'

Months ago, on the island, one of Piper's own advisers had tried to kill me, to take out Zach. I'd thought, since then, that I'd proved my worth to the resistance. And I'd believed that Piper's watchfulness was because of The Ringmaster. I hadn't realised that he still believed I was at risk from our own soldiers, our own people.

Piper spoke gently. 'It was only a precaution,' he said. 'And I don't think they'd kill you directly – they've seen you fight for us, and they know what you've done for the resistance. You helped us evacuate the island, and free this town. I think our people understand that we need you, even if that means that Zach lives.' He cast a glance at the door through which Zach had been taken. 'But if Zach's here with us, it's a provocation. If they caught him on his own, with that sneer on his face, it would be easier for them to see you as collateral damage. At best, they'll rough him up, hurt him badly enough that it'll hurt you too. At worst, they'll finish him off, and you with him.'

'We can't keep him with us, though,' shouted Zoe. 'I won't do it.'

'This isn't about you,' snapped Piper. 'You think I wouldn't like to give him a beating myself?' Piper's voice was rigid, but then it softened. 'Hell on earth, Zoe. I was next to you when we pulled those kids out of the tanks. And you weren't even on the island – you didn't have to see what I saw there. The Confessor executing my soldiers, one after another – all on Zach's orders. Stop acting like you're the only one who hates him.'

'If we don't take him in, they'll kill him?' Paloma said. She'd been standing silently to the side while we argued. Now she spoke up. 'Kill him, and Cass too?' she went on.

The Ringmaster gave a quick nod.

'Then we keep him,' Paloma said. She made it sound as if it were simple: the only choice.

Zoe's face twisted in disgust. 'He'll be spying on us. Manipulating us. And he'll find out about Paloma—'

'We need Cass,' Paloma interrupted her. I was surprised to hear her put it like that. I'd seen how she watched me when I had a vision. How she'd avoided being close to me, since she'd first understood that I had seen Elsewhere burn.

'It's not that simple,' I said, but I was grateful nonetheless for the certainty in her voice.

'Don't patronise me,' she said. 'I hate your visions, hate that you've seen my home burn, my people massacred.' She choked a little on those words, and pressed her lips tightly together before she could continue. 'But I believe you. It's coming. And you're the one who's warned us. You know more than anyone about the blast. We can't save the Scattered Islands without you.'

We were all watching her. She stood very straight, arms wrapped around herself, waiting there in the middle of us all for a response.

'We keep him here,' Piper said.

'Under guard,' The Ringmaster added. 'And away from Paloma.'

Zoe was about to speak again, but she looked at Paloma, and then said nothing.

So he stayed. I thought I might feel relieved – it was true, after all, that we would both be killed if the others hadn't agreed to take him in. But an unease had settled in my guts. Zach had come to us, bruised, desperate and alone, and still we had no option but to do what he demanded.

CHAPTER 5

The next morning, when I woke, I lay silently for a few minutes. I stretched, feet jammed against the bars that made up the foot of the bed, trying to forestall the moment of getting up and facing the day, which meant facing Zach.

Piper had slipped away the night before, while the rest of us were eating in the kitchen. When he'd come back it was nearly midnight, Paloma rolling over with a half-asleep grunt as the door clattered shut and he strode to his bed. I didn't need to ask him where he'd been – I could tell that he'd been talking to Zach. I could see it clearly enough in the way he kicked his boots off and halfway across the room, and in the way he shoved and punched his pillow into shape beneath his head. Now, even though it was barely dawn, Piper was already awake and out in the courtyard with Sally, the two of them talking in low voices.

Zoe and Paloma were awake too, talking by the dormitory window. Paloma was nodding at something Zoe was saying. She was wearing Zoe's shirt, too large for her, the sleeves rolled and bunched over her pale arms. I left the two of them alone.

I found Elsa in the kitchen. While she busied herself with sifting weevils from the flour, I stirred the porridge. The pot held only a dusty handful of oats, thickened with water until it was more like paste than porridge.

'Been like this ever since the last weeks of winter,' Elsa said, seeing me grimace at the grey mixture. 'The grain stores are nearly empty. Half the farms around here weren't even planted last season. The Council only maintained a handful of the fields – enough for the troops stationed here.'

The Council hadn't planted the farms, because they'd thought that by the time the wheat was shoulder-high and ready for harvest, the thousands of Omegas who lived in New Hobart would be tanked, just as the children had been.

'Even now,' she went on, 'some of the farmers are reluctant to work their smallholdings outside the wall. A lot of them have packed up and left.'

I couldn't blame them. The area surrounding New Hobart clung to a semblance of normality, but it was hard not to feel as though the town occupied a pause between battles.

I was still hungry after I finished my porridge, every last scrap of it; I scraped my spoon against the inside of the bowl until the clay squealed.

Walking up through the town to the Tithe Collector's office, the four of us passed a patrol of The Ringmaster's soldiers on their way down to the wall. A year before, if I'd passed them in the street and glanced at their faces, I'd have assumed they were Omegas. Each face had been forced to remember its skull, the bone outlines hard against the flesh. Not since the drought years, when I was a child, had I seen Alphas looking so gaunt.

When we reached the Tithe Collector's office I looked closely at The Ringmaster. Even he had lost weight about the face, though his mass of curly hair disguised the worst of it.

I asked him about the rations.

'I've secured the grain silos at Deadmeadow and Landfall. Most of the western plains are still held by garrisons loyal to me. The tithe takings, too.'

Piper's lips tightened – that money had all been taken from Omegas, often at the lash of a whip.

But if The Ringmaster noticed, he paid no heed. 'The problem is getting it here,' he continued. 'The Council's holding Wreckers' Pass – the convoys from my garrisons can't get through any other way without getting dangerously close to Wyndham. The General's soldiers have picked off two convoys of grain in the last month, and one of weapons. As long as The Council holds the pass, and the plains around Wyndham, we're going to struggle to feed all the troops, let alone the townsfolk.' He added, with a glance at the guards by the door, 'My soldiers aren't used to such short rations.'

'Our troops have worked on less than this for years,' sniped Zoe.

'That doesn't make any difference,' said Piper. 'We need to do better, for all of them. We're asking them to take on the Council, in open battle, when The General attacks – and she will, eventually. We can't defend New Hobart with disgruntled troops. Forget about principles or loyalty – nothing breeds mutiny like a hungry army.'

'And what about new recruits?' I said. 'Have there been more, as the news of the refuges spreads?'

For generations the refuges had been the last resort of the Omegas: places where they would be fed and housed by the Council in exchange for their labour. Though they'd always been little more than prison camps, they were supposed to be the last safety net of a Council that could never endanger Alphas by allowing Omegas to starve. In recent years, under Zach and The General's rule, they had become something more sinister: places where desperate Omegas in their thousands turned themselves in, only to be tanked, permanently preserved to protect their Alpha counterparts.

'You can't be the only one who's decided not to stand for the Council breaking the taboo,' I added.

The Ringmaster shrugged. 'The news of the refuges is spreading – that song you started did its job, I'll give you that, and Omegas have been trickling in, though many are reluctant to come into a town that I'm holding. As for the Alphas – most of them don't believe the rumours about the tanks. And even for those who do, it's a question of what they fear most: the machines, or the Omegas and the fatal bond. Of how far they'd be willing to go to be free of their twins.'

This was the same question I asked myself about him, every day. Every time he spoke of twins, I couldn't help thinking of his own twin, locked away somewhere.

'They fear The General, too,' he went on. 'And rightly. It's one thing for them to want the taboo upheld. Another for them to be willing to oppose her.'

'It would be different if they actually saw the tanks,' I said. I could never forget what I'd seen in there. The melding of tubes and flesh; the heavy silence of the floating bodies. 'Hearing the rumours is different from having to see the reality. Except for the soldiers actually working in the refuges, the Alphas never have to see the tanks. They never have to confront what's actually being done in their name.'

'Your brother and The General know that well enough

– their plans depend on it,' The Ringmaster said, a little impatiently. 'Anyway, while they hold Wreckers' Pass, we couldn't feed more recruits, even if they were pouring in the gates.'

Piper must have seen how my shoulders slumped.

'It's not all bad news,' he said. I raised an eyebrow. 'If The General's concentrating on starving us out, then they might not be planning a major counterattack. Not yet, anyway.'

How long did we have, I wondered, before the Council found out about Paloma, and about Zach? If The General knew that we were sheltering both of them here, would she crush New Hobart? And would The Ringmaster and his troops be enough to defend us, if the Council turned its whole force against us? Would he even try?

*

The Ringmaster was the first person to comment aloud on Paloma and Zoe, the day after Zach's arrival. It was late afternoon; Paloma and Zoe were on the far side of the main hall in the Tithe Collector's office, talking with Simon and Piper. As Paloma walked behind Zoe, she let her hand trail briefly across the back of Zoe's neck.

The Ringmaster spoke so that only I could hear. 'Of all the people she could have chosen,' he said, shaking his head.

'Because Zoe's a woman?' I shot back.

'Don't be stupid,' he said. 'Because Zoe's as spiky as a blackthorn shrub.' He gave me a conspiratorial look.

I didn't return it. I didn't want to discuss Paloma and Zoe – least of all with him. So much of our lives was already under his control; I didn't want to have him sullying this as well.

'Paloma's our only emissary from Elsewhere,' The Ringmaster went on. 'I might not be as keen as the rest of you to join ourselves to them, but I'm not fool enough to think we should risk alienating them. Paloma's goodwill is no small thing. The last thing we need is to have a lovers' quarrel jeopardise our only contact with them.'

'There haven't been any quarrels,' I said. Zoe was as prickly as ever with the rest of us, but around Paloma she had a new calmness. Across the room, Paloma was standing in front of Zoe, and Zoe had tucked her chin to cup the top of Paloma's head.

The Ringmaster was staring too.

'The soldiers are already asking about Paloma,' he said. 'They're not blind, or stupid. They know she's not from here – they're asking where she's from and why she's here. What it means for the future.'

'You know what it means,' I said. 'You can't expect us to ignore what we've learned. If we can save Elsewhere, we'll be able to end the twinning. Look at Paloma.'

'I have,' he said coolly. I followed his gaze. With Zoe standing close behind her, Paloma's false leg was barely visible, a few shades darker than the rest of her flesh.

'She's free of the twinning,' I said. 'They all are, over there.'

'And they're all mutants,' he said. 'You're asking us to make a huge sacrifice.'

I noticed that he still spoke of the Alphas as *us*.

'No,' I said. 'We're asking you to take your fair share. We've carried the burden, for centuries. Not just the infertility, but everything else too. We've done it alone, while you've lived comfortably in your intact bodies.'

'Do you realise what you're asking? You're asking us to give that up.'

'It must be nice,' I said, 'to be so convinced of your own perfection.'

His nostrils flared slightly. 'Easy for you Omegas to claim the moral high ground. You're not the ones who'll be taking this medicine. You want us to risk everything by taking a taboo medicine that you don't even understand.'

He was right: I didn't understand how it worked. Even Paloma didn't know the details of that. The only proof I had was Paloma, and a handful of documents from the Ark. And The Ringmaster was right, too, that it wouldn't be the Omegas taking the medicine. The treatment was for the next generation, so it would be wasted on us, since the one mutation that all Omegas shared was our infertility.

He continued. 'Untwinning – the kind that you're describing – it wouldn't have saved my wife.'

His wife had died in childbirth, when the Omega twin, with an enlarged head, had become stuck. Since confiding this to me, he'd never mentioned it again, until now, and the one time I'd raised it he had responded with fury. But now he raised it himself, unprompted, his voice tired.

'It wasn't the twinning that killed Gemma,' he said. 'It was the freak she gave birth to. And you want me to help you make this untwinning happen – to make the whole next generation into freaks.'

There was a long silence.

'This isn't for us,' I said. 'It won't save us, or change us, or raise the dead. But there's a chance for the next generation's lives to be their own.'

He was still staring across the room at Paloma's false leg, and at Piper and Simon.

'But what kind of life can it be, really?' he said.

I looked at him, and pity mingled with my anger. How

could he ask? I followed his gaze. There was Piper, his wide shoulders bent over a map as he spoke with Simon, and Paloma, whose bond with Zoe sometimes felt like the only growing thing in a scorched world. How could The Ringmaster look at them and speak of imperfection, or of meaningless lives?

'For all your perfection,' I said, 'you see nothing.' The Ringmaster looked at me strangely – I hadn't meant to, but I'd laughed as I spoke. 'Do you really think it's the deformations that make our lives impossible? I'm not stupid enough to say the deformations aren't hard. But the real problem's the settlements, the tithes, the curfews, the whippings. The Alphas who spit as they ride past us, and the raiders who raid our settlements, knowing the Council won't protect us.'

'But I have protected you,' he said. 'I freed this town, and fought alongside you, because we agreed that the taboo had to be upheld.'

'We agreed that what Zach and The General were doing was wrong,' I said.

'And what if I think what you want to do, with Elsewhere's medicine, is wrong?' he said.

I did my best to keep my breath steady. 'Then you must make your choice,' I said. 'Just as I have.'

*

When one of The Ringmaster's soldiers brought a tray of food to the table, Piper glanced towards the room where Zach was locked up. 'We should take him some food,' he said.

'Why?' snapped Zoe. 'Let him go hungry. It's the least he deserves.'

'We need him healthy,' Piper said. 'If he weakens, or sickens, it puts Cass at risk.'

'I'm not suggesting we starve him to death,' Zoe said. 'But it won't kill him to miss a few meals. I'm not going to be waiting on him hand and foot, that's for sure.'

'I'll go,' I said, standing. I bent to spoon more stew into my bowl, and grabbed the last hunk of flatbread.

The Ringmaster and Piper were both watching me as I straightened.

'See what you can get out of him,' The Ringmaster said.

'You don't need to tell me what to do,' I said. 'I'm not going to see him for fun.'

Even as I walked down the corridor towards where Zach was kept, I felt the sweat sting my underarms, and my heart pummel my ribs; I walked faster, to make my footsteps match its pace.

During the years that he'd kept me imprisoned in the Keeping Rooms, I used to wait for his visits. I'd counted the days, the meal trays, the steps outside my cell. Even though I'd hated him, he'd been the only person who ever came, except for The Confessor. My hatred for him, and my longing to see him, had curdled in me.

Now it was my turn, taking those steps down the corridor to the room where Zach waited.

Simon had been given a break, but there were still four guards outside the room, stepping aside and unbolting the door for me as I approached.

It was barely a room, really – more like a cupboard, though a narrow window up high let in some light. Dust mounted in the corners, where empty crates were stacked.

When I stepped inside, ducking under the low lintel, Zach raised his hands to show me how his shackles had been passed through a metal ring screwed to the wall. I put the bowl on the floor and slid it towards him, but he ignored it.

'This is how you choose to treat me?' he said.

The door closed behind me. 'You came to us,' I said. 'You knew what to expect.'

'I didn't expect this,' he said, shaking his hands so that the chain rattled.

'You did worse to me,' I said. 'Four years in the Keeping Rooms. Be grateful that you've got fresh air, and sunlight. It's more than you gave me.'

'Four years?' he said. 'Try thirteen.'

'What are you talking about?'

He cocked his head to the side. 'You think this is the first time I've been your prisoner?' he said. 'What about the first thirteen years of our lives? You kept me trapped. You made my own parents wary of me. I couldn't start school; couldn't make friends; couldn't do anything, fit in anywhere, until I was free of you.' He stared at me unflinchingly. 'Thirteen years,' he said again, dragging the words out, making each syllable last. 'My life couldn't start until I'd got rid of you. I've had to make up for lost time ever since.'

'Don't blame me for what you've done,' I said. 'It was your choice – all of it.' I looked at his hands, and thought of the things they had done. Looked at his mouth, and thought of the orders he had given. 'You've done unspeakable things.'

'What alternative was there?' he shouted. 'Let things continue as they were? Everyone subject to the whims of Omega bodies, that could sicken at any moment?'

I ignored him. 'Tell me what you know,' I said. 'Where did you move the blast machine? What's The General planning?'

He went rigid. 'I've told you. The General's been freezing me out, ever since you destroyed the database and retook this town.'

How quickly we were back to his old refrain: everything was my fault. Mine.

'But you still must know,' I said. 'You were in the Ark, when they were moving the blast machine out.'

Night after night, I had groped after that blast machine. I'd forced myself to reach for it, against every instinct that recoiled at the thought of such a weapon. I'd reached for it, clenching my eyes so tightly that I saw white shapes moving in front of the blackness. It made no difference – however hard I strained to see the place, I felt nothing, or worse, a wavering impression: north one day, and two days later gone altogether, or to the west. My seer's knack for finding things was failing me. Or the blast machine had broken it, as it would break everything in the end.

'I've got nothing to tell you,' Zach said. 'The General ordered the relocation. I never saw the new site. I already told that to your friend Piper, when he came to badger me.' Zach's lips tightened at the memory. 'Him and The Ringmaster together, asking me the same questions, for hours. Trying to scare me, intimidate me. I told them what I've told you: I never went there. I don't know.'

'You're lying to me,' I said.

'What are you going to do about it?' he said. 'Torture me?' There was a smirk at the edges of his lips.

I banged on the door. While the guards were unbolting it, I kept my hand to the door, pressing my palm hard against the rough wood and trying to stay calm. Zach eyed me appraisingly. He knew that I would share any pain inflicted on him. Last night, when I'd guessed that Piper and The Ringmaster were in here with him, I'd slept with my body half-braced, awaiting the pain. It hadn't come – but I didn't know how long I could expect Piper and The Ringmaster to spare me. It didn't matter that Zach and not I was responsible for his crimes. It made no difference: my body had become an obstacle between the resistance and what we needed to know.

Before I rejoined the others in the main hall, I stood for a moment with my back against the wall of the corridor. The guards were locking the door of Zach's room again, and I felt my breath slowing with the scrape of each bolt sliding home, but flames still hissed at the edge of my vision. The blast was stalking me. How much longer, I wondered, before I joined Xander in the Kissing Tree, and in his silence? How much longer before I surrendered to the blast?

Piper watched me carefully as I entered the main hall; conversation stopped when I entered.

'Did you get anything out of him?' The Ringmaster said.

I shook my head. 'He says he doesn't know anything.'

'Do you believe him?' asked Zoe.

'I don't know,' I snapped. 'I can't read his mind.'

Zoe raised her hands in mock surrender, rolling her eyes. 'Take it easy. Nobody's suggesting that the two of you are best friends.'

I busied myself with pouring a cup of water at the side table, so that I could turn away from their stares. The water splashed from my unsteady hands.

Piper picked up his cup and joined me. 'Zach's trying to mess with you,' he said, without looking at me, as he took the jug and filled his cup. He kept his voice low, so the others couldn't hear. 'Don't let him in your head.'

I nodded. But he didn't know that Zach had never been out of it.

CHAPTER 6

Sally, Elsa, Xander and I sat in the front room of the holding house as the town's evening noises rattled past the window. Soldiers off duty; the more orderly footsteps of those still on patrol; the voices of passing townsfolk. When I was last in New Hobart, it had taken me a few days to realise why the town sounded strange. It wasn't only the aftermath of the battle that had left the town damaged and the residents nervy and furtive. Even after the repairs had begun, and people had returned to the streets, the sound of the city remained different. Eventually I'd realised that it was the nearly total absence of children. At Elsa's house, around the market, and in the streets, only adult voices were to be heard. There was a whole layer of noise missing: the high voices of children's chatter; the crying of babies; the sudden shout of a child ambushed in a game. The town was far from silent now – thousands of people lived here, and went about the business of their days – but like a dented bell, New Hobart didn't ring true.

My gaze kept straying to where Xander sat, leaning against Sally's chair with his eyes closed. I thought of Zach, locked in his cell at the Tithe Collector's office. Zach was my past, Xander was my future. And ahead of us all: the blast, which would be the end of Elsewhere, and the resistance, and any futures that I could envisage.

Below the large window, another patrol passed – twelve mounted soldiers on their way back from the wall.

Sally saw me watching them.

'We've increased the size of the patrols, since the Council seized Wreckers' Pass and started picking off the convoys. We've set up some permanent outposts on the supply routes, too.'

It wasn't the size of the patrol that had caught my attention, though. It was the two men in the centre of it, who didn't wear the same uniform as the rest of The Ringmaster's soldiers. They wore the blue of the island's guards, and they were Omegas. The first man's left arm was a stub, a clawed hand protruding directly from his shoulder. The taller man, behind him, had a hunchback that forced him to lean forward over the pommel of his saddle.

'They're patrolling together now?' I said to Sally.

She nodded. 'Neither side was that keen on it – The Ringmaster's men in particular. It was never a decision we made. It just happened. There was the fire in the northern quarter while you were away, and everyone had to pitch in together, to stop the whole town going up in smoke. And at times, they were a few hands short for some of the Alpha patrols. Drafted in a couple of our troops – not without some muttering, on both sides.'

'But they've kept doing it?' I said, my gaze following the last of the riders as they turned the corner at the top of the hill.

'Don't get dreamy-eyed about it,' Sally said. She took a deep pull of Elsa's pipe, held the smoke in her mouth for a few seconds. 'Nobody did it because they wanted to. Like I said: it just happened. Still only happens when a patrol's shorthanded, or there's some kind of emergency.'

I nodded, and leaned my face against the window frame to hide my smile. This was how it happened: daily familiarity, not grand gestures. You could only pass a fellow soldier so many times, at shift handover, and see him unbuckle his sword, and grunt about the weather, before you learned that he was a man just like you, no more mysterious or terrifying than that. The Council's policy of segregation had been a key part of its attempt to stoke tensions between Alphas and Omegas. Sharing a latrine might do more to bring the two together than any inspiring speeches could have done.

'It's not all been smooth sailing,' Elsa said. 'There's been bickering, and some big flare-ups, especially since rations got so tight. While you were away at the coast, some of The Ringmaster's men tried to claim the biggest well, in the market, saying it was for Alpha use only. They were trying to get everyone worked up about it. Muttering about contamination.'

Sally rolled her eyes. 'We share a womb, but they reckon they'll catch something if we share a well?'

I knew what she meant, but I also knew that it was *because* we shared a womb that they flinched from us, not in spite of it – I'd learned that from Zach. Nothing frightened them more than the realisation that we were not so different after all.

'There were arguments,' Elsa went on, 'and more than a couple of fistfights.'

Sally nodded. 'The Ringmaster came down hard on both sides – he was fair about it, I'll say that. Didn't take any nonsense, not from his own soldiers any more than ours.'

She gave a slow chuckle. 'It was laziness that put an end to the idea though – not discipline, let alone principles. Most of the Alphas quartered on the eastern side of town were too lazy to go across town to the market for water. The whole thing petered out after a few days.'

She still spoke of them that way: *his soldiers* and *ours*. But for the first time since Zach's arrival I permitted myself a moment of hope that in this half-starved town, we were building something new. In its own small way, the sight of those riders, Alphas and Omegas together, felt as monumental as Elsewhere itself.

*

Sally came to the dormitory that night, when I was alone. I heard her distinctive gait across the courtyard: a slow step, each movement precise because it cost her so much pain.

'I've seen you watching Xander,' she said.

His name was enough to make me stiffen. What she said was true. I didn't like to be near Xander, but when I was, I couldn't stop watching him.

'I don't mean to stare,' I said. 'But I can't help it. When I see him, I can see what I'm becoming—'

She spoke over me. 'I don't have time for your platitudes.' She waved a hand impatiently. 'You're a seer and I need your help. I can't reach him any more. Tell me what can be done for him.' I thought of Xander's face, blank as the burnt-out buildings that still lined the streets of New Hobart. 'He's barely said a word, for weeks,' Sally went on. 'Not even the usual fire-talk.' His old refrain: *Forever fire*.

'What's the point of him saying it, now?' I said. 'You don't stand in the middle of a burning forest, shouting, *Fire!*

The blast is upon us. It's too late for warnings. He knows it. We know it.'

'So how can I help him?' she said.

'You can't,' I said. 'I mean, not any more than you already are. Talk to him. Keep him fed. Let him go to the Kissing Tree, if it helps to calm him.' All the hundred things that she did for him each day. That same morning, from the dormitory window, I'd seen her kneel on the gravel to trim Xander's toenails, though kneeling seemed to take her minutes, both hands on the small of her back as she lowered herself.

'Does he even know what's going on around him?' she asked.

'He's living in the blast,' I said. 'It's all he sees now.'

'Nothing else?'

'I think he's aware of things passing. He hears what we say. But everything that isn't the blast doesn't count. Everything else . . .' I paused, trying to find a way to describe what I felt each time I saw Xander. I remembered what Paloma had said, when she was telling us what had happened to the mines and oil wells when the blast came: *Everything that could burn, burned.* 'Everything else,' I said to Sally, 'is just fuel. It burns away.'

*

Orders had been sent for the ships to be readied. The General held most of the coast, but The Ringmaster had two ships at a garrison to the south, and they were to be sailed to the north-west coast to join *The Rosalind*. It was dangerous – the Council had increased its coastal patrols, even that far north, and mooring the ships at deep anchor meant exposing them to the storms. And we all knew that the Council would attack New Hobart at some point – if they didn't starve us out first. But it was some comfort to know that if we could survive for a few months, the fleet should be ready. As soon as the last of the northerly winds carried spring away, Paloma could lead us back to her homeland – if the Council hadn't found or destroyed the Scattered Islands first.

Although he'd given the orders to prepare the fleet, I noticed that The Ringmaster was still wary around Paloma. If we sat around the table in the main hall, he always made sure he was at the far end, opposite her. When the rest of us asked her questions about Elsewhere, he just watched her, arms crossed over his chest. He was silent when the topic of the medicines was raised.

Piper noticed it too. 'You have an objection?' he asked.

'I've already said I'll provide the ships, and do what I can to protect Paloma,' The Ringmaster replied. 'But I can't make a promise that will expose my people to taboo medicine.'

'You won't even offer them the choice?'

'We Alphas have preserved proper humanity for four hundred years. You want to undo all of that.'

'Proper humanity?' I said. 'You mean Alphas – ideal people like Zach, or The General?'

'You know what I mean,' he said impatiently. 'Physical perfection. Strength. It might not be the Long Winter any more, but this is still a hard world. We need hardy people to survive it.'

From the other end of the table came Paloma's voice. 'You really think everyone was perfect before the bomb?' She was leaning back in her chair.

The Ringmaster stared at her. 'We know the blast caused the mutations. We've always known it – and the papers from the Ark confirmed it. They talk about the mutations, and how they developed after the blast.'

'Yes,' Paloma said, leaning forward. 'I can't deny what the blast did. But do you think all bodies were the same before then?' She bent, chin almost to the table, and there was a clicking sound as she twisted her false leg free of the socket. 'This technology,' she said, placing the leg on the table, 'was from before the bomb.' The Ringmaster's nostrils narrowed as he watched the leg rock from side to side, and then settle. 'At home we have other technology taken from back then as well,' she went on. 'Wheelchairs, and artificial hands. The doctors only managed to preserve a fraction of what they used to have, but it's enough to know for sure that there were people born then like we are today.'

'They had the words for it,' I said. 'In the Before.'

'What are you talking about?' The Ringmaster's head snapped around to face me.

'In the Ark papers, when they were writing about the mutations,' I said. 'They already had the words to describe them.' It had been a jumble of syllables to me: *polymelia; amelia; polydactyly; syndactyly*. But it had meant something to the people who wrote it. They were horrified at how many people had mutations, since the blast, but the conditions they were witnessing were already named, already known. These were things that had preceded the blast. 'They knew what these problems were,' I said. 'They had names for them.'

'And medicines, for some of them,' Paloma added. 'We haven't been able to preserve many of them, but there are some conditions that can be improved, or managed, at least, with the right medicines. My youngest sister has seizures, or she used to. The doctors gave her a medicine, to take every day. She's hardly had a seizure since.'

The Ringmaster shook his head. 'Just because there used to be a few freaks, in the Before, doesn't mean it's right. Doesn't mean that we should just give up, and let everyone here become like that.'

I started laughing. Paloma looked at me as though I'd gone mad. Perhaps I had. But I could see it all, now. I'd seen it with Zach, and now again with The Ringmaster. How frantically they shored up the walls that collapsed around their beliefs.

'Freaks?' I said. 'You're just drawing a line in the sand. It doesn't mean anything. It's arbitrary.'

As the argument continued over the table, I kept thinking about how things used to be clearer. The clear line between Before and After had been blurred by the discovery of the Ark, and Elsewhere, and what we had learned about the past. And the line between Alphas and Omegas was fading, despite the best efforts of Alphas to maintain it.

But what about the line between me and Zach?

*

That night I woke with a shout of pain, clutching my forehead. Across the dormitory Zoe gave a grunt, and tugged at the blanket that Paloma had dragged to her side of the bed.

At first, I made the same assumption as Zoe: that the pain in my head was a vision, or a dream. I lay in the bed and waited for it to dissipate, but it grew worse, and I curled tightly, knees to face, hearing my own moan. When I sat up, Zoe was kneeling in front of me, her face a mixture of irritation and concern. Paloma was behind her, blanket wrapped around her shoulders. The courtyard door banged open and Piper ran in, but I closed my eyes against the agony in my forehead. It had the insistence of a burn. I hadn't felt anything like it since I was thirteen, the day that I'd been branded, the Councilman's breath on my face as he'd pressed the brand into my skin. Then the sound of skin extinguishing fire.

'Show me,' said Zoe, peeling my hands away from my face. I fought her – as if pressing my hands against my forehead could somehow contain the pain – but she was so much stronger.

'There's nothing there,' she said, looking around at Piper.

He guessed first.

'Zach,' he said.

*

By the time we got to the Tithe Collector's office, The Ringmaster had found him.

I'd stumbled through the darkened streets, one hand gripping Piper's arm to keep me steady, the pain so hot that I had to bite my lower lip to stop myself from shouting.

Beside the Tithe Collector's office, six soldiers stood with their backs to the wall, heads lowered. Two men wore the red of The Ringmaster's soldiers; the others, three men and a woman, were in the blue of the resistance. Facing them stood The Ringmaster, a lamp raised in one hand. He kept his anger tightly contained, which only made it more frightening.

Sitting on the ground by the wall, a few feet from the soldiers, was Zach. His hands were cupped over his forehead, just like mine.

The Ringmaster saw us. 'Simon was off duty. Four of them jumped Zach on the way back from the privy,' he said. 'Two of his guards were escorting him. They didn't do their job.' Each of his words was as tightly clenched as a fist.

'I tried to stop them,' said the woman. I recognised her: it was Meera, one of Simon and Piper's senior soldiers, whom I'd spoken to often enough.

Piper stepped forward. 'How hard did you try?' he said.

She gave no answer. Her tunic was ripped at the neck, but there were no bruises or wounds on her – however hard she'd battled to protect her ward, it hadn't been enough to mark her. Even while my teeth were gritted against the pain in my forehead, I didn't think I could blame Meera. Hadn't I swung my fist at Zach myself, only the night before?

'If they'd got carried away,' Piper spat, 'Cass could be dead. You understand?'

'Yes sir,' Meera said, head lowered. I didn't know whether she was hiding her contrition, or her lack of it.

The Ringmaster turned to give a dismissive glance at Zach. 'I think no more of him than you do,' he said to the soldiers. 'But he's under our protection. And any attack on him is an attack on our seer. She's valuable to us.'

He looked carefully at each of the soldiers, memorising each face.

'Get back to your barracks,' he said. 'But this isn't over. There will be consequences for each of you.'

They left in silence. I looked at their retreating backs, red and blue tunics together. I had not wanted it to be this way; I didn't want hatred for Zach to be the one thing that could unite our fractured army.

Piper grabbed Zach by the back of his shirt, and hauled him upright. Only then, when he came within range of The Ringmaster's lamp, could I see what they had done to him.

They must have planned it in advance, because they'd made the brand. It lay on the dirt by the wall, just a piece of metal, crudely bent, the farrier's tongs fallen open nearby. Zach must have struggled, so the burn sat crookedly on his forehead, a lopsided A with no crossbar. It didn't matter that it was barely intelligible – the message was clear enough. Already, one side of the Alpha symbol was a fattening blister; the other was a red indentation, black at the edges. I remembered my dream: Zach, his forehead branded like mine. When I leant in to look more closely at his wound, he flinched away.

'Pull yourself together,' Piper said to Zach, releasing him to stand on his own. 'It's only a brand, no worse than nearly every Omega gets as a child.'

He led Zach into the main hall, and let him sit down. Elsa had followed us up the hill, slow on her bowed legs; she came in now, looked at Zach with distaste, then rummaged through her medicine bag to find a salve.

'Put it on his burn – it'll ease the pain,' she said, giving me the small jar. 'For you, I mean. I couldn't care less about him.'

On the far side of the room, the others were talking quietly and urgently around the big table; in the corner, I stood over Zach, but he didn't meet my eyes. The salve smelled of lard and rosemary, and it was so thick that I had to rub it between my hands to warm and soften it before I could apply it Zach's wound. He was sweating – a hot, urgent sweat of fever and panic, dampening the underarms of his shirt.

He flinched when I put the salve onto the burn.

I looked down at him. 'I know how it feels.'

We were both remembering the same thing: the brand on my flesh, while the Councilman held me down. Zach standing with my parents on the other side of the room, watching. I remembered him giving a grunt of pain; he must have felt, back then, a taste of my own agony. Now it was truly his.

'I dreamed you would be branded,' I said. 'Weeks ago. It didn't make any sense, back then.' I picked up a cloth and wiped the last of the salve from my fingers. It left a greasy film on my skin.

'I would never have come to you, if I'd known you can't even control your own soldiers,' Zach said.

I shrugged. 'It was your choice to come to us. You want to leave now?' I looked at the doorway. Even if there were no guards behind it, we both knew that Zach would never dare to go. If she got hold of him, The General would not stop at branding him. The soldiers who had just attacked him were the only thing keeping us both alive.

*

It wasn't only pain that kept me awake that night. Piper had stayed up at the Tithe Collector's office to guard Zach himself, and even though Zoe was close by, I found it hard to sleep without Piper's breath in the next bed, or his silhouette at the window, when he sat overlooking the courtyard.

I had been afraid, in different forms, for as long as I could remember. Afraid, when we were growing up, that Zach would expose me and I would be branded and sent away. Afraid, in the settlement, that Zach would come for me. And when he had come for me, and I was in the Keeping Rooms, I was afraid that I would never get out, and never see the sky again. The six months since my escape had been a collection of different fears: pursuit, hunger, imprisonment, battles.

For a long time after Kip's death, I had cared little for my own life, or for anything else. But now I had fought my way through that, and found there were things in the world that I wanted, and relished. So when I'd seen Zach huddled on the ground, and felt his pain in my own skin, my fear had a new simplicity: I did not want to die. I did not want Zach and his enemies and treachery to snatch this life from me, just when I'd learned to occupy it again.

The next day, the soldiers who'd branded Zach were whipped. Piper had warned me, first thing in the morning, when he came back to the holding house.

'Is it really necessary?' I said. 'Most of them are Omegas. They joined the resistance because they wanted to fight the Council, and they've found themselves taking orders from The Ringmaster, and now seeing Zach here too. It's hard for them.'

'If we can't control our army, we've no hope of beating the Council's,' said Piper.

I couldn't argue with him. I knew that it wasn't only my own life, or Zach's, that depended on our army holding together. But through those long morning hours as I worked with Elsa in the kitchen, Zach's brand still pulsing on my forehead, the sky outside was smeared grey, as if the news of the whippings had spread an ugliness over the day.

I refused to watch the whipping. Paloma, too, had scrunched her face with distaste when Zoe asked her if she wanted to see, so she waited with Zoe in the holding house, while I went to the Tithe Collector's office to check on Zach.

When Piper and Elsa and I passed the square on the way, the whipping post was being fixed in place. Months before, Kip and I had witnessed a man whipped bloody by Alpha soldiers in the same square. The raised platform they'd used had long since been torn down, and probably burned for firewood. Now, two Omega soldiers were sinking a thick post into the ground. With each pound of the mallets, the ground spat back dust. I walked faster, yanking on Elsa's arm as she craned her neck to see. The soldiers who weren't on patrol had all been summoned to the market square. They were gathering already, the crowd thickening as we shouldered our way through.

In the main hall, The Ringmaster was waiting, along with Simon. To my surprise, so was Zach.

The Ringmaster stood as we entered. 'I'm leaving him here with you,' he said. 'Piper and I are needed in the square, and I want you both properly guarded.'

I knew I was being protected, and that I wasn't wearing shackles like Zach, but I still looked to Piper for reassurance.

He nodded. 'Simon will be here the whole time. And three guards, hand-selected, on the door.' He gestured at the doorway, where soldiers waited. Two of them were The Ringmaster's, but I was relieved to recognise Crispin, too.

At first, after Piper and The Ringmaster left, the massed soldiers in the square beyond the northern window were a background hubbub of noise. But at noon they fell silent. The cries of the market traders, too, were hushed. And even from where we sat, with the shutter closed, we could hear the strokes of the whip. Ten strokes each for the four soldiers who had attacked Zach. Five strokes each for Meera and the other soldier who had been guarding Zach, for failing in their duty.

Simon sat by the door. He was leaning back, arms crossed over his chest, but one of his hands rested on his axe hilt, and he didn't take his eyes off Zach.

Zach and I sat on opposite sides of the room, and heard each stroke. It seemed to take a very long time: a pause after each blow, and then the crack of the next. The noisiest thing of all seemed to be the silence between me and

Zach. We stared at each other, him on a chair at the table and me on the windowsill, my back against the closed shutter. Zach fidgeted from time to time, reaching up to his burn, and prodding gingerly around its edges.

'Don't touch it,' I snapped. 'You'll only make it worse.'

There was another stroke of the whip. I couldn't stop myself from wincing, a sharp intake of air through my closed teeth.

'You can stop glaring at me,' Zach said. 'It's hardly my fault that your soldiers attacked me.'

I kept my expression blank, my eyes on his. 'It's your fault that they wanted to.'

'And your army's weak discipline that meant they went ahead with it.'

Another thwack. I didn't want Zach to know how I felt. That his arrival had left me exposed, as though the walls of New Hobart had fallen.

'He's whipping them himself, you know,' Zach said. 'Piper.'

Yet another whip stroke cracked the silence.

'You didn't know that?' Zach said. His voice was like a knife, probing flesh.

'I knew,' I lied.

Zach just raised an eyebrow.

I ignored him. We sat there together, under Simon's gaze. The pain in my head had lessened already, just a reminder of last night's searing, but periodically Zach would ignite it again by touching the burn, grimacing as he tested the tautness of the blister.

When the whippings were over, Piper came back. He let the door slam behind him. He was sweaty, but I was relieved to see no blood on his clothes, or on the leather whip that he tossed to the ground. Whatever he'd done, it had not been as brutal as the whipping I'd witnessed with Kip. The length of plaited leather lay on the ground between us.

Zach had stood as soon as Piper entered; he moved to the far side of room, eyeing the whip as though it were a snake that might strike at him.

'You can stop cowering,' Piper said. 'I'm done for today.'

He came to stand by me at the window. I kept my voice low, aware of Zach watching us from the far side of the room.

'Couldn't it have been The Ringmaster who whipped them?' I said. 'Or couldn't you have got one of the other senior soldiers to do it? What about Simon?'

'I don't ask my men to do things I'm not willing to do myself,' he said. 'And it had to be me, not The Ringmaster. Can you imagine the response, if we put The Ringmaster up there, to whip mainly Omega troops, in defence of The Reformer?' He exhaled. 'It had to be me.'

He was probably right. But when he put his hand on the windowsill, close to mine, I couldn't help thinking of the whip.

'This isn't what we wanted,' I said in a whisper. 'This isn't what we're doing this for.' I didn't want to say it in front of Zach – didn't want to show him the cracks that I could see, spreading everywhere. But I was thinking of what I'd said to Piper and Zoe, back in the deadlands: that if we didn't find Elsewhere, we would build our own. That we would find a way to make a better world here. This wasn't what we'd dreamed of: the whip on the floor, the beaten soldiers outside.

'You're not different from me, Cass, for all that you'd like to think you are,' Piper said. He was leaning forward over the sill, his weight on his arm. 'You've made the same choices I have, to survive, and to do what has to be done.

You think that because you can't throw a knife, or wield a whip, that you're somehow innocent?'

I wasn't angry because I disagreed with him. I was angry because everything he said was true.

'I have done only what's been necessary,' he said. 'I am what the resistance has needed me to be.'

'I know,' I said.

'Then what do you want from me?' he said.

What could I have told him that wouldn't have sounded wistful, impossible? A different world, in which he didn't have to be those things. In which neither of us did.

'Nothing,' I replied.

CHAPTER 7

'We're moving Zach to stay with Cass,' The Ringmaster announced. 'We—'

'No,' I said, interrupting him. 'No way. Absolutely not.'

It had been such a relief when Simon led Zach back to his cell, and Elsa, Zoe and Paloma had joined us in the Tithe Collector's office. Now The Ringmaster's words struck me like a kick. I turned to Piper for support, but his face was firm.

'I'm trying to keep you alive,' he said. 'We need to have both you and Zach guarded, by people we can trust. And we have Paloma to worry about as well. If Zach's with you, that's one location to cover instead of three. I'm posting guards outside the holding house. I'll be there too, when Zoe's not.'

'You can't be serious,' I said. 'Even if he has to be with me, he can't come to the holding house. Not with Paloma there. And you can't expect Elsa to have him.'

Piper's face remained set.

'I'll move up here,' I said. 'Don't bring him to Elsa's.'

He lowered his voice, brought his head close to mine. 'I

want you where you can be safe.' He looked across the room at The Ringmaster. 'Not here, with him, in the thick of his soldiers.'

Even though we gathered daily in the Tithe Collector's office, there was still a sense that it was The Ringmaster's territory, and that Elsa's was ours. Perhaps it was the residue of the building's former role: this was a place where Omegas used to come in supplication, to hand over their tithes. Even after the battle, and the hungry months since, the rooms still had a scale and grandeur that marked them as Alpha territory. We were all more at home admidst the half-trashed furniture of the holding house, than on the leather-upholstered chairs of the Tithe Collector's office.

'It's not just that,' Piper said, stepping back again. 'You can watch Zach in a way that we can't. You know what happened when you were travelling with Zoe.'

Zoe's face hardened at the reminder. In those weeks of sleeping close together, I had glimpsed her dreams. I'd never meant to, but each morning I'd woken with the memory of her dreams as well as my own. That was how I'd discovered her endless scouring of the sea for the drowned Lucia.

'I can't read minds,' I said. 'It's not as tidy as that.'

'I know that,' Piper replied. 'But anything that you can glean from him could still help us.'

Elsa spoke. 'I'll take him.' She had stepped forward a little, chin high. 'I can't promise I'll be civil to him. Or even that I won't spit in his food. But if it's the best way of helping, and of keeping Cass safe, I'll take him.'

'You don't need to do this,' I told her. 'It's asking too much.'

She shook her head. 'I want you safe, and with me.' She shrugged. 'He's just a side effect.'

I remembered how The General had said that Omegas

were only side effects of Alphas – the same phrase that had been used in the Ark papers – and I smiled to hear Elsa use it now, to describe Zach.

For half a day the holding house was noisy with the sound of soldiers fitting bars on the windows, and a thicker door for the dormitory, with bolts on the outside. Elsa said nothing, just followed the soldiers with her broom and scolded them when they left iron filings and nails on the floor. A roster was drawn up, for the soldiers that we trusted, to watch the front of the holding house while Zoe and Piper guarded it from within. It wasn't a long list. Simon, and his long-time adviser, Violet, were on it. Having seen her come to blows with Piper once, I trusted her candour, and her courage – and since their fight, she'd shown herself loyal to him. Crispin, who had served Simon and Piper on the island, and ever since, was on the list too.

The Ringmaster had offered us some of his senior soldiers as well. I doubted that we had a choice, but in the end I was glad of those he'd chosen: Tash, a tall woman from his personal guard, who spoke little but met my eyes without the disgust or evasiveness of many of the Alpha soldiers. Adam, a bluff man who was quick to laugh, and who, when stationed at the holding house door, seemed to laugh and chat as readily with Elsa and Sally as with his fellow Alphas.

Paloma and Zoe shifted their things out of the dormitory, to sleep in the small room Kip and I had once shared on the other side of the courtyard. Piper moved out too, dragging his bed out to the courtyard, under the covered porch by the main door.

'It's warm enough now,' he'd said, over the scraping of the bed on the floorboards. 'And I'll be able to keep an eye on Zoe and Paloma's door, as well as the dormitory.'

That was true – but we both knew that he also wanted to avoid sharing a room with Zach. I looked at the two drag marks left on the floor by the legs of his bed. It would just be me and Zach now, alone each night in the dormitory.

So he came. They kept the shackles on his wrists, and Piper and Zoe made sure that one of them was always in the holding house. At night, in the dormitory, his shackles were fastened to a chain bolted to the wall. I had measured it out myself: the chain reached just far enough for him to lie comfortably in bed, but fell short of my bed on the opposite wall.

During the day, when Zoe or Piper was nearby, his shackles were kept on but we let him take some exercise in the courtyard, or eat with the rest of us.

'I don't want him being waited on, like he's still in the Council chambers,' Zoe said. 'And I'd rather have him where I can see him.'

The clanking of Zach's shackles quickly became a familiar sound in the holding house.

'I'm sorry,' I said again and again to Elsa, whenever we were alone. 'I'm sorry that you have to see him every day.'

She just smiled at me, and gripped my hand. As for Zach, she never spoke to him, but she met his gaze squarely, and filled a bowl for him at mealtimes and placed it on the table. It was a kind of courage I'd never seen before, the way she faced him each day, in her home, where the children he'd killed used to live.

I wondered, at first, how Zach himself would react to being in the holding house. Most of the children's possessions had been destroyed in the raid when they'd been taken, and half the holding house had been trashed. But the signs of them were everywhere. Behind the dormitory door, a row of hooks barely at hip height, where the children used to hang their winter coats. In Elsa's smashed-up kitchen, the handful of cups that had survived the raid were all the children's, and so we drank each day from the tiny cups, our lips where their lips had been.

If any of these things made Zach uneasy, he never showed any sign. I watched him at dinner, that first night. He wrapped his long fingers around the small cup, drank, and left it on the table for Elsa to tidy away. He never mentioned the children, who were absent and present everywhere.

*

The first night, alone in the dormitory, Zach and I lay on either side of the long, narrow room. He had his back to the wall, facing me. I blew out the candle so I wouldn't have to look at him any more.

'Light the candle again,' he said.

'Go to sleep.'

His chain clanked a few times as he shifted. 'I don't like the dark.'

'Get used to it,' I said, rolling over. 'This isn't the Council chambers. We don't have an endless supply of candles.'

'I never used to mind the dark,' he said. 'But since you flooded the Ark, I hate it.'

I remembered it too: the total darkness of those corridors. Black water rising in black air.

'I only just made it out,' he said. His breathing grew faster at the memory. I listened unwillingly, my arms crossed over my chest. I had enough of my own memories of the flooded Ark, and no time to waste on his.

'Even when I made it to the surface,' he went on, 'it wasn't over. The river burst through the western door. I was nearly caught up by it. Half the camp was swept away.

At least four of our soldiers died. Men were tangled up in the canvas when the tents were washed away.'

More bodies to add to the tally of the dead. There were so many people that I had killed, directly or indirectly. Sometimes I felt tangled in them, like the soldiers drowning under the sodden canvas.

'A hell of a way to die,' Zach continued.

'You've condemned many people to worse,' I said.

He ignored me. 'I dream about it,' he went on. 'If it's dark, I dream about the Ark. The water in the corridors, and that flash flood by the western door.'

I tried not to listen, but I was remembering how we used to talk at night when we were children, while our parents were downstairs arguing about what they could do about us, their unsplit children. We'd lain there and whispered across the gap between our beds, just as we were doing now.

'I have worse dreams,' I said.

'What about?'

I was silent. I wasn't going to explain my dreams to him – he already knew too much about the blast.

'What about?' he said again.

'Nothing,' I said. 'Now shut up – I'm trying to sleep.'

'You're lying to me,' he said.

'I don't owe you the truth,' I said. 'I don't owe you anything.'

He spoke over me. 'You're lying about your dreams, just like you did when we were kids. You never really talked to me, even then.'

'What are you talking about? We used to talk all the time.' It had been just the two of us, after all, under the scrutiny of the whole village.

'Not properly.' He spoke quietly. 'You were lying to me the whole time.'

For a while I didn't answer. I didn't want to agree with what he'd said, but I couldn't argue with it. My seer visions were the only thing that revealed me as an Omega, so I'd concealed them for years, to prevent being branded and exiled.

'I had to,' I said eventually.

'And I had to do what I did,' he said. 'I had to claim my life.'

'Have you forgotten how close we were?' I asked. 'Have you convinced yourself that it never happened, because you're ashamed of being close to an Omega?'

He laughed. 'You talk about those years as if it was some kind of paradise – you and me, the best of friends, together against the world. It wasn't like that. It was never like that.'

'But we were always together,' I said. 'All the time.'

'Only because we didn't have any choice,' he shouted. 'Because you made the whole village think we were freaks, and nobody would come near us.'

I could hear how he forced his breath to slow, his voice to lower.

'It didn't end, even when you'd finally gone. The taint didn't go with you. It should've, but it didn't. For years, people didn't trust me. That's why I had to leave the village so young.'

'I left it when I was younger,' I said, acid in my voice.

He overrode me again. 'Even when I got to Wyndham, there were rumours about me. The word had spread, about how late we'd been split. I had to prove myself more than anyone else. Had to work twice as hard, prove my loyalty, over and over. Do things that others weren't willing to do.'

The Council chambers at Wyndham were already notorious for their viciousness and ruthlessness. I looked through the darkness towards Zach, and thought of the depths of brutality to which he had sunk.

'I never felt safe,' he went on. 'Not even when you were in the Keeping Rooms. Not for a moment. You took that from me, with all those years you made me live a half-life. You were the one who showed me how dangerous Omegas could be, what a burden they are. You're the reason I had to come up with the tanks.'

I closed my eyes. I knew his excuses and justifications were madness, and that the tanks were his madness made solid, and not my doing. But I couldn't stop picturing the children in the tanks, their hair drifting across their dead faces. I kept my eyes closed, trying not to remember.

'You made me what I am,' he said.

They were the same words that The Confessor had said to Kip, all those months ago in the silo.

*

That night, I waited for his dreams to come to me. With Zoe's dreams, it had been an accident, her dreams seeping into me as she slept close by. Even when I'd tried not to sense them, her dreams had come to me, as full of loss and longing as the sea is full of salt. But Zach didn't dream – or if he did, his dreams meant nothing to me. We had so much in common, and so little. If he dreamed, during those nights in the dormitory, nothing of them reached me. I wondered if our childhood, when I had worked so hard to hide my seer nature from him, had built some kind of barrier. All those years of lying in my small bed and training myself not to react to my visions, not to cry out at what I had seen, meant that I couldn't reach out to him now, asleep or awake, nor feel any sense of what passed in his mind. I felt no closer to him, lying only a few yards away in the dormitory, than I had when I'd been on the island, hundreds of miles away.

I got no glimpse of his dreams, but he could not help but know something of mine. Before dawn I woke from a glimpse of the blast, my shouts bouncing back at me from the dormitory ceiling. He made shushing noises. At first, still reeling from the shock of waking from flames to darkness, I had forgotten whose voice it was nearby, soothing me. Then, when my breathing had settled, Zach spoke: 'What did you see?'

I had never heard a hunger like I heard in his voice, and I knew hunger well. The whole of New Hobart was hungry. Only that night, the eight of us who now lived in the holding house had shared a stew made with two squirrels that Zoe had caught on the roof – and we'd boiled the bones clean.

I didn't answer him. After that, I tried harder than ever to keep silent when the visions came. I couldn't always manage to quell my screams – my visions were more frequent and more vivid than they had been when we were children. But I tried. I didn't want to give him any hint of what I saw, nor the satisfaction of seeing me scream. Some nights, when I woke from dreams of fire and ground my teeth against the screams that I would not allow myself to make, I felt like nothing had changed: that Zach and I were still there, in our childhood bedroom, me hiding my visions, him watching and waiting.

*

From the very first day, when he saw her crossing the courtyard with Zoe, Zach stared at Paloma. I wished that her appearance didn't announce her difference quite so loudly, but everything about her stood out: the bone-white hair and skin; the washed-out blue of her eyes. I watched him watching Paloma, and I felt my fists tightening. I didn't want his eyes on her. He had always taken everything. I saw him stare at her and I wanted to shout: *Not this. Not her. You can't have this too.*

'It's true, then,' he said, his eyes following her as she and Zoe walked over the gravel.

I said nothing.

'I knew you were searching.' He shook his head. 'But I didn't believe you'd succeed. Piper and his rag-tag bunch of sailors. How did you do it?'

'I'm not talking to you about her.'

'I'm not an idiot,' he said.

'I never thought you were,' I said. 'You're something much worse, and much more dangerous.'

When we went to the kitchen to eat, he didn't hide his staring, and Paloma stared back, her curiosity matching his. This was the man who had unearthed the blast that might destroy her whole family, and everything that she had known. I saw how she narrowed her eyes, head cocked a little, as if straining to understand what could make a man do terrible things. And I wanted to shout at her: *Stay away. Stay away.*

Zoe did the shouting. When she saw Zach's eyes lingering on Paloma, she stepped between them.

'Keep your distance,' she said to him.

He raised his arms before him, shaking them so that the shackles jangled.

'I'm just a prisoner here,' he said. 'It's not my choice where you people take me.'

'You don't need to stare at her all the time,' Zoe said.

'I'm just curious,' he said, his voice gentle as a blade. 'Nobody's introduced me properly to your new friend.' His eyes were scanning Paloma, coming to rest on her face. 'I'd love to learn more about you.'

Paloma spoke: 'I've heard more than enough about you,' she said.

'And you believe it?' Zach said quickly. 'What makes you think you can trust these people?'

Zoe opened her mouth, but Paloma spoke first. 'I make my own judgments.'

'And you've judged that this is the best alliance your homeland can hope for?' Zach cast a glance around at the rest of us, and the shabby kitchen.

Zoe shoved him backwards. It was only a light push, but with his arms chained in front of him, he could neither balance nor break his fall, stumbling and landing on his back by the fireplace.

Piper moved to pull Zoe away, but she was already leaving, Paloma beside her.

'Keep your distance,' she repeated to Zach, without looking back. She slammed the kitchen door behind her.

Zach raised his eyebrows, heaving himself upright and doing his best to brush the dust from his trousers with his shackled hands.

'What are you all so afraid of?' he said.

My vision answered: the flames burst behind my eyes. *Forever fire.*

*

For all the years of my childhood, I had done everything I could to stay with him. I had lied, and hidden, concealed the truth about my visions from everybody, so that I could stay with him and my family. Now he was here, and all that I wanted was to get away from him.

There were moments when I was ambushed by the similarities between us. I heard his inflections in my own words and so fell silent. At meals, sitting with my chin on my hand and the other hand rubbing the back of my neck, I'd look across the table and see that he was doing exactly the same thing. I didn't know who was mirroring whom. But I always jerked away, placed my hands awkwardly by my sides, glancing to see if any of the others had noticed.

Often he was silent, just watching. When he did speak, it was always for a purpose.

He singled Sally out, one morning over breakfast.

'Have you thought about the other potential uses for the tanks?' he said.

I froze, a spoonful of porridge halfway to my mouth. Sally ignored him, and Zoe made a point of turning her body away from him to face Paloma, at the far end of the table.

'We've seen enough of your tanks,' Piper said.

'You've all been so quick to dismiss the tanks.' Zach waved his hand around the table. 'A kneejerk reaction, because you're afraid of the taboo. But there are other uses for them.' His burn was healing: the blisters gone, the dried skin cracked like summer earth. Soon enough he would have a scar in the same place as mine. 'For the sick,' he continued, 'to keep people alive until they can be cured. Or for the elderly.' His voice was soft now, his focus back on Sally. 'Who knows what medicine might achieve in future years, if this uprising of yours isn't allowed to derail our progress? The tanks could allow you to stay alive decades longer, until we have the ability to help with your condition.'

Sally had been continuing to eat, as if he weren't even there. Now, though, she put down her spoon and laughed loudly. 'I'm not *elderly*,' she said to him. 'I'm old.' She rolled the word on her tongue, relishing it. 'And my *condition* is that I've been on this earth for more than eighty years, and I've seen and done things you can't even dream of. There's no cure for that.' She pushed back her bowl. 'You think I'd go into a tank, in the hope of scavenging a few more years?'

She leaned in, her face so close to Zach's that he drew his head back, barely hiding his distaste. 'I'm going to die, son,' she said. 'And so are you. The only difference between us is that I'm wise enough to know that dying's far from the worst thing that could happen to me.'

The bench creaked as she stood up. She took Xander's hand and led him from the room.

*

I thought it was rain that had woken me, but it was just the claws of rats on the roof. There was a plague of rats in New Hobart. It had started in the western quarter, and before long they were all through the town, scrabbling under the floorboards of the holding house. Like us, they were suffering from the absence of crops in the surrounding farmland, and so they swarmed to the town to scavenge what they could, which felt like everything. Each morning we swept their pellets from the kitchen floor. The leather upholstery in the Tithe Collector's office had been completely gnawed away, and one day I found a nest of eight baby rats sleeping in the horsehair stuffing of the largest chair.

The Council ban on Omegas keeping animals meant there were no cats in New Hobart. Even The Ringmaster had to laugh when he reported that he'd sent two small patrols into Council territory, to steal cats from towns and villages. I was there when they returned, and when they opened the two sacks that hung, thrashing, from the rear rider's saddle, the cats sprang out with a hiss like water on a hot skillet, scattering and howling, sending one of the horses shying into a fence. Within a few days the cats had settled in as the guards of our grain stores, and they grew fat and glossy while the rest of us grew thinner.

Despite the cats, the rats kept coming, and they grew bold. One afternoon I saw one scuttle across the courtyard in broad daylight, dragging a pilfered potato in its mouth. When I threw a stone at it, it didn't even dodge, just turned to stare at me briefly before continuing its steady progress across the gravel.

The worst was at night, on the way to the latrine, when my candle showed a roiling mass of dark fur, and eyes shiny and black as beetles, in every corner.

In the kitchen one morning, I found Sally making snares. A pile was beside her on the table; she had one wire raised almost to her face, squinting at it as she twisted it into shape. Precise work was hard, with her stiffened hands; it was easier for her to wield a dagger than a needle.

'What's the point?' I said. 'Zoe says the snares in the forest have hardly caught a rabbit for weeks. Even the squirrels are getting scarcer.'

Sally had always been thin; now, after the long months of hunger, when she lowered her hands, her loose skin settled in folds at her wrists.

'These aren't for rabbits,' she said, and I looked again at the snares on the table. They were tiny – each loop barely big enough for a finger to slip through. Too small for a rabbit, or even a squirrel.

So right through those months, when we should have been harvesting the spring crops of root vegetables, instead we were harvesting rats. They weren't easy to catch – they wised up quickly to the snares, and we had to use increasingly elaborate traps. One night Elsa caught thirteen rats by laying boards coated with a thick paste of resiny glue on the ground of the courtyard, by the kitchen door. In the dormitory, with Zach lying in the next bed, I put my pillow over my head to muffle the scrabbling of the trapped rats. But the next day, I ate them anyway.

The town was starving, and still the Council held Wreckers' Pass, and no food convoys from The Ringmaster's territory could get through. We were still readying ourselves for the Council's attack, but as I watched the listless, gaunt faces in the streets, I wondered whether The General would need to attack us at all, or whether her stranglehold on Wreckers' Pass might be enough to crush New Hobart from a distance.

It was fiddly work, skinning the rats and salvaging the little meat that they gave. One morning, Piper joined me in Elsa's kitchen. Without being asked, he sat down to help, clamping each tiny body between his knees and slitting them neatly from chin to tail, then gutting them before tossing the carcass to me to be skinned. I was getting quicker at it now: I'd learned to peel the black, oily skin off in one piece. I cut the flesh from the back legs, and scraped it from the ribs, fine and sharp as the teeth of a comb.

From the corner of my eye I watched Piper working. I was pleased to see that he still did things like this. Sometimes, when we were in the Tithe Collector's office and he and The Ringmaster were arguing over the maps, or when we walked together through the town and the Omega soldiers sprang to salute him as he passed, he felt a long way away. I preferred the moments when we were together like this, even if we were knuckle-deep in rat guts.

'If we survive this war,' I said, 'and if we manage to get

Elsewhere to help us, and bards one day tell the story of all that happened, it will never include this.'

Piper laughed. 'You know it wouldn't. It will all be battles, and bravery, and magic visions.'

I smiled with him. 'Not rat guts, and soldiers sent on missions to steal cats.'

But this is what I would remember, I promised myself. If we survived – an *if* that seemed less likely by the day – then I wanted to remember all of this. The messy business of living. Ever since I'd discovered that the Council planned to bomb Elsewhere, I kept being struck by glimpses of beauty. I found them in unexpected places: in the way the light fell through the bars of the dormitory window; in the patience of Elsa's hands as she mixed herbs for Xander; even here, sitting amongst the rat guts with Piper. I had found a way to live again, and to allow myself moments of hope, all the sharper for their unlikeliness. Even while I savoured those moments, I was aware of how fragile they were. The more things I treasured, the more I could lose. Everything was doubled, everything was sharpened. We had found Elsewhere – something worth fighting for – yet we also stood to lose more than we could have imagined.

There was another moment that gave me hope. I was crossing the courtyard, and the door to Zoe and Paloma's room was open. Paloma was combing her hair, and Zoe was sitting on the bed, bent forward with her elbows on her splayed knees, sharpening her knife in strong sweeps down toward the floor. Paloma laughed at something Zoe had said, and Zoe smiled. I couldn't hear what they were saying: just the tone, laughter around the edge of each word.

It was a perfectly ordinary scene – one that could have taken place in bedrooms and kitchens anywhere, in any time. It was a moment of happiness, and I felt as though it had been smuggled like contraband into this walled town, in wartime. Sally saw it too. She was tying snares in the shade of the courtyard, but she lifted her head and smiled as she looked at the two of them.

*

'Come here,' Sally said to Paloma, that night. 'You should have this.'

She was holding something out towards Paloma; it swung from a leather cord. A pendant, the size of a tooth and much the same colour, set into a metal clasp that hung from the cord.

Paloma came to stand in front of Sally, reached out and took it, lifting it close to her face to see it more clearly.

Piper and Zoe had already recognised it; I saw Piper stiffen, and Zoe take a deep, slow breath.

'I've had it for years,' Sally said, as Paloma peered at the pendant. 'You should wear it now.'

It might have seemed a sentimental gesture, to anyone who didn't know Sally. Anyone who hadn't heard the story of how she and her fellow infiltrators had been issued with poison capsules. She had watched one of her friends crush his capsule and die, frothing and thrashing, rather than be tortured. Sally herself had put a knife in her other friend's neck, to spare her from the same fate. Sally had managed to escape, and had never had to use her poison capsule. It had never occurred to me, until now, to wonder what had become of it.

'It's never been unsealed,' Sally said, as Paloma peered at the pendant. 'It should still work. You should wear it.'

Paloma still didn't understand.

'That's the last one,' Sally went on. 'We haven't been able to make them for years. There was a stand of snakewood trees on the hills of Merricat, but it was burned along with the settlement, in a raid.'

Paloma had been holding the capsule in her palm, but when Sally mentioned the snakewood trees, she let it drop as if it were hot, and held it only by the cord.

Sally took the pendant back for a moment, and lifted it over Paloma's head to place the cord around her neck. 'Keep it with you, all the time. If you need to, bite down, hard, and swallow.'

Paloma swiped her hand along the back of her neck to lift her hair over the cord. When her hair fell again, you couldn't even see the pendant. But none of us was likely to forget it was there, least of all Paloma.

'Thank you,' she said to Sally, and it sounded sincere. But as Paloma moved around the kitchen, for the rest of the night, I saw how her hand kept straying to her neck. It was a gift, but it was also a noose, and we all knew it.

Later that night, when I crossed the courtyard, Zoe was sitting on the step to the room that she shared with Paloma. I opened my mouth, but she raised her finger to her lips and jerked her head back towards the door.

'She's sleeping,' she said.

I nodded, and sat beside her on the step.

Zoe broke the silence first. 'I'm glad she has the capsule,' she said, keeping her voice low. 'But I hate that she needs it.'

'We'll keep her safe,' I said. 'It won't come to that.'

'You can't promise that,' said Zoe. She shook her head. 'I keep thinking that I should wish she'd never come here. I know it would be safer for her, and all of Elsewhere. But I don't.' She gave a hushed laugh, just an exhalation through her nose. 'It's selfish, I suppose. I can't bring myself to wish it.'

I matched her whisper.

'Piper offered it to me, once,' I said. 'Not a capsule – but it's the same thing. When we were overrun, in the battle outside the walls. He turned to me, and I saw what he was ready to do.' I raised my own arm, the remembered knife balanced in my empty hand.

It was on the plain outside New Hobart, when the battle had seemed lost, and all was hopeless. Nothing ahead but the certainty of torture, or the tanks. Piper had turned from the advancing soldiers to face me, and brought his knife up. I'd known, then, that he would kill me before I could be taken. It had been very cold, I remembered – the oncoming soldiers riding hard, the breath of their horses turning the air white. I'd seen Piper, and his blade, and he hadn't looked away, or hidden his intention. He'd met my stare, and I'd nodded, and between us had passed an understanding that I had not been able to forget. I kept returning to it. There was an intimacy to that – greater than if I'd shared a bed with him. I knew what he was willing to do for me. What he was willing to do to me. It lodged in me, as if the knife had been thrown after all, and I lived now with its sharpness tucked deep in my throat.

'You would have been tanked,' Zoe said. 'Piper was only offering to spare you that.'

I nodded. 'I know that.'

'And if you'd seen him being taken, and if you were able, would you have done the same for him?'

'I can't throw knives. I can't fight – not like you and Piper.'

'That wasn't what I asked you,' she said.

We both knew the answer. I would have done it, if I could. It was a promise I couldn't remember making – like the promise of a shared death between me and Zach. I hadn't asked for that either, but it was no less a part of me.

CHAPTER 8

I hated hearing the marching of The Ringmaster's private guards down Elsa's street, and the way he entered without knocking. I knew that the whole town was under his control, and that his soldiers massively outnumbered ours – but I still clung to the illusion that the holding house was our own.

He gave no greeting. 'Get ready,' he said. 'We're riding out. There's a message from The General. She's willing to talk.'

Sally, Xander and Zoe stayed at the holding house with Simon, to guard Paloma and Zach. Piper and I rode out from the eastern gate with a squadron of soldiers, blue and red tunics together.

We rode for several miles through the secured territory around New Hobart. It was nearly midday before we passed the last watch post on the eastern road, and the sun was hot on my bare arms. Last time we'd ridden out to meet The General, there had been snow on the ground. And Zach had sat beside her, joining her in her threats. Now he was in shackles in Elsa's dormitory.

His absence didn't seem to have dented The General's

confidence. She sat there, amidst her own soldiers, on a white horse taller than any of the others. Her arms were crossed over her chest.

When we were twenty feet from her, The Ringmaster raised his arm for us to stop. Before our horses had even stopped shuffling into place, The General spoke.

'I've come for The Reformer,' she said.

'He's your problem, not ours,' said Piper.

The General spoke over him. 'He's not to be trusted. He'll use you for his own ends.' She addressed all her statements to The Ringmaster – as though the rest of us weren't there at all.

Just behind her right shoulder, I noticed that one of her guards had an arm that ended just below the shoulder. He was unbranded; where his stump emerged from his tunic, the scar tissue was thick and an angry pink. A recent wound: seeing it, I couldn't help but think of Kip, and what had been done to him.

'Even if we had The Reformer here—' The Ringmaster said.

The General interrupted again. 'Don't waste my time with lies. He was spotted heading this way. And he had nowhere else to run.'

The Ringmaster continued as if she hadn't spoken. '—we would never hand him over to you.'

'You want to protect the man who began the tanks? It was all his idea, you know. Him and his pet seer, The Confessor.'

'You know as well as I do that it's not The Reformer we're protecting,' Piper said.

The General turned her head to face me. The movement was slow and relaxed, as if I was barely worthy of her attention.

'And is she really worth so much to you, this seer of yours?' she said.

'Enough to make you turn on your closest ally,' Piper said. 'Enough to bring you here.'

'Enough to continue a war that you can't win?'

'What are you offering?' called The Ringmaster.

'Terms,' she said calmly. 'Hand over The Reformer, and share whatever you know about Elsewhere, and we can come to terms.'

'You'd stop the tanks?' The Ringmaster said. 'And destroy the blast machine?'

She gave an impatient shake of her head. 'We have to be able to preserve our sovereignty, as a nation. We need weapons to protect us against interference or attacks from Elsewhere. But we can consult with you on how we continue to implement the tanks. And I'm offering the chance to discuss a newly configured Council. Perhaps even with a forum for Omega representation.' She turned back to Piper. 'You've shown yourself a strong leader. You could work with us. Instead of leading your people into war, you could work with the Council to negotiate the best options for Omegas.'

'I'm not going to be your puppet,' Piper said. 'Your token Omega, helping you to consign my people to the tanks. And I want no part of any Council whose only interest is tanking Omegas, and destroying the only place that could help us.'

'You want to avoid bloodshed and destruction?' she said. 'Forget about Elsewhere – it's thousands of miles away. What about this war? Give us The Reformer, and details of Elsewhere, and it could end.'

'If you want to end this,' I said, 'stop the tanks. Destroy the blast machine. Accept the help that Elsewhere can offer us.'

Her voice was very calm, and very quiet. 'Listen to me. If you don't hand over The Reformer, you will all die in this town. Look at yourselves. Your troops will starve, or be killed, and those of your people who survive will be tanked.'

I was the seer, but she spoke of the future with far more certainty than I was ever able to muster.

'Elsewhere will not be permitted to corrupt what is left of our humanity. It will burn.' She had raised her voice now, to ensure that all of our guards, and hers, would hear her. She laid each word before us as though it were its own proof. As though all that she had described had already happened. And, of course, it had: the blast had come before. It would come again. There was such a sense of inevitability about it all, and her voice left no room to imagine any other way.

The one-armed soldier behind her shifted in his saddle. I tried to catch his eyes, but he kept them fixed on our soldiers opposite him.

The General caught me staring at him. 'Don't be fooled,' she said. 'He lost his arm at New Hobart – but even with his injury, he could still best the strongest Omega.' She cast a scathing glance in Piper's direction.

Piper ignored her, but I bridled. 'And what's the difference between his left arm and Piper's?' I said.

'He wasn't born that way,' The General said. 'He's not a freak.'

Piper just laughed. 'And does knowing that make it any easier for him to tie his bootlaces?'

Throughout the whole exchange, the soldier had looked straight ahead. Now, though, he glanced toward Piper. I could read nothing in that stare. Did he recognise himself, in Piper's body? Or was he disgusted by what he saw? I'd learned that the two could go together.

He turned his gaze away.

'Don't think that this chance to negotiate will last forever,' The General said, again addressing The Ringmaster. 'With or without you, I will end this. End it more absolutely than you have ever imagined.'

I thought of Paloma, and her family, and all those in Elsewhere who had no idea of the flames that were coming for them.

The General spoke to The Ringmaster again. 'Give me The Reformer.'

'Why is he so important to you?' I asked. 'What does he have that you need?'

She ignored me, and addressed The Ringmaster again. 'Give him to me.'

'Stop this madness with the machines,' The Ringmaster spat back.

She looked at him, her face revealing nothing. 'You're a man of principles,' she said. 'I've always known that. I can even understand your opposition to some of my projects. I respect your reverence for the taboo. But if you continue aligning yourself with them' – she glanced at me and Piper – 'you'll find yourself dealing with technology more terrifying than anything we've seen here. Don't be seduced by the idea of ending the twinning. They're talking about the end of humanity as we know it. All for the sake of getting rid of twins – when we've already solved that problem.'

'The tanks aren't a solution,' I shouted at her.

Neither she nor The Ringmaster responded to me – the two of them were staring at each other. I looked from one to the other, trying to sense what was passing between them.

'Give me The Reformer,' she said.

'In exchange for what?' he said.

'For you?' She raised an eyebrow. 'A chance to get out of this alive.' She kept her eyes fixed on his face.

He looked away first.

'This isn't only about me,' he said briskly.

'You're right,' she said. 'If you give me The Reformer, I'll spare some of your soldiers when I take this town, as you know I will, if I don't starve you out first. If you refuse to hand him over, your selfishness and paranoia will cost lives. Thousands of lives. This is your last chance. Keep him, and I will show no mercy.'

Piper spat on the ground. 'The same mercy you showed to the children of New Hobart?' he said. 'We've already had a taste of your mercy.'

He turned his horse. I moved to follow him, but The General called after me.

'You're a seer. Tell them what you've seen.'

Everyone was watching me. Behind The General, the one-armed soldier shifted so he could see me more clearly. The Ringmaster, too, had turned in his saddle to stare.

'I know what all you seers see. Your brother told me, when you were in the Keeping Rooms: you see the blast.'

Each of my breaths was coming faster than the last, my mouth dry.

'Why do you let them follow you,' she said, 'and fight for you and risk everything, when you know how it ends?'

'It doesn't have to end that way,' I told her. I wanted my voice to ring out as hers had, but there was a tremor in my words. I had seen the blast too many times to be able to deny it. 'It can be different,' I said, and tried to make it sound as though I believed it.

She looked at me with something like pity. 'You know I can't be stopped,' she said. 'You can see the future, but you can't change it.'

CHAPTER 9

All the way back to New Hobart, I felt the stares of our soldiers on my back. Most of them already knew about my blast visions – many of them had seen Xander, too, reeling from the flames. But The General had made each of my visions sound like a betrayal: proof of the Council's victory. *You can see the future, but you can't change it.*

My visions had allowed me to warn the islanders about the Council invasion – but the bloodshed that I had seen had still taken place. And before the battle for New Hobart, I'd had visions of bloodshed and death. I'd secured The Ringmaster's help, and we'd managed to win the town – but the bloodshed and death had still come to pass on the plains outside New Hobart.

'She came here to scare us,' Piper said, spurring his horse forward to join me. 'She's trying to make you doubt yourself.'

'I know,' I said. 'But that doesn't mean it's not true.'

'So what?' he said impatiently. 'We give up, and wait for the flames?' He gave a smile that was half a snarl. 'I've been in this fight for more than ten years. You going to tell me I should stop fighting now?'

He didn't wait for an answer – just pressed his heels into his horse and rode forward to join The Ringmaster. I watched him, and wondered about Xander. Was that what he had done – given up and waited for the flames? Did he know that our visions could warn us, but not save us? What was the point of all that we were doing, and had done, if it would end in fire anyway? For all the hours that I'd spent, teeth clenched and fists pressed against my scrunched eyes, seeking the blast machine, and for all Piper's and The Ringmaster's attempts to interrogate Zach, nothing had brought us any closer to finding the machine, let alone stopping the blast.

Riding behind Piper through the gates of New Hobart, I thought about The General's voice. There had been such urgency in her words as she'd said it: *Give me The Reformer*. Was it only revenge that led her to pursue him – to ride out to meet us, face to face? Or was there something else that she wanted from him? When he'd come to us, bruised and desperate, I'd been as convinced as Zach that The General wanted him dead. But today she'd come in search of him. She'd been willing to negotiate with us, even to make some concessions, in order to get him back. She didn't seem like the kind of person who let herself be driven by emotion – not even vengeance. She was a woman in control of everything, including her own feelings. What did she want from Zach, other than his death, and mine?

*

'We need to strike back,' I said. We were gathered in the dining room of the holding house, Zach shackled and under guard in the dormitory.

'You heard what The General said,' I went on. 'She's going to retaliate. It was a blow to her, when we took back New Hobart, but she's been gathering her strength. Her stranglehold on Wreckers' Pass is weakening us every day. She'll be getting ready to make her move. And readying the bomb, too, and closing in on Elsewhere. And there are thousands in the tanks – and more being tanked each day.'

'She doesn't have the numbers for an all-out assault on us,' Piper said. 'Not while The Ringmaster's troops stay loyal, and she has Wyndham and the refuges to defend. She's making empty threats.'

'She doesn't make empty threats,' The Ringmaster said calmly.

Nobody spoke. There was no noise from the streets outside – the quiet of a town without children. That silence was proof enough of The General's ruthlessness.

'So we need to strike first,' I said.

'We can consolidate the gains we've made, if we don't do anything reckless,' Zoe said. 'Hold New Hobart. Wait until the end of spring, while we ready the fleet to take Paloma home.'

'Hold New Hobart for what?' I said. I waved my arm at the window, beyond which were the fortifications and the barracks, soldiers patrolling the hungry streets where no children ran. 'What's the point, if we let The General continue with the tanks, and the blast machine?'

'We have a base, and an army that can withstand the Council's. We have Paloma,' Zoe said. 'And Zach. If we jeopardise those things, it's all over. We can't keep Paloma safe, or work with Elsewhere to undo the twinning, if there's nothing left of us when they get here.'

'If they get here and we haven't done anything to weaken

the Council – really weaken them, I mean – they'll be doing nothing but walking into a trap,' I said. 'Elsewhere will burn.'

'She's right.' It still surprised me to hear Paloma speak in support of me, given how she'd kept her distance since learning of my visions of the blast. 'We can't sail until the end of spring. Until then, the best thing we can do to help the Scattered Islands, and ourselves, is to keep bringing the fight to the Council.'

I took a deep breath, and tried to make my voice sound forceful. 'We need to hit the Council where it will really undermine them: strike the refuges.'

The Ringmaster snorted. 'And what would we gain?'

'Freedom for thousands of tortured people,' I said. 'Is that enough for you?'

'They're heavily guarded, and out of the way,' he said. 'We need supplies, and more soldiers. Not an outpost in a wasteland, full of half-dead Omegas.' He didn't try to conceal the contempt in his voice. 'I hate the machines as much as you do, but that's just bad strategy. We don't even know if those people would survive being taken out of the tanks, even if we could free them.'

'What's the biggest refuge of them all?' I said, turning to Piper.

'Refuge Six,' he said without hesitation. 'It was the first place they expanded, when Zach came to power – the first big tank complex. It got so huge they consolidated, shut down Refuge Seven altogether, since it was only thirty miles further north. And they've kept expanding it, since then.'

'How many Omegas are in there now?'

'Six thousand,' Piper said, 'give or take. Almost all of them tanked. But it's also the best-defended of the lot.'

'There's a whole garrison there,' The Ringmaster said.

'Six hundred soldiers, last information I had. And it's close to Wyndham – we'd have reinforcements on us within half a day—'

I ignored him, kept my gaze on Piper. 'Six thousand?'

He nodded.

'That's where we strike, then,' I said. 'If we want to make a difference, Refuge Six is where we have to go.' I felt giddy at the thought of it: six thousand people freed from the tanks.

Once I had promised a man, as he bled to death in front of me, that I would find his niece and rescue her from the tanks. His name was Lewis, and Piper had killed him when Lewis tried to assassinate me. When I'd heard about his niece, taken and tanked by Zach, I'd understood why Lewis wanted me dead, and I'd made him my promise. I had no way of knowing whether she was in Refuge 6 – refuges had sprung up like mould spores in recent years. It had been a stupid thing to promise, and Lewis would never know whether I had even tried to keep my word. But I would know.

Paloma was speaking again. 'Wouldn't it make sense to tackle one of the smaller refuges? See how that goes, before we throw everything at the largest?'

Piper shook his head. 'Cass is right. After the first attack, they're going to tighten security in all of them – it's going to be harder, if not impossible, to do it again. If we only get one chance at this, then let's make it count. Get the most people we can out of the tanks.'

'It's bad strategy,' said The Ringmaster again. 'It's too close to Wyndham – before we even had the place freed there'd be reinforcements sweeping in. We'd never succeed. And even if we could somehow free them, what would we do with those people?' I tried my best to ignore the way he spat the words: *those people*. 'We don't have the numbers to set up another stronghold there without sacrificing New Hobart. How could we shift the untanked Omegas back to New Hobart, or feed them if we got them here? Thousands of them, in who knows what kind of state.'

'It's because of those thousands of people that we have to do it,' I said.

'The Council won't be expecting it,' Piper said.

'They won't be expecting it,' The Ringmaster said, 'because it's insane.'

'What would they be expecting?' I asked, looking at The Ringmaster. 'What would you do, if it were just up to you?'

'I wouldn't be wasting time on the tanks. I'd be consolidating my gains, like Zoe said. Making strategic strikes to allow me to challenge the Council's power.'

'Where?' I said. 'What strikes?'

He leaned forward, over the map that he'd spread on the table. 'Here.' He pointed without hesitation. 'Noose Canyon. If I had more troops, that's where I'd strike. Seize the canyon, and we'd have a strong, defensible position, from which to lay siege to Wyndham itself.'

Wyndham. For four years I'd been trapped beneath the city, in the Keeping Rooms. Hundreds of feet above me, in the fort that clung to the side of the mountain, the Council had lived and worked in their luxurious chambers. Below the fort, and spread out on the hills, was the city itself, hub of the Council and the biggest city I'd ever heard of, before Paloma arrived with her tales of Blackwater. Wyndham was ten times the size of New Hobart. No – twenty times, or more. I'd glimpsed it properly only once, from the battlements where I'd launched my escape. Street upon street, crammed with houses and carts, blurring into the horizon.

'If we want to take over the Council,' The Ringmaster said, 'we need to take Wyndham, eventually. But first, we'd need to take Noose Canyon.'

I looked at where his finger sat. Halfway between Wyndham and Refuge 6, to the west of the town itself, there was a gash in the mountain – a deep ravine. Within a mile of the city, the two sides narrowed to a neck.

'Why?'

He waved at the map again.

'There's a reason Wyndham was chosen as the Council's base. It's built into the cliff, with the mountain behind it to the south, and the river wrapping in front of it to the north. It's compact, and defensible. Its natural defences protect it on three sides – the mountain cliffs are too sheer, so the only way it can be attacked is from the north. But even then, an attacker has to cross the river, and there are only two bridges. Even if they manage that, they're attacking up the hill. Wyndham's lower slopes reach all the way down into the plain now, but under attack its citizens can draw back behind the fort walls. There's a lot of space below the fort itself – it's only used for the Keeping Rooms.' He spoke so casually of the Keeping Rooms, and didn't seem to notice how my jaw tightened at the mention of them, and at the thought of his own twin, in her private keeping room somewhere. 'And, these last few years, the tank complex is down there too,' The Ringmaster continued, in his offhand way. 'But there's room under there to house most of the city, if it came to a siege. Grain stores, and wells, too.

'But here—' he prodded again at the canyon on the map '—Noose Canyon cuts through the mountainside. It gives access to the western roads, cutting straight through the mountains – saves a full day's ride going over the river and around to the north. It's the key to defending the city. It wouldn't be an easy fight – it'd take every soldier we have, and even then we'd be looking at a long siege, and high casualties – but it's the weakest point in their defences. Wyndham can't be held if Noose Canyon falls. And you can't take over the Council without seizing Wyndham.'

I smiled. 'Perfect,' I said.

The Ringmaster looked blankly at me. 'You're deluded. We don't have the numbers. We can attack, but you'd be talking about a siege that would last months, at best.'

I nodded. 'But we don't want to take over the Council. We want to destroy it.'

*

'They'll expect us to do what they would do,' I explained. 'To go for Wyndham. They think we're interested in power – in taking over the Council.' I looked at The Ringmaster. 'You heard what Zach said to you, the night he arrived. And what The General offered us today: the chance to be involved in the Council. They think that's our goal: to take what they have. And if we let them think that's true, they'll protect what matters most to them: Wyndham. The Council Halls, the seat of their power.'

'A decoy?' Piper said, pulling the map towards him.

I nodded. 'If we can convince them we're mounting an attack on Wyndham, they might even draw off some troops from the refuge to the canyon. And if we can hold the canyon for a while, they won't be able to send reinforcements to Refuge Six. It could give us the chance we need to free it.'

'If we march east,' The Ringmaster said, 'they won't need convincing that we're planning to attack Wyndham. It's the only target of any strategic value out there.'

'Only if you share their definition of *value*,' I said.

He shook his head. 'If we can draw them to the canyon and hold them there, it will slow down reinforcements for the refuge – but they'll come the long way, over the bridges and skirting the northern plains. It'll add a day to their riding time, but they'll still come.'

'Not if we take out the bridges,' Zoe said.

'Won't they just ford the river?' Paloma asked.

'They won't be able to,' Zoe said. 'The snowmelt's still coming off Wyndham Peak. It'll keep the river high until late spring. They'll try to ferry soldiers across, but that won't be quick – especially if we take out the landing stages on the southern side.'

'It would give us enough time to free Refuge Six,' I said. 'Get them out, get them back here.'

'Could it work?' Paloma said. They were all looking at me.

I spoke to The Ringmaster. 'You're our best decoy – more important than the soldiers we send to the canyon. Because they'll expect us to do what you would do. They assume that you're leading us now.' I was remembering the way The General had addressed her demands to him, ignoring the rest of us.

The Ringmaster looked nearly amused. 'And wouldn't that be a reasonable assumption?' he said. He looked past me, to the window. 'Those are my soldiers out there, keeping this town safe.'

'They're not all yours,' said Zoe quickly. 'Resistance soldiers serve here too. Resistance soldiers led the charge against New Hobart.'

'I saved New Hobart,' he said.

'You didn't even have the courage to turn on the Council until we'd already made a stand,' Piper said.

The Ringmaster stood. 'Not only are they my soldiers

out there now, patrolling,' he said. 'They're my horses. *My* garrisons, holding most of the west. *My* convoys, bringing the food that keeps this town alive.'

This last point fell flat; we were starving.

'Do you want to do what The General's expecting?' I said. 'Is Zach right about you? Did you come here because you saw your chance to overthrow the Council, and take power for yourself?'

'I want to stop the tanks,' he said. But I noticed that it wasn't a denial.

'We have a chance to do more than just stop the tanks. We can end the twinning. Change everything. But only if we can bring down the Council. Only if you're willing to be more than what they think you are.'

The tiny muscles at the corners of his eyes were twitching, as he kept his stare on mine. 'And you think you know what I am? Who I am?'

I shook my head. 'No,' I said, and I meant it. 'But I know what you could become.'

CHAPTER 10

The seconds passed in silence. The Ringmaster dragged his eyes from mine, pulled the map back to himself, and planted a hand on each side of the parchment as he bent over it. He narrowed his eyes for a few minutes as he examined the map, then took a stub of chalk from his pocket and marked the canyon's mouth with an X.

'Noose Canyon,' he said. 'We've no realistic prospect of winning it, not without sending our full army there – we don't have the numbers, and they can withstand a long siege – but if we can take out the southern bridges too, we could hold them, keep their forces contained. It'll give us a chance to free Refuge Six.'

Paloma asked, 'But how many of the decoy force would be killed?'

We all looked at the map, the narrowing mouth of the canyon ending in The Ringmaster's X. 'If we send them in, outnumbered,' Piper said finally, 'they're not coming out of that canyon alive.'

Paloma snatched the map from the table. 'I want to challenge the Council. I do. But our soldiers aren't just figures on a map.' She pushed back her chair with a screech as she stood. 'They'll be massacred,' she said, waving the map. She walked to the other side of the table, her uneven footsteps loud, her false leg echoing on the wooden floor.

She stood in front of Zoe, holding the map, and there were tears in her eyes. Zoe rose and reached out, and for a moment I thought she would take Paloma's hand, but instead she took the map from her, and laid it on the table again.

'I don't see any other way,' she said.

'Please,' said Paloma.

And Zoe shook her head. 'This is what happens in a war.'

If she had struck Paloma, Paloma could not have looked more shocked, or sickened. She turned and walked out. Zoe followed her.

I felt a chill, like sweat left to cool on my skin. Just a few months ago, it would have been me making Paloma's point. Arguing to defend our troops against a massacre. This was how war worked: it deadened even those who lived. A hardening, like the calloused skin on the palm of my knife hand.

'Is there any other way,' I asked, 'to free the refuge?'

The Ringmaster stood. 'There are no guarantees, even if we use the decoy attack. But I'd say it's the best chance.' He paused. 'The only chance.'

I looked to Piper. 'And you think we can free Refuge Six?'

'There will be casualties. Not just at the canyon, but at the refuge too.' I could count on Piper not to dodge the truth in situations like this. He spoke it bluntly. 'If we can hold the canyon,' he went on, 'it'll give us a chance. But the refuge is still tightly guarded. And we'll struggle for numbers – we'll be fighting on three fronts: the canyon, the refuge, and maintaining our hold here.'

'But if we succeed,' I said, 'thousands will be spared from tanks.'

He nodded.

So we were choosing death over torture. It was the same choice that I would make; the same choice that Sally had offered Paloma with the snakewood capsule; the same choice Piper had offered me, when we were about to lose the battle of New Hobart and he'd trained his knife on me. But this wasn't my own death I was choosing: it was the deaths of hundreds of soldiers. I could barely raise my head under the weight of all those deaths.

*

Late that night, I crossed the courtyard slowly. Zach was waiting for me in the dormitory. I didn't like being near him at the best of times, and now I felt more reluctant than ever to go into the dormitory. I felt as if just being near to him might somehow reveal something about our plans for the refuge and the canyon. I stood in the courtyard and took deep breaths of the night air.

'Not tired?'

I hadn't realised that Piper was out there too, in the darkness, until he spoke. He was sitting on the bench beneath the kitchen window.

I shrugged, joining him.

'Or afraid to sleep?' he said.

I sat beside him, stretching out my legs next to his. Piper was right: it wasn't only Zach I was avoiding. It was sleep, and the dreams that came with it. I didn't want to witness another doom, Elsewhere's burning was enough. A glimpse of a massacre at Noose Canyon, or at Refuge 6, would be more than I could bear.

'I never wanted this,' Piper said. He tipped his head back, rested it against the wall, and stared up at the sky as he spoke. 'I never wanted to lead the resistance – not in the first place, and not again, when Simon handed it back to me.'

Across the courtyard the rats were starting their nighttime patrols, rattling the tiles of the roof and clawing up the drainpipes. We listened to them together, and I let the dark ease the words from him.

'I did it,' he went on, 'because I knew I could do it well. But I don't want to be the resistance leader who lost everything. The one who presided over the end of the resistance.'

'It is the end,' I said. They were hard words, and they sounded hard: no comfort in them. I knew him too well, and trusted him too much, to lie to him – and he had seen me screaming enough times to know that it would end in flames. 'Not just for the resistance – it's the end of everything. Everything's changing, no matter what you do. They have the blast, and the tanks; we have Elsewhere, and the power to end the twinning. Whether we win, or lose – nothing will be the same. Staying here, and barricading ourselves in this town, might delay it a little, but it isn't going to change it.'

He gave a jerk of his chin at the town beyond the holding-house walls. 'Every resistance soldier who followed me here – I'm responsible for their lives,' he said. 'When I send them into that canyon, most of them won't come out again.'

I nodded. 'I know.' I felt it too: the weight of sheer numbers, when I thought of all that rested on our decisions.

'But there are others to think of. The tanked, and those who'll be tanked soon enough. Paloma's family, and everyone in Elsewhere. Just because they're not here, doesn't mean we're not responsible for them too.'

He swallowed, and looked at me. 'I don't want to be remembered as the resistance leader who led them to their deaths. I don't want to be the one here at the end.'

'It is the end,' I said again. 'And we are here. These are the times we were born in. We can't change that.' I was glad to feel his shoulder next to mine. I leaned into the solid warmth of him. 'If it's the end,' I said, 'let's make a good end of it.'

He looked at me, and gave a slow nod.

We sat together and watched the silhouette of the rats on top of the courtyard wall. I tried to hang on to all of it: the feeling of the rough brick behind my head, snagging my hair. The air, which had been mild all day, but at night still remembered the winter. Piper beside me – the warm smell of him.

If I had known, then, what he would decide, would I have changed the words I spoke to him? I think perhaps I already knew.

*

Zach was still awake, the candle by his bed burning low.

'What did The General offer you, to hand me over?' he asked.

I ignored him.

'Don't play dumb with me. I know why you all rushed off today. It was only a matter of time before The General came.'

'I don't have to tell you anything,' I said.

'What did she offer you?' he asked again.

I sat on the edge of my bed and stared at him. He lay on his back, his legs poking out from under the blanket. His wrists, where the shackles gripped them, were scrawny. It was so hard to reconcile the sight of him – this ordinary body, with bony ankles and long shins – with what he had done. What he had planned to do.

'I saw the old men,' I said. 'When we were in the Ark. The old men who ruled the Ark, and had themselves tanked at the end.' I could never forget those floating men, with their naked, puffy bodies. Skin as white as freshly peeled garlic.

He raised an eyebrow, but kept his gaze on the ceiling. 'So?'

'So the tanks,' I said, 'weren't even your idea. You just took it, and twisted it.'

'I improved it,' he said. 'I saw how we could use them, in a different way, to solve the Omega problem. I developed them, and improved them, with The Confessor's help.'

'You're just like them,' I said. 'Those cowardly old men floating in the Ark. We're the ones in the tanks, but you Councillors are the ones who are just like them. It's grotesque. And it's a delusion. The same with wanting to attack Elsewhere. It's cowardice – just trying to preserve yourselves, at any cost.'

'And you think the alternative is better?' he said.

I was facing him, but he kept talking at the ceiling. 'We're the last stronghold of humanity. It's better for everyone if Elsewhere's wiped out, before they have a chance to spread their madness, making us all into Omegas.'

'No more Omegas – no Alphas, either. They'd be freeing us all. No more twins.'

'It won't free me,' he said. 'Or you.'

'So nobody should benefit from it, just because it's too late for us?'

'*Benefit?*' he said. 'Ask any Alpha. Ask them: would they rather have a twin, safely in a tank, and be as they are – be perfect? Or would they rather all be born as freaks?'

'If I asked Zoe, I know what she'd answer.'

'Her?' His mouth contorted into a grimace, as he sat up and turned to me. 'Something went wrong with that one. She's been contaminated, from spending her life with Omegas. She's as freakish as any of you. And don't think I haven't noticed what's going on between her and Paloma. Zoe's as bad as any Omega – she's a disgrace to Alphas.'

I didn't want to hear Zoe and Paloma's names in his mouth. He spoke of the contamination of the Omegas, but everything he touched, he polluted. I spoke over him. 'You really think you can just put all Omegas away, close the doors and forget about us? Live as if there were never any Omegas, and it was all just a bad dream? Bomb Elsewhere, pretend that it never existed either? How much do you have to destroy just to preserve this fantasy, that Alphas alone matter?'

'And you? Your little fantasy of Alphas and Omegas all getting along, all living in harmony – how's that working out for you?' He looked around the dormitory. Elsa had repaired the worst of the damage, but scorch marks were still visible by the door, from when the Council had raided the holding house and taken the children. A rat scurried in a corner, stopped, scurried again.

'Your resistance is in shreds,' Zach said. 'You're half-starved, living amongst the rats, waiting to be crushed by

The General. And you've thrown in your lot with The Ringmaster. Do you really think you can trust him?'

'More than I can trust you,' I said.

This wasn't true, I knew, as I lay back and listened to his breathing. Zach had said he would destroy the Omegas, and he had done his best to keep that promise. In that sense, he was the most trustworthy of us all.

*

Preparations for the two-fold attack on Wyndham and Refuge 6 began the next day.

At the armoury, blades were sharpened and distributed. Half of the market square had been cleared to use as a training ground, and soldiers were working through drills, and sparring. But I'd seen how the chaos of battle would sweep aside the most careful strategies. On the day, we would all be subject to luck: a blade swung too high, a shield lifted too late; a sentry who spotted something or missed something. Refuge 6 would fall, or not, accordingly, as we would live or die.

We told nobody our precise plans – the troops were told only that they were preparing for an attack. But the scale of the preparations was clue enough, and I heard the word *Wyndham* muttered enough times in the streets to know that the soldiers had guessed that much. In fact, the attack wasn't the part of our plan that required the most preparation – that was the retreat. If we freed the people from the tanks, they would be our responsibility, and under our protection. The first thing we needed was time, and for that we would rely on the decoy army. We were asking a lot of them: not just to draw The General's troops to the canyon, but to hold them there long enough for us to make our escape.

The other things we needed were wagons. Even if we could get the six thousand people out alive, we had to assume they mightn't be fit to walk – let alone to race more than a hundred and fifty miles across the central plains and marshes, pursued by the Council's forces. Two of the garrisons still held by The Ringmaster's forces were within half a day's journey to the north of the refuge – they were small, but defensible, and The Ringmaster reckoned they could, between them, take two thousand of the refugees, for the short term, at least. That journey they would have to make on foot, escorted by our mounted soldiers. For the rest of them, the only secure stronghold was New Hobart.

So we built wagons – wagons as big as the long fishing boats that they used on the island. Their wheels stood taller than Piper's head, and each would take a team of six horses to pull when fully loaded. Seventy people per wagon, we calculated.

'Lucky they'll all be so thin,' The Ringmaster said, when we were drawing up the plans. I shot him a look. If he had seen what I'd seen – the wasted bodies, the atrophied muscles and the softened skin – he wouldn't have said it so glibly.

And if they weren't thin when they came to us, they would be soon enough. The Ringmaster's food convoys still couldn't reach us. He'd sent a squadron to try to reclaim Wreckers' Pass, but they'd been repelled, suffering heavy casualties. The General's troops were well ensconced, and the narrow pass was a natural stronghold. We couldn't afford to lose another convoy, or to wait forever. The spring crops, such as they were, could be harvested soon, but it wouldn't be enough for the town, let alone for thousands more.

Time was running out, and the whole world seemed to be counting down: spring's northerly winds softening; the snow receding from Wyndham Peak; The General's army gathering. Somewhere, the blast machine was being readied. The visions of the blast left me gasping for breath, and stealing glances at Xander's closed eyes and his open mouth. Each day my ribs protruded further, sharp lines like a tally of days marked on a wall. There was so much we needed to do, and so much stacked against us. We were all so hungry, but above all I was hungry for time.

The first ten newly-built wagons were sent off as soon as they were ready, to wait in the fell country until it was time to bring them south, on the day of the attack. Another ten were being constructed further north, at one of the garrisons under The Ringmaster's control. The remaining wagons, hastily being constructed, would be used in the march to Noose Canyon, and diverted away to the refuge only at the last minute.

We needed more horses, too – enough to move more than sixty loaded wagons, fast, for five days. The accompanying soldiers would also need to be mounted, if we were to have any chance of spotting and fighting off attacks during the journey. Soldiers were sent to raid farms and stables in Alpha territory to the east. I heard Adam and Tash joking about it, at the holding house door.

'If I'd wanted to be a horse thief,' Adam said, 'I could've done it years ago and spared myself the drills and the crap rations.'

In addition, The Ringmaster sent for horses from each of his garrisons, all the way to the coast.

'It leaves some of my battalions without a decent cavalry,'

he said, over the maps in the main hall as we tallied the numbers. But he gave the orders, and the horses kept coming. It was the greatest proof I had of The Ringmaster's commitment to the plan: hard to argue with those horses, the sheer muscled mass of them, and their numbers. Each day another mounted patrol or messenger arrived, until the tank building had to be converted into stables. I was glad, when I passed it, to see the grooms coming and going, and to hear the sounds of the horses, the whinnies and stomps, and to smell the rich warm stink of manure. The reek and busyness of life, instead of the tanks' sterile silence.

For weeks, the town had rung with axe and hammer blows, as the wagons were built. It seemed a strange thing for so much to rest on. In the attack on New Hobart, pumpkins had been the unlikely weapon, carved with our warnings and smuggled to the Omegas trapped within the walls. Now, the unexpected weapons were these wagons, hurriedly built from un-sanded green logs hauled from the forest, and from whatever spars and beams we'd been able to salvage from the ruined buildings of the town. Some of the wagons had beams bound together with rope; others had nails protruding, ready to snag unwary flesh.

'They won't be comfortable,' said The Ringmaster, coming up behind me as I watched the horses being hitched to one of the wagons. 'But they're as light as we can make them, so they'll travel fast, and carry a good sized load.'

Comfortable would mean little, I suspected, to those freshly hauled from the tanks. If we could get into the refuge. If we could get them out of the tanks alive. The more I thought about it, the more the *if*s began to mount, and I ran to help the hitching team, to keep my hands busy and my mind quiet.

Zach knew better than to waste time asking me what all

the hammering and the axe blows were about. He was working too, there in his shackles. I saw it: how attentively he watched us all as we came and went in the holding house. How he slept rarely, instead lying on the bed gazing at the ceiling. I could glean no more of his plan than he could of ours, but I didn't doubt that he had one.

We'd continued our attempts to interrogate him. Again and again we'd questioned him about where the blast machine had been moved, and what The General wanted from him. Our demands earned us nothing. When Piper or The Ringmaster grew enraged, shouted or stood above him as he sat, chained, on the bed, he just raised an eyebrow.

Then, 'What are you going to do?' he'd say, with a glance at me.

Every time, I cast my eyes down, ashamed of my body, linked to his; ashamed to be his guarantee of freedom from torture.

*

The date was set: we had fourteen days remaining before the march on Wyndham and Refuge 6. Any earlier, and the wagons and troops wouldn't be prepared. Any later, and the snowmelt would be gone, the river low and tame enough to be forded by the Council's reinforcements. It was such a precise balance, and so much depended on it.

I had started dreaming of blood and blades. Zach had learned not to ask me about my dreams – he knew he would get no answer. But despite my best efforts to show Zach nothing, and to quash my screams, I couldn't hide the effects of the visions entirely. After each vision my body refused air, and my gasping and aborted breaths were enough to make him smug, and watchful. There was no disguising it:

something was coming, and it would not be good. But the dreams revealed little to me. They gave me no clues as to whether we would win or lose. The blood that I saw, and the bone-jarring clashes of blades, would come either way. And there would be no winning, this time. Even if we freed the refuge, our troops in the canyon would pay the price in blood.

CHAPTER 11

Two days later, scouts came from the west with news that repairs on *The Rosalind* were almost complete, and the other two ships had been stocked. When the spring northerlies stopped working against us, the fleet would be ready to sail.

Other scouts came, regularly, but none of them reported any leads about the blast machine. They brought nothing but news of more raids on convoys, and on settlements. Of more and more Omegas being forced by rising tithes to go to the refuges.

The Council had perfected the system: pushing the Omegas onto bleaker and bleaker land, and charging ever higher tithes, until people were desperate enough to turn to the refuges, which they saw as the final bulwark between themselves and starvation. I'd seen the sign myself, on the road outside Refuge 9: *Securing our mutual wellbeing. Safety and plenty, earned by fair labour. Refuges: sheltering you in difficult times.* When they were destitute enough, our people turned themselves in to the refuges willingly, and their own tithes had paid for the walls that contained them, and the gates that closed behind them.

The scouts reported that these days, the Council no longer waited for Omegas to turn themselves in voluntarily. One scout had come upon a whole settlement being marched by armed soldiers into Refuge 6.

'It's a new strategy,' Piper explained to me, when he and Zoe came back from hearing the scout's report. 'They declare a settlement *unviable*, for whatever reason – bad harvest, a flood, some other problem. Even failure to pay tithes. They post warnings – what they call a *protection order* – telling the whole settlement they have to move to a refuge instead.'

'The usual stuff,' Zoe chimed in. '*For your own safety*, all that crap.'

Piper nodded. 'They give them a week, apparently. And if any Omegas are left after that, the Council moves soldiers in to clear them out.'

If the Council was marching people to the refuges by force, it was a sign that they were accelerating their tanking programme – but it was also a sign that Omegas were not going willingly. I could not be glad at the news of people marched from their homes at swordpoint, and dragged off to the tanks – but I was glad, at least, that the truth was leaking out, and that Leonard had not died for nothing. It was months since the bards Leonard and Eva had begun their work of spreading the song about the tanks and the refuges; now scouts were reporting that the song had spread, and was spreading still.

And when the soldiers broke down the doors in an 'unviable' settlement, they didn't always find what they were looking for. In recent weeks, since the snow had cleared from the lowlands, the Omegas had begun to come to us instead.

'Just what we need,' The Ringmaster said, as he and I stood on the balcony of the Tithe Collector's office and surveyed the latest potential recruits. 'More starving people to feed.'

Below us, Simon and Tash were inspecting the three women and a man who had presented themselves at the gates. The new arrivals were thinner even than the rest of us in New Hobart. The tallest woman wore a loose dress, and her shoulder blades protruded from her back like the stumps of wings.

'We can always use more soldiers,' I said.

'Do they look like soldiers to you?' he asked.

'They can be trained. Strengthened.'

'We both know that wasn't what I was talking about,' he said, keeping his eyes fixed on the recruits.

The array of mutations they displayed among them was not out of the ordinary – one was a dwarf; the fingers of the man's right hand were fused into one fleshy mitt – but The Ringmaster's face announced clearly enough what he thought of them.

'We can make soldiers of them yet,' I said to him. 'You've seen our army fight.'

'I rescued your army from certain defeat.'

'Because we were grossly outnumbered. But we still fought, and well.'

'You were being slaughtered,' he said.

'We had the courage to take on the Council without your help.'

'Courage doesn't win wars,' he said.

'Perhaps not,' I said. 'But what I know for certain is that fear starts them. And you need to decide whether you're more afraid of Omegas than you are of the tanks and the blast. You and all the rest of the Alphas. Are you willing to help us, your allies, to bring a cure for twinning from Elsewhere, and share the untwinning with us?'

'You can't blame us for not wanting to see the next generation become like that,' he said, with a glance down at the recruits.

'The machines ended the world,' I said. 'That's why you came here, to fight with us against Zach and the tanks. Why you've agreed to try to free Refuge Six. But you and Zach are just the same: you think that being an Omega would be the end of the world, too.'

He'd turned to face me now, his eyes on my face for so long that I felt my cheeks reddening.

'You don't look like them,' he said, jerking his head toward the window. 'I forget, sometimes, that you're one of them.'

His voice had lowered. For a moment, I almost felt pity for him, watching his face, and his outstretched hand hovering an inch above my arm. I had felt that same hunger, in the months since Kip died. Months of cold and starvation, when the body seemed to offer nothing but suffering – I could understand The Ringmaster reaching for some comfort. But even as his hand reached for me I saw the corner of his mouth stretch, pulling back into a grimace.

When he grabbed my shoulder, his grip was tight. I didn't know who he was angrier at: me or himself.

'There are times,' he said, swallowing loudly, 'that I forget, for a while, about my wife, and how she died.' He paused. 'I forget what you are.'

'Don't,' I said, pushing him away. His fingers left angry red marks on my shoulder. 'You're helping us, and we need you. But make no mistake—' I crossed to the door '—I know exactly what I am, and what you are.'

*

Back at Elsa's, as the sun crept over the wire-topped wall, I thought of my own words: *I know exactly what I am.* I was thinking, too, of Xander.

That morning, he'd gone out of the kitchen door without speaking. Sally hadn't needed to ask him where he was going – it was the same every day. She'd just heaved herself upright. 'I'll go with you as far as the gate,' she'd said, shuffling beside him. 'See you on your way, make sure you've got your sentry.'

I knew I'd been neglecting Xander since I'd returned from the coast. Despite my defiant words to The Ringmaster about knowing what I was, I'd been avoiding Xander because of what he revealed to me about myself. I helped Sally to feed him, if he needed help, and I'd learned to mix the night-time dose of herbs to help him sleep. But I touched him only when necessary, and had found myself looking away when he flinched under the whip of a vision. I never took the time to sit with him, as Elsa and Sally did, while he stared at the kitchen wall, rocking slightly. I had been avoiding him, just as I'd been trying to avoid my visions.

But the visions came anyway. My days were splintered into segments, divided by fire. For all my efforts to conceal the visions from Zach, I could not prevent them, or what they did to me: my hands shaking; my eyes rolling back in my head. All the things that I had seen in Xander, time after time, and had turned away from.

I asked Piper to take me to the Kissing Tree. When the sentries waved us through the gate, I took a deep breath, and let it out slowly. The marks from The Ringmaster's fingers were still on my flesh, and Zach was waiting in the holding house – it felt good to be outside the walls. Crops were being sown, farmers walking patiently along the freshly tilled rows. Handcarts and wagons moved along the road, stopping at the sentry posts.

Beyond the cultivated land, the burnt forest was showing new growth. Ivy was growing up the scorched trunks, and scrubby undergrowth made it hard to walk once we'd dismounted and tied our horses to a tree. A patrol passed us, nodding to Piper; a little to the east of us, where more trees had withstood the fire, a team of soldiers was felling timber for building wagons.

Even with its upper part burnt away, the Kissing Tree was the biggest trunk within sight. It was several yards wide, a hollow ring of blackened wood reaching higher than Piper's head. Xander's sentry, a tall Omega, was sitting on a stump nearby; he jumped up and saluted when he saw us approach.

'This is sentry duty, not a picnic,' Piper said curtly. 'Look lively.'

'Sir,' the man said, snapping his heels together and keeping his eyes down.

I had to pull some ivy aside before I could find the narrow gap where the sides of the trunk didn't meet. I poked my head through first. Xander was sitting with his feet drawn close, his knees up to his chin. He'd taken off his shoes and placed them neatly beside him, his bare feet in the ashy dirt. His eyes were open, but they didn't turn to greet me.

'Can I come in?' I asked.

I hadn't expected an answer, and I got none.

I crawled all the way in, ivy dragging its fingers over my face. Above us, where the roof of the tree's cave had burned away, the trunk rimmed a circle of sky.

I sat facing him, my leg squashed against his in the cramped space. It felt unfamiliar to be so close to him, after avoiding his touch since my return from the coast.

'Why do you come here every day?' I asked.

Again no answer.

I said, clearing my throat, 'I should have been spending more time with you.'

It made it easier that he didn't look at me, his gaze still fixed on the ground.

'Things have been so chaotic, with Zach here,' I went on, my words speeding up, the rush of words making the tiny space feel even smaller. 'So complicated. It hasn't been easy.' I stopped myself. I was making excuses again, and I hadn't come here to do that.

'I should have tried harder,' I said. 'I'm sorry. I'm the one who should have understood.'

'You do understand,' he said. He lifted his head and looked straight at me. There wasn't any recrimination in his voice – it was a simple statement.

He was right. I feared him not because I didn't understand what was happening to him, but because I understood it all too well. I'd been keeping my distance from Xander as though that would spare me from becoming him.

'It's happening to me too,' I said. 'More, since we found out the truth behind the blast.'

At my mention of the blast, his whole body stilled, his eyes glassy.

'Forever fire,' he said.

'I know.' I tried to take his hand, and he twisted his hand from mine. I didn't know if he was deliberately brushing me off, or if it was just his body's habitual churning. I stayed beside him nonetheless. We sat like that for a long time, the two of us, huddled in the tree amongst the flames that only we could see.

*

I noticed that Piper kept his arm on his hip, close to his knives, as we passed back through the southern gate. When I stopped to look at the growing stockade of wagons, a long line of them parked end to end, he drew me back slightly, into the shelter of a doorway.

'Why are you so jumpy today?' I said.

He looked around to check there was nobody in earshot.

'I didn't want to tell you back at Elsa's, with Zach underfoot.' He ran his tongue over his lower lip. 'A scout was approached, on patrol. An Alpha soldier came to him, unarmed, and handed him a message from the Council. It's a list – a bounty. Names of people they're after.'

'Who?'

He smiled. 'Who do you think? You and Zach. Me, Zoe. Xander, too – they know the value of seers. Sally, as well – they haven't forgotten about her.'

'And Paloma?'

He lowered his head, nodded. 'Not by name. *The pale woman from Elsewhere*. That's what the list said.'

A nugget of ice was forming in my stomach. 'Who told them we have her?'

He looked around at the streets. 'It could be anyone who's seen her in the street, or heard the rumours we were searching for Elsewhere, and put two and two together. Or maybe a traitor in the inner circle.' He exhaled heavily. 'We should never have brought her here.'

'We had no choice,' I said.

Each time somebody passed the doorway, my body tensed. A tall man came past, pushing a handcart loaded with water buckets, and turned to look at me. Such stares happened often enough: everyone knew I was the seer, after all. But this time I felt my guts clench as he stared at me. It lasted only a second, before he turned away and kept walking, but I was prickling all over with sweat.

'The scout came to you?' I said.

He nodded. 'We were lucky. It was Crispin. They'd promised him money, and amnesty. He wasn't swayed by the Council's offers. But others might be, if that list is in circulation. Crispin won't be the only one they approach. They've probably tried others already.'

I felt such a sense of helplessness. We were waiting: for the wagons and the troops to be ready to march on Wyndham; for The General to make her next move; for a betrayal that was coming, as surely as summer.

*

That night I dreamed of the blast, and woke with one hand clutching the iron frame of the bed, cool and solid, the other hand braced against the dormitory's stone wall. But the blast had shown me how solidity was an illusion. I had seen bridges lift and ripple like banners in the wind. Huge buildings that sheared away like a bank of sand. As for people, they simply disappeared: there, and then not there, as if the world had forgotten them.

I'd gone to bed early; now the rats had started their midnight scratching in the roof gutters, and the moon was high. There were eleven days left, before we marched towards Wyndham. There was still no word about the blast machine, and my own efforts to sense its location still gave me nothing but confusion. I felt a stranger to my own mind, during those silent nights, alternating between visions of the blast, and fruitless attempts to track the machine that would unleash it. As for Zach, he'd remained silent on the topic of the blast machine – to me, and to The Ringmaster and Piper.

There are so many different kinds of silence: The comfortable silence that I could share with Elsa. The silence between lovers, like when Zoe and Paloma sat together by the fire and said nothing. And the silence between me and Zach, as we lay in our parallel beds in the dormitory. It was a silence full of things that could not be said, and would not be said.

When The Ringmaster slid back the bolts outside the door, I heard the rats scattering on the roof.

'I need to talk to him alone,' he said.

'I'm not leaving you alone with him,' I replied. I pulled my blanket up to cover my thin nightshirt as I sat up, remembering his gaze on me the last time he'd seen me, and his fingers clutching my shoulder.

Piper was behind him. 'Don't worry,' he said, pushing past The Ringmaster to join him in the room. 'I'll be watching him.'

Zach was sitting up, watching The Ringmaster and Piper from beneath lowered eyebrows. With his hands shackled in front of him, the chain passing through the bolt on the wall, he sat twisted sideways. He looked very small, compared to The Ringmaster and Piper. If he had been anyone else, I would have felt sorry for him.

I shrugged on my coat over my nightshirt. Zach caught my eye when I was nearly at the door.

'Cass,' he said.

I waited, but if he'd been going to ask for my help, he couldn't bring himself to do it. He just stared at me. I watched his throat rise and fall as he swallowed slowly.

'Go,' said The Ringmaster, and I left.

Zoe and Paloma were still awake, in the kitchen with Elsa, Sally and Xander, who sat quietly on a stool in the corner. Sally and Elsa were chatting, but I couldn't concentrate on anything they were saying. I was trying to recall whether The Ringmaster had been wearing a knife.

When Paloma passed me a mug of tea, I hoped she didn't notice my hands shaking.

Zoe, though, missed nothing. 'Piper's not going to let The Ringmaster get out of control in there,' she said to me, impatiently.

I nodded, wanting to believe her. We waited in silence.

Then there was a crash from the dormitory, and raised voices. Zoe jumped up so quickly that she sent a cup smashing to the ground as she moved between Paloma and the window. A door slammed. Piper and The Ringmaster were in the courtyard grappling by the dormitory door, the two of them just shapes in the half-dark. Then I heard a low grunt from The Ringmaster and saw him double over. Piper's hand moved to The Ringmaster's shoulder. From where I crouched at the window, I couldn't tell whether he was comforting The Ringmaster, or holding him at bay.

Zoe's shoulders relaxed, and she lowered her blade. Across the courtyard, Piper had let his arm drop. Straightening, The Ringmaster said, 'Stay out of my way. I'd have any other man whipped for interfering like that.'

'That would be a mistake.' Piper's voice was calm. 'Nearly as big a mistake as the one you were about to make in there.'

Sally had clambered to her feet and joined me at the window to peer into the courtyard. 'False alarm?' she said.

Zoe nodded, turning her back on the scene. 'Piper's got this,' she said.

Elsa was on her knees, gathering up the fragments of the broken mug. 'The Council didn't quite manage to smash everything I own,' she said to Zoe. 'Good thing you're here to finish the job for them.'

'All part of the service,' said Zoe, with a quick grin. She bent to help Elsa pick up the fragments.

But I stayed at the window, listening to Piper and The Ringmaster outside.

'We've both seen what that kind of pain can do to somebody,' Piper was saying.

'I'm not a novice,' The Ringmaster said. 'I can make him talk.'

'I'm not talking about him,' Piper said.

'We need what he knows,' The Ringmaster said.

'We need her,' Piper shot back. 'If it weren't for her, we wouldn't even know about the blast machine.'

'If it weren't for him, there wouldn't be a blast machine,' said The Ringmaster.

'She's this close,' Piper said, holding up his hand with thumb and forefinger pinched tight, 'to cracking up. Torture him, and we'll have lost her completely.'

Behind me in the kitchen, Sally said something and Elsa gave a chuckle. The Ringmaster turned. He saw me watching. For a few seconds we stood like that, him and Piper both staring at me, silhouetted in the window. Then The Ringmaster strode across the courtyard. He didn't come into the kitchen – I heard his footsteps through the corridor, and the front door closing behind him.

I went out to the courtyard. Piper was waiting for me, leaning on the wall by the door.

'I won't let him hurt Zach,' he said.

I just stared at him.

'I'm trying to protect you,' Piper said.

'Why?' I said. 'What's the point? You can't protect me, can you, from *cracking up*?'

I was angry at all of them: Zach. The Ringmaster. Piper. Even Xander, poor Xander, rocking in the kitchen with his eyes closed. He was what I'd thought of, when I'd heard Piper's words. *Cracking up.* There was nothing they could do to Zach that would be worse than what was happening to Xander already. What was happening to me.

'Cass—' Piper started.

'I'm going to sleep,' I said, talking over him. 'You should too.'

I unbolted the dormitory door, and slammed it behind me. I heard Piper slide the bolts again.

*

Zach was standing by his bed. His shirt had been pulled crooked, but he was uninjured – no marks on him except for the healing scar on his forehead. He tried to straighten his shirt. It was awkward, with his hands shackled. I tugged his sleeve down for him, and sat opposite him on my bed.

'You can't trust The Ringmaster,' he said. 'He had his knife out. He was one step away from sinking it into me.'

'Piper didn't let him.'

'For tonight,' Zach said. 'But his troops outnumber Piper's. If The Ringmaster decides to torture me, how long do you think Piper can hold him off?'

'I don't know,' I said. 'That's why I have to do this instead.'

Since Zach had moved into the dormitory, I'd worn my knife next to my skin, on a thigh strap. I pulled it out now. He stiffened.

'If you kill us, you won't find out where the machine is.'

'I'm not going to kill you,' I said. 'I'm going to hurt you.'

He ran at me. He came at me with such force that when the chain yanked tight, it spun him around, arms jerked backwards toward the wall. I felt, at my own wrists, the jolt of pain.

He was still four feet from me, and could get no closer. I walked calmly to the door. I dragged one of the empty beds across the floor, wedging it between the door and the wall.

'You won't do it,' he said, eyes darting from door to windows and back again. The bars on the windows had been put there to keep him safe. One by one, I closed the shutters.

'I'll scream,' he said.

'I probably will too,' I replied, closing the final shutter. 'But even if they hear us, I'll have a few minutes.' I gestured at the thick door, the shuttered windows, behind which the bars waited. Everything designed to protect both of us from an attack from the outside.

Piper could protect me against everything except myself. I sat on the bed, facing Zach, and tried to keep my breathing steady as I lifted my knife.

CHAPTER 12

I pressed the blade to my thigh, the fleshy part just above the knee. Zoe had taught me to keep my knife sharp, and I was glad of it now: it cut cleanly, with less pressure than I'd thought.

I'd expected the pain. I hadn't expected my body's protest – the vomit rising in my throat, acid sharp. Everything was very slow. I saw the whiteness of the exposed flesh, before the blood rushed to fill it. My hands mutinied, turning weak as I tried to push the knife deeper. It hovered at the edge of the wound; when the blade shook, it snagged on my skin, a small pain amidst the larger pain. A noise came out of me that I did not recognise, a hiss like a cornered cat's.

Zach yelled, kicking out, as though he could kick the pain away. He knocked over the chair that stood by his bed; it rocked from side to side on the ground, while he squatted, clutching his leg.

'You've always been determined,' I said. 'Clever, too – brilliant, even, in your own sick way. But you've never suffered, like the Omegas have.' I thought of him wincing when I'd put the salve on his burn. 'And you've never been physically brave.'

I pressed onwards. At that moment, if I could have cut him out of myself, carved him from my flesh like dead skin from an infected wound, I would have.

'So you're going to tell me, right now: where was the bomb machine moved to?' I said, through clenched teeth. 'Where is it?' I made each word the length of a breath, forced myself to keep breathing, keep talking. 'And what does The General want from you?'

'You're insane,' he said. I pushed the knife deeper, and he yelled.

'Do you think I want to do this?' I shouted, hoping my voice would drown his; that if Piper or Zoe heard us, they would think we were just arguing. The blood was a hot trail on my leg, soaking into the sheets. I heard the drops falling to the floor, a spattering that started slow and then sped up.

'Where's the machine?' I said. 'And what do you have that she wants?'

I pressed my left hand over my right, forcing it down, making a second, parallel slice into my flesh. And suddenly I felt very calm. There was so little that I could control. Not this war, with us in the middle of it. Not The Ringmaster, or Piper, or The General and her army. Least of all my own mind, which turned on me with visions of the world's end. But this, the knife on my flesh, I could control. It wasn't easy – but it was simple. I was doing it, my body, my blood, my choice, and Zach's face blanched with pain.

'I told you already,' he said. 'The General didn't let me near the new installation, not for months. And she'll have moved it since then. I have nothing to tell you.'

'Cass?' Piper's voice at the door.

'Leave me alone,' I shouted back, doing my best to keep the tremor out of my voice.

'Stop her,' yelled Zach.

I made another slice, quicker this time, and deeper. The blood surged, followed my knife along the flesh.

'Tell. Me. Where. You. Moved. It.'

Only when I saw the sweat on Zach's face did I realise that I was also drenched in sweat, the knife handle slippery in my hand.

'Stop,' he said. He was yanking at the shackles, the chain slackening and then clanging tight, again and again, the weight of his whole body thrown against the chain's limits.

'Tell. Me.'

'Stop,' he yelled. The shackles had left a ring of blood on one of his wrists. He'd fallen to the floor, curling into himself, both hands clutching his leg.

'Tell me,' I said. I could no longer feel the pain – just a strange sensation of coldness, where my flesh was opened to the air.

'You crazy bitch,' he spat. His eyes were clamped tight shut. When he opened them, they opened too wide – pupils rolling in the whites. There was loud banging on the door now, Zoe's voice along with Piper's, and Elsa yelling something.

I raised the blade again, then let it rest on its tip, its own weight pressing a dimple into my flesh. The blood from the nearby wounds ran into the hollow.

'Tell me,' I said.

'No,' he said.

The door was shaking, crashing against the bed wedged in front of it. With a shriek of steel the bed shifted a few inches across the floor, then jammed tight again. There were more thuds. I pressed the knife in, sharply. I felt the flesh parting, and the tip of the blade jar against something hard – bone. Each barb of this new pain was Zach's pain too. I pushed harder.

Zach gave a scream – a sound as harsh and urgent as the cry of a crow taking off. I prodded the bone again. 'Blackwood,' he yelled, the word a strangled shriek. I paused. 'Blackwood,' he said again. 'Near the west of Blackwood.'

An axe blade came through the door. I counted its blows: four, five, six. Piper kicked at the split wood and shouldered his way into the room, stepping over the bed.

I let myself fall sideways, head on the pillow. A few feet away, Zach gave a retch, and then vomited – a pale, liquid pool on the floor beside him.

'What have you done?' Piper said, standing over me.

'You wouldn't do it,' I said. 'You wouldn't let The Ringmaster do it either. So I had to.'

*

Elsa wouldn't touch Zach, to clean the wound his shackles had made on his wrist – but she brought a tin of warm water and a jar of salve, and dropped them with a clatter on the floor within his reach. Zach said nothing to her.

My wounds, Piper stitched up himself, one by one, bending low over my leg. We were in the courtyard outside the smashed door, and he'd given me a clean cloth to staunch the bleeding.

'I've sent word to The Ringmaster,' he said. 'But The General will have moved the blast machine.'

'At least we have somewhere to start,' I said, wincing at the snag and pull of the thread through my flesh. 'Do you know this place – Blackwood?'

He nodded. 'It's not far south-west of here. Proof that

they started shifting the stuff there a long time ago – they'd never have based it so close, if they'd had any idea that New Hobart would become our stronghold, or that The Ringmaster's garrisons would hold much of the west.'

More reasons why it was unlikely still to be there.

'We have to go there,' I said. 'To be sure.'

I'd expected him to argue with me – we were due to march on the refuge in eleven days – but he nodded. 'I'm not crazy about the idea of taking you beyond our territory, but I don't think we have a choice. Nothing's more important than the blast machine. If there's anything to find at Blackwood, even if it's only a lead, you're our best chance of finding it.'

He worked for another minute at my wounds. When he spoke, his voice was lower. 'A slip of the knife, and you could have died.' He narrowed his eyes, concentrating on each stitch. 'There's still infection, that might kill you yet.'

'We need to know where the machine is,' I said.

'We need you,' he said.

I shook my head. 'You said it yourself: *cracking up*. It's only a matter of time before I end up like Xander. We both know I won't be useful for much longer.'

'I need you,' he said. He didn't break the rhythm of his stitches, or alter the pressure of his fingers on my leg. He didn't even raise his eyes to mine. He just said it, as if it was a fact, and kept stitching.

*

Zach turned his back on me when I entered the dormitory to sleep. The only bond between us through that long night would be our pain.

I had expected Zach's fury, but Elsa's caught me by

surprise. We were woken at dawn by hammering as she nailed new boards onto the broken door. When I offered to help, she walked off, and I could hear her clattering around in the kitchen.

'I worked hard to get this place back together,' she said, when she came back out to finish the door. 'Then it gets smashed up again, because of your damn-fool tricks.' She drove another nail into the wood.

I passed her the next nail, and she took it without looking at me.

'There's a limit,' she said, closing one eye as she aimed her hammer. 'I can't keep putting this place back together.'

'Can we stop pretending that we're talking about the door?' I asked.

She turned to me. 'I was willing to have him in my home, Cass. That man, who killed my children. Because I wanted to keep you safe. There's a lot of people who've done a lot of things, to keep you safe. Don't screw it up, trying to be a hero.'

'I'm not trying to be anything,' I said. 'I'm trying to save Elsewhere.'

'By torturing yourself? And what for? That brother of yours isn't stupid.' I noticed that she avoided using Zach's name. 'Nor's The General,' Elsa went on. 'She'll have moved the blast machine.'

'Perhaps,' I said. I knew that she was probably right. My leg hurt, I was tired. I had taken no joy in hurting my body – this faithful body, that had kept me going. When I'd taken that knife to my flesh, I had shocked myself. I knew that I'd shocked Piper and Elsa. But I remembered Zach's words: *You won't do it.* I'd shocked him, too, and I was glad of that.

*

The Ringmaster was waiting on the porch of the Tithe Collector's office as Piper and I approached. He watched us as we came up the road, me limping slightly. Was he glad, I wondered, to see me in pain? To see this body, that had refused him, limping?

But he was all business. 'We march for the refuge in ten days,' he said. 'If you're going to get to Blackwood and back first, you need to travel fast, and light. Two days there, two days back, if you don't run into trouble. Another day for reconnaissance, to see if you can confirm what's going on there.'

He turned to Piper. 'You'll need to wait until night, for cover. Tash is ready to ride. Tell Simon to be ready to leave as soon as it's dark, and Crispin too.'

I nodded. That would leave Adam, Zoe and Violet to guard Zach and Paloma. The Ringmaster would be watching them too. I didn't relish the thought – but I knew that everything in New Hobart was subject to his mercy, however much we might reassure ourselves by staying at Elsa's, or posting our own guards at the door.

But it wasn't only Zach and Paloma who needed protection – I thought about the bounties, and the list of names.

'You should post extra guards on the holding house, for Sally and Paloma,' I said. 'And make sure that Xander's properly guarded when he goes to the Kissing Tree.'

The Ringmaster snorted. 'I've got sentry posts on all the roads, and patrols for miles. There are farmers in the fields, for crying out loud, and traders. We're not under siege yet. The only reason I've granted Xander a sentry at all is so he doesn't wander off and get lost. I'm not allocating more soldiers to him just because he insists on taking himself off to the forest every day.'

How could I begin to explain to The Ringmaster what it was like for Xander, for a seer, living under the certainty of the blast? 'He does what he needs to do,' I said.

'So do I,' he responded. 'I have a town to protect, and feed. An attack to prepare. The wagons aren't even finished yet. I've got bigger concerns than a deadweight boy who hasn't strung two words together for months.' He looked down at my bandaged leg. 'And my job would be easier if you weren't interfering.' He paused. 'You took an unacceptable risk.'

'I only did what you were trying to do yourself.'

He nodded, but his face remained stern. 'I'm more experienced at torture than you are.'

'I don't doubt it,' I said, meeting his gaze. He looked away first.

*

I didn't have to tell Zach where we were going.

'The blast machine will be long gone,' he said as I stuffed my things into my rucksack. 'They'll be ready for you. The General will have expected you to torture me. She knows the limits of your morals.'

'Then she also knows the limits of your courage,' I said, blowing out the candle. I left him there, chained to the wall.

Paloma, Zoe, Sally and Elsa were gathered in the courtyard to say goodbye.

'You come back safe,' Elsa said to me. It was an order, and so I saluted, and for the first time since I'd cut myself, she gave a quick smile.

Outside the front door, I grabbed Paloma's hand tightly before I mounted my horse.

'Be careful out there,' she said to me. She looked so pale that I could see the veins in her face, beneath the skin. I didn't have the heart to say to her that it might be no safer within the walls – that there might be traitors inside New Hobart as well as out. I thought of the bounty list: *The pale woman from Elsewhere.* Inside the collar of her shirt, I could just make out the dark stripe of the leather cord, where the poison hung. It was a cold comfort, but a comfort nonetheless.

Zoe kept a hand lightly on Paloma's shoulder. She met my eyes, and gave a slow nod. If I could count on nothing else, I could count on her vigilance.

Sally, too, was quiet. Standing close by my horse, she reached up to hold my leg with fingers that were surprisingly strong.

'Be alert,' she said, voice so low that only I could hear. 'Bring him home.' She gestured at Piper, who was mounted and waiting for me. He had been only a boy when he and Zoe had first found their way to Sally. In the way she looked at him now, and in the pincer grip of her fingers on my knee, I understood that part of her would always see him that way: a boy, in need of her help. I opened my mouth to say something, but she was already shuffling away, not looking back.

Beyond the walls, our small group rode south, through the remnants of the forest, past a sentry post where a patrol was readying itself in the light of burning torches. Timber felling was still going on to the east of us, the sound of axe blows measuring out the night as we rode. Heading west, we reached the marshland, where the horses foundered and slowed. Each lurch of the horse jolted my wounded leg, and blood seeped through the bandages.

When we paused to rest at the end of the first night's riding, Piper looked to the south-west, and asked me, 'Can you feel anything?'

Beside him, Simon, Tash and Crispin were pretending not to stare. I did my best to ignore them, and to keep my concentration to the south-west, where Blackwood lay. I could feel the space: the marshes petering out, the ground drying and growing stony, and then the foothills of the Spine Mountains. The thickening of the night where Blackwood Forest itself grew. Farther to the west and north, I could even sense the Ark, now nothing but the river's intricate gut. But I could feel nothing of the blast machine. There were none of the strident flames that had beset my visions when I'd been in the Ark, where the machine had lain for centuries.

'Nothing,' I said. Simon shifted in his saddle; I couldn't work out if it was disappointment or relief in his eyes.

At dawn after the second night of riding, we reached the slopes that overlooked Blackwood. It was well named: lying in a low valley between hills, a dense patch of forest where the trees grew so thickly that it looked as though the light would never penetrate. Had we not known what to look for, we might never have spotted the clearing. But Zach had told true: it was near the forest's western edge, a gap, just visible from our vantage point. Running from the clearing to the forest's southern edge was a road, a line of absence where there should have been trees.

Piper made us circle to the north of the forest, to approach the clearing and the road from the west. 'If they're expecting us, they'll be expecting us to come from the east, from New Hobart,' he said.

Before the trees had even begun to thicken around us, the blast vision came. My whole body tensed, startling my horse into a jigging trot. But the vision passed quickly, the blast stripped of its usual power – the flames in shades of grey, not the blinding white of the forever flames I'd seen at the Ark. It was no more than a residue: a spark that flared and would not catch.

Soon riding was impossible, the trees tightly clustered and the undergrowth thick and scrubby. Somewhere, outside Blackwood, it was morning, but the forest refused the daylight, and we moved through heavy shadows, searching the dimness for signs of ambush. When Piper calculated we must be about half a mile from the clearing, we tethered the horses, leaving them saddled in case we needed to make a quick escape. They were shifting and flaring their nostrils, shying at each brush of fern. This forest was ill at ease. I had not heard such a hush since the deadlands. It was the absence of birds, I realised; nothing moved in the scrub, or overhead.

We came to the edge of the road, where the light at last was allowed to reach the ground. The road was wide, and rutted with cart tracks. Piper moved carefully out of cover, and bent to the ground at the path's edge. There was new grass on the ruts, and ferns and ivy were already narrowing the road. No carts had travelled this way for weeks, at least.

In silence, staying in the trees, we traced the road to the clearing. It was bigger than it had looked from above, an island of light in the forest's grey. No building waited for us there – not even a ruin. Whatever had been there had been removed, brick by brick. All that we found, as we crept closer, was a shape on the ground, an outline of the building that had once stood there. Ferns and moss had begun to reclaim the clearing, but nothing grew on the concrete foundations of the building.

At the clearing's edge, I thought of the Ark, its twisting depths. I knelt and pressed my hands and the side of my face to the ground. There was nothing there: no hidden tunnels, or buried passages. Just the earth, impatient with spring, and the urgency of new shoots finding their way upwards. I looked up to see Piper watching me, and I shook my head. *Long gone*, Zach had said. He was right.

'There's nothing here for us,' Piper said.

Not nothing. Amidst the stillness of this abandoned place, something was stirring. I tasted iron at the back of my mouth, the taste of blood, and the swords that spilled it. Then another, stronger smell: something burning, acrid, clutching at my throat.

I whipped around, scanning the clearing.

'Take cover,' I whispered, as I sprinted for the trees. 'Someone's coming.'

CHAPTER 13

Simon, still half in the cover of the trees, responded immediately, crouching down and drawing back, but Crispin and Tash looked first to Piper for confirmation.

Crispin's height saved him: the arrow passed inches above his head. It hit Tash in the side.

The arrow struck her like a horse's kick to the chest: a rib-splintering whack, knocking her backwards. She fell, hands to her side, the arrow's feathered shaft poking out of her like some misshapen wing.

I dived for the ground, and scrabbled on hands and knees to reach her. I looped my arms beneath Tash's armpits and dragged her. We were close to the trees, but there was no time for gentleness and the arrow snagged and jerked against the ground as I pulled her. Another arrow scudded past me and lodged deep in the base of a tree nearby. The arrow was burning. The fire spread up the shaft, until the feathers themselves were burning, a nasty, pungent smell that I recognised from my vision, only moments before.

I scrambled to drag her to cover, her blood soaking both of us. I could hear Piper shout something, only yards away, but I couldn't see him. All I could focus on was the smell of the burning feathers, the heat of Tash's blood and the trail it left on the ground as I dragged her. I seemed to be moving very slowly. How can she have lost so much blood, I thought, and still be so heavy?

At last there were trees shielding us. I tried to lower her carefully, but my hands were slippery with blood. She thudded down on her back, face grey, her lips drawn back into a wordless snarl.

Reaching us, Piper lifted Tash's legs and together we hoisted her over a fallen trunk and huddled in its shelter. Crispin was beside us now, Simon flanking us to the right. Back at the edge of the clearing, where the flaming arrow had lodged, the tree's dry bark was smoking busily.

Piper squatted for a moment next to Tash. He looked at the minced flesh of her side, and the arrow's shaft wedged between her ribs. He pulled out his knife. I remembered Zoe slitting the throat of the wounded horse, and was about grab at Piper's arm to stop him. But he braced the arrow's shaft with his knee and sliced through it, so that only a short stub protruded. Tash grunted, her eyes closed against the pain.

'Get her to deeper cover,' Piper said to me and Crispin. Piper was already turning his back, knife raised. He and Simon didn't speak, just moved silently together towards the clearing.

Crispin took Tash's arms this time, while I grabbed her legs. The trees grew thickly here, so we were shielded from arrows, but with Tash slung between us we made slow and awkward progress, and trunks and branches kept jolting and jabbing my wounded leg. Barely twenty yards from the clearing's edge, a stand of trees grew in a cinched circle, and I panted to Crispin to head that way. When we laid

Tash on the ground between the trunks, she didn't seem to notice; her eyes were open, glazed, and her face was slick with sweat.

Crispin had his sword out. We were caged by the trees around us. I pressed my hands against Tash's wound, felt the flesh around the truncated arrow. Her heart was beating light and fast, a woodpecker drilling at her ribs.

Piper and Simon were visible through the trees, amidst the smoke at the clearing's edge. Piper, his knife raised, was craning around a tree to scan the clearing beyond. He looked back at me, one eyebrow raised.

I jerked my head towards a thicket on the clearing's western side, twenty yards beyond him. I didn't know if it was the archer, or somebody else, but I could feel them, crouching there, as if their breath was on my neck, and as if their shaking was my own.

I raised a finger and pointed. I knew that outstretched finger would unleash blood. I just didn't know whose blood it would be.

Piper gave a curt nod, then gestured with his knife at Simon. Simon waited a few seconds, then burst from cover, dashing from one broad trunk to dive behind a stump a few yards away. His movement was answered by movement across the clearing – the trees revealed a glimpse of red tunic, racing towards Simon. The first of Piper's knives took flight. The man fell forward from behind a tree: a tall man, hands to his face where a glint of metal was lodged.

Piper had moved back, closer to where Tash and I were hidden. Her flesh, under my hands, was growing colder, the blood stickier as it began to congeal. 'We need to move her now,' I said. 'We need to get back to the horses.'

'Not yet,' Piper said. 'The archer's still out there.'

'How do you know?' I said.

He jerked his head at the soldier's body. 'No quiver.'

I hadn't thought to look, but he was right: the fallen man, now face down and motionless, wore no quiver of arrows on his back. There was at least one Council soldier still out there – probably more.

'Run,' Piper said to me, drawing a fresh knife from his belt. 'Take Simon, get back to the horses, and ride for New Hobart.'

'Not without Tash,' I said. It was true – I wasn't going to leave her to drown in her own blood-curdled lungs – but we both knew that I was not going to leave Piper here, either. So we waited, the four of us standing with our backs pressed against the tight ring of trees that held Tash's bleeding body. The same trees that shielded us from arrows also made Piper's throwing knives useless. There was a metallic snick as he slipped his knife back into his belt and pulled out his sword. Simon and Crispin already had their swords at the ready; I clutched my knife.

The first two soldiers came charging at us from the west, a man and a woman. They moved quickly, half crouching as they darted from tree to tree. The woman, red-haired and grim-faced, was coming around to face Simon, while the man bore down towards me.

Crispin darted forward to meet him. Crispin's small stature had spared him from the arrow that hit Tash, but it worked against him now. The soldier used his height and reach, bearing down on Crispin with three swings of his sword. At the second swing, Crispin managed to jab upwards, and the man gave a yell of pain, but his third blow, a backhander with the hilt of his sword, caught Crispin on the side of the head and sent him reeling. It was all over in a few instants, Crispin face down on the ground and the man charging towards me.

To my side I could hear the impact of steel on steel as the woman reached Simon. I saw sparks from the corner of my eye. Then Piper stepped in front of me to block the man's charge. Blood dripped from the soldier's right elbow – Crispin must have wounded the soldier's sword arm, I thought, seeing him swipe clumsily at Piper with his left hand. Nonetheless, he matched Piper for size, and nearly for strength, and Piper was panting as he blocked the thrusts, always manoeuvring himself so that he remained between me and the attacker.

Between strikes, Piper kicked out at the injured soldier and sent him stumbling. I darted closer and tried to slash at his arm from the side, but I couldn't get near enough with my dagger without offering myself to his sword. He blocked my strike without even looking at me and the sheer weight of his sword was enough to jar my arm and throw me against a tree. My head crashed against the trunk, and I fell to my knees while the soldier turned back to Piper. They were only yards away from me. Piper was faster than the wounded man, but was unable to press his advantage. With his back against the stand of trees, to shield Tash, he had less room to manoeuvre than his opponent.

I turned at a sound from the other side of the clearing: the archer had emerged, bow still slung over his shoulder with his quiver, and was running through the trees towards me, a long, curved knife in hand.

I was on my feet again, my dagger raised before my face, its blade splitting my vision. This is how death comes, I thought: this frightened-looking man with his archer's glove clutching a long knife. I could hear my breath, or his – he was so close now that I couldn't tell. A final step, and the bow on his shoulder snagged on a branch, yanking him backwards. It halted him for only a second, but it was all I needed. I jumped forward, under his raised weapon, and slashed.

Zoe would have told me to focus, to aim for arteries, or eyes. But that swing of my arm was all that I had in me, and it was pure luck that it caught the man's throat. I felt the snag of a ligament, magnified through my blade's tip, and then there was a line across his neck, surprisingly tidy, and everything below that line was red, while his face above it blanched. His eyes bulged and his head dropped backwards. And when I closed my eyes, I saw a woman at a table, one hand still wrist-deep in a lump of half-kneaded dough while her other hand grasped at her throat.

When my eyes opened again to the scene in front of me, I was still standing, but my knife was somewhere on the ground, amidst the blood and the leaves. Crispin was stirring, a few yards away, but still face down on the ground. Both Piper and Simon were fighting their opponents at close hand. Simon didn't fight with the same efficiency or precision as Piper; instead he moved with a kind of explosive energy, brawling and thrashing his way through the fight, an axe in two of his hands and a short-sword in the third. He and the woman were both grunting and swearing as they fought.

I couldn't find my dagger. On my knees, I swept my hands over the ground, snatching them back when I found the outstretched hand of the man I had killed. I looked around for another weapon. Nearby, Piper was gaining ground against the injured man, who was slowing, tripping slightly when Piper wrong-footed him. But behind him another soldier, with a blond beard, slipped from between the trees, sword raised at Piper's neck.

I shouted a warning, still groping for my dagger, and

Piper, between grunts, swung at the bearded soldier, leaning back at the same time to dodge a thrust from the injured soldier. But he couldn't hold them both off at once. As he blocked a blow from one, the other threw his whole weight into a strike, dashing Piper's sword from his hand.

'Cass, run,' he shouted.

He was unarmed now, his back to the tree, both men in close. Crispin was still face down to our left, and Simon was caught in his own struggle with the woman. The bearded man drew back his arm for the final thrust, sword levelled at Piper's stomach. Even as I ran at the soldier I knew that I would be too late, and that my fists could never stop that blade.

I should have seen this coming, I thought. How could I not have sensed Piper's death, of all things?

In that same instant, before the thrust, the soldier was staring at Piper's face, and something like recognition crossed his own. He froze, his arm still drawn back. 'Not him,' he said to the injured man next to him. I knew the expression on the wounded soldier's face, because it was the same terror and uncertainty that was on mine. Piper, too, looked uncomprehending.

'Not him,' the bearded soldier said again, panting. He stepped back. 'Get the seer.'

The other soldier nodded, turning to me. I'd halted, barely ten yards from them, and now I moved backwards. The distance between us was scattered with trees, and the two of us moved warily: when he stepped one way, I stepped the other, keeping the trees between us.

Beyond him, the bearded soldier still had his eyes fixed on Piper's face. His sword was lowered slightly, and he'd drawn back further.

'Go,' he said to Piper. 'Go,' gesturing towards the trees with his sword.

Piper took half a step back, eyes narrowed, then another step. He moved hesitantly, as though if he looked down to where he had been standing, he would see himself lying there, the sword in his chest. The bearded soldier opened his mouth to say something else, when Crispin's axe found the back of his head. It was a clumsy throw, the small axe juddering through the air rather than spinning neatly. But it did its job, lodging in the back of the man's head. Behind him, Crispin was leaning heavily with one arm against a tree.

There was no time to think about what had happened. The other soldier and I were still performing our uneasy dance between the trees, and he sped up now. I ducked behind a tree as the man took his first swing. He had aimed low, for my legs, but the sword jarred against the tree. I remembered the bearded soldier's words: *Get the seer*. He didn't want to kill me, only to capture me. That was no comfort.

He grunted as he wrenched the blade free of the wood. It bought me a few seconds, and I sprinted further into the trees. It was a mistake. Unarmed, my only chance was speed, but there was no room to sprint, roots and scrub grabbing at my ankles as I ricocheted from tree to tree, squeezing myself through ever-tighter gaps. The man was right behind me, his breath loud. Then he had hold of my arm, tight, jerking me backwards so that I fell.

'Give it up,' he said. It was more of a plea than an order. He was bleeding, and his face was pale and sweaty with exhaustion and fear. But he pinned me hard to the ground with his foot while he used his good hand to raise his sword over me, pointed at my stomach.

Then Piper's sword came through him. It pierced his chest

from behind, ten inches of steel poking through his tunic. The soldier dropped his sword, both hands clutching the blade emerging from his chest. He wrapped his palms around it gently, as though it were a treasure he had found. Then his legs crumpled and he fell, face forwards.

Now there was nothing between me and Piper, staring at each other over the body.

CHAPTER 14

I could hear my heartbeat, loud in my ears. On the ground, the dead man's blood was spreading towards my boots. But it was the other soldier I was thinking of: the bearded soldier who had been about to kill Piper, but had spared him. The soldier's words: *Not him*.

'What happened back there?' I said. 'Why didn't he kill you?'

'Are you all right?' Piper said. I followed his eyes to my blood-soaked clothes. The blood was not my own: it belonged to Tash, and to the injured soldier who had grabbed me. I wore Piper's blood, too – his hand, now on my shoulder, was warm and wet, his arm bleeding from several cuts.

'Piper!' Crispin was calling through the trees, and I heard his running footsteps a short distance away. 'Cass!'

I shrugged Piper's hand off.

'What did that soldier mean, when he said, *Not him*?' I asked.

From somewhere behind Piper, Simon's voice had joined Crispin's, calling for us.

'I don't know,' Piper said. He didn't avoid my gaze.

'He could have killed you there and then. He was about to.'

'I know that,' Piper said, with an exhalation that was nearly a laugh. I could see that he was still adjusting to the novelty of not being dead.

'Why did he let you go?' I said. For a moment I wished I had my dagger, even though I knew it would be useless against Piper and his sword.

'I don't know,' Piper said again. 'Maybe he lost his nerve. Maybe he had orders to take me alive.'

'He didn't try to take you alive,' I said, shouting now. 'He let you go.'

He threw out his arm, raising his voice to match mine. 'I don't know why he did it. But we don't have time to argue about this. We need to get out of here.'

Crispin reached us, his face already swollen and purpled, one eye forced closed.

'Boss?' he said.

Piper ignored him. 'You know me,' he said to me quietly.

I couldn't answer. Piper turned away.

'Get to Tash,' he said to Crispin. 'If she's still alive, bind her wound.'

I followed them back towards the clearing. Simon was striding through the trees, gathering the fallen weapons. The woman he'd been fighting lay slumped against a tree trunk – her face looked wrong, somehow, her whole head misshapen by the force of the blow she'd taken. Her skull was a puzzle that could not be remade.

'No sign of any others,' Simon said. Like Piper, he had several slashes on his arms. He was sweating, the sweat spreading the blood on his shirt into a pink blur.

Piper was wiping his sword on the tunic of one of the

dead men. 'Find your knife,' he said to me. 'We need to go, now.'

I found it, the handle poking out from beneath the arm of the man whose throat I'd slit. I had to touch his skin to retrieve the knife. His flesh was still warm – the skirmish felt like it had taken forever, but only minutes had elapsed. I wiped my hands, front and back, in the leaf mulch on the ground. They still smelled of blood.

Tash was alive, but looked little better than the dead that we left behind us. Her skin had the clammy greyness of an oyster. She was still conscious, somehow, though I wished for her sake that she wasn't. Crispin had wrapped her wound as carefully as he could, but there was no time to be delicate. Simon hoisted her on his shoulder, holding her firm with his three arms, and we all jogged through the forest. I was behind Simon, Tash's face staring back at me as she hung over his shoulder. She didn't yell, but each time she was jolted against a tree, she seemed to turn greyer. A red stain spread from Simon's shoulder, and it was not his blood. When we reached the horses, Simon laid Tash down for a few minutes; one of the horses sniffed her idly, and then continued to tear grass from around her outstretched arm, as though she was already dead.

We rode out of the forest into the glare of the morning sun. Crispin held Tash upright before him; Simon led the spare horse as he rode. Grazes and scratches all over my body, which I hadn't even noticed when the soldier was chasing me through the scrub, were now stiffening into scabs, and my sliced leg was a constant ache. Every time a bird moved, I imagined ambush. If I closed my eyes, just for a moment, I could still feel the ligament snag on my blade as I'd slashed open the soldier's neck. I pictured his twin, too – caught unawares, her dying fingers twisting the dough. Five bodies had been left in the clearing, and the twinning's unflinching mirror doubled it: ten dead.

All through that long day of riding, my horse's hoofbeats ringing loudly in my head, the bearded soldier's words became my own refrain, as I stared at Piper's back, just ahead of me: *Not him. Not him. Not him*. I'd thought that I could bear almost anything. Now I knew that wasn't true. I could not bear that: for him to be a traitor.

*

By a marshy pool, when the horses had drunk their fill, we dozed a few hours in the darkness, taking turns to watch. Tash lay with her hands clutched to her wound; twice I tried to check it, and each time she hissed at me with a ferocity that I found reassuring, curling her whole body around her smashed side and swiping at me with a clenched fist.

'Should we try to take out the arrow?' I whispered to Simon.

'Not here,' he said. 'It'll restart the bleeding, and we have to ride again soon. Wait for New Hobart, and the doctors.'

If she was strong enough to make it to New Hobart, I thought, she would be strong enough to live.

My own wounds were slight in comparison: I had grazes, and a bruise along my cheekbone, and I'd ripped open the stitches of one of the cuts on my leg. I hadn't even noticed it during the frantic chase through the forest, but now I inspected it and found that the torn stitches had left shreds of skin, and a wound that gaped each time I moved. I bound it as well as I could, and said nothing of it to Piper.

I avoided him, and busied myself with taking care of Tash, but when I went to fill my flask he followed me down to the pool.

'Cass,' he said, keeping his voice low. I was squatting, feet sinking into the damp ground as I leant over the water. 'I don't know what happened back there,' he said, 'any more than you do—'

I straightened, jammed the stopper back in my flask and walked back to the others, before he could say anything further.

By unspoken agreement we said nothing in front of the others. They were oblivious to what had happened to Piper in the ambush. Perhaps I kept silent because I didn't want to expose Piper to their scrutiny, or perhaps I just didn't want to make it real. But I watched Piper, and I turned the moment over and over in my mind. The recognition on the soldier's face. His words: *Not him*. The moment clung to me, like the smell of burning feathers that still lingered in my hair.

I slept for barely an hour, lying close to Tash to try to keep her warm. I dreamed of Xander. It wasn't a long dream: a few seconds, flashes of images, but enough to know he was in peril. It was strange to wake to that certainty, because Xander was in peril all the time. For the last year or more, his mind had been aflame. Peril was his permanent state. But this was a different kind of peril: men on horseback. Swords. An axe thudding into the Kissing Tree.

I sat up, shook Simon's arm. It was after midnight, the moon half hidden by clouds.

'There's an ambush,' I said, my voice still croaky with sleep.

On the other side of Tash, Crispin squinted up at me through his black eye. 'I'm not sure you understand how this seer thing works. The visions are meant to come before the thing.'

'Not the ambush on us,' I said. 'At New Hobart. It's Xander.'

We rode. The ground was treacherous, once we reached the marshland, but we pushed the horses as fast as Tash's injuries would permit us. Each time we stopped to rest or water the horses, I didn't even attempt sleep. We rode as the light returned, and through that long day and night. I stared at the sun's progress across the sky, and then the moon's, and thought of Xander. I knew that we would get to New Hobart too late, and I cursed the vision for coming early enough to taunt me with the knowledge, and too late for me to save him.

There's an ugliness to all war, all deaths, but what I felt in the vision, when I saw Xander being snatched, was something unclean, souring the air. It was betrayal.

We came within sight of New Hobart when it was nearing dawn. Even if I hadn't had the dream, we would have known something had happened. The perimeter around the town had been tightened, and swarmed with our soldiers. A patrol spotted us and rode to meet us even before we reached the first sentry post, miles from the walls.

'We've orders to take you straight to The Ringmaster,' the tall Alpha soldier said, reining his horse nose-to-nose with Piper's.

'There's been an incursion?' Piper said.

The man nodded. 'A Council raid. No substantial losses, but they got to within a few miles of the wall.'

'*No substantial losses*,' I repeated. For a moment my heart clutched at the words, and I allowed myself to hope – but then I thought of how the Alpha soldiers regarded Xander. How The Ringmaster himself had called him *a deadweight*.

'They took the seer boy?' I said.

The soldier muttered, 'That's right,' but he was staring at Tash. Her uniform no longer matched his – the whole right side of her tunic was blackened with blood, and with flies that kept settling on her, no matter how many times Crispin shooed them away. Tash was lapsing in and out of consciousness, and Crispin's arm around her chest was the only thing keeping her upright.

'Will she make it?' the soldier asked.

In one swift motion, Piper drove his horse forward and leant over, grabbing the soldier by the throat.

'If your comrade Tash makes it, it will be because we kept her alive. But you sit there and talk about *no substantial losses*, as though Xander were worthless.' He released the man as quickly as he'd grabbed him, pushing him backwards and sending his horse shying. The soldier had his hand to his neck, and his other on his sword, but kept himself under control, though I could see that it didn't come easy to him to submit to an Omega.

Piper went on, enunciating each word carefully, through a tensed jaw. 'You have no understanding of what that boy was worth.' He took a slow breath. 'Any other casualties?'

'They killed a sentry too,' the soldier said, following with a reluctant, 'sir. One of yours – he was guarding the boy.'

To the east, the sun was rising over the burnt forest where the Kissing Tree stood. The patrol escorted us all the way to the gate, but my thoughts stayed with the Kissing Tree and Xander as I'd last seen him, his thin knees bent up to his chin, his mind a vessel of fire.

*

'How many men did you send in pursuit?' Piper demanded.

'Zoe sent some of your soldiers. Violet, and a patrol of

ten,' said The Ringmaster. He was in the Tithe Collector's office, working, the table littered with candle stubs and maps. Crispin and Simon had taken Tash to the barracks to be tended by the doctors there.

'They've got a full day's lead,' The Ringmaster said. 'When a patrol found the sentry last night, he'd been dead for hours. Cold and stiff, and shoved inside the tree – they had to break his legs to get the corpse out.'

I would never get used to the casual way that The Ringmaster spoke of such things. Piper didn't flinch. He too was fluent in the language of death.

'It was a targeted raid,' The Ringmaster went on. 'They knew what they were after, and they must have got him pretty much as soon as he got to the tree, first thing. They were in and out, quick and efficient.'

I had been clinging to the hope that Xander's capture might have been random, a raiding party that happened to stumble upon him, rather than a deliberate betrayal. I'd wanted to believe that Xander's location had been let slip by a gossiping sentry, or some sharp-eyed person in the street who'd gleaned that Xander went to the forest most days. But there was too much detail to the betrayal – it was too tidily planned. The raiders had known I was away, and couldn't give warning. They knew exactly what they were looking for. They'd penetrated miles into our defended territory, snatching Xander early in the day, giving them time to get away before his loss was discovered. It spoke of a traitor familiar with Xander's movements. Somebody who knew them well.

'And you?' I said to The Ringmaster. 'What have you done to help with the search? Did you send any of your soldiers?'

'There was no point,' he said. 'They had a twelve-hour lead already.'

'If you're going to be ruthless, at least be honest about it,' Piper said. 'You didn't send anyone because you don't think Xander's worth it.'

'Fine,' The Ringmaster said. 'The boy can't give them any information.'

'A *deadweight*,' I said. 'Isn't that what you called him, when you refused to give him more protection?'

'I stand by what I said,' he replied. 'He's of no use to them. They won't get anything out of him.'

'There's a reason he was on the bounty list,' I said.

'They don't know the state he's in,' The Ringmaster said. 'They want a seer – not a kid who talks in riddles and doesn't know what day it is.'

'That's what a seer is,' I yelled. 'That's the reality of it.' Living with fire in your head, and time that wouldn't stay in place. 'Xander was the one who knew about the Ark,' I went on, 'long before me. He knew the Council had found it.'

'He wasn't privy to any of our plans. There's nothing operational that he can give them.'

'You don't know what he knows,' I said.

'*He* doesn't know what he knows.' The Ringmaster slammed his palm flat on the table. 'He doesn't know anything.' He closed his eyes for a moment, exhaled, then wiped his hand down his face. 'Look,' he said. 'I don't relish this. I wish no harm on Xander. But I have to make hard decisions. I can't risk more soldiers by sending them chasing after a boy who can't even wipe the drool from his own chin.'

He paused, looking from me to Piper.

'And there's other news,' he said. 'You don't understand the full picture. At noon yesterday we heard from the scouts: The General's troops have withdrawn from Wreckers' Pass.'

His words settled in my stomach, cold and hard.

'Did you hear me?' he said. 'It's good news. The only good news we've had in weeks. I've deployed a squadron, to secure the pass and escort a convoy coming through from the west. They're half a day away now.'

There was a ringing in my ears. I closed my eyes, but all I saw was fire. I was swaying; normally I would have reached for Piper to steady me, but since Blackwood I didn't even want to do that. I concentrated on my breathing, and waited for the earth to stop tilting underfoot.

'Are you listening to me?' The Ringmaster said. 'It's the biggest convoy to have made it through. It'll be enough food to see us through to the end of spring. Enough to guarantee that we can feed your precious Omegas, if we get them out of the refuge.'

'Why would The General concede the pass?' Piper said.

'There're any number of reasons,' he said. 'Her scouts will have picked up on all our preparations. She could be beefing up the defences at Wyndham. She could be—'

'Don't lie to me,' I shouted over him.

I stepped closer to The Ringmaster; my shirt crackled with Tash's dried blood as I moved.

'Did you betray him?' I said. 'Did you tell The General where he could be found, in exchange for Wreckers' Pass? Are you trading with her?'

'Be careful what accusations you throw around,' The Ringmaster said. 'I might not think much of the boy, but I think even less of The General.'

Piper walked to the door. 'I'll be sending more of the Omega troops after Xander.'

'Do what you must,' said The Ringmaster. 'But don't forget who runs this town.'

CHAPTER 15

Piper gave the orders, and ten of his troops rode out from the southern gate, in search of Xander.

'It's too late,' Sally said. It was the first thing she'd said, since we got back to the holding house. She stood at the window staring out at the street, and not even Zoe dared to talk to her. Now Sally had finally spoken, there was a certainty in her voice that scared me more than tears or hysteria would have done. 'Too late,' she said again. 'They've had him since yesterday morning.'

Elsa was distracted, black circles under her eyes. She checked my wounds. My bruises and scrapes were already yellowing and faded; the worst injury was the reopened cut on my leg. It was too late to restitch it, Elsa told me, but she cleaned it and bandaged it tightly.

'Sally hasn't eaten since he was taken,' Elsa said. She was bent low over my leg, her tongue out of the corner of her mouth as she fastened the bandage.

I saw it myself, when we ate breakfast. Sally didn't even look at the bowl that Elsa put in front of her. The Ringmaster was there too – he'd come in without knocking, with more questions about what we'd seen at Blackwood, and the ambush. In the kitchen, we all watched each other, monitoring every movement, trying on our suspicions and our fears.

When we were young, Zach and I had found a wasp nest in one of the willows by the river. Zach had thrown rocks at it. When the first rock hit, the whole swarm had risen, vibrating with rage. If we hadn't dived in the river and swum downstream, surfacing only for air, it would have been the end of both of us. The whole holding house was like that swarm, now: seething and shifting, abuzz with distrust.

Piper led Zach out of the dormitory, his chain dragging from his shackles, leaving a trail in the dirt across the courtyard. When they reached the kitchen, Zach surveyed my exhausted face and roughed-up hands and arms.

'You should have listened to me,' he said. 'I told you you'd find nothing at Blackwood.'

His gaze lingered on my bruised face; he turned to Piper and looked at Piper's wounded arm.

'Run into trouble?' Zach asked. He turned back to me. 'You should be more careful. You know there's a traitor about.'

'Be quiet,' snapped Piper.

'Are we not supposed to talk about it?' Zach said. 'If there's a traitor in New Hobart, none of us are safe – including me.' He scanned the room, then shrugged. 'Though, from what I've seen, Xander's hardly a great loss.'

It all happened very quickly: Zoe reached across the table and had Zach by the throat. She grabbed a handful of both shirt and flesh, and twisted it as she jerked him forward. One of his elbows sent Sally's bowl skidding to the floor, porridge spraying on the flagstones; then Zoe pulled him to the ground.

'Don't hurt him,' Piper said.

Zach's breathlessness clutched at my own breath, my hand pressed against my neck as if that could protect it. Zoe knelt over him.

'Zoe,' said Piper again.

She turned to look at me without releasing her grip on Zach.

'Let him go,' I said. The words came out as gasps, short of breath.

She shoved her hand down, slamming Zach to the floor with a jolt of pain that made me cry out. Then she let go and stepped back, wiping her hand on her trousers.

'We don't need to talk about the traitor,' she said, glaring down at him, 'because we know who it is.'

'You don't know it was him,' I said, when I had enough air to speak again.

'Oh, come on,' she spat. 'You're not really going to defend him, even now?'

'Of all of us, he's had the least chance to betray Xander,' I said.

'He's the only one here who would do it,' she shouted. 'You know what he's like. Hell on earth, Cass – he worked with those people for years. He built the tanks. You can't tell me you don't think he's capable of betraying us.'

'I think he'd do it, and readily,' I said. 'But I don't think he's capable of breaking steel chains, or sneaking out when he's been under guard the whole time. And I don't see why he'd care about Wreckers' Pass enough to risk trading with The General.'

'He told you about Blackwood to get you out of here, so you wouldn't be around to warn us,' The Ringmaster said.

'You think I'd set up my own torture?' Zach raised an eyebrow. 'You're clutching at straws.'

'Who else would do something like this to Xander?' asked Elsa.

It wasn't a question I wanted to contemplate. I looked at The Ringmaster, remembering how he'd called Xander a *deadweight*. If we couldn't trust him, we were all lost.

'You despised Xander,' I said. 'And you were thrilled with the news about Wreckers' Pass.'

'We should all be,' he said. 'It might not seem as important to you as one mad boy, but it'll keep this town alive for months. All of our other plans depend on it.'

'And that justifies letting them take Xander?' I said.

'It might have,' said The Ringmaster. 'But I didn't do it. And if you weren't so blinkered, you'd be looking to your own twin.'

'The Ringmaster and I aren't the only Alphas here,' said Zach quietly, fixing his gaze on Zoe. 'She never liked the boy.'

He was right that Zoe had avoided Xander whenever she could. I'd seen her snap at him, or stalk away when he muttered and rocked. But I knew why she did it. And I couldn't bring myself to suspect Zoe. It wasn't just that I'd relied on her for months, during our travels together. It was more that betrayal and treachery weren't in her – she would be more likely to take a knife to Xander herself, if her frustrations grew too much.

I looked around the table. Zach had been under lock and key. But for any of the rest of us, the task would have been easy enough: a whispered exchange in the street; a note slipped into a hand during a walk around the walls. Any one of us could have had the opportunity to betray Xander. Even Simon, or one of the other guards we trusted to watch the holding house – they would have seen Xander come and go each day, and known where he was headed. Tash; Violet; Crispin; Adam.

Even Piper. A deal – Wreckers' Pass, and his life, in exchange for Xander's? It seemed impossible. But what was impossible, these days, while a woman from Elsewhere sat opposite me at the table, along with The Ringmaster and Zach? While the Council had found the blast machine, and was ready to use it? I no longer knew how to make sense of this world.

One thing I knew for certain was that I could not suspect Elsa, my old friend, who treated Xander with the same steadfast tenderness she'd shown to all the children under her care. It would be as absurd as suspecting Sally, who had protected Xander for years, and who sat, now, at the table, with blank eyes and a face collapsed in on itself by grief.

'You had a lucky escape yourself,' The Ringmaster said to me. 'Convenient, isn't it – that you went out there to visit him, the day before you left, and just before the raid?'

I did my best to keep my voice calm. 'I'd never betray Xander,' I said. I was looking at The Ringmaster, but hoping that the others believed me.

'Wouldn't you?' he asked. 'It's not like you were fond of him. You could hardly bear to be in the same room as the boy.'

He was right. I knew that I had indeed betrayed Xander. Not by handing him over to the Council, but in every other way. I'd betrayed him each time I'd stared at him, or flinched at his slack-mouthed silence.

'You don't know what it's like,' I began. 'Being a seer—'

The Ringmaster cut me off. 'Exactly. We don't know what it's like, or what you're capable of. Sending messages, maybe. Reading minds. Finding a way to communicate with the other side, to make some kind of deal. Get rid of Xander.'

'This has to stop,' Piper said. Even though he was injured and exhausted, his voice still carried enough authority to silence us all. 'This is madness. Flinging accusations around isn't going to help Xander.'

'Nothing's going to help Xander,' said Sally. 'We all know that.'

Not one of us dared to deny it.

*

Our own news – the empty clearing, the missing blast machine, the ambush – was lost in the chaos of Xander's capture, and the arrival of the food convoy from the west, which came the next day. Eight wagons, axles straining under the load of grain. I heard the whooping in the streets, but couldn't bring myself to celebrate.

Paloma, though, hadn't forgotten about Blackwood. She came to me in the courtyard.

'Is it true? No sign of the bomb?'

I checked to see that Zach was nowhere near. I didn't want him gloating. 'It was like Zach said: they'd moved it. Weeks ago, at least. The whole place had been taken apart.'

She nodded. Her lips were pressed tightly together.

'I was on that list, wasn't I?' she said. 'The one with Xander on it. Zoe refused to tell me, but I heard Elsa talking to Sally. And Zoe's been jumpy ever since the news of the list – hardly wanting us to leave the house.'

I didn't want to lie to her. She had already risked so much for us – I thought she deserved to know the truth.

'Yes,' I said.

She looked back towards the kitchen, where Zoe was with the others. 'She wants to protect me. She doesn't think I could handle it – if I knew everything.'

I looked at her, that long neck, the eyebrows so pale that they were nearly invisible. She was like a white feather that had blown to shore.

'I was never much of a fighter, or even a politician,' she said. 'I joined as an emissary because I had some trading experience, and because they always need volunteers. Caleb was the main emissary, really. He was meant to be in charge —' her voice caught, and she paused before continuing. 'Until the storm killed him.' She gave a slow shrug. 'Zoe's so brave. Sometimes I think she'd despise me, if she knew how afraid I really am.' She looked up at me. 'I'm afraid that they'll catch me,' she said. I saw how her hand moved to the neck of her shirt, and I saw the lump where the snakewood capsule hung. 'But worse than that,' she said, 'I'm afraid that they won't. That they'll find home without me, and bomb it, and I'll still be here, alive. I'll have to live and know that I brought it all on them.'

I touched her arm. The tiny hairs of her forearm were standing up in the cool evening air. 'It wasn't you who did this,' I said.

'I left my home,' she said. 'I said goodbye to my parents and my sisters. I was ready for the possibility that I might not come back. The expedition ships don't come back, more often than not.' She shook her head slowly. 'But I wasn't ready to lose them all.' Her voice faltered. 'That wasn't how this was supposed to go.'

I couldn't say what I was thinking: that this was exactly how it was supposed to go. That I'd seen it go that way, in all my visions. That every one of us who walked this scorched earth had already seen it go that way, once. The war, and the tanks, had come before, and had come again. That it was all a circle. The blast had come before as well, and when I woke from visions, my mouth too full of flames to scream, I knew that it was coming again.

*

There were six days left until the march to the refuge. While the preparations continued outside, in the holding house we busied ourselves with stares and whispers, passing suspicion between us like a glass of soured wine. Violet and her soldiers had returned, and the second group as well – both with nothing to report of Xander but a trail that was lost in the marshes. Sally barely responded when the troops reported to her; she took the news with a fatalism that I found more alarming than tears or rage.

Piper was nervy, snapping at me and Paloma every time we got too close to the window in the front sitting room, overlooking the street. The third time, I snapped back.

'We both know that Xander was betrayed by someone who knew him, Piper. Keeping me away from the windows might make you feel important but it isn't going to save me.'

He said nothing – just slammed the shutters closed, sealing us off from the street. And leaving the accusation hanging in the air didn't make me feel better.

Later, Piper cornered me in the corridor outside the kitchen.

'You know it wasn't me,' he said.

'Stop telling me what I know,' I said.

He didn't let me pass, and I was reminded of the sheer size of him. When he stood in front of me, blocking the corridor, little light from the courtyard door got past him.

His voice dropped low. 'I trusted you, even when you nearly killed us both in the Ark. I have never doubted you.'

'Never?' I said. 'You told The Ringmaster I was cracking up.'

'And aren't you?'

I had long felt it, myself – the madness waiting for me, certain as the blast. But it was something else to hear him say it like that.

'Why did that soldier let you go, at Blackwood?' I asked.

'I've told you. I don't know. Believe what you like about that. But you must know that I'd never betray Xander.'

I was looking at Piper's hand. I'd seen it rest on Xander's shoulder as he calmed the boy. I'd seen the same hand deliver death with a flick of a knife. The many times he'd saved me. The many times he'd killed for me.

'Tell me that you believe me,' he said.

I wanted to, so much. But after seeing that soldier spare him, I had no answers any more. I pushed past him, the stone wall cool against my arm, and walked away.

Those days, each time I entered the dormitory, Zach seemed relieved to see me. 'Be careful,' he said to me, again and again. 'Don't trust them.'

I didn't reply, didn't even look at him, but his whisperings still got to me. We Omegas were supposed to be the tainted ones, carrying the contagion of the blast. *She's poison*, Zach had once warned Piper about me. But Zach was the poison, now. His shackle and chains didn't stop his whispers reaching me even when I pulled the pillow over my head. In those long nights, he spoke of The Ringmaster, his old ties to The General, his lust for power. Piper and his ruthlessness. Even Paloma – 'You've no idea what her real motivations are,' he said. 'And Zoe and Paloma are loyal only to one another now.' All night, his words insinuating themselves into my ears.

I knew what he was doing, and why, but I couldn't ignore him. Everything he said, through those days and nights when Xander was missing, only gave voice to my own fears. All the doubts and suspicions that I tried to keep at bay, he brought into the room where I slept, and released them, to scuttle around us like the rats in the rafters.

*

Word came from the barracks that Tash had died. The doctors had taken the arrow out, the messenger said, but she'd lost more blood, and had died within a few hours of us bringing her back to New Hobart.

I closed my eyes. I didn't want to show the messenger how I was feeling. It was anger, as much as grief – the waste of it. We'd brought her so far, and yet she was as dead as if we'd left her on the ground in Blackwood with that arrow in her side.

'There's something else,' the messenger said.

I braced myself for more bad news.

He was a young Alpha soldier, one of The Ringmaster's, and had seemed ill at ease when he first knocked on the holding house door with his report, eyeing Elsa's crooked legs as she'd led him down the corridor, and keeping his distance from me as though my visions were contagious. But when he spoke now, he looked me straight in the eyes.

'They said it was you – you and the rest of them – who brought her back from Blackwood alive. You could have left her, and you didn't.'

I shifted in my chair. Beside me, Piper spoke.

'We did for her what we'd do for any of our soldiers,' he said.

'Hasn't always been that many in our barracks that would've done the same, sir,' the soldier said. He was just a boy, really – probably a few years away from twenty, his chin covered with a patchy, downy growth that could only charitably be called a beard.

'Tash was well-liked, sir. When I joined up, she kept an eye on me. There's a few more now,' he said, 'like me, who've heard what you did for her. Who'd repay the favour, if it came to it.'

He then left quickly, red-faced and head down. But during those cloistered, angry days after Xander was taken, the young soldier's words gave me something to cling to. We were building something, here in New Hobart. I only hoped that we would have a chance to complete it.

In my dream that night, Xander came back to us. He walked up the road from the east, right up to the gate of the town. When I ran to him, and tried to clasp him to me, he started to fall apart in my hands. It was like trying to clutch armfuls of wet sand.

Awake, I ran to the door without even lighting a candle. Zach called after me, and I heard his shackle clatter as he sat up. I ignored him – I was already shouting for Piper.

For all my wariness of Piper since Blackwood, I was grateful that he listened, and never doubted what my vision had shown me. He led the patrol of fifteen soldiers himself, riding down the eastern road towards Wyndham while it was still dark. The rest of the holding house was roused too; we gave up on sleep, and waited in the kitchen, blankets thrown around our shoulders, while Elsa boiled pot after pot of tea. It was nearing mid-spring and while the days were hot, the nights were still sharpened by a chill.

Zoe and Paloma sat closest to the door, shoulders leaning against each other. Elsa clattered about the kitchen, as though if she scrubbed and wiped enough, and boiled enough water, she could somehow reassemble Xander. Sally sat alone, saying nothing. She'd turned to face the east. It left her perched sideways on the bench, staring at the wall beside the fireplace. I doubted she even realised she had done it; it was instinct, her body's vigil, as we all waited for news from the eastern road.

I even took a cup in to Zach, just to break up the waiting, and to get away from the stares of the others in the kitchen. I placed the cup carefully on the floor between our beds, at the edge of where his chain would reach.

'It's Xander, isn't it?' he said.

I looked up at him from under my lowered brows, and nodded.

'Is he dead?'

I gave no answer.

'It wasn't me,' he said. It was a whisper.

I didn't say: *Then who?* Because I didn't want to hear his answer. All the possibilities – Piper? The Ringmaster? Zoe? – were too awful to contemplate.

He looked very pale. 'I know they all think it was me. If the boy's dead, they'll blame me for that too.'

'Thirty children used to sleep in this room, before you and The General had them drowned.' I made no effort to keep the disgust from my face. 'Nobody here needs another reason to hate you. Nor do I.'

CHAPTER 16

Before dawn, when Simon had finished his shift at the holding house door, he agreed to escort me to the eastern watchtower. The sentries ignored us when we climbed to the tower. They stolidly watched the horizon, and spoke only to complain when my pacing irritated them. Before the rest of the city had even stirred, Sally came shuffling up the ladder to join us. It was a slow process, and I heard her breath rasping, long before her wrinkled hands appeared at the top of the ladder.

'Are you sure it will be today?' she said, when she was finally beside me.

'I thought so. I could be wrong. You know how the visions can be.'

She gave a grunt. She had cared for Xander for years, with more patience than I'd ever been able to muster. She knew, more than almost anybody else who wasn't a seer, how capricious the visions were.

We waited together in silence. The sentries changed twice, and it was past midday when the soldier to my left raised her arm and pointed east at a column of dust rising on the road, and we saw the distant shapes, nothing more than a shimmer on the horizon. I knew what they would be carrying long before they came into view and I saw the hessian bundle laid across the front of Piper's saddle.

When the riders were nearly at the wall, Simon started down the ladder. I followed, then paused, one foot already on the first rung, waiting for Sally – she hadn't even moved from the railing at the tower's far side. I stepped back up to the platform. She leaned a long way forward against the railing, hands clutching it. I saw how she had shifted her eyes from the approaching riders to the ground below. I took a step closer to her, and then another, trying to move quietly. She bent her head further to peer at the ground, assessing the fall.

Before I could speak, or reach for her, she turned, breathed in slowly, and walked towards the ladder. If I had ever needed proof that living in this world was harder than dying in it, it was in the set of Sally's shoulders as she walked past me and began to climb down.

We were at the gate, waiting, when they rode through. The Ringmaster was waiting too, standing a little apart from me, Simon, and Sally. I wondered whether he would have come here to meet Xander's body if it weren't for the suspicion that hung over each of us.

Piper dismissed the other soldiers who had ridden with him. They dismounted in silence and led their horses to the guardhouse along the wall. There was none of the chatter that usually came at the end of a patrol; their heads were down, their lips tight.

Piper remained mounted, his hand on his burden, and we walked beside him, a parade of death, up to the holding house. When he dismounted at Elsa's door, I stepped closer, and together he and I lifted the bag down. I gripped it by the corners, the hessian dragging at my hands; it was heavy, sagging in the middle as we carried it inside, manoeuvring carefully down the long corridor to the kitchen.

Zach was there, at the far end of the table, a plate of bread half-eaten in front of him while Zoe guarded him. He sat up straighter when he saw me and Piper enter, the sack hanging between us. I wondered how many dead bodies Zach had seen, apart from Kip's and The Confessor's. He had never been a fighter. Even back in our village, he'd been more likely to hide from the children who bullied us than to stand and fight; more likely to find a way to strike back later. The piece of broken glass placed carefully in the shoe of our neighbour's son, lined up with the other shoes on their porch, the day after he'd thrown stones at Zach from the schoolyard. I doubted Zach had ever led his troops into a battle, like The Ringmaster had. Zach had given orders for the massacre on the island, and the drowning of the children in New Hobart, but he hadn't been present for either. He'd given his orders and made his plans from the safety of his strongholds. Here, in Elsa's kitchen, there was nothing between him and the mess of death: just a few yards, and a bloodstained layer of hessian.

Piper and I laid Xander's body in front of the fireplace, and stepped back. Elsa closed the shutters; already flies were gathering at the window. The Ringmaster put his hand on a jug of wine on the table, but did not drink. Piper dragged a chair to where Sally stood. She ignored it, and him. All of us were quiet, and moved carefully around the room. We orbited the body as though it were a hole, a grave already dug.

Zach hung back, close to the wall. He kept his distance, but he was looking at the sack, his chin slightly forward, and a crease beneath his brand as he peered.

Zoe glared at him. 'Does he have to be here, even for this?' she said.

'Make him see what he's done,' Elsa said.

Piper silenced them both with a look. Then he glanced back to the sack. 'He was left in the middle of the eastern road,' he said.

'Was he strung up, like Leonard?' I asked.

Piper nodded, but he offered no further details. I thought of the pinched lips of the soldiers who had returned with him, and I remembered Leonard's broken fingers, snapped like twigs. I didn't want to know anything more.

Zoe and Paloma were standing close, and Piper stood a little way from Zoe, alone. Whatever Piper had seen when he found Xander's body, it had placed him somewhere where none of us could reach him.

'No note? No message?' Elsa asked.

The Ringmaster scoffed. 'The message is clear enough.'

Sally knelt with aching slowness, and went to peel back the hessian. Piper squatted beside her, reached out and placed his hand over hers.

'You don't need to look,' he said quietly. 'There's nothing you can do for him now.'

'Don't tell me what I need,' she said, without even turning to look at him. There was no anger in her voice – only a steely calm. Her head still down, she said: 'Elsa – get me warm water, and rags. The rest of you, go.'

None of us, not even The Ringmaster, would have dreamed of disobeying her. Elsa moved quickly to fill a bucket. The rest of us left, heading for the courtyard, Zach's chain clanking as he walked.

Sally called Piper and Zoe back, when we were nearly at the door.

'Make yourself useful, you two,' she said, still not looking up. 'Dig his grave.'

*

Piper and The Ringmaster could have ordered soldiers to do it, but this was a job that we wanted to do ourselves. Piper chose a spot just outside the walls, on the northern side. I was glad it was on the other side of the city from the battleground on the southern plain; enough bodies had been buried and burned there already, and I wanted a quieter place for Xander, who had known little peace in his own life. Simon went in search of shovels, but came back only with two, so we took turns. We had even brought Zach with us; in the current climate, none of us wanted to let him out of our sight.

The General had not given us back the body to be kind. She'd done it for the same reason they had left Leonard's body hanging on the road outside New Hobart: so that we would see what they had done to him.

Except that this time they hadn't acted alone. Somebody we trusted had betrayed Xander, and that person was as responsible for his ruined body as The General. Perhaps that was another reason they had made sure that we got Xander's body back: so that we would do what I was doing now, looking sideways at the others, nausea rising in my belly, knowing that likely somebody here had likely handed Xander over to the enemy. I looked at them, one after another: Simon. Zoe. Paloma. The Ringmaster. Piper. Zach.

I had seen so much death, but this was only the second proper burial that I'd ever witnessed. The first had been our father's. Zach had stood beside me then, as now.

All the other dead, too many to count, had been left where they lay, or hastily hidden in shallow graves. The children had been drowned when the winter earth was frosted and would not take so many graves; Piper had ensured that their small bodies had been given a proper burning, at least, but I had not witnessed it.

For Xander, we dug a deep hole. There was satisfaction in that. I dug, stamping on the shovel to slice the earth, and hefting the dirt over my shoulder. My healing leg and scratched arms hurt, and it felt right. We only slowed when water began to seep into the base of the grave. This close to the swamps, the water was never far below us.

Sally and Elsa came, after an hour, walking side by side, with Crispin escorting them. Behind them, two soldiers wheeled a handcart, with the shrouded body inside. The hessian sack had been grubby, and stained with blood. Now Xander was tightly wrapped in white.

We stopped our digging, and Piper stood back from the nearly finished grave so that Sally could inspect it. She walked around it slowly, before giving a nod.

'It needs to be longer,' she said. Piper didn't question her – just went back to digging. After all, she knew Xander's body better than us: she had cleaned him, dressed him, lain beside him at night and calmed him when he babbled and yelled.

I worked beside Piper, with Zoe at my back. I was grateful to have an excuse to keep digging, to have a few more minutes of work to do before we had to turn back to the body and bury him.

When the time came to lower the body into the hole, Piper and Zoe picked up the shroud, one at each end. They were gentle with him, but I hated seeing the water waiting at the bottom of the grave as they lowered him in. It was stupid, I knew – he was already dead, and there was nothing that the few inches of brown water could do to harm him – but I still winced at the slight splash that came when Zoe let his legs down.

Sally threw down the first shovelful of earth on top of him. It didn't scatter lightly – the soil was too laden with water. Instead, it landed with a compacted thud across the shroud that had been Xander. Two tears chased themselves down her cheeks.

It had started to rain. Sally turned away and left the rest of us to fill the grave. Next to Piper, I shovelled the earth back into the grave, trying not to wince at the *thunk*, *thunk* of the soil as it hit the body.

'It's done,' said Piper, and Sally turned around and stepped closer to the grave. I'd thought that perhaps she might say something, a few words about Xander to soften this burying – but she said nothing. What we could do, we had done with our hands, digging the grave and laying him in it. There was nothing to be done with words, and nothing that would unbreak his body. No neat story in which his death meant something other than what we had seen for ourselves: the fallibility of flesh; the willingness of the earth to take our dead, and not to care.

We left no marker on the grave – just the mound of disturbed dirt, a scab on the earth that a few more hours of rain would heal.

CHAPTER 17

I moved around the dormitory silently that night, readying myself for bed. I stayed on my side of the room without even thinking, these days – it had become a habit, to stick close to the wall, and to avoid the orbit of Zach's chain.

He didn't move, just sat cross-legged on his bed, watching me.

'Who else knew about Xander?' he said. 'Who else knew he'd be at the Kissing Tree, and where to find it?'

It was easy to forget how Zach existed on the margins of the rest of us. He shared a house, and even many meals, with us, so he could not help but know a little of what went on. But when he was led into the kitchen and we were talking about anything substantial, we all fell silent. He knew only what we let him see – though I suspected he saw more than we realised.

'Nobody else knew,' I said. 'Those who live here, and The Ringmaster. Perhaps the guards: Simon. Violet. Tash. Crispin. And the sentry who was with him on the day.'

'Were there other sentries, on other days?'

I shook my head. 'He had the same one assigned to him.'

I thought of the young sentry, and his embarrassment when Piper had reprimanded him. 'But he was killed.'

'Sentries talk in the barracks.'

'Perhaps.' I wanted to think it could be the case – a loose-lipped sentry, revealing Xander's whereabouts to somebody we didn't know. But I felt the betrayal, inescapable as the swamp water over which New Hobart sat.

'They still think it's me,' he said. 'And as long as they think that, we're both in danger. You realise that?'

'Can you blame them for thinking it's you?' I said.

'But you don't think it was.' He wasn't asking – he was telling me.

'Don't think for a second that I trust you,' I said. His face remained impassive. 'But you've been under lock and key. And the last thing you want to do is help The General. Not while your life depends on us holding her at bay.'

'You think it's The Ringmaster,' said Zach. Another pronouncement.

'You don't?'

'Do you care what I think?' he asked.

'No,' I said. 'But you've known The Ringmaster longer than I have. You worked with him for years. You sat with him on the Council.'

'And look how that turned out,' Zach said. 'He betrayed the Council.'

'So you don't trust him?'

'I don't trust anyone,' he said. 'But that doesn't mean that he's the traitor. What reason would he have to help The General?'

'A compromise. Wreckers' Pass freed. And maybe more: some kind of backup plan, to ensure he can crawl his way back onto the Council, if this uprising doesn't succeed?'

Zach gave an abrupt laugh – almost a bark. 'Compromise?

If he wanted compromise, he'd have stayed in the Council, and worked with us. But he's a fundamentalist, as much as The General ever was. He wants the machines destroyed, and her brought down.'

I thought of what The Ringmaster had told me about his wife, and his children. He blamed the blast for their deaths – I couldn't see him helping The General, when another blast was her goal.

'You wish you could believe it was him,' Zach went on. 'Or me.'

I said nothing.

'Because then you wouldn't have to consider the other options.'

'I'm not talking about this with you.' I reached for the candle.

'You're happy enough to talk about it with me, until it gets too close to home.'

I pinched out the flame. In the dark, I ran through the options: Simon, who had fought beside Piper on the island and at New Hobart. I couldn't forget the relief in his face when he'd handed the leadership of the resistance back to Piper – he was not a man to crave power for himself, or to manoeuvre secretly. Elsa, a more steadfast mother to me than my own mother had ever been, and a woman with more reason than most to hate The General. Paloma, alone in a strange world, with nothing to gain from The General but torture and the destruction of her people. Zoe, loyal to the resistance her whole life. She had already lost Lucia; she would never aid The General, when doing so would jeopardise Paloma's safety. Sally, the hero of the resistance, who had cared for Xander for years, and loved him fiercely.

And Piper. Piper, who had protected me for months.

Saved my life many times. Who used to carry Xander to his bed if he fell asleep in the kitchen.

Piper, who had whipped the guards. Who had kept me and Kip imprisoned on the island. Who I had seen kill, time and again, as efficiently as The Ringmaster.

Zach's voice cut across my thoughts.

'What about Sally?' he asked.

'Go to sleep,' I said, rolling over.

'She's a tough old bird,' he said. 'You should have heard the way people talked about her, back in Wyndham, after her stint as an infiltrator.'

'You don't know anything about her,' I said. 'She cared for Xander for years.'

'She killed one of her fellow infiltrators herself. Threw a knife at her throat – her own friend. Did you know that?'

'I knew,' I said. 'And I don't blame her. It was a kindness. Her friend had been captured and was about to be tortured. She saved that woman from a slow and painful death.'

'I'm just saying: Sally can be as ruthless as any Councillor, when she needs to be.'

'Go to sleep,' I said again. I thought of Sally's hand on Xander's head. The tears on her face at his graveside.

'I was with them in the kitchen when the soldier came to report that they'd found the sentry's body,' Zach said. 'Sally and Zoe.'

'I'm not going to listen to you,' I said. 'You're poison.'

'The Ringmaster sent a messenger – a young soldier.' I tried to ignore him, but his voice kept coming – and his insinuations could not be more poisonous than the speculations that my own mind had been conjuring in the dark. 'He came to the door, reported to Zoe and Sally in the kitchen. Said the sentry had been found dead.'

'And?'

'It was Zoe who asked about Xander. Not Sally.'

I shook my head, even though he couldn't see me in the dark. 'Can you blame her for assuming the worst? If the sentry was dead, she knew what that meant.'

'I'm just saying,' Zach said. 'She didn't ask. She just sat there, looking pale. It was Zoe who asked about Xander, who started on about getting The Ringmaster to send some troops in pursuit.'

'That doesn't mean anything. Sally would've been in shock.'

'I've yet to see anything shock that woman,' he said, and rolled over.

*

For an hour or more I tried my best to sleep. I listened to the wind testing the loose tiles on the roof, and to Zach's breathing. Twice, the blast bloomed in my head; I braced my whole body against the mattress, and tried to calm my breathing. I thought of Xander, for whom the visions were ended now.

When I looked out the window, the rats were the only movement in the courtyard, under a waning moon. The candles were out in Paloma and Zoe's window, and Elsa had put out the kitchen lights too. Across the courtyard, by the main door, Piper was stretched out on his bed under the porch. I couldn't tell if he was awake.

'Zach,' I whispered across the room.

'What?' His voice was bleary.

'What exactly did the messenger say to Sally and Zoe, when he came to the holding house that day? What information did he give about the dead sentry?'

He thought for a minute, staring at the ceiling.

'He said: *They found Xander's sentry dead in the forest. There's been a raid.* Told them The Ringmaster was on his way.'

'Was that it? No other details about the sentry, the body?'

He spoke quickly, with certainty. 'He was just a messenger, sent running from the Tithe Collector's office. That was all he knew. He gave us the message, then waited. And Zoe started in on him, badgering him about Xander, about sending troops. But the messenger didn't know anything else. Just said he'd report back to The Ringmaster.'

I remained silent for a long time.

'Are you going to tell me what that was about?' Zach said.

'No,' I said, and walked to the door in the dark.

'Cass?' he called after me.

*

When I opened the dormitory door, Piper sat up in his bed on the other side of the courtyard. 'What is it?' he said, keeping his voice low.

'It's nothing,' I said. 'I just wanted to check on Sally.'

'Leave her in peace,' he said. 'She buried him today. She isn't going to want to talk about it.'

'It's not that.' It was only partly a lie. 'And it's important.' That wasn't a lie. 'I need to ask her something.'

'Don't push her,' he said. 'Not after today, of all days.' As he lay back down, I caught a glimpse of moonlight on metal. Poking out from under his pillow was his dagger, out of its scabbard.

Inside, I passed the kitchen and made my way quietly down the corridor. Towards the front door, a stripe of candlelight showed under the closed door to Sally's room.

I knocked. When there was no answer, I entered anyway.

I hadn't been inside this room since Sally and Xander had moved in. Two narrow beds stood with their heads against the wall. On the other side of the room, by a small table, Sally sat in the chair by the window. She didn't look at me when I stepped across the threshold.

'Have you come to commiserate with me?' she said. 'Don't bother. You never liked him much.'

'It's true,' I said. 'I didn't like being around him. That was my fault, not his.'

'And you want me to offer absolution? Tell you I understand?'

'No,' I said.

'So what do you want?' She turned her head to face me now, the rest of her body rigid in the chair, still facing forward. 'What are you doing here?'

I took a few steps closer, edging around the table. It felt wrong to be standing over her, so I sat down on the foot of the closest bed.

'Not there,' she snapped. Then she forced her voice back to calm. 'That's his bed.'

I stood quickly, looking back at the bed behind me. It was neatly made, but dust had begun to settle on the white coverlet. It had not been touched in the four days since Xander had disappeared. I felt suddenly embarrassed. What was I doing here, intruding on this old woman, her grief as tangible in that small room as the smell of cheap candle fat?

But I thought of Paloma, lying in Zoe's arms beyond the courtyard. Of Elsewhere, and all that was at stake. I walked around Xander's bed, and stood closer to her.

'You didn't ask whether Xander was missing,' I said.

'What are you talking about?'

'When the messenger brought the news of the sentry's body being found. You didn't even ask about Xander.'

She sighed, and hauled herself to her feet. 'You weren't there,' she said. 'Have you been listening to your twin? Letting his lies get everything twisted?'

'I despise Zach as much as you do,' I said. 'But that doesn't mean he's wrong. So tell me: why didn't you ask?'

I looked at her carefully. She stood with her back to the candles on the windowsill, so that it was hard to see her face.

'I don't know what you're thinking, Cass. But be careful that you don't say something you'll regret.'

'Just tell me: Why didn't you ask about him? Why wasn't that the first thing in your mind?'

'Are you questioning my love for that boy?'

'No,' I said, shaking my head. 'I know how much you loved him. That's why I need you to explain why you didn't ask about him. Why you weren't pushing The Ringmaster to send troops after him.' The longing in my voice was real. I wanted nothing more than for her to give me an explanation. To have it all make sense again.

'I've been fighting this war a lot longer than you have,' she said. 'I knew it was too late. They'd had him since the morning. There was no way we were going to catch them.'

'You didn't know that,' I said. 'Zach told me exactly what the messenger said.'

'Zach,' she said, her voice thick with disgust.

I ignored her and kept speaking: 'The messenger said: *They found Xander's sentry dead in the forest.*' That's all you knew, at that point. All the other details – the sentry's body being cold and stiff, and how it was shoved into the tree – you didn't find out until later.'

'Perhaps,' she said. 'It was a terrible day. I can't remember every word of every conversation. It might have escaped your notice that I'm helping Piper to run an army, Cass. I don't have time or energy to notice every detail.'

'No,' I said again. 'You don't get to be in your position – running an army – unless you're exactly the kind of person who notices everything. You don't survive as long as you have, and achieve all that you've achieved, without being alert to details. I know how sharp you are.'

She said nothing, so I went on.

'You knew he'd been taken first thing in the morning, because you'd told them where to find him, and when.'

'I loved that boy,' she said.

'I know that.'

'Then why would I betray him?'

I thought about what she'd said to Zach more than a week earlier: *I'm wise enough to know that dying's far from the worst thing that could happen to me.* She'd been talking about the tanks, but I thought of Xander's twisting hands, his endlessly burning mind. I had experienced enough of it myself to know that it was its own form of torture.

She'd reached back to the windowsill, where her dagger lay. Her hand clutched it tightly, a vein on the back of her hand tracing her pulse.

'Did he know what was coming?' I asked.

She looked at me appraisingly. There was no hint of shame in her eyes.

'Did he know?' I asked again.

She shrugged. 'He was a seer, Cass.' A moment's silence. 'He never said anything. Never said anything anyway, these days. But I think he knew. He still chose to go to the Kissing Tree, that last morning.'

I could hear each of her breaths, the slight wheeze of each intake of air. When I moved towards the door, she moved too, taking a single step that placed her between me and the doorway. She was watching me as warily as I was watching her.

'You betrayed him.'

When I moved to the left, she moved with me.

'I freed him,' she said.

'That wasn't your choice to make.'

When she'd come to ask me how to help Xander, I'd said, *You can't*. Had I signed Xander's death warrant with those two words?

I stepped to the right. She did the same, quicker this time. She moved heavily, on her twisted legs, but faster than I'd thought her capable of. There was no longer any pretence that she wasn't trying to keep me in the room.

The knife she held was the one she usually wore at her belt: it was heavy, wide-bladed, with a curved serrated edge – the sort I'd seen people gutting fish with on the island. I pulled my own dagger from my belt, and tried to remember everything that Zoe had taught me. The thought of fighting Sally seemed absurd, even as I stared at her and the blade's sharp-toothed grin.

'I did what I needed to do,' she said.

'You sent him to his death. His twin, too.'

'I had no choice.'

'What are you talking about?'

'That was the deal,' she said, her voice perfectly calm.

'What deal? Wreckers' Pass, and your own life? Did you buy yourself a promise of safe passage out of all of this?'

She scoffed. 'Do you really think my life, what's left of it, is worth anything to me?'

I believed her.

She stepped forward, knife raised. I swiped at her, but it was only a feint: I couldn't bring myself to cut that old flesh, thin and wrinkled as the muslin bags that hung in Elsa's kitchen, stuffed with herbs.

I hadn't realised that she still had such speed in her. Without even taking her eyes from my face she blocked my knife with her own, sending it spinning onto the floor.

'Calm down,' she whispered. 'Cass, listen to me.'

My knife had slid beneath the bed and out of sight. She still held hers, but didn't press her advantage. Instead she just blocked the door, watching me.

'Was it worth it, for Wreckers' Pass?' I asked again, watching the candle flame reflected on her wide blade.

'The town was starving, Cass. You want to rescue Refuge Six? If we free those people and bring them here, we need to feed them. And it wasn't only Wreckers' Pass,' she said.

'So what else was it? What did they offer you that could be worth Xander's life?'

'I couldn't protect him any more,' she said. 'He was already lost. He was in so much pain. He didn't know about the plan to attack the refuge – he had no information to give. You said it yourself: all that he knows these days is the blast. He had nothing to give them, if they tortured him. But I could save something. Stop the town from starving. Give you a chance to feed the Omegas from Refuge Six—'

She stopped, mouth still open. There was something else she wasn't saying. I was about to ask her, and then it all fell into place. Her smile, when she and I had glimpsed that moment between Paloma and Zoe, through the open door of their room. Her hand on Piper's shoulder, as she'd passed him in the kitchen of her house on the Sunken Shore. The soldier at Blackwood, registering who Piper was, and stepping back. *Not him.*

CHAPTER 18

'Don't tell Piper and Zoe,' Sally said. I realised that I had never before heard her ask for anything. 'I don't want them to blame themselves.'

'They would never have wanted any part of your deal. They wouldn't want their lives traded for Xander's blood.'

'Is it so different, what I've done, from what you're doing, with your plan for the decoy attack on Noose Canyon?' Her eyes were fixed on mine. 'We both trade in lives, Cass.'

I shook my head. 'It's not the same.'

'I've been fighting this battle for such a long time.' She let out a long, slow breath. 'I don't even believe that we can win it any more. So I made the choice: give up what we could afford to lose. What was no longer any good to us. Because I wanted to save something. This town. Piper and Zoe.'

I made a rush for the door. I half expected to feel her knife in my back, but she just grabbed me, wrapping her knife arm around me from behind, her other hand around my neck. Her bony hands gripped my flesh like the pincers of the river crabs that used to nip at me and Zach when we were children.

'Piper and Zoe came to me years before I'd even met Xander.' She adjusted her grip on my neck. 'They were so young, and so alone.'

'They wouldn't have wanted this,' I said. I could barely speak, let alone cry out; her fingers were tight around my windpipe.

'I've never minded that Omegas can't have our own children,' she continued, her voice a hiss in my ear. 'I had my work – it was more important than anything. But then they came to me. I helped them. I taught them everything. They continued my work, when I couldn't do it any more. I've loved them more fiercely than you can know.'

I didn't doubt that she loved them. I'd seen Zach, stitching Kip back together and keeping his and The Confessor's bodies in the tanks, because he couldn't bring himself to accept that she was dead. I'd seen how love, as surely as hatred, could twist the world into terrible shapes.

Her grip was unrelenting. I thought again of what Zoe had taught me, and stopped struggling. I let my body relax, my head slump forward a little.

She exhaled, and I felt her hold loosen, barely perceptibly. For a moment, it was more like an embrace than a fight.

I clenched my teeth and threw my head backwards. I must have hit her nose, because I felt something give way, and heard a smaller crunch within the bigger thud that had set my head ringing.

I suspected it hurt me as much as it hurt her – but she wasn't expecting it, and her grip loosened enough for me to slip free of her arms. I turned. Through my blurred vision, I could see her clutching her face, trying to hold back the blood pouring from her nose. My knife was somewhere behind me, out of sight beneath the bed. Sally was still blocking the door. The table still stood between us – I leaned backwards and kicked it over towards her. She grunted when it struck her hip, but didn't let go of her knife. I pushed by the overturned table, but she was there first, blade out.

Her knife nicked my arm. If she'd wanted to kill me then, she could have, but instead she pressed the knife against my hand, holding it back against the wall. One shove and the blade would go straight through, pinning my hand to the wall. With her other hand, she grabbed my neck again. Her fingers were slippery with the blood from her nose.

'I'm old, Cass,' she said, 'but I've been a fighter for a lot longer than you have.' She took another step forward, forcing me backwards against the wall, until the back of my head banged against the mantel.

'You're a traitor,' I said.

'I gave this town its only chance.' Her body was pressed close to mine. The blade against my hand was shaking with the effort of holding me off. 'Securing Wreckers' Pass, and getting that food convoy through, will do more to help this uprising than any heroics at the canyon.' The blood from her nose was dripping off her chin. 'And I wanted to save Piper and Zoe. I only gave the Council what was no longer useful to us.'

'Who were you planning to sell off next?' I said. Through her clamped fingers, my voice didn't sound like my own. I couldn't have cried out, even if I'd dared. 'Has Paloma finished being useful yet? What about me?'

My right hand was pressed between the blade and the wall, but my left hand was free. I groped along the mantel, and found the wide neck of a jug, still full of water.

When I smashed it over her head, it was probably the shock of the cold water as much as the impact that made her shout. I snatched my other hand free, feeling the blade leave its trail across my palm. With my bleeding hand I grabbed her wrist, twisting her knife away from me. A bone in her hand cracked, and she gave a small grunt, but her other hand's grip on my throat only tightened, and the yell I tried to give made no sound at all. I heard a scream, but it wasn't my own: Zach's voice, from the far side of the house. I thought I heard other shouts, too, but by then lights were moving in front of the blackness in my eyes, like lamps on a dark sea.

*

The door crashed open. Piper ran in first, Zoe just behind him, both with knives raised. There was a moment of chaos; Piper moved quickly to pull Sally away from me, but I could see his confusion as he looked from her bloodied face to my slashed hand; behind him, Zoe was scanning the room for an intruder. Violet, who had been on duty on the street, beyond the front door, was moments behind them, sword drawn.

It took a few instants for them to gather that there had been no ambush, and no attack. I was leaning against the mantel, gasping noisily for air. Sally, her nose still dripping blood, stood very erect. She didn't even look at me now – her eyes moved from Piper to Zoe and back again.

'It was her,' I said. There was no triumph in my voice. Hands at my throat, I slumped to the floor and sat amongst the broken pieces of the jug. 'She betrayed Xander. She did it to win Wreckers' Pass, and to get amnesty for you and Piper.'

Sally still held her knife. Her chin dripped with a pink liquid. Blood and water.

'Get to the courtyard,' Zoe said to Violet. 'Keep an eye on Zach, and Paloma. And tell Elsa not to disturb us in here.'

Violet nodded, staring as she withdrew.

'Is it true?' Piper asked Sally. His voice was low, as if he didn't want to hear the question, let alone the answer.

Sally said nothing.

'Deny it,' Zoe whispered through her teeth.

Sally finally spoke. 'I had to make a choice.' She placed her knife, very slowly, on the foot of the bed. Piper and Zoe watched her every movement as she stepped back, hands raised, and then slumped in the chair.

'Crispin wasn't the only one they approached. A messenger stopped Elena too, when she was on a courier run.' I remembered meeting Elena. She was young, barely twenty, and gangly as a foal. She looked too slight to be a soldier. 'She came to me,' Sally continued, 'told me everything. I told her I'd tell The Ringmaster. I did – but I didn't tell him one of the details. They'd told Elena about a place where messages could be left – just outside the outer perimeter. I rode there one night, left a message. Had a parley the next day.'

'With The General?'

She shook her head impatiently. 'Not the first time. That was a few days later. And we made our deal.'

'You know as well as I do that The General doesn't stick to deals,' I said.

'She wanted a seer.'

'She wanted a seer she could use,' I said. 'You think she'll stick to her side of the bargain now that she's finished with Xander? She'll retake Wreckers' Pass. She'll come after all of us harder than before.'

'Xander wasn't all that I offered her,' she said.

'Who else did you trade away?' I asked. 'Me? Zach? Paloma?'

'I told you.' Her voice was slow and calm. 'I only offered what wasn't any use to us any more.'

I looked at her. She looked down at her hands, gnarled and knotted.

'You,' I said.

Sally gave the smallest incline of her head.

'When?' Piper asked.

'I told her two weeks. Long enough for us to get more convoys through the pass; late enough that I could betray nothing of the decoy plan.'

'And did you really think The General would continue to honour the bargain, after they'd taken you, and Xander?' I said.

'Perhaps not. But Wreckers' Pass will be hard for her to seize back, now we've taken it,' she said. 'As for Piper and Zoe's amnesty? I haven't allowed myself many indulgences in this life, Cass. That hope – that one small hope – was the only one I've permitted myself.'

*

'Give me your weapons,' Piper said. He'd already picked up the knife from the bed. Sally nodded, walked stiff-legged to the far side of the room, where a larger dagger was hanging, in its scabbard, from a belt thrown over the wardrobe door. On all fours, I crouched and retrieved my own knife from where it had spun beneath the bed. My hand left a bloody print on the floor.

'I did what I had to do,' Sally said.

'No,' said Zoe, her voice tight. 'You made a choice. And it wasn't your choice to make.'

Sally didn't argue with them, or bow her head under their stares.

'You were wrong,' Piper said.

'It's been years since I've been able to believe in right and wrong,' she said. 'I don't see how we can win this. I don't believe we can save Elsewhere. There are days I don't even believe in tomorrow. But I didn't want this town to starve. And know this: I do believe in the two of you.'

Piper and Zoe looked at her.

'I believed in you too,' said Zoe. At the past tense, Sally flinched, but did not speak.

Piper and Zoe moved together towards the door. I stepped through first, but paused at the threshold.

'It did save him.' I turned back. 'What you did was wrong. But it saved them both. At Blackwood, a soldier spared him. He was about to kill Piper, but he let him go. I didn't tell anyone, because I didn't understand what had happened. I even suspected that he might be the traitor. But it did save them.'

She gave a slow nod. She was still standing there, perfectly still, as Zoe walked past me, Sally's knives in her hands.

I turned to wait for Piper, who had paused in the corridor, just outside the doorway. Neither he nor Sally spoke, but their eyes were fixed on one another. I could not read Piper's face; I did not understand what was passing between those two, in those seconds that they stared at one another in silence.

Then Piper pulled the door firmly shut.

'Fetch Violet,' he said to me. 'Tell her to post two guards at this door. And get your hand seen to.'

*

By the time Elsa had bound my hand, Piper was already leaving for the Tithe Collector's office. I ran to catch him at the end of the corridor, pushing past Violet and the sentries at Sally's doorway, and grabbing his arm before he could march off up the hill. My hand throbbed; the cut had bled a lot, and Elsa had grimaced as she washed it, but it was clean and not deep enough to need stitching.

'Do you need to tell him?' I said.

'I don't have a choice,' Piper replied. 'I can't be seen to shield her. It's bad enough that the traitor should be one of ours. It's already going to weaken our standing with The Ringmaster.' He exhaled. 'It's not only a betrayal of Xander. It's treason. Xander could have revealed secrets under torture. Sally couldn't know for sure what he did or didn't know. He could've jeopardised the whole attack.'

The lamp outside the door cast harsh shadows on Piper's face. 'What will happen to her now?' I said. 'What will The Ringmaster do?'

I thought of the soldiers who had branded Zach, and been whipped. Would The Ringmaster do the same to Sally? Would they do worse? Would it be Piper, again, who would have to carry out the punishment?

'Whatever he decides to do with her,' I said, 'it won't be worse than what The General would have done, when Sally handed herself over.'

'Even that was madness. It doesn't matter how determined she was, or how brave. Nobody can guarantee they won't give up secrets under torture.'

I wasn't so sure. I was thinking of Sally's words: *Do you really think my life, what's left of it, is worth anything to me?*

'Are you OK?' I said to Piper, putting my hand on his arm.

'I'm fine,' he said abruptly, then gave a bleak laugh. 'That's the whole point, isn't it? That's what she wanted. I would have died at Blackwood, if it weren't for Sally.'

He didn't need to say what we were both thinking: And Xander would have lived. From the set of Piper's jaw, I knew that he carried Xander's death with him as he walked into the night.

*

I was waiting in the kitchen for Piper and The Ringmaster. I tried to stay calm, tried to listen to Elsa as she talked. 'I don't believe it,' she kept saying, and I could give no reply, because I believed it all too well. All the things that had made it impossible for me to suspect Sally – her single-minded dedication to our cause; her love for Xander – made it impossible for me to doubt her guilt.

'Are you listening to me?' Elsa said. She reached out her hand to my leg; I looked down at it, and for an instant it wasn't her hand, but Sally's, knuckles jutting and skin wrinkled like an empty leather water flask. The hand was dripping blood. Not just the blood I'd seen an hour earlier, from the nosebleed I'd given her; this was thicker, pooling in the deep creases of her hand. I pinched my eyes closed. When I opened them again there was nothing there: just Elsa, her hand outstretched and her face close to mine, a mixture of irritation and concern. 'Are you listening to me?' she said again. And I nodded, trying not to think about what The Ringmaster would do to Sally. He would want to make an example of her, I knew. I could not argue that she didn't deserve it. But in that flash of a vision, there had been so much blood. Would The Ringmaster go that far? Would she be killed?

The Ringmaster didn't knock at the holding house door – he just slammed it back against the wall. His footsteps on the wooden floor were faster than usual. When I stepped into the corridor to see him, his eyes were narrowed, his lips tight. Piper was behind him.

The Ringmaster didn't have to give any orders – the sentries at Sally's door jumped aside as he and Piper approached. But when he pushed the door, it opened only half a foot, and then jammed.

'Sally,' The Ringmaster called. Silence. Zoe had joined us in the corridor, pushing me aside to stand with The Ringmaster at the door. Only Piper hung back, leaning against the corridor wall behind them.

The Ringmaster slipped his knife from its sheath as he pressed his shoulder into the door. There was a scraping sound as the door was forced open. I could see nothing past the crush of Zoe, The Ringmaster and the guards.

Zoe was the first one to step inside. 'Hell on earth,' she said.

I looked down. Where the door had opened, there was a smear of blood, tracing the curve of the door's sweep. The Ringmaster had followed Zoe inside; I came after them, stepping over the pooled blood.

Sally was on the floor, against the back of the door. She lay awkwardly, half-rolled where the door had pushed her. Her left arm bore two wounds: each one a decisive slice, tracing from elbow to wrist. Her throat, too, had been slashed, a neat two-inch opening beneath the right side of her jaw. There were no tentative first attempts, or smaller wounds where she'd worked up the courage or flinched at the pain: just the gashes, the skin loose at the edges and blood-blackened inside. Her right hand still held the tiny dagger, its bone handle smeared with blood.

The floor creaked. I looked up; Piper had entered, and was looking down at Sally's body.

'It's finished, then,' Piper said.

The Ringmaster turned on him. 'She shouldn't have been allowed to escape justice,' he said. 'Why was that knife overlooked?'

'She must have had it concealed,' Piper said. 'And even if we'd taken it away, she'd have found a way. She would have used a candlestick, or hanged herself with the sheet.'

'She should have been made an example of.'

'What are you going to do?' Zoe said. 'Stitch her up and kill her again, in the market square?'

Piper spoke before The Ringmaster could respond. 'It's finished,' he said, again. 'There's nothing left to be done here.'

The Ringmaster stepped back.

'This has been an ugly business,' he said. He reached out with his foot and prodded Sally's elbow. Zoe and Piper were both watching him minutely, but neither of them moved.

'Have the body cleared out,' The Ringmaster said to the guards. He turned back to Piper and Zoe, watched them as he continued issuing his orders. 'Dump it in the open pits, on the eastern plain.'

Then he was gone. The guards were arguing in the corridor about where to get a handcart for shifting the body.

Zoe's face was closed. There was nothing to be seen there. She left without looking back.

Piper was leaving too. I put my hand on his arm.

'You didn't rush in, just now, when the rest of us did.'

'So?'

'You knew what we'd find,' I said. He didn't respond. His eyes closed for a moment, his breathing slow.

'You knew about that knife,' I whispered, aware of the guards in the corridor, and The Ringmaster somewhere nearby. 'You'd lived with her for years. You knew she kept it in her boot.'

He shrugged. 'And what if I did?'

'You knew she'd do this,' I hissed. 'You could have stopped her.'

'And then what?' Piper turned on me. 'Let her be whipped, as a traitor? Let her be lynched by the soldiers, once word got out? Let the resistance tear itself apart, arguing about what to do, and who to blame?'

He looked down again at Sally. The blood on the floor was thickening already, black clots forming amongst the red.

'It's better this way,' Piper said.

I shook my head. 'How could you let her do this?'

'You knew about the knife too.'

My breath stopped. It was true. I'd seen that bone handle before; seen Sally slip it from her boot to chop tobacco with Elsa by the kitchen fire; seen it when she'd eased the gravel from Zach's wounds.

'I forgot,' I said.

'Maybe I forgot too,' he said, as he left.

CHAPTER 19

They took her body away immediately. I pressed my face against the bars of the front sitting room as I watched two of The Ringmaster's soldiers load the body onto a handcart, near where Violet and Crispin stood guard at the front door. There would be no burial, as there had been for Xander. She would lie in the pits with the dead from the battle, ours and the Council's together. I was so exhausted by not knowing how to feel.

'How long have you known it was her?' The Ringmaster was right at my shoulder. I'd been watching the soldiers haul the cart up the street, and hadn't heard him approach.

'Not until today.' Up the road, the cart jolted to a halt as a wheel jammed on a loose stone. One of the soldiers shoved it back into motion, the body jerking with the cart. Blood had already soaked through the sheet.

'It was Zach, actually,' I said. 'He worked it out.'

The Ringmaster nodded. 'He's never been stupid, your brother.'

The soldiers had rounded the corner now. Across the corridor from us came the sound of Elsa's scrubbing brush, already at work on the floor. It would take her a long time to clean up all the blood.

'And all this time, you thought it was me?' The Ringmaster said, his voice quiet.

I turned impatiently to face him. 'Does it matter? You thought it was Zach. All of you did. You were wrong too.'

We had, each of us, found so many new ways of being wrong in these last few months.

'I'm not wrong about this,' he said. 'Listen. Zach might have seen through Sally, and he might not have been the traitor this time, but never forget: he can't be trusted.' He looked at me. 'Be careful.'

*

The Ringmaster came back the following day, gathering all of us except Zach in the kitchen.

'I'm moving the attack forward,' he said. 'We can't risk any more leaks, any more betrayals.' He looked pointedly at Piper. 'And this fiasco with Xander will have angered The General. We ride tomorrow, before she strikes back.'

'Are the wagons ready?' Paloma asked.

'They will be.' He jerked his head towards the street. Since dawn, the town had been quaking under the sound of the hasty assembly of the final wagons. The hammer and axe blows beat like battle drums, and my pulse kept time, faster and faster.

As he stood to leave, The Ringmaster said to us, almost as an aside: 'I'll be leading the attack into the canyon.'

His voice was grave, but if he was afraid, he didn't show it.

'I know the area best,' he went on. 'My soldiers are brave, but they'll know what they're heading into when we ride into that canyon. They won't do it without me.'

Even Zoe had no criticism, no barbed words to throw at him.

'How long will you be able to hold them at the canyon?' Paloma asked.

'They'll see the bridges come down. They'll see us marching towards Wyndham,' he said. 'Their fortifications will be in place. They'll be ready to make a stand at the canyon. If we're lucky, we'll be able to hold them there for a day or two. Long enough to buy the time we need to free the refuge.'

During the few minutes before he left, I wanted to say something to him, but I couldn't find the words, and there was nothing in his closed face and brisk manner to encourage me. For all that he still frightened me, I could not deny that there was real courage in what he was doing. For the rest of the day, his words ran through my mind. *Long enough to buy the time we need.* It was blunt, even for him. It was as Sally had said: this was a deal, a trade in lives. I wondered when our blood had become currency. Our soldiers' bodies, an offering to the carrion birds.

The first squadron left that same morning: a small group heading south-east to bring down the bridges. Piper and I went to see them off. They were gathered by the gate, forty soldiers, already mounted and wearing no uniforms. Alphas and Omegas together. They were going as saboteurs, not fighters, though there would be sentries at the bridge to deal with too. For weeks they had been poring over the plans for the bridges, with details of the towers, the braces, the truss supports, the taut wires. Reports from our scouts about patrols, sentries, and traffic across the two suspension bridges that spanned the wide river. The saboteurs' packhorses carried a strange assortment of equipment: not only weapons, but barrels of lamp oil, fine-toothed hacksaws, and even two tiny wherries, for reaching the posts in the river itself. These needed to be light, for speedy travelling. Paloma's island upbringing had come in handy here. She'd advised on their construction, using a method I had not seen before, stretching animal skins tightly over wooden frames. She'd been glad to be useful, and had done much of the work herself, Zoe watching while Paloma coaxed the frames into shape.

'Are you sure they'll take the weight?' I'd asked, watching as she'd surveyed the finished boats in the courtyard. 'They'll have oil casks, and the river's quick.' I was thinking of the river I had unleashed into the Ark – how that place had survived four hundred years, and the blast itself, but could not withstand the river's force.

Paloma had tapped her fist on one hull, tight and hard as an oak barrel. 'My sisters and I fished in these every day, growing up,' she said. 'In Blackwater Bay, to be fair, and not in the open sea – but it's still rougher than any river.' She let her hand linger on the hide hull, and I was reminded that she had left a world behind her.

The boats were loaded now, upside down, making the packhorses look like pale-shelled turtles. We watched them leave. I closed my eyes and strained for a glimpse of what would befall them, but all I could see was flame. I didn't know if this was the triumphant flame of a bridge burning, or just my mind's habitual state now: *Forever fire.*

While the town thrummed with preparations, Elsa had found her own way to be busy. In the front sitting room, yards of cloth draped over her knee, she was stitching a flag.

We saw the Omega symbol everywhere, staring at us from mirrors, and the faces of those around us. But only twice had I ever seen an Omega flag. Piper's troops had planted one above the crater, before the attack on the island.

And when we'd freed New Hobart, June had raised an Omega flag from the eastern tower in the walls. Both of those had been makeshift: tar or paint smeared onto bedsheets. Elsa's flag was more elaborate, made of canvas sailcloth, neatly hemmed. She'd outlined the Omega symbol in chalk on the pale cloth, and had begun to stitch a strip of black fabric into place.

'I'm used to being busy,' she said, needle held in the corner of her mouth as she snapped the thread with her fingers. 'There's nothing else for me to do now.'

Now. It contained so many things that we couldn't speak out loud: *Now that the children have gone. Now that they've been torn from me, and drowned in the dark. Now that I've pulled their bodies from the tanks, and shrouded them for burning. Now that Xander, too, has gone, and I've cleaned Sally's blood from the floor of my house.*

'This was Piper's idea,' she said, nodding down at the flag.

I was touched that, in the midst of all the preparations, he had noticed Elsa's empty hands, her restless pacing around the kitchen.

I watched the Omega symbol take shape under her fingers. At Wyndham and the refuge, the Council's army would be fighting under its own flags. Even The Ringmaster's troops still had the Alpha insignia embroidered on their tunics. It was fitting that our own soldiers should have a proper flag. It was time that we claimed as our own the mark that they had made us wear on our faces.

'You want to know what would make it even better?' I said to Elsa.

I took up the chalk that sat on the window ledge, and knelt over the flag. I drew slowly, trying to keep the line straight when the canvas bunched beneath the chalk.

When I was finished, I stepped back. Elsa, next to me, pursed her lips.

'They won't like it,' she said. 'Our own troops, any more than The Ringmaster's.'

'And The General's troops least of all,' I said, shaking out the flag so that it lay flat, and surveying my work. 'But it's what we're fighting for, isn't it?' I gestured to the window. All day patrols had been marching past, Alpha and Omega troops training together for the attack. 'We're not talking about some kind of truce, or some kind of alliance. We're talking about the fact that we're the same.'

Elsa looked again at the flag, the sharp diagonals of the **A** overlaid against the curve of the Ω.

'You've made more work for me, you know. That's another two hours' stitching, at least,' she said. But she slipped me a smile as I passed her back the flag, and she took up her needle again, sewing to the rhythm of the marching outside.

*

Piper came back to the holding house before the sun had set. He had been with The Ringmaster for most of the day, going over the final plans, and doing final drills with the troops. Sweat marked his shirt, and his trousers were grey with dust. It had been a long day, coming after a long night. It was hard to believe that only yesterday Sally had been alive.

'You're going into the canyon with The Ringmaster, aren't you,' I said.

He hadn't needed to tell me. I knew – had known, I supposed, from the first moment I'd announced the idea of the decoy attack – that this was what he would choose. If there had ever been any chance that he might choose not to, Sally's betrayal had put an end to that. He would never spare himself now, knowing that he had been spared already, and at what price.

There were many reasons why it was the right thing for him to do. He started to explain them: the Omega troops would follow him; The Ringmaster would not be left alone in charge of the attack. So many practical reasons, and moral reasons, all of which my body was ignoring now as panic took hold. Piper was still talking, explaining calmly, but all I could hear was noise, a scrabble of words over my pulse. Sweat in my hands, and my breath too loud in my own head.

'I have to,' he said. I heard the words, but didn't respond. It was a double fear that had seized me: if I lost him, I would lose Zoe too. At the thought of their absence, my mind stopped working and my breath began to tighten in my chest – a world without them seemed impossible.

I swallowed, tried to force my breath back into submission.

'If it goes wrong,' he said, 'protect Paloma. Watch her. Trust nobody. Find a way to keep her safe.'

I looked into his face. There was a small cut, just below his right eye, from the ambush at Blackwood. It had nearly healed – the scar raised slightly, pinkish white. I could see the strain of the new skin holding together.

'What Sally said, before she died—' I began.

He waited.

'She said she didn't know what to believe in now – except that she believed in you and Zoe.'

He looked down.

'What she did to Xander was wrong. But what she said about you,' I said. 'I believe that too.'

It wasn't a smile that moved over his face, but there was a kind of softening. His lips widened; the lines at the outer edges of his eyes relaxed.

Before he stood, he took my hand, covering it in his large one.

'It's not over yet,' he said.

'Do you think there's any chance?' I asked. For so long, people had been asking me that question. Now I asked him.

'On the one hand, there's a certainty of casualties. And a small chance of freeing the refuge, at best.'

I nodded. 'And on the other hand?'

His wide smile – I had missed it, I realised, now that I saw it again. 'You forget,' he said. 'I only have one hand.'

*

I had farewelled Elsa enough times by now to know that she was impatient with goodbyes. When dark had come, and it was time for us to ride out, she clutched me to her for a fierce second, then straightened her arms, just as quickly, pushing me away. I put my hand to my shoulder where her hand still rested, and felt the small bones under her skin, the ridge of each knuckle.

'You get those people out,' she said. 'And then you come home. Stay safe.'

I almost laughed. What did *safe* even mean, in a world where the blast machine had been resurrected? Even if we were, somehow, to succeed in freeing Refuge 6, the bomb was still out there, and Elsewhere still doomed. *Safe* was just a sound now, and not a word – it had been knocked loose of its meaning.

But Elsa had also said *home*, and I found that word still

meant something. The holding house was a run-down building with rats in the roof, in a town surrounded by soldiers. But when I heard Elsa say *come home*, it was enough to stop the tears that had threatened to come, and to let me muster a small smile before we left.

*

We rode out in the dark. It would buy us a few hours at most, but every hour counted. Before dawn, Council messengers would be on their way to Wyndham, warning of our approach. We were ready for that: ready for them to man the defences at Wyndham; ready for them to harry us on the journey; ready for them to mount counterattacks on New Hobart itself, while it was sparsely defended. All of these prospects, frightening as they were, would mean that the Council was expecting us to lay siege to Wyndham. So we moved with purpose, a thousand of us, on the eastern road. None of the soldiers knew what they were riding towards, though the rumours passing up and down the column still whispered of Wyndham. It would only be in five days' time, when part of our army had committed itself to the canyon, that a separate force would peel off to head further north to the refuge.

We travelled quietly, but the soldiers seemed resolute, some even cheerful; since the convoy had arrived through Wreckers' Pass, they'd had full bellies for the first time in weeks, and there was some satisfaction in doing something, rather than waiting in New Hobart for The General's next strike.

Zach and Paloma rode with us. We had argued about it, Zoe, Piper, The Ringmaster and I, in the holding house a few days earlier. None of us relished the thought of taking

Paloma into battle, however carefully guarded, or of risking Zach at the front line. But the alternative was just as unappealing: to leave them in New Hobart, a town guarded only by a skeleton force. Who could we trust to watch and defend them?

'With me and The Ringmaster at the canyon,' Piper had said, 'I need Zoe and Simon at the refuge, leading the attack with you.' He didn't say *protecting you*, but I knew well enough that was what he meant. 'We need Paloma and Zach where we can keep them safe,' he went on.

'I'm riding to the refuge,' Paloma said.

We all turned, but Piper shook his head immediately. 'I know you want to be where Zoe is,' he said. 'But it's a battle. I have to think about strategy, not sentiment.' He turned back to me. 'If we keep her and Zach here, we'll need—'

'Stop talking about me as if I'm not here,' Paloma interrupted him. 'This isn't about me and Zoe. And I don't only want to be where it's safest.'

'Then you're a fool,' said Piper.

Zoe bridled, and went to speak, but Paloma spoke for herself.

'I don't want to sit here, surrounded by guards, until you put me back on a boat at the end of spring,' she said. 'I didn't know what being an emissary was going to be like. None of us did. To be honest, none of us ever really believed we'd find another land. But we did, and I am the Scattered Islands' emissary, if not a very good one. I answer to the Confederacy of the Scattered Islands, and not to you. And as emissary, I need to see what you face in the battle, and witness what you find at the refuge.' She spoke calmly, though I could see by her clenched fists that it cost her some effort to keep her voice steady.

'I'm not kidding myself that I'm going to save the day

on the battlefield. But I should be there. I should be part of this.' She paused. 'I am part of this already.'

Zoe and Piper looked at each other, and then Piper gave a slow nod.

'Then you'll ride with Cass, Zoe and Simon,' he said. 'Zach too – I want you all guarded together. You're to hang back from the front line, and I want a cordon around you at all times. We'll have Violet and Crispin guarding you too, and Adam.'

'And if we fail at the refuge?' I asked.

'Then New Hobart will fall too,' Zoe replied, 'and Paloma and Zach will be no safer here. If our army's destroyed at the refuge and the canyon, it'll only be a matter of time before The General crushes New Hobart.'

Back in the dormitory, Zach was waiting. He could tell that something was going on.

'Get ready to leave,' I said. 'We'll be on the road for a while. You'll need your blanket, and a water flask.' I tossed him a small bag. 'We ride at sunset.'

'You're attacking Wyndham?' he asked.

I didn't reply.

'The Ringmaster's ambitions will cost you,' Zach said, his voice low. 'Wyndham won't fall easily. It can withstand a long siege. He's leading you to your deaths. To all of our deaths.'

'You're the expert in deaths,' I said softly.

We kept his hands shackled as we led him to the courtyard, where Paloma and Zoe were waiting. Even Paloma carried weapons now.

'Can you fight?' Piper had asked her, the previous day.

She'd nodded. 'Well enough,' she'd said, with a glance down at her false leg, 'if I can stay on my feet. I'm better with a sword than an axe.'

I was reminded, once again, that Elsewhere was not some place of peace and plenty.

'Fine then,' Piper had said, and turned to Zoe. 'Go to the armourers. See she's issued with whatever weapons she chooses.'

So now Paloma carried a short sword, and a small curved dagger on her left hip. Next to her, Zoe had a broadsword.

'And me?' Zach asked, looking from Zoe to Paloma, and then to my own sword and dagger.

'You'll be guarded,' I said. 'And given a shield.'

'You're going to march me into a battle unarmed?'

I faced him; I saw his jaw muscles tense when I placed my hand on the hilt of my dagger.

'Unarmed, and shackled,' I said. 'I told you that you'll be guarded. Be grateful for that. I will not have you armed, let alone at close quarters with Paloma.'

He said nothing. His nostrils narrowed with each intake of breath. He looked at me, and then at Paloma. I wasn't sure who he hated more.

CHAPTER 20

We rode near the middle of the column: me, Zach, and Paloma. Zoe kept her horse close to Paloma, with Simon, Crispin, Violet and Adam flanking us.

In the daylight, when we stopped to rest, our improvised camp was hushed but unsettled. It wasn't even the patrols surrounding the perimeter, or those who still clustered by the campfires talking. It was the sound of nearly a thousand soldiers trying to sleep without dreaming.

I'd been surprised to see The Ringmaster himself overseeing the hoisting of the flag, near the centre of our first camp. He directed the soldiers, watching while Elsa's banner was raised on a pole strapped to one of the wagon joists. A hot wind kept the flag moving, the intertwined symbols shifting in the air above the tents.

'I wondered if you'd even let us fly it,' I said as he came back to his tent.

'It's a good idea.' He bent under the flap of the door. 'A clear statement. We need the troops to feel united – fighting for a common purpose.'

'And you?' I said.

'What do you mean?'

'Do you even believe in any of this?' I said to him, nodding at the flag and the troops who moved around below it, blue and red tunics interspersed. 'Not just as a good strategy for motivating the troops. But really believe in it?'

'We've been through this,' he said. 'I know you suspected me, when there was a traitor. You were wrong then. You're wrong now, to keep doubting me.'

'I know that you're no traitor,' I said, 'and I know that you're going into battle with us, as you did at New Hobart. But I still don't know what you're doing it for. What you really believe in.'

He spoke without turning, keeping his gaze fixed ahead. 'I believe we have to stop the machines.'

'And if we do? Then?'

'Then we'll need stability. A steady hand, to guide us in this new era. Assess the situation with Elsewhere, and where we should go from here.'

'Stability,' I repeated. 'And what about change?'

'What more do you want?' he said. 'Isn't this enough change for you? I sacrificed my place on the Council. I gave you an army. I've brought this land to its knees. I'm even flying that damned flag. And I'll be riding into that canyon myself when we reach Wyndham.'

'And if you survive? What then? What do you see yourself getting out of it?'

'This Council will fall.'

'And you'll take its place?'

He didn't answer.

*

The attacks on our convoy began at dawn on the second day. We'd been riding all night, and for hours I had felt the unease stirring my guts, like a sickness.

'Archers,' I'd said to Zoe, drawing my horse closer to hers. 'When I have visions, that's the sound I hear.'

The Ringmaster rode back to consult with me.

'It's Crow Pass,' he said. 'A few miles further east. It's a likely point for an ambush. If they've had time to muster troops from the nearby garrisons, that's where they'll be waiting for us.'

I nodded, gesturing to the north. 'The arrows will come from that side.'

He nodded, calmer than I could comprehend. 'I've sent a squadron. They're in place, to flank the ambush if it happens. I've ordered our troops to have their shields ready when we approach the pass.'

At the pass, where the road narrowed between walls of stone, the arrows began. The first two volleys came in high, and both times we raised our shields, closing off the sky. A few horses across from me, an arrow came clean through Crispin's wooden shield, close to his forearm, stopping half an inch from his face. From the shadow of my own shield I watched him exhale, then breathe in again, testing each breath carefully, not convinced that he was still alive. When he tried to jerk the arrow out, the shield split clean in half. He moved his shield arm tentatively – the force of the arrow's impact had sprained it, if not broken it.

When the archers saw that we had shields at the ready, they shot low, and several horses screamed. Just ahead of me, a horse took an arrow to the side. He didn't stop moving forward, but his front legs buckled, so he ploughed onward into the ground, his rider pitched over the horse's lowered head, while its back legs were still thrashing. All around us horses reared and shied, and soldiers were shouting and swearing. I gripped on tightly with my legs, but the only thing that stopped my horse from bolting was the fact that it was penned in on all sides by other riders. Close to me, Paloma was grim-faced, though she held formation and kept her shield raised.

Zach, too, had paled, cringing below his raised shield. I saw him stare at the thrashing horse on the ground, the arrow still lodged in its side.

'You'll have seen worse than that, before the week's out,' I told him.

He didn't respond.

From the north, a small force charged out of cover to ride at us: perhaps forty soldiers, coming fast. Our front squadron rode to meet them, and I sought out Piper's tall silhouette amongst them. He'd swapped his shield for his sword now – he could not wield both at once – and whenever a new volley of arrows came at our advancing squadron my breath halted, my whole body a knot yanked tight.

The attackers were outnumbered, but it was an ugly skirmish, with the archers still shooting, now hitting their own riders as well. Each time a volley came, I threw up my shield, and each time I lowered it, I was afraid of what I would see in the fighting ahead. Afraid, above all, that I would no longer be able to pick out Piper's broad back. But he was still there: a glimpse of him, low over his horse's neck. Another, his sword swinging at one of the Council riders. I saw The Ringmaster too, fighting near Piper. In the centre of the fight, they looked like the hub of a wheel, the rest of the skirmish rotating around them. Soldiers and horses on both sides were foundering, fallen figures spat out from the centre of the battle.

The sounds of the arrows in flight were replaced with

shouts from the hill to the north, as the flanking squadron sent by The Ringmaster came upon the archers from behind. And then it was over: no more arrows, no more shouts. The front squadron rode back to the head of the column; soldiers gathered the injured and loaded them into the wagons, and we were moving again.

'Will there be more attacks?' Paloma asked Zoe.

Zoe grimaced as she craned around to pull from her arm a splinter of a broken shield. 'They'll be coming at us all the way,' she said, flicking the shard of wood from her hand, and not even looking down at where the blood welled on her arm.

'But will their whole army ride out to meet us?'

It was Zach who answered. 'They won't want to risk open battle on the plains, without a stronghold, and leaving Wyndham undefended, when they know they can hold you off there. They'll be drawing back already, readying Wyndham for a siege.'

I said nothing. Zach, like all the soldiers, still didn't know that the attack on Wyndham was only a decoy.

'Do you have any idea what you're doing?' he said, lowering his voice to speak only to me. 'You can't win at Wyndham, even if you attack Noose Canyon – not without more troops, more support. The Ringmaster must know that,' he hissed. 'This crusade of yours will kill us all. I came to you to keep us both safe.'

I waved back the way we had come, where the dead lay on the narrow road, along with horses studded with arrows.

'Go back then,' I said. 'Go on. Walk back to your people. Go to The General and see how that works out for you.'

He turned away from me, gripping his shield tighter with his shackled hands, and we rode on in silence.

*

At sunrise the next day I looked to the east, squinting into the rising sun and trying to conjure a sense of the distance that still lay between us and Wyndham.

'They'll be ready for us now,' Piper said, joining me. 'Not just the local garrisons, who've had news that we're on our way, but the messengers will have reached Wyndham. They'll be preparing for a siege – and sending more troops out to block our way.'

He was right. The next attack came the following afternoon; I sensed it coming, felt its snare tightening around us, and was able to send a warning up the column before the Council soldiers rounded on us from the south and charged. The skirmish was quick and deadly: we had far greater numbers, and of the fifty Council soldiers who made a stand on the road, forty at least were left on the plain when we rode on.

It was strange to be in the battle but apart from it, flanked on all sides by our own soldiers while the fighting went on a few hundred yards away. I didn't see the full extent of it until it was over, and we rode past the ground where the fighting had taken place. Our horses stepped gingerly over the fallen bodies. By that point, as the blood seeped into the ground, it mattered little whose dead they were.

The third attack, half a day out of Wyndham, caught us all by surprise. I had dreamed, the night before, of a mountain collapsing. I had seen the world crumble many times before, seen the blast shatter mountains as well as bodies. But the next afternoon, as the road passed into the shadow of a grey slate hill, there was a sound like the world grinding its teeth.

I looked up at the scree slope above us; it was moving, the loose rock face shimmering like water. Towards the top, a huge boulder had been pushed loose and was crashing its way down, unleashing a cavalcade of smaller stones. Half a hillside sloughing away, and the middle of our column was directly in its path.

There was no order given to flee – each horse and each body gave its own order, instinctive as breath. We surged forward, and the world became a series of sounds: the skittering of the smaller stones racing towards us; the bass crash of the larger boulders; hoofbeats on the stone road.

I was leaning so far forward that my face touched my horse's neck; when I dared to glance to the side, Zach was doing the same. To my other side, beyond Paloma, the avalanche tore down the hillside, a slippage of the world. The nearest rocks were only a few hundred yards away now, close enough that I could make out individual stones amongst the grey blur. Ahead of me, a horse stumbled, and the horse behind it had no time to swerve. Both horses and riders went down, and my own horse only avoided them by swerving sideways, my leg crushing against Zach's. I could hear the jangle of his shackles and his fevered breath. I looked over my shoulder; Paloma and Zoe had avoided the fallen horses, and were right behind us.

Further back, one of the wagons was losing ground fast, its white-eyed horses throwing themselves against the traces. The driver stood at his seat, wielding his whip and shouting, but the sound of the rocks was close enough to bury any noise he could make.

Just ahead of me, the hillside above the road thickened with trees rather than rocks. We were perhaps a hundred yards from safety now, but the avalanche was gaining on us. I risked another look over my shoulder. There seemed no way that anyone behind us would make it, least of all the lumbering wagon.

Zoe, riding on the far side of Paloma, veered away from

us. She had to wrestle with her horse to slow its pace and move to the right, letting the wagon gain on her. For a moment I thought she might try to seize the driver and carry him to safety on her own horse. But instead she swung her sword wide and low, and severed the traces. The wagon continued, jolting for a few seconds; the horses darted forward in a streak of fear, Zoe's horse beside them. Then the wagon juddered to a stop. The driver gave a yell that grabbed at my guts like a hook.

The rocks reached the road. I was barely clear of their path, and the impact made the ground lurch, and rock fragments chipped at my legs and sent my horse careering.

I was glad I did not see the wagon being hit. By the time I had my horse under control, and turned to look back, the rocks had claimed the cart and everything around it. One minute, a throng of riders; the next, a plain of settling rocks.

Zach, Paloma and I, and those closest to us, were only twenty yards clear of the stones; Zoe had barely got clear. Ahead of her was a crush of panicked horses, the soldiers just as wild-eyed. Behind her, nothing but stones.

I waited for the cries from those injured or buried, but the silence was worse. At least thirty soldiers, and as many horses, were buried there. The fallen stones gave away no clues: even the huge wagon could not be seen under that mass of stone.

A few of the soldiers closest to the edges of the rockfall had dropped to their knees and begun to dig, scrabbling at the stones. I wheeled my reluctant horse to join them; it danced on the spot, would not be persuaded to head back. Then the arrows began: one bounced on a rock a few yards away from me; beyond me, one of the men digging at the fallen rocks was hit from behind, cast forward like another piece of the fallen hillside.

'Ride on.' It was The Ringmaster's voice. He had ridden back, Piper beside him, along the broken column. 'Ride on,' he shouted, over the sound of arrows. His voice as heavy and hard as the stones themselves. 'Ride on,' he called again, and the word was passed down the column. I looked around for Piper, hoping to hear him countermand the order. But he was riding south, leading a squadron towards the thicket from which the arrows came. The rest of the column staggered back into motion. Those at the back had to detour widely around the expanse of the stones, which had swallowed the road and expanse beyond it onto the plain. Loose horses were being caught; the line of the column, where the rocks had shattered it, was being reassembled.

Zoe had rejoined us now.

'Keep your shield up,' she shouted, seeing me looking back towards the rocks.

'Couldn't you have saved the driver?' Zach asked her. He was still panting, still glancing back at the rocks every few seconds. I could hear, in his question, my own voice; it was the same question I would have asked, a year ago.

'No chance,' she replied, riding on. 'And we need the horses.'

*

The final camp, within sight of Wyndham, was subdued. We had expected to be attacked on the way to Wyndham, but there was something unanswerable about the avalanche, and our helplessness in the face of it.

Beyond the perimeter of our camp, Council patrols moved in the darkness – flashes of torchlight along the plain, and the sound of hoofs in the distance. They watched, and waited. They would have time enough to attack us when we were hemmed in at the canyon.

To the north, a few miles away, we could just make out a column of torches moving along the ridge.

'There,' The Ringmaster said, finger outstretched. He had come to our tent. I was sitting outside, away from the others; I didn't want to be cramped in that small space with Zach.

'Reinforcements,' The Ringmaster went on, 'heading for the canyon. A whole squadron, at least. My advance scouts said troops have been coming in since yesterday – from every garrison within fifty miles.'

'Including the refuge?' I asked.

He nodded. 'At least two hundred soldiers marched in from that way before sunset yesterday.'

I didn't know how to feel. Hope – for all those thousands in the tanks in Refuge 6. And hope for those of our soldiers who would, in a few hours, be following me to steal off to the refuge, where hundreds fewer of the Council's soldiers now waited. But those riders we were watching, that trail of lights in the dark, would be massed at the canyon's neck, to meet Piper and The Ringmaster and the rest of our army.

Back in the tent, I knew there was no sleep to be had. I stared at the dirty canvas ceiling, listening to the sounds of the camp. Zach lay barely a yard away. His eyes were closed, but I could tell from his breathing that he was still awake. Beyond him, Paloma and Zoe had given up on sleep. Paloma lay with her head on Zoe's lap, and the two of them were speaking in low voices, Zoe absently stroking Paloma's shoulder with the backs of her knuckles. I thought, for a moment, of Kip, and of his long fingers. The perfectly round scar on the inside of his wrist where the tube used to enter his skin. But this was not a time for self-pity. I looked instead at my own hands: this was what I had. These hands.

Piper startled me when he touched my shoulder. He was squatting in the doorway, reaching in to me. 'Come and see this,' he said, already standing to go.

A long way to the south-east, a glow of flame had taken a chunk out of the darkness. Smoke was rising, white against the night. Two columns, blurring into one as they climbed.

'The bridges,' I said. I was used to flinching from fire – to waking in screams from my dreams of flame. But now there was a smile spreading across my face, and Piper's.

'It's time,' he said.

'Time for what?' Inside the tent, Zach had sat up.

Piper ignored him. I didn't find it so easy – I could feel Zach's eyes on me, as I turned to Piper.

'We're mustering now,' he said, his voice low so that Zach couldn't hear. 'Your squadrons will be able to slip away as soon as we begin the charge.'

I took a step closer to him.

'Back at Elsa's,' I said, 'you told me you didn't want to be the leader at the end.' He smiled ruefully. 'I don't mind that so much,' I went on. 'I've been seeing the end coming for so long now. But I had thought, when it came to the end, that we would be facing it together.'

'We already have,' he said. 'More ends than most will ever imagine. The island. New Hobart. The Ark. We've stood together before and seen the end come – and we've got out the other side, too.'

'And this time?' I said.

'You're the seer.'

'You know what I see these days.' I was thinking of Xander: *Forever fire.*

'I know you see the fire,' he said. 'But not all the time. Not now. Look around you.'

He gestured at the rows of tents, the hungry faces lit by firelight. By the nearest fire, one of the soldiers injured in an ambush was bent over his wounded leg, wincing as he tightened the bandages. Three women were sharpening weapons, the throat-slitting scrape of steel on steel. There was no beauty in the scene. But these people had gathered, Alphas and Omegas together, to fight against the Council. Through the tent walls, lamplight showed the silhouettes of Zoe and Paloma, Zoe's head bent to Paloma as they talked.

'There are still things worth fighting for,' he said. 'There's more to the world than fire and ash.'

CHAPTER 21

The Ringmaster was already mounted. He looked calm, but his horse had picked up on the atmosphere and was shifting from hoof to hoof, its eyes too wide, its tail flicking from side to side. I looked over the soldiers nearest to us. The moonlight made all the faces grey. Near us, a soldier on foot had his head lowered and was muttering to himself, some private wish or incantation. He made no sound, just his lips moving, and he reminded me of Xander and how he used to mutter to himself. That was what this canyon did: it made every one of us a seer. You only had to look at those narrowing cliff walls ahead, funnelling down towards the Council's stronghold, to know what this night would bring.

'Have you seen anything?' The Ringmaster asked. 'Anything that can help us?'

I shook my head. What I had seen of the battle was blood, swords and arrows, and how the sides of the canyon became two jaws that would crush our army. It was nothing that he didn't know already, and nothing that could be useful.

'Then tell me this,' he said, gesturing beyond the canyon to the east, where Wyndham lay. 'The General – is she in there now?'

'Yes.' I didn't even have to wait, or to try to sound out the city beyond the canyon. The General was waiting for us inside – I could feel her.

Years ago, before we had been split, Zach had found the pet bugs that I had collected and kept in a jar, and he had pinned one to the windowsill. *An experiment*, he'd said, when I'd found him watching the bug dragging itself in an endless circle around the needle. I felt The General now, waiting for us with the same distant curiosity with which Zach had watched the bug. She had contrived all of this, and we were just squirming on the pin.

'Good,' The Ringmaster said.

He turned his horse away, and I didn't get a chance to see if his face matched the strange glee that I had caught in his voice.

Then it all happened quickly: the troops fell into formation; Piper rode to his place, beside The Ringmaster. There was no time for words, or farewells, or speeches. The Ringmaster waved his arm, and the mass of troops began to move.

Piper and The Ringmaster led the army into the night. Everything had been done to make the attacking force seem larger than it was. The horses and foot soldiers were ranked widely apart, to add the appearance of mass to the column. At the front, with torchbearers on either side, rode The Ringmaster, with Piper beside him. The torchlight threw shadows against the canyon's walls: a horse's head, distorted; the shape of a sword bent by a wavering flame. The march had all the appearance of a folly: a mad, doomed attack, The Ringmaster's desperate attempt to seize back the Council.

It was all counterfeit, but there was nothing counterfeit about the blades that waited for them at the neck of the canyon.

Only at the last minute, barely a mile from Wyndham, when the cliff walls had begun to rise around the back half of the column and we were all but committed to the canyon, did we peel off. Four hundred soldiers entered the canyon, to face off against the assembled mass of The General's army. Five hundred of us slipped away, heading north towards the refuge. Zach and I were near the front, surrounded by Zoe, Paloma, Simon, Violet, Crispin, and Adam. We rode without torches, trusting the horses and the slender moon.

As we rode, we heard sounds of the fighting behind us. The canyon, and distance, muffled some of the noises, and twisted others. Arrows made a distant purr, instead of the air-shredding rip that I knew so well. Sword clashes and screams were muted: a general clamour, a long way away. The sound made me angry: it seemed a kind of lie, that those noises of horror and death should be softened like this. A trick played on us by the canyon and the darkness.

'Where are you taking us?' Zach's whisper was insistent in my ear; he had been badgering me ever since we had slipped away from the canyon. When I ignored him, he reached over with his shackled wrist and yanked at my arm.

Simon, riding close, had his sword out in seconds, but I had already slapped Zach's hand away and spun to face him. 'Do you want to go with them?' I whispered, keeping my voice even, and jerking my head back towards the canyon. 'Do you want to march into that canyon, and face what waits for you there?'

He was silent.

'I thought not,' I said, spurring my horse away from his. 'So shut up.'

*

We were at the refuge within three hours, the night still heavy on the plains. When we'd planned the attack, I'd seen the refuge on maps, but when we passed the ridge and saw it ahead of us, the scale of the place was still enough to halt my breath. Sitting above us on a low hill, the sprawling complex was choked by its high fence. Months earlier, when Piper, Zoe and I had seen Refuge 9, there had been fields visible, worked by those Omegas who had not yet been tanked. Here in Refuge 6, even that pretence had been abandoned: there were no fields, and no crops. Only the long buildings, windowless, splayed around a central hub from which smoke emerged, white on the black sky.

'What's all that smoke from?' Paloma asked.

Zach answered, instead of me. 'It's the fuel – to power the tanks.' He had been quiet for the last hour, ever since he had worked out where we were going. 'You have no idea of how valuable that is. We've poured so many resources into keeping the Omegas safe. If you charge in there now, you could kill them all. And even if you manage to get them out alive, you don't know what kind of state they'll be in.'

I had seen what the tanks had done to Kip – his memories hollowed out of him. And Kip had been an Alpha; Omega bodies, more susceptible to sickness, might respond differently. But I also knew that anything was better than the tanks and their endless, airless near-death. I thought of Sally's words: *Dying's far from the worst thing that could happen to me*. It felt strange to be seeking reassurance from Sally now: a dead traitor. But I ran her words through my head all the same.

Simon and Zoe had been issuing their whispered orders to the soldiers. The refuge had only one gate, and we were massed half a mile from it, on the slopes. Our archers had crept slightly closer, in the scrubby ground a little to the east. Ladders had been unloaded from the wagons, which we had left just beyond the ridge, out of sight of the refuge.

I had been so busy being afraid for Piper and the army we had left behind in the canyon, that I had forgotten to be afraid for us. At least four hundred soldiers waited for us in that refuge. We had more, just about – but a third of those were Omegas, many with mutations that limited their ability as fighters. The Council's soldiers had the advantage of the walls, and the hill.

The sharp, fox stink of urine reached me. I glanced to my left and saw the wet stain spreading in the trousers of the young soldier standing to the left of my horse. If he even noticed what he'd done, he gave no sign. His lips were clenched so tightly that they were white. The buckles that fastened his tunic at the sides rattled slightly, his whole body trembling. He was one of The Ringmaster's men, but so young that he must have been recruited only within the last year or two. When he'd joined up, he could have expected nothing more arduous than breaking up tavern brawls, or roughing up some Omegas who had tried to dodge a Tithe Collector. Not this: lining up in the dark to charge towards hundreds of well-armed soldiers. The certainty of blood.

I would have liked to say to him: *It will be all right*. But my mouth was too dry to form words, and this was not the place for lies. My own hands were shaking, my sweaty palms dampening the leather of my sword's hilt. My mouth was so parched that my lips clung to my gums.

My body was a nest of fear; every part of me wanted to run, so much that I could barely believe that I was still here, feet braced apart, shoulder to shoulder with Crispin on one side and Zach on the other.

Simon and Zoe rode together to the front of our lines and stopped there, facing the soldiers who stared up at them. It was Zoe who spoke, raising her voice against the night.

'You did not know, before we rode away from the canyon tonight, what would be asked of you. We will not be overthrowing the Council, or storming the fort of Wyndham. But what we do here is no less important, and no less of a blow to the Council. We will be freeing those imprisoned in the refuge, and bringing them to safety.

'We are the lucky ones: in the canyon, people are already fighting and dying to hold the Council's forces at bay. We must repay that sacrifice with victory here.

'Outside these walls, you will each see things on the battlefield that will horrify and disgust you. But once we have won, and thrown the gates open, you will see things more horrifying still. Some of you have seen, as I have, the drowned children of New Hobart. All of you will have heard the rumours of the tanks. You will see them confirmed, tonight, and you will wish that you had not. This is what we take up our swords against: a world where this is possible. A world that divides us, and imprisons us, and leaves drowned children floating in glass tanks.'

Behind the walls of the refuge, lights were moving, voices calling and answering, orders being given. A very light, warm rain had begun to fall; I felt it on my face, and wondered if I would feel such a rain again. I looked to my right and saw the tiny droplets of rain settling on Paloma's eyelashes as she stared at Zoe.

Zoe spoke again. 'For those of you who, like me, are Alphas, and fight tonight to free Omegas, I give you no more thanks than I give to the Omega soldiers who ride beside us.' I glanced around me; the faces of the Alphas were grim, but Zach's was the only one to display anger.

'Each of you is doing what is right and necessary,' Zoe continued, 'for the freedom of all of us. None of us, Alpha or Omega, will be safe while the tanks are allowed to continue. There is no end to the Council's plans, or to their willingness to destroy.'

The blast flared in my mind. I clenched my eyes shut and tried to keep myself still, but I must have jolted or stiffened – my horse shied to the side, jostling into Zach's. For a moment we were crushed together, my leg pressed against his, and I felt the slight trembling of his body – our shared fear.

It took only a few seconds to regain control of my mount. Zoe had turned to look at the refuge behind her. Torches were marching towards the gates; shouts carried through the rain.

She continued, her voice clear and loud. 'I have wished, often enough, that I had been born in different times, in a different world. I am learning, only now, that the different world is the one we build here, with our own hands.

'If you seek hope, and if you seek courage, nothing I say tonight can give you those things.' She paused for a moment, and I saw her search our lines for Paloma, her eyes settling on that blonde head for an instant. 'There is hope in this world,' she went on. 'But it is not given to us – least of all by the Council. Such hope as there is, we must make ourselves. Such courage as there is, we must find in ourselves.'

She lifted her chin, raised her sword. 'Find it now.'

CHAPTER 22

Simon stayed in the front line; Zoe slipped back to rejoin me and Paloma, closer to the centre of the troops. I rode between Zach and Paloma. Encircling the three of us was our own small guard: Zoe, Crispin, Violet, and Adam. Ash, too, the young Alpha soldier who had brought us the news of Tash's death, and who since then had taken regular sentry postings at the holding house. Next to me, Zach hid his fear better than I did. His mouth was set, his eyes fixed on the refuge gate. His breathing was steady but noisier than usual, each breath a concentrated effort. I looked along the row of soldiers beside me. All of us were clutching our weapons; Zach's hands were gripping tightly too, though he had only a shield to hold.

They were ready for us when we charged. I was oddly comforted by the fact that they met us on the slopes. If they had faith in their fortifications, or in reinforcements from Wyndham, they would have waited it out, and done their best to repel us from the walls. But they knew that they were alone now, cut off from Wyndham, in a refuge never built to withstand an attack from without. So three squadrons spilled from the gates, one riding straight at us while the other two spread wide, aiming to flank us.

Our archers shot first, breaking the first line of their charge. Those first few deaths struck me like blows – I felt each one, my body flinching and my throat tasting of blood that was not my own. Then their archers answered, the arrows sounding their deadly cry. There was moonlight, but not enough for us to spot the arrows until they were too close; we huddled blindly under our shields. Close to me, Violet's horse took an arrow to the neck and slumped to the ground, pitching her off sideways. She leaped clear, but then I lost sight of her amongst the crush of horses and the darkness. The rain had increased, so heavy at times that the noise of it on my raised shield almost drowned out the sounds of the battle around me.

Between volleys, when I lowered my shield, I could see our front line lit by the torches of the Council troops. Simon had held his place, leading the attack. When the Council's riders reached him, he swung his axe and swords with a brutality and speed that was awful to watch. I saw him strike one man with the butt of his axe, a blunt blow that smashed the cheekbone and eye socket. Blood spurted, but the worst was the face's collapse, as though the geography of the man's face had been transformed to swamp and sinkholes, everything sunken into that central impact.

From then on, it was a haze of fighting. When the moon was behind clouds, the darkness made everything harder – I could see little but blades slicing the night, and an indistinguishable press of bodies. I kept my sword and shield raised, but the fighting itself hadn't yet penetrated our tight circle of guards. Nothing reached us but a single arrow that struck the edge of Paloma's shield, almost knocking her off her horse. She managed to cling on, hauling herself awkwardly back into the saddle, but she had dropped her shield.

The battle was spreading now, the ordered lines giving way to smaller skirmishes. It was like being in one of my visions: time became unruly. Some moments took forever; a spray of blood arcing from a distance and spattering onto Paloma's face seemed to last for minutes, one dark drop at a time landing on her white skin. At other moments time slipped, everything moving too fast, a blur of blades and bodies.

I could see Violet again, down amongst the churn of horses' legs and mud. Zoe was sticking close to Paloma; she'd tossed Paloma her shield and was wielding the broadsword two-handed now, in combat with a mounted man. There were times I'd wondered whether her closeness with Paloma had softened Zoe; now, instead, I saw a new fierceness, her face twisted into a snarl as she slashed and jabbed at the man who was trying to get past her. But another Council soldier, on foot, slipped around the rear of Zoe's horse and stood suddenly within a few feet of Paloma.

His swing was low, swiping at her leg. At first he thought he'd wounded her; I could see the confusion growing in his face as he pulled back his sword and waited for the blood to come. The horse screamed and reared, but Paloma only winced at the jarring of her false leg. Before the man had grasped what had happened, she'd regained control of her horse, and leaned forward. Her sword stroke was precise: a jab, in and out, opened a loose-lipped second mouth in the man's neck, and he fell beneath her horse's hoofs.

On my other side, beyond Zach, Crispin was swinging his axe, but he had a shorter reach than his opponent, and caught a blow to the chest. It was the flat of the sword, not the sharp edge, but it was enough to send him backwards to the ground. As more and more riders fell and more horses foundered, I began to feel exposed on my saddle: conspicuous amidst a battle that was increasingly taking place in the mud below me. Zoe, too, was on the ground now, fighting in a frenzy of blades.

Up the hill, ladders and grappling chains were going up; each time I snatched a glance towards the gate, there were more, clambering up the wall like ivy. Simon was there, somehow still mounted, directing the charge with hoarse shouts, and still swinging his weapons at any Council soldiers who got close to him.

But I couldn't afford to watch what was happening up the gate. Paloma and Zach were close on either side of me. Zoe was holding her ground, but she was hard-pressed. Ahead, both Crispin and Violet were unseated and fighting in the scrum, while young Ash, still mounted, was fighting strongly behind me. Beyond Zach, Adam was holding his place, exchanging blows with a soldier who held a broadsword with both her hands, but I could hear the panic in his short, rasping breaths. The cordon around us was tightening. Adam ducked under one of her blows, a sweep of the blade that sliced the night air. It passed within half a foot of me and Zach, and we ducked in unison. It felt strange to be moving with him like that, and to want the same thing that he wanted. For those few minutes, both of us had only one goal: to stay alive.

It should not have been this close. The plan had been for our small group to hold back, to keep me, Zach and Paloma out of the worst of the danger while the gate was seized. But the Council's soldiers, with little faith in their defences, and had ridden out to meet us in the field. It was brave, and stupid, and while it might have cost them the refuge, it cost us too. There was no front line any more, just blades and skirmishes spreading out from the gates. In the chaos and darkness, I doubted that any of the Council soldiers knew who Zach, Paloma and I were – they charged indiscriminately, and the guards surrounding us were wearying. An arrow came again at Paloma – I wondered if her paleness made her an easy target in the darkness. The arrow missed her, but struck her horse in the shoulder. The horse screamed and bucked, and Paloma was thrown.

Zoe was still struggling in combat to my left; ahead of us, Violet and Crispin were barely holding back a press of red tunics. To the other side, Ash and Adam were fighting hard and hadn't even seen what had happened. I swung my leg over the saddle and dropped close to Paloma, who was struggling to stand, her false leg slipping in the mud. Zach shouted as I jumped. 'Don't leave,' he yelled, or it might have been, 'Don't leave me' – but I ignored him.

Down on the ground, the battle took on new shades of horror. We were in the midst of grappling soldiers and panicked horses, flailing hoofs as deadly as the blades that surrounded us. Paloma's horse refused to lie down and die, even with the arrow buried a foot deep in its shoulder. Paloma was dazed but didn't look injured; her shield was gone again, but she had kept her sword, and had it raised in front of her face. Twice she stumbled as her own horse jostled her. I thought of the waste: to have come all this way, the first emissary of Elsewhere, and to die in the mud, trampled by horses. It was too stupid, too ugly and pointless, and the rage that flared in me was almost a relief after all that fear.

Somewhere nearby, a sword was knocked from a hand, or perhaps thrown; it came hurtling towards Paloma, end over end, while she was looking the other way in search of Zoe. I blocked the flying sword by instinct, my own blade raised just in time, the clash of steel on steel jarring my bones and knocking a grunt from me as the other sword fell into the mud. Paloma turned at the noise, but by then there was nothing to see except me, standing there clutching my sword, which was still vibrating with the impact.

A few yards beyond Paloma, the tall man blocked one of Zoe's swipes, and their swords snarled together, jerking both from their grip. For a moment they were both empty-handed; he had stepped back a few yards, then charged at her just as she reached to the back of her belt for one of her small knives. I thought she would be able to dodge him, or hold him off, but she went over easily, knocked flat to the ground beneath him. I sprang to help her; behind me, Paloma too was moving, a sound coming from her that was both a yell and a sob. It was only a few steps through the clinging mud, but there was no way we could reach Zoe before he had time to pull out his dagger or to get his hands around her neck. For a long moment they were both still, his body stretched full-length atop hers. But his head never lifted, and he didn't move. Only when she shoved his body to the side, with a grunt, and I saw her bloodied knife held at her stomach, did I realise that she had made her body into a trap, letting him throw himself onto her raised knife and impale himself with the force of his own weight.

She squirmed free of his dead weight, and he settled on his back, both hands still at his stomach, where his tunic was soaked a darker shade of red. Zoe staggered to her knees and turned to Paloma. Paloma reached out her hand and the two of them touched – they didn't even grasp hands, just touched, palm-to-palm, for a moment – before Zoe turned away, picked up her sword, and resumed her guard.

I looked back up to Zach; he was standing in his stirrups, turning from side to side as he searched below him for me and Paloma. Just behind him, something caught my eye:

a sudden stillness, the abrupt stoppage of a blade that has sunk home. It was Adam, still mounted, on the far side of Zach, an axe nested deep in his stomach. He dropped forward, folded double over his horse's neck. A dark-haired woman had seized his reins; Adam's body subsided to the ground as she jerked the horse aside and stepped into the gap. There was nobody between her and Zach now, and she grabbed his leg and began to haul him sideways from his horse.

I looked to Zoe, but she was facing the other way, already exchanging blows with another Council soldier. Crispin was not far from her, with his own battle to fight, and neither Violet nor Ash, both fighting to my right, was near enough to close the gap that Adam's fall had created, or to reach Zach.

Zach tried to kick his leg free, and slammed down at the woman's hand with the butt of his shield, twice, but she hung on, and when he struck a second time she managed to wrench the shield from him. His kicks had driven his horse into a greater frenzy now, shying and jerking its head, but the woman still clung to his leg. Her other hand held a curved knife, and she swiped up at Zach. He blocked her slash with the chain stretched between his wrists, but she kept hold of her knife. I ran towards her and swung my sword, but the horse kicked out at both of us, a hoof clipping my blade and sending my sword jerking back at me, nicking my ear. The horse turned on the spot, bucking all the way, the woman somehow hanging on so that she was swung around too. Zach, unarmed, was between us now, his horse blocking my view of her except for her knife, raised high for another strike. Zach looked down, not at her but at me.

I held out my knife, and he grabbed it, his hand over

mine, then turned and plunged it in one movement. There was a scream, and from under the horse's belly I saw the woman fall, hands to her face.

Before I'd ever seen a battle, I'd thought it would mean quick deaths: a neat slash of a blade, a clean cut with an axe, and life gone swiftly, like a candle snuffed out. But that was true only for the lucky, and there were not many lucky that day. Adam had been one of the fortunate ones. The woman Zach stabbed was not lucky: she lay in the mud and bled, and made screams that were not words, but whose meaning was perfectly clear. It paralysed me – it was the sound of my own fear, given voice.

The screams ended, and when I opened my eyes to see why, Paloma was there, on the far side of Zach's horse, standing over the woman's motionless body.

Bending slightly, Paloma wiped the flat of her sword on a tussock of grass.

'I'd have done as much for a sheep with a broken leg, at home,' she said, meeting my stare.

Zach had half-climbed, half-fallen, from his horse. He stood facing me, my dagger still in his hand.

'Give me back my knife,' I said. It wasn't that I feared him. It was that the dagger was mine: the one that Piper had given me, all those months ago, before we'd fled the island. I didn't like the thought of Zach touching it.

He looked down at the dagger. A little of the woman's blood had pooled around the hilt and spread down his hand.

'Give it to me,' I said, 'or I'll make you.' I picked up my sword, hefted its weight in my hand. I could see him assessing it. He glanced to the side, where both Zoe and Paloma stood now, then he looked back at me.

He held out the knife, offering me the hilt, but as I took

it he kept hold of the blade for a few seconds, so that we held it between us.

'I knew you'd save me,' he said.

I snatched the knife. If it cut his hand, it wasn't deep enough for me to feel his pain.

'I didn't do it for you,' I said. 'I saved myself.'

*

The fighting around us had eased, but was no less ugly. Zach, Paloma and I were a tight circle now, facing outwards, shoulder to shoulder, with Zoe, Violet, Crispin and Ash rotating around us, and a press of our own soldiers around them. Several times the Council soldiers reached them, and were repelled; one man broke through, between Crispin and Ash, and came running at us fast. His eyes unnaturally wide, he seemed to be fleeing as much as attacking, and he fumbled his axe as he raised it. Paloma and I both swung our swords at him. I was grateful for the dark and the mud, which meant I didn't see the details of what we had done, nor know which of us had struck the killing blow.

The gate of Refuge 6 was never designed to withstand a concerted attack from outside. It was a gate to keep out prying eyes, or to stop the occasional panicked Omegas who came to the refuge and then changed their minds. The ones who noticed, at the last minute, the uncanny silence of a refuge where thousands of people were supposed to be living and working. When Simon and his squadron finally gained the ground in front of the gate and went to work with their grappling hooks and battering rams, it took only a few minutes before half the gate was torn right from its hinges, and the other half gaped open.

With the gate fallen, the Council's army could only defend

the refuge with their bodies. So it was a battle without complications or strategy – instead, it became a battle of numbers. The awful simplicity: a press of Council soldiers in front of the bowed gate, and a crush of our soldiers pushing back at them. We ground steadily onwards, me and Zach and Paloma, jostled and guided within our cordon of guards, until the slight climb to the gate was made steeper by the mound of bodies in front of it.

It was supposed to be a triumph. It was the victory that we hadn't allowed ourselves to imagine, and it was ugly beyond anything I had seen.

I saw a woman step on the body of her fallen comrade, not yet dead, to reach up and slit the stomach of a man on horseback. I saw a man pull an arrow from his own guts, then sit there staring at it, holding it in his hands and contemplating it as if it were a shell he had found on the beach. I saw a woman duel for long minutes with a man, defeat him finally with an elaborate feint and slash, and then, before she'd had time to wipe her blade, be killed by a kick to the back of her head by a panicking horse.

What I learned that day: every death is total. Every blade is the blast for the person whose throat it slits.

CHAPTER 23

In the leaden stillness that came when the fighting was over, I walked up to the gates of Refuge 6 with Zach at my side. It was nearly dawn, the darkness leaching from the sky. My shield was gone, my sword filthy with mud and blood. The side of my neck was crusted with blood from my nicked ear, but my only wounds were minor: grazed knuckles, and bruises already surfacing on my arms. My right forearm, which had never healed properly after it was broken in the battle for New Hobart, had taken enough knocks to awaken its old pain.

I looked behind me to the battlefield. Our soldiers were catching the horses, ours and theirs, and clearing the road of bodies so that the wagons could be brought inside the walls. Simon, outside the gate, was directing our sentries to take up their posts, and organising lookouts and patrols. More of our soldiers walked, bent low, amongst the dead and wounded. They were looking for those who could be helped, and finishing off those who could not. Zoe and Simon had given clear orders that prisoners were to be taken alive. I didn't kid myself that this was an act of mercy: we needed their information.

There was no time to linger – the tanks were still waiting. Gaining entry to the refuge was only the first step – and every hour we spent here was an hour that Piper and The Ringmaster had to hold the canyon. Every moment we spent at the refuge would be measured in blood.

I took a deep breath before I stepped through the gates. Twenty yards ahead, the door of the nearest building had been kicked in. Zoe, Ash, Violet and Crispin stayed close as we approached. Even within the refuge, there were skirmishes and shouts as our troops cleared the buildings, one by one, of the handful of soldiers that had retreated there.

'It's clear,' Zoe called from the doorway, ushering us forward. The three of us – me, Paloma, and Zach – stepped together into the windowless building.

After the battlefield, for a moment the tank room seemed peaceful. The neat rows of cylindrical glass tanks, each one as big as Elsa's kitchen. Ladders led to the metal gangways that criss-crossed overhead; above them stretched an orderly array of pipes and wires. It was quiet, barely lit, with just the glow of a few small lights on the panels, and the dawn light seeping through the broken door.

But this was horror nonetheless – just a different kind of horror, sterile and gleaming. Often enough, when I was deep in dreams of flames and blood, I tried to scream – but no noise came. In those dreams, I would open my mouth again and again, but my body refused to make a sound. The silence of the tanks was the same: the scream of a dreamer who cannot summon a sound.

There were so many. I had known, in the abstract, that there were six thousand people tanked here. But that number was just syllables, shorn of meaning. The reality of it was different. The rows mounted, one after another, each tank bulbous, fatly full of our people. And the smell – the awful sweetness of the preserving liquid, perched on the cusp of foulness, like the water in a jug of flowers left to rot and turn rank. I was besieged by memories: the tank rooms beneath Wyndham, where I'd found Kip; the tanks in New Hobart, where we had dredged up the bodies of the drowned children; the tanks buried deep within the Ark, where I had found Kip once more. I couldn't move, my breaths reluctant. Each memory was its own tank, in which I was trapped.

Zach yanked at my arm. 'I don't know how long you think your army can hold the canyon, but it won't be as long as you think. If you stand around like that, you'll get us killed.'

'Watch him closely,' Zoe ordered me and Violet, while she herself stuck near to Paloma. We moved down the rows, and the figures came into view. Each of the tanks was large enough for forty or more people. Within the glass, the people were crammed together like the dead piled outside the gates. All of them were naked, their flesh the same texture I remembered from Kip and from the other tanks I'd seen: sodden, white and wrinkled, like the skin that forms on top of boiled milk.

Paloma had slipped her hand into Zoe's, but even Zoe, who had seen the tanks in New Hobart, had paled, her jaw clenched. Around us, Crispin, Violet and Ash craned their necks back to take in the tanks' full height. Violet reached out a hand to touch the glass, but snatched it back before she had made contact. In the tank closest to me, a woman's hair floated like seaweed. Her eyes were closed, and I closed mine too, for a moment, to shut out everything that I had seen.

'You won't get them all out alive,' Zach said.

'You'll help us,' I said, turning to him. 'You'll tell us everything you know.'

'There isn't anything to know,' he said, throwing up his hands. 'It's theoretical, at best.'

'What do you mean?' said Zoe. She shoved Zach hard in the chest. Without thinking I stepped my own leg back to brace myself against his fall. He stayed upright, brushed her hand from him.

'We never wanted to take anyone out of the tanks. Why would we? The Confessor said it should be possible, in theory. But the only time it's been done was when Cass took out The Confessor's twin. And it damaged him.'

I interrupted him. I didn't want to hear Zach talk about Kip, let alone hear him discuss the ways in which Kip had been damaged.

'We're taking them out,' I told him. 'With or without your help. But if you know anything that could help us, fewer will die. Fewer of their twins, too. That's six thousand Alpha lives.'

He looked at me appraisingly, then up at the panel, with its blinking lights, that sat on the gangway near the centre of the room.

'How long have we got?'

'You know the answer,' I said. 'Not long.'

He shrugged. 'I can equalise the pressure, and raise the temperature. It might ease the transition when you take them out.'

I nodded. Zoe leant close to him. She had one of her throwing knives in her hand, and she held it next to his cheek. It barely touched him – she ran it slowly down his face, so gently that it might have been mistaken for tenderness. Zach kept perfectly still. I watched how the blade traced his cheekbone, then parted the stubble on his chin. His breath was loud, his lips pressed tightly together. The knife came to rest just beneath his jaw. She placed it very precisely, angled inwards and upwards. I had seen Sally's body with a wound in that exact place. She had taught Zoe well.

'If you do anything to sabotage this, or to cause them more harm – if you so much as sneeze without my permission – I will slice you up.' The knife moved again, caressing his cheek, stopping below his right eye. She lifted the blade from his flesh and held it barely half an inch from his eye. He managed to keep it open, watching the blade, but his eye twitched with the effort of fighting his body's instinct to clench it closed. 'I'll start with the eyes,' Zoe continued. 'And when I'm finished with you, I'll leave you here for The General to deal with, when she comes. And I will not care what it does to Cass.'

We all knew that she was telling the truth.

I leaned in to Zach's other ear. 'If you try anything,' I said to him, 'I'll knife you myself.'

Zoe lifted her knife away from his face, and Zach took a single deep breath.

'Start it,' Zoe said to him, pushing him towards the nearest ladder. 'Whatever you've got to do to get them out safely. Start now.'

'You can't rush this,' Zach said, shaking her hand from his arm. 'It's risky enough as it is.' With one foot on the ladder, he turned back to Zoe. 'It'll take ten minutes, at least, to equalise the pressure. Have your people ready to drain the tanks quickly, when I say the word.' I could see Zoe bridle at taking orders from him, but she turned to Crispin, waiting by the door, and nodded.

I followed him up the short ladder, Zoe and Paloma

close behind. Zoe kept the knife in her hand, even when she was climbing, and never took her eyes from Zach as he walked to the central panel, embedded with buttons and dials. There was just enough light for me to read the various labels: H_2S. CALIBRATE O_2 LEVELS. COMMENCE INDUCED HYPOXIA. The words meant nothing to me. As with so much of what I'd seen in the Ark, the letters became mere shapes etched in metal – they carried no meaning.

But Zach understood them well enough. He turned the dials, pressed the buttons, and once or twice bent low to look more closely at small glass panels behind which colours flashed and moved.

There were shouts outside. Fifty or more of our soldiers filed in, and followed Crispin's directions to station themselves in front of each tank. I saw how each one slowed after entering, and how they cringed as they looked around, some of them halting altogether and having to be prodded back into motion by those behind them. Zoe had warned them that they would encounter horrors inside the refuge, but nothing could have prepared them for this. Everything that the taboo had taught them, everything that they had feared about the machines, was confirmed in this dark room. They stared at the wires, pipes, and tanks, and several of them instinctively drew their weapons, as if the machines could be fought that way.

Zach ignored them, even as some of them passed near us on the gangway, carrying rope ladders to access the tanks from above. They walked hunched over, flinching from the wires overhead.

I tried to concentrate on the people in the tanks, to see whether Zach's busy fingers on the controls were having any effect, and ready to sound the alarm if I saw any changes for the worse. In the tank immediately below me, a young man floated above the others, suspended in the liquid, his head thrown back and arms out wide. His long blond hair drifted upwards, massing near the surface. I would have guessed he was a few years younger than me, though the thick glass lid, and the liquid itself, made it hard to tell.

The minutes passed, and Zach kept working at the panel. I might have imagined it, but I thought that some colour was returning to the floating man's face; I was sure that his right arm, which had no hand, twitched slightly.

'OK,' said Zach. He placed both palms on the panel and exhaled as he looked up. 'Now.'

The soldiers on the gangways opened the lids; I watched their faces contort at the fresh onslaught of the smell. In unison, our soldiers on the ground pulled the levers as Crispin had shown them. A grating sound echoed through the room, and the people in the tanks shifted as the liquid began to slip away. As the fluid lowered, the bodies took on their own weight, and the soldiers had to climb down into the tanks quickly to stop those at the bottom from being crushed.

I was there, beside the top of the tank, when the soldiers carried up the blond boy. He was already stirring. They eased the tube from his mouth and laid him on his back on the gangway. His long hair hung through the metal grating. His flesh was as pale as Paloma's, and so delicate that when he lifted his arm to his face, the ridges of the gangway had already marked the back of his arm, nearly breaking the skin.

He coughed, his stomach drawing up under his ribs with each convulsion. I put my hand under his head to stop it banging on the floor when his coughs seized him. His eyes were open now, and he said a single word: 'Who?' He spoke it to the ceiling, and we had no way of knowing what he meant: *Who am I? Who are you? Who did this to me?* It might even have been no more than an accidental sound, spat from his throat along with tank liquid and phlegm.

All around me, soldiers were rushing. Some were hauling more people from the tanks; others carried them from the gangways down to the floor, and draped them in blankets brought from the carts. Only Zach was motionless, standing by the controls and staring at what he had wrought. Those people, limp as fresh-caught fish, hauled from the tanks and placed on the ground where they twitched, or groaned, or sat up and looked blindly around them.

They were not OK. There was no way of knowing whether any of them would ever be OK again. But they were out, and the raw panic of the tanks, the heavy quality of the underwater silence, had lifted from them. The blond boy close to me was looking around, his eyes focusing first on the ceiling, then on the backlit door, and then on his own hand as he raised it before his face. He turned his hand from one side to the other and back again, examining it minutely. His own body had become unlikely – something he had to learn to believe in.

*

It took most of the day, and none of us thought of stopping to rest. In the complex of buildings there were twelve tank rooms, with hundreds of people in each room. Each time, Zach worked at the control panel and gave the orders. Zoe and I still watched him, the knife never leaving her hand. First we got quicker, as everyone became used to the process, and the soldiers moved more confidently amongst the machines. Then we got slower, as everyone grew tired.

We did not get them all out alive. Some never took a breath; some breathed only a few times; one man had a series of seizures in the tank before they could lift him out, thrashing against the side of the glass. But most found their way back to breath, and even to some form of words. Many cried out. The ones who worried me most were those who didn't: those who sat or lay silent, mouths slack and eyes glazed.

There was only one room left, a smaller antechamber off the last of the main tank rooms. Crispin had gone in ahead of us. Before I could follow him, Zach grabbed me.

'Don't go in there,' he said, a new urgency in his voice.

I looked down at where his hand gripped my forearm, the chain hanging slackly between his shackled wrists.

'Don't tell me what to do,' I said, drawing back my arm.

'This is where we kept some of the early experiments,' he said, lowering his voice. 'The first ones that we tanked. There's nothing you can do for them.'

I paused, still holding the door handle.

'They won't make it,' he said. 'It's only forty people or so. There's no point. Take my word for it.'

I enunciated each word slowly, carefully. 'What did you do to them?'

He spoke quickly. 'It was early days, and we had trouble, at first, replicating what we'd found in the Ark. Didn't have all the right materials. Before we mastered the oesophageal valve tubing, we had to . . .' He paused. '. . .take other measures, to prevent drowning.'

'Stop hiding behind your fancy words,' I spat. 'Tell me what you did.'

'Cass,' Crispin called from within. 'You'd better see this.'

Crispin had been with us when we had dredged the drowned children from the tanks – but there was a tremor in his voice that I had never heard before.

I shoved past Zach and into the room.

These were individual tanks – smaller even than those I'd seen beneath New Wyndham.

It was so dark inside that it was hard at first to see what was different. Then my eyes adjusted to the darkness; in the tank closest to the door, a woman drifted, her red hair floating above her. I stepped close, to see her face.

I had seen so many different variations of the human face. Nina, with her single eye; Crispin, with his blunted features; Paloma, bleached bone-white; Eva, with the second mouth at the back of her neck. So many branded, scarred and starving faces. But I had never seen anything like this: the sealed line of flesh around the tube, where her mouth should have been; her nostrils stitched shut too, so that the whole face was puckered.

'We had to,' Zach said behind me. He was looking with distaste at the woman in the tank. 'They'd have drowned otherwise. It was The General's idea. We sewed the mouth and nostrils shut.'

Crispin's fists were clenched, his knife still in his right hand.

'It's not as painful as it looks,' Zach went on. 'We had their Alpha twins to consider, after all.'

Crispin swallowed, and tried to control the speed of his breath, as he took a step towards Zach.

I got to Zach first. He looked relieved for a moment, when I put my body between him and Crispin. Then I drew back my elbow and swung my fist, hard, at his guts. We doubled over at the same time, with the same noise: a deep grunt of pain. We stayed bent like that, heads nearly touching. I waited for my lungs to accept air again, and for the pain in my stomach to recede.

'Know this,' I said to Zach, as soon as I could muster a wheeze. We were still bent over, bowing at one another, heads close. 'You are the only monster in this room.'

*

Zach had been right: they did not survive. Whatever they had endured, in those first clumsy attempts at tanking, was more than just the mutilations of their faces. When our soldiers, pale-faced and silent, drained the tanks, their occupants never regained consciousness. One man reached up a hand and pulled the tube from the centre of his sealed mouth, leaving a narrow hole that fluttered with each breath, giving a wet purring sound. But there were only five or six breaths, each of them slower than the last.

Paloma and I sat with them. I was glad to have her beside me, for those few minutes in the half-dark room, while the breath ran out of those people like water dripping from a cracked glass. This horror had nothing to do with her, but she shared it with me nonetheless, kneeling beside me while we held their hands and watched them die. She pressed her hand against one man's forehead, her flesh the same white as the scars of his mutilated face. I took the hand of the red-haired woman and held it between my own. I did not pretend to myself that she knew I was there, or that it eased her death. But at such times, skin seeks skin.

I looked across at Paloma, and the emptied tanks behind her. I was thinking of the tanks that Piper and I had found in the Ark, where the leaders of the Ark had entombed themselves. So much had changed since those men had witnessed the blast, and so little.

'The mutation we really needed, after the blast,' I said to Paloma. 'It never happened, did it?' Our bodies had changed, but the human capacity for cruelty was the same as ever. I looked down at the dead woman's face, my brother's handiwork. 'Look at what we've done.'

CHAPTER 24

They were already loading the untanked into the wagons. Beyond the battlefield at the refuge gate, smoke was rising from the south-east. Each time I tried to think of the canyon, and of what Piper was facing there, my breath seized in my throat. I saw how Zoe also kept looking over that way, searching the horizon for clues.

Some of the untanked could walk; draped in blankets or sheets, they staggered in a line towards the wagons, where we helped to lift them up. They settled without complaint on the uneven floor. Others had to be carried. I watched as one of The Ringmaster's Alpha soldiers grimaced and craned his head back as far as possible from the pale woman in his arms. I didn't know if it was her wasted, sodden flesh that repulsed him, or the fact that there was a third eye beneath her brand, but I took a breath to say something.

Zoe had been watching too, and she put her hand on my shoulder before I could speak.

'Enough, Cass,' she said. 'They fought here, they're helping. Don't demand too much of them too soon.'

I was too tired to argue, and turned back to my task.

Zach, close beside me, was helping too. I doubted that he had any desire to, but helping the rest of us in the line made him less conspicuous than standing aside by himself. Even then, every soldier who passed him glared and muttered – the Alphas as much as the Omegas – and we made sure that Zoe or the other guards we trusted were near him at all times. Only the untanked ignored him. They had more right than anyone to lash out at him, but they moved past him, glassy-eyed, and when he reached out to help me lift and steady them as they climbed up onto the back of the wagon, they took his arm without looking in his direction.

'There's somebody here that you should see,' Simon called to me. He was at the front of the next wagon, which was now fully loaded. I climbed up, stepping carefully over the rows of people crammed together. Some were conscious, or at least had their eyes open; others were sleeping while seated – they were packed so tightly that it wasn't possible to fall over. Soldiers were checking them, holding water flasks to the lips of those who were awake.

One man was staring at the sky and shouting, again and again: 'Neil. Neil.' That's what I thought at first: that *Neil* was his name, or the name of somebody he cared for. But then I realised that he might equally have been saying, *Kneel. Kneel.* The final order he'd been given, perhaps, before they tanked him.

Right at the front of the wagon, Crispin was squatting beside a young woman.

'This is the one?' said Simon. 'You're sure?'

Crispin nodded. 'Rhona,' he said. 'Lewis's niece. I knew her most of her life – since Lewis took her in, when she was just a kid. He only came to the island after the Council got hold of her.'

Simon nodded and Crispin left, squeezing the young woman's shoulder as he stood.

She didn't respond. She was sitting against the wagon's wall. Somebody had propped her upright, but she'd slumped down and now half-lay, her head tilted to the side, leaning against the woman next to her.

'You heard what Crispin said?' Simon asked me.

I nodded. I would never forget the name Lewis – not since his blood had soaked up my sleeve, my hand pressed to the wound in his neck that Piper's knife had made. Lewis had been one of Piper's advisers, and had tried to kill me on the island. The girl who now slumped in front of me was the reason he'd tried to kill me, and Zach.

'I knew your uncle,' I said. 'Briefly.'

Zoe, who had followed me, snorted. 'That's one way of describing it.'

Rhona said nothing. Her dark hair was long and tangled, her eyes scanning the sky above my head. She kept lifting her hand and trying to run it through her hair, but her fingers couldn't pass through the matted strands.

I had not made many promises. I'd learned that they were too hard to keep, that the future was slickened with blood. Even Kip and I had made each other no promises – only the promises that the body makes, and all the things that go unspoken.

But back when I knew no better, I'd made Lewis a promise. Now I'd kept it: I had found this girl, her skin still wearing the puffiness of a dead body. I held my water flask to her mouth; she ignored me, and the water trickled down her chin and into the blanket that Crispin had wrapped around her. Her only movement was her hand, trying and failing again and again to pass her fingers through her hair.

'Your uncle was a brave man, in his own way,' I said to her. 'He cared about you.'

She might have nodded, or it might have just been her head dropping forward a little.

I had a comb – a rough, small thing made of wood, which Zoe had carved for me months before. 'To stop you complaining about your hair tangling,' she'd said as she tossed it to me one night across the campfire. I pulled it from my pocket, and shuffled closer to Rhona. Her hair had dried, but the tank liquid had left a sticky patina, and the knots clung. With one hand I bunched all her hair, close to her scalp, so I could work at the ends without hurting her. She closed her eyes after a while, but I kept brushing. I pulled the broken strands of hair from the comb's teeth, until I had made a small dark bird's nest on the floor by my side. One of the clumps was too thick and I couldn't untangle it without hurting her, so I held the comb in my teeth for a minute and carefully sliced the matted patch free.

It seemed a frivolous thing to do – an insignificant thing, in the face of everything that was going on around me. But I did it, insignificant as it was, because it was the only thing that I could do for her.

Twice Simon came, and once Violet, to consult with me. I heard what they said – *Patrols for the outer perimeter; Loading the final wagons, but some will have to ride, even walk* – I may even have responded. But I didn't leave Rhona. I had made few promises, and had even fewer chances to keep them. Lewis was dead – he had died at my feet. Something in me would not allow me to leave this girl clawing at her own hair.

It was perhaps ten minutes that I spent there, and in the whole time she never spoke to me, nor even met my eyes.

I didn't kid myself that I was healing her, or doing anything other than chasing the knots from her hair. But when I'd finished, her impatient hand returned to her head, and she could run it from her scalp to the ends without snagging. She kept doing that, even while she seemed to be sleeping.

One girl, out of the tanks and born again into the air. It was a small thing to set against the blast, and the tanks, and the dead on the battlefield. But when I looked at her, I knew that it was not nothing.

*

The last thing we did before we left was destroy the tanks. It was satisfying at first: the soldiers took their axes to the glass, while others set fires against the wooden walls. I took my turn, borrowing one of Simon's axes and swinging at one of the tanks, watching the crack spread from the point of impact, and swinging again until the tank collapsed into itself, spitting shards back at me.

The whole refuge shrieked with smashed glass, the sound dampened by smoke. But after a while, I gave Simon back his axe, and stepped outside. I'd had enough of broken things.

There was no time to bury the dead. Those who had not survived being taken from the tanks, we had to leave on the floor for the Council's army to find. Outside, the dead of the battlefield had been left where they had fallen – even our own dead. Only those blocking the road had been moved, dragged aside to clear the way for the wagons. We had to prioritise the living now, and every hour's delay would see more dead mounting in the canyon.

We left in the late afternoon, the sun still hot. When we rode out, near the front of the column of wagons, it was the first time I had been beyond the broken gates since the battle.

During the night of fighting, the dark had felt like a curse. But now that I saw the battlefield by daylight, I longed for darkness. Two layers of haze sat over the slope: the shimmer of heat, coming off everything and blurring the horizon; and the second haze, the swarms of flies that buzzed, discordant, over the dead.

The bodies we passed, as we rode through in our jolting convoy of wagons and riders, were only half the story. All across the land, more dead lay in their homes, killed by swords they never saw, in a war they never fought.

Zach was riding next to me, his voice close to my ear. 'Is this what you wanted?' he asked.

I kept my gaze straight ahead. 'I wanted to save people,' I said.

'You wanted to feel like a saviour,' he replied.

'That's not true.' My voice lacked conviction.

'Look around you.'

The road had been cleared of bodies, but the horses moved uneasily, jerking their heads and skittering at the swarms of flies. My nostrils narrowed at the stench, and I had to press a hand to my mouth and take shallow breaths, to hold back the vomit.

'You can't tell me that this is better than the tanks,' he said, gesturing at the dead on either side. Even without the flies and the blood, there would be no mistaking those bodies for anything other than dead. The shapes they made were wrong: something about the angles of their necks, and the stiffness in their splayed limbs.

'It doesn't have to be war or the tanks,' I said. 'They're not our only choices.'

I glanced, without thinking, at Paloma, riding a little way

to my right. When I turned back to Zach, I saw that his eyes were on her too.

*

Getting the people out of the tanks was only the beginning. The refuge was no stronghold – our victory had shown that. The hardest part would be moving the untanked back to New Hobart. On horseback, travelling by day, Refuge 6 would have been nearly a week's ride from New Hobart. We didn't have that long. Piper and The Ringmaster couldn't hold the canyon for much longer, and The General probably realised already that the march on the canyon had been a decoy. Her soldiers would be finding a way to swarm over the river, to the north. They would flank our force at the canyon, and they would come after us. If they caught up with us, battle-weary and laden with the helpless untanked, before we reached the stronghold of New Hobart, then everything we had done would be for nothing. So we rode all day and into the night, stopping only for a few hours at a time, when the horses began to flag. When darkness blinded our lookouts, I didn't dare to sleep; I concentrated fiercely, trying not to think about Piper or the hundreds of soldiers in the canyon.

Crammed in the wagons, the untanked were mainly silent as we rode, and did whatever they were told. It had made our job easier, but I would have been happier to see some signs of defiance, instead of the blankness of the faces we'd shepherded into rows, helping the weakest onto the carts. Those who could walk, the strongest two thousand, were marched off north, surrounded by a squadron of The Ringmaster's soldiers, towards his garrisons. It should have been half a day's journey, but as I watched the untanked stumbling slowly across the plain, I knew what a vulnerable position we had placed them in.

Zoe rode close to me. 'Can you feel anything, from the canyon?'

'Nothing useful,' I said to her. The worst aspect of my visions was that the horrors I saw were all part of our plan. We knew there would be fighting and death – we had planned it ourselves. Nothing that I saw – not the blood, or the swords – was unexpected, or of any use to us. What we needed to know was how long it would last: how long before the Council repelled the charge completely, overthrew the army or flanked them from the north, and came charging back through the canyon. We had sent scouts east, back to the canyon, to carry the message to Piper and The Ringmaster that we were on the road. In another day our wagon convoy should have a safe lead, and our soldiers could retreat from the canyon. But we did not know whether by then a retreat would be possible, or whether there would be anyone left to retreat.

Even if our army was still holding the canyon, there were Council garrisons and squadrons that had not been caught in the trap of Wyndham. One of them came at us on the dawn of the second day. Eighty soldiers or more, riding hard from the south. Our scouts spotted them from a mile away, the dust that their hoofs raised on the dry road. It was a brief skirmish – we outnumbered them, but had to shield the lumbering column of wagons. Simon shouted for the wagons to be circled, and for the guard to draw tight around them. Zoe herded me, Zach and Paloma close to the wagons. Our horses jostled against one another, and we huddled between our shields and the wall of the nearest wagon.

The strangest thing about the fight was how the untanked

didn't react at all, not only when the attackers were grappling with our soldiers around the perimeter, but even when arrows came at the wagons themselves. Even when an arrow struck a dark-haired man in the wagon nearest me, he didn't make a sound, and those around him didn't react. They just continued to sit, packed close together, the arrow's shaft protruding from the man's bare back. I waited for his scream, but it didn't come. It was as though his body didn't belong to him, and nor did its pain. His mouth was open; blood trickled from the corner, and after a few moments he tipped forward slightly, coming to rest against the back of the woman in front.

The Council squadron could not have expected to win – they were eighty men against hundreds. They concentrated, instead, on causing maximum damage, hurling themselves against our ranks. Even from where I huddled, shield raised, with rows of soldiers between me and the attackers, I could feel the desperation of their assault. I could hear it, too: the low grunts, and the swearing, and the screams. A frenzy of sound and movement, closing in around the silent wagons. More arrows were unleashed; they punctured flesh, but they didn't puncture the silence of the untanked.

When the fighting subsided, the attackers were dead. It was all for nothing, I thought, as their bodies were dragged from the road so that the wagons could proceed. Paloma, on my left, was grim-faced. We were moving again, riding west. I closed my eyes and the flames came. For the first time, I thought: *Let them come. Not just to Elsewhere – everywhere. If this is what we've made of the world, then let the flames come.*

Zoe was shouting something at me, but I could only see her lips move, the angry motions of her sword slicing the sky as she gesticulated. All I could hear was the flames, and their promise to wipe this ugliness away.

'Throw down the dead,' she shouted again, to me and to Crispin, Violet and Ash beyond me.

She must have seen us hesitate.

'Do it,' she yelled impatiently. 'Lighten the load for the horses, and make room.'

We obeyed. There were at least twenty dead in the wagons, propped upright by the crush of people. Two were in the wagon closest to us. Violet had already clambered aboard, and was dragging a dead man to the side. I passed Zach my reins, climbing from the horse straight to the side of the wagon, and picked my way through the seated people to where a dead woman sat. Her long blonde hair hung over her face; the blanket had slipped from around her shoulders, and was held up only by the arrow buried in the back of her neck. I picked her up. The tanks had left her lighter than any adult woman should have been, but it was still hard to lift her. My arms hooked under hers, hauling her backwards on the unsteady wagon, as her hanging legs dragged over the heads of the others, who didn't even have room to shift out of the way.

I meant to lower her gently over the side, but the wagon was jerking, and her right side was slick with blood. She slithered from my grip, tumbling several yards to the ground. The silence of the rest of those in the wagon was worse than the small gasp that came from Paloma.

When I was mounted again, Zach looked behind us at the woman's body, dumped in the dust at the side of the road.

'Do you think she was grateful?' he asked.

I didn't look at him. My hands were coated with the woman's blood, growing tacky on the reins.

'Zoe made a speech about building a different world. Do you think that woman enjoyed her time in this brave new world of yours?' he went on.

I turned to look at him. 'You keep needling me,' I said. 'Trying to provoke me, trying to make me doubt what I'm doing.'

He raised his left eyebrow slightly.

'Everything you do only proves my point,' I said.

He waited, his eyebrow frozen in its cocked position.

'You know exactly how to provoke me,' I said. 'Exactly what to do to frighten me, or set me against the others.' I paused. 'It's because you know me so well. Just like I know you. Because we grew up together. You can pretend, as much as you like, that we're different creatures, from different worlds. And you're right: we're not the same. We've made different choices. But you know me.' I shrugged. 'Just like I know you.'

I looked back at the woman's body, already just a shape in the distance. 'You did this. You and The General.' I gestured at the wagons around us. 'Stop telling me that this is my choice,' I said. 'You chose this. I won't be made to feel guilty any more. I'm your twin. I grew up with you, and I'll die with you. But in between, I won't carry your crimes.'

*

I'd never imagined it would be possible to sleep while riding, but there were moments, during those nights and days of our retreat to New Hobart, when I'd have sworn I was asleep, my body propelled by nothing but urgency and the hoof falls of the horses at either side. When Crispin passed around jerky to eat, I was so tired that even chewing felt impossible. And every time we stopped, half of the rest period was spent making sure that the untanked ate, or at least drank.

In the morning of the third day, we paused at a pond by the road, in a clear spot safe from ambushes. As soon as we dismounted, the horses jostled to the water's edge, pushing each other aside to drink before we could fill our water flasks. That was what saved us. Within a minute, the first horses began to thrash. A grey mare dropped to her knees, then subsided, thrashing, on her side, churning the water with her kicks.

Simon screamed his orders, and the soldiers scrambled to get the rest of the horses away from the water.

'They've poisoned the pond,' Zoe said, spitting at the ground. 'They knew we'd be coming this way.'

Eight horses died: five instantly, and the rest when Simon ordered their throats slit to stop their agony. From then on we only refilled the water flasks and barrels from fast-moving streams.

*

When we were half a day from New Hobart, we saw dust darkening the horizon, and for a moment my stomach clenched. But the fear didn't stick – I knew already that these were our own troops, marching out from New Hobart to usher us home. I exhaled and breathed in again, and it felt like the first breath I had taken since we had left New Hobart more than a week ago.

When they were close enough I could see June leading them, the soldiers marching behind her hunched back. Zoe, Paloma and I rode forward to join Simon at the front, to ask June whether there had been any reprisal attacks on New Hobart.

'They came at us two days ago,' she said. 'But it was only their locally stationed troops – they didn't even breach the outer perimeter. No sign yet of any reinforcements from Wyndham.'

Simon nodded. June was looking down the convoy, the long tail of wagons crammed with the pale men and women. Six thousand people had been in the tanks at Refuge 6. Four hundred had not survived, and another two thousand had been sent off to The Ringmaster's garrisons further north. On the journey, we had lost another fifty – mostly in the ambush, and some who had refused to drink or eat and had quietly died in those cramped wagons, and been lowered over the sides as we moved. Their bodies marked our road from the refuge to New Hobart like milestones. But there were still more than three and a half thousand of the untanked with us now.

The dead that we had left on the road meant there was enough room on the wagons for some of us to climb aboard. It wasn't only that I wanted a break from riding – I also wanted to be with the untanked for this final stretch, as we brought them home. Zach and Paloma climbed onto the wagon with me, though Zach stayed pressed against the back wall, leaning away from those who sat nearby. Crispin, Ash, and Violet rode beside the wagon, and Zoe was standing at the front, close to the driver.

Some of the untanked looked up the hill towards the town, as we neared the gate. Many were still silent and listless, but some, in the last few days, had begun to edge closer to language again.

'I know this place,' said one of the men, pointing up the hill, and grabbing the shoulder of the man sitting in front of him. 'New Hobart,' he said, the words surprising him as much as they surprised me. He was smiling, and even though the last week had been one of the hardest in my life, I was smiling too.

Our journey from the refuge was an evacuation – but in that moment, as we came through the eastern gate not long after dawn, it felt like a victory march. At the front of the wagon, Zoe was standing with one arm wrapped around the corner post. She swung around to look back at me, grinning as she squinted at the bright sun. Paloma, sitting by Zoe's feet, looked up at her and said something – I could see her lips moving but couldn't hear her words over the rattling wagon, and the whoops of the soldiers who rode beside us, and the sound of the hoof falls clanging as we reached the cobbled roads of the town. We were home.

I should have known not to trust my joy.

Zoe swung her head around to the east, as if looking for something; then her whole body went slack, and she dropped from the wagon like a hanged man when the rope is cut.

CHAPTER 25

Paloma screamed, already scrambling over the wagon's side. The wagon was still moving when I jumped over the back and ran alongside it, pushing Violet and Ash aside to reach where Zoe lay, face down. I scanned the wall behind us, looking for an archer, trying to work out whether we'd ridden into a trap. But there was nothing to be seen, and when I grabbed Zoe by the shoulder and hauled her over onto her back, there was no blood on her. Just the scabs and bruises of the battle, already yellowing at the edges.

I knew then that it was out of our hands. Crispin bent to help me with Zoe, but when he saw that she bore no new injuries he straightened, swearing, and turned to look back through the gate, beyond the last wagons, towards the way we had come. Zach was craning over the edge of the now-stopped wagon, sharp-eyed, assessing the situation.

Only Paloma still didn't realise what had happened.

'What's wrong with her?' she shouted, and pulled at Zoe's shirt, as if that would reveal some bloodless wound that we had missed. 'Do something!' she screamed, so close that I felt her breath on my face. 'Do something.'

There was nothing I could do. When I pressed my finger to Zoe's neck, I could just make out a pulse, the vein barely twitching beneath my fingers.

'It's not her,' I said to Paloma. 'It's Piper.' And it had never seemed crueller, this trick of history, this knot that the blast had tied between bodies, twin to twin. Zoe, pale as the dust she lay in, and Piper so far away. Her body wearing his dying.

She was heavy – so tall and muscular that it took three of us to lift her into the back of the last wagon when it came through the gate. I laid her head and shoulders down, but it was Piper's body I pictured, broken somewhere in the middle of battle. He was alive – but based on Zoe's barely breath, he was no more than that.

People were gathered in the town's streets to see us coming in. I didn't know what they were expecting when they'd heard we were approaching, or whether they had planned to be cheering for us. Instead, they were silent and still, except for those at the back, jostling and craning to get a better glimpse of what had come through the gate: the wounded soldiers; the wasted, motionless people crammed into the wagons, oblivious to the watching crowds. And, in the rear of the final wagon, Zoe laid out, and me and Paloma scrambling to find something to wrap her in.

It seemed to take us a long time to reach the Tithe Collector's office, past the rows of staring faces. Soldiers were waiting at the doorway, ready to help the untanked from the wagons, and escort them to the beds that had been prepared for them. Two of the large rooms at the back had been set aside as makeshift dormitories. There, we laid Zoe down with the others. She looked the worst of any of them. Her skin was grey now, and clammy. The rows of people next to her were quiet but conscious, but Zoe was utterly still, her mouth hanging slackly open.

Elsa found us there, in the half-darkened room. She stepped over the others to reach us, moving as fast as her twisted legs would allow.

'Where is he?' she said, as soon as she had taken in Zoe's stare.

I shook my head. 'They were still holding the canyon when we left the refuge. It was the only reason we were able to get away safely. It's five days' journey, even after they retreat . . .'

My voice trailed off. I didn't add the *if*. There were too many *ifs*: if Piper lived that long. If he wasn't left to die, slowly, on the battlefield. If somebody dragged him to safety. If they were able to pull back from the canyon, and to make it all the way back here. Too many reasons why every breath of Zoe's felt like a miracle.

From the moment I'd announced my plan for the decoy attack, I had known that Piper would choose to lead them into the canyon. And I had known that there would be a cost for the lives of the thousands we'd freed from the tanks. It felt selfish to find myself staggering now that the dead might include Piper and Zoe. If I had to make the choice again, knowing exactly what that cost would be, would I do it? This was a question that I couldn't answer, not even to myself. And it was not my choice, I knew – Piper had made the choice himself, and so had Zoe.

*

We moved her back to the holding house that night. Forty people from the tanks were also carted down, to be housed in Elsa's dormitory. All the beds were used, and even then some of the untanked had to make do with the floor. My bed and Zach's had been dragged into the dining room. I'd suggested Sally and Xander's old room, but Simon had insisted on a room that overlooked the courtyard, not the street, and I was glad not to be sleeping in the room where Sally had died. In the corner of the dining room, above Zach's bed, Simon affixed the steel ring himself, for Zach's shackles to pass through.

The holding house was full again, as it had been when I'd first come there. But instead of the noisy children, it was the untanked, carrying with them the silence of the tanks. They wandered, in ill-fitting clothes that the townspeople had donated, or that Elsa had pieced together from sheets and blankets. Many of them spent the days sitting in the courtyard, and even though their skin burned easily, I couldn't blame them for wanting to feel the sun, after years in the tanks.

I'd made sure that Rhona was amongst those brought to Elsa's house. I watched her the next morning, sitting on the ground in the courtyard and sketching in the dust with a stick. I sidled closer, to see if I could make out what she was drawing. They were childlike outlines: a house, and then a few letters, the start of a word that she never finished. Then a mountain, and then the house again. After each sketch, she swept her stick sideways, scraping it through the dust, erasing what she had made, to start again. When I came back through the courtyard, hours later, the sun had shifted west, the shadows creeping towards the roof, but she was still there, drawing in the dirt.

Paloma moved through the house like an angry ghost. She spoke only to ask for things that she needed for Zoe: a fresh sheet; something to pin over the window to keep the flies out. When we brought her food, she seemed to eat and drink not by choice but only because her body remembered how.

All of us were just waiting: keeping a vigil over Zoe, and waiting for news of Piper. If the news was good, it would come via the eastern road. If it was bad, we would hear it first through Zoe, when her breath stopped altogether.

Scouts had brought news from Wyndham, but it was days old by the time it reached us. The fighting in the canyon had been vicious. Our saboteurs had brought down the bridges completely, and The General's forces had quickly realised that they were trapped. But they had the canyon's natural defences in their favour, and greater numbers. They had pushed hard and ceaselessly at our soldiers blocking the canyon. By the second day, Council soldiers were crossing the river in a hastily assembled fleet. Our archers, on the river's northern shore, had held some of them back, and the river itself, always hungry, had claimed many lives. The General's army had built rafts to shift horses across, though at least one raft had been tipped by panicked horses, and all aboard drowned. But eventually a force had made it across – enough to attack our archers, and to secure the crossing. Some of the Council troops had ridden to Refuge 6, and found the place emptied, and us gone. There had been attacks on our convoys sent north – *substantial casualties*, the young scout had reported to Simon, and I'd slammed my hand on the table.

'Don't skirt around it,' I'd said. 'What does that mean? How many?'

She had bitten her bottom lip, and taken a big breath.

'The convoy to North Haven reached the garrison intact. But the Council soldiers caught up with the second convoy, in the Ithon valley. They killed about half of the untanked,' she said. 'Nearly five hundred – and at least fifty of our soldiers, too.'

I wished I had not asked. Simon swore, all three of his hands clenched. I looked beyond him, through the window into the courtyard. Rhona was there, and several others, eyes closed as they turned their faces to the sun. She was still drawing in the dirt with her stick. I felt that all my plans and calculations had been as pointless as her scrablings in the dust. How to calculate the value of those lives, and the lives lost?

I turned back to the scout.

'That's it?' Simon said to her.

She nodded. 'Last I saw, our forces were flanked at the canyon, the Council pressing them from both sides.'

Simon dismissed the scout with a gesture, and took a deep breath as she left.

'They held the canyon, Cass,' he said. 'Longer than we could have hoped.'

'Don't talk like that,' I said.

'Like what?'

'Like you've given up already. Like it's all over.'

He exhaled. 'You've seen Zoe. You heard the scout. We need to work out where to go from here. Try to secure the loyalty of what's left of The Ringmaster's army, so we can hold on to New Hobart without him. Concentrate on getting Paloma to the boats, and back to Elsewhere.'

Fire scorched my mind at the mention of Elsewhere, and I staggered as I stood.

'It's not over,' I said through the flames. 'I know Zoe. I know Piper. It's not over.'

*

For those five nights, I was afraid to sleep, and afraid to be idle. When Xander had been missing, I'd dreamed of his body, and known that he was dead. I didn't want the same thing to happen with Piper. If he and Zoe were going to die, I didn't want to know. Instead, night and day, I kept myself busy. I helped Elsa: sewing clothes for the untanked; cooking and scrubbing pots until the skin of my hands cracked and bled. The visions came anyway, both awake and asleep, but they told me nothing new: only that the world would burn. At times, after the visions, I found it took minutes, or longer, for me to be able to speak again, and even then my tongue stumbled. The words were being scorched away.

Many of the untanked had injuries that were still healing – sores on their too-soft skin from the days of riding on the wagon; wounds from the attacks on our convoy. We dressed their wounds, gave poppy tincture and henbane for the pain, and valerian at night to help them sleep. We tried to get them to eat, too. It might have been a mercy that they didn't eat more – even since regaining Wreckers' Pass, we had little to give them – but I saw Rhona's collarbones propping up the flesh above her sunken chest, and wished that she would take more of the broth that I offered her.

There was no denying it: Kip's quick physical recovery from the tanks seemed to have been due to his strong Alpha constitution. For the Omegas, the process was slower, and less certain. And even Kip had suffered the mental effects. His past had been lost to him – erased like a boat's wake, forgotten by water. He'd had to reassemble himself, without any idea of who he was, or what he had done.

Now the thousands we had pulled from the tanks would have to do it too: take whatever pieces of them we had been able to dredge from the tanks, and try to assemble them into a life.

Most of them struggled to sleep. At night, while Zach and I lay in the dining room, I could hear their footsteps wandering through the house. They existed out of time. They had woken from a past they couldn't remember, into a present that they couldn't grasp. Perhaps that was why I felt at home with them – my own grasp of time was so uncertain that I shared their sense of being unmoored, adrift in days.

Paloma ignored the untanked and their wanderings, just as she ignored our pleas for her to rest or eat. She refused to leave Zoe's side. When I went into their room, on the second day, she didn't even look up.

'She's worse,' she said, one hand pressing a cloth to Zoe's head. She was right: Zoe's skin was dry and pale, her lips flaking. Occasionally her eyes flickered open, but her pupils had rolled back, so that all that showed were the whites. I listened to her breath. After each exhalation there was a pause, so long that when the inhalation finally came it felt like nothing more than chance. Paloma was holding her breath too, each time, listening for Zoe's next breath to start.

'This is the first time I've understood your brother,' Paloma said. I looked up, and she spoke again, quickly, her words falling over one another. 'It's not that I think the tanks are right. I know it's wrong – I knew that even before I'd seen Refuge Six. But now—' she paused and looked down again at Zoe. 'Now I can understand, at least partly, what drove him to do it. And why some of the Alphas have gone along with it.'

I remembered how, when Zach and I were children, we had watched our father die, his twin's sickness slowly killing him. I'd seen the fear and anger in Zach's face then, and I recognised it now in Paloma's.

That was when the vision came. Vision wasn't the right word, though – I saw nothing but darkness, and pinpricks of light. But I could hear Piper's breath and feel the horse beneath him, jolting his broken body.

'They're coming,' I said.

Simon sent two squadrons out to meet them. I begged to ride with them, but he was firm. 'There's danger enough without seeking it out. If they're coming back, The General's troops won't be far behind.'

Instead he allowed me to go to the gate, escorted by Violet.

'Is this the advance group?' she asked me, as she watched the bedraggled cluster of soldiers trace the eastern road, towards Simon and his riders.

I shook my head. 'That's all of them.'

Of the four hundred who had marched into the canyon, barely sixty had made it back in this limping convoy. The majority of the soldiers were on foot; a few were mounted. Stretchers were swung between horses to carry the worst of the injured. As our soldiers drew closer, I couldn't see a single one without injuries. As he came into view, I saw that even The Ringmaster had his left arm in a sling, and a slash running from his eye to his jaw, twisting his mouth upwards at the side. *Physical perfection*, he'd said about Alphas when we'd argued about the untwinning – but I could take no joy in seeing his mutilated face.

He was on foot – he had given up his horse for one of the more seriously injured. When I greeted him at the gate, he didn't bother with small talk.

'They're coming after us. Harried us on the Asher Pass, and again at the western edge of the swamps. They've been to the refuge. Reprisals already, at Shute Gully. Raids, and whole settlements torched. Sounds like they've taken them all to Refuge Three.'

'It's not going to stop, is it,' I said.

'It's easier to start a war than end one,' he said. 'We made a choice. Not just when we attacked the refuge – even before that, when we freed New Hobart. The General was always going to strike back.'

His words were hard, but his shoulders slumped, and he looked tired. 'How many did you get out alive?'

'More than five thousand, all told,' I said. I think he smiled – with his newly twisted face, it was hard to tell.

'Can we hold them off?' I asked.

He looked back at his diminished army, the rows of hobbling and bloodied soldiers filing through the gate. 'For now.'

*

They brought Piper to Elsa's – four soldiers carrying the stretcher, walking as solemnly and slowly as if they were taking him to his grave.

If I'd had questions about what had happened in the canyon, his body told me the whole story. On his arm and hand, the half-healed nicks and slashes of the initial fighting. Bruises days old now, and settling into purple and yellow. Then the newer wound, messy and total, from when they had been overrun. It was a blow to the side of his head: not the clean slash of a sword, but a knock from an axe or a sword hilt, leaving the flesh crushed, rather than cut. Elsa did her best to stitch the wound, but much of the left side of his scalp was a mass of blood and pulped flesh. In several places, the skull was visible. The sheer whiteness of it looked oddly clean, amidst the mess of bloodied skin.

'I think it broke the skull as well,' Elsa said, as I bent to peer at the wound. 'But sometimes it's best if that happens. If the skull doesn't break, then there's nowhere for the swelling to go . . .' She trailed off, and I thought of Piper's brain, crushed against bone.

There was a line of blood from the corner of his mouth to his chin. It had dried into black scales. I washed it off, pressing the wet cloth against the scabbed blood to soften it.

I didn't realise, until I looked down, that I had put my hand on his chest, to reassure myself of its slight rising and falling. On the next bed, Zoe's chest moved in time with his.

I only learned on the second day how he'd been saved. Elsa had sent me to the sitting room to fetch more tea tree oil for Piper's head. The window was unshuttered, only the bars between me and the street. Violet was on duty outside the front door, talking to an Alpha soldier who had been at the canyon.

'You see the state of him?' said the man.

'Not looking good,' said Violet.

'Should've seen him when the boss hauled him out,' the man said. 'I thought he was already dead. Couldn't work out why the boss was bothering to carry a body back to our lines.'

*

That night, when The Ringmaster came back down to Elsa's, I was in the kitchen washing the blood from Piper's shirt. I'd soaked it in cold water all day – that was best for blood stains, I'd learned. I had learned a lot about blood, these last few months.

I turned, my hands still in the basin, to look over my shoulder at The Ringmaster as he poured himself a mug of water. I tried to picture him carrying Piper's unconscious body. Piper was taller than him, and stockier. It couldn't have been easy, let alone in the midst of the battle.

'I heard that it was you who carried Piper out of the fighting,' I said.

He didn't stop pouring the water from the jug. 'It doesn't matter who got him,' he said.

For a few moments there was no sound but the clatter of him setting the jug down on the table.

'Thank you,' I said.

He shrugged stiffly. 'We need him. Especially after what happened with Sally.' He sat down, took a swig from his cup. 'We need somebody for the Omegas to rally behind.' He drank again. 'And he had my back, when we were holding them off at the canyon mouth. Saved me a couple of times.'

Less than a month ago, Piper and I had been skinning rats in this same room and laughing together about the things that would be left out of histories, if anybody ever wrote them. I wondered, now, about the stories that The Ringmaster and I would tell ourselves, if we survived long enough to look back on this. How much we would leave out. Those who had died because of orders we'd given, decisions that we'd made. The bodies in the canyon. The bodies we'd left at the refuge.

I kept scrubbing the shirt. The stain had gone, except around the edges. A stubborn brown outline of blood, like an island drawn on a map.

When the shirt was hanging in front of the fire, The Ringmaster and I crossed the courtyard into the small room where Zoe and Piper were laid out, side by side. Paloma gave no sign that she'd registered our presence. She was sitting by Zoe's bed, the chair pulled close so that she could lean her arm and head on the mattress, close to Zoe's. The window was open, but the room was still steeped in that sickroom smell – too much breath and not enough air.

Piper's breathing was loud, each inhalation a scraping of air through bloodied lungs. I thought nothing could be worse than that sound, the gurgling and wheezing noisy in the cramped room. Then his breath went quiet, and that was worse: time and again I had to press my ear close to his face to check that he was still breathing at all. With his stillness, and the precisely carved ridges of his muscles, he looked like a statue. His dark skin had paled and his lips were blue at the edges. When I took his hand, his fingers were cold and stiff in mine.

'Aren't there more blankets?' I asked Paloma.

'He left half of his blood in the canyon,' The Ringmaster said. 'Blankets aren't going to change that.'

I ignored him, and pulled the blanket high under Piper's chin, letting my hand linger for a moment there.

'You should rest,' I said to Paloma. 'Eat something, too.'

She ignored me. Her hair was so dirty that it looked darker than its usual white blonde. It hung forward over her face as she stared at Zoe. When The Ringmaster left, she didn't even look up.

'Are you all right?' I asked her, when his footsteps had retreated across the courtyard.

It was a stupid question, and she didn't bother answering. I tried again.

'You need to go to the coast,' I said. 'We'll take you to the ships. In another few weeks the winds will turn, and you'll be able to sail.'

The Ringmaster's scouts had reported from the west: *The Rosalind* was fully repaired and fit to sail, with two ships from The Ringmaster's own coastal squadrons nearly ready to accompany her. But the scouts also reported increased activity from The General's fleet: patrols of the black ships sweeping along the coast, and the Council's dockyard at Whitcliff noisy, night and day, with building. When spring ended, the southerly winds that would carry Paloma and our fleet north to warn Elsewhere would also carry the Council's ships, searching. That was if Elsewhere's own ships didn't reach us first, and stumble into the Council's hands.

'I'm not leaving her like this,' Paloma said.

'The General's troops are gathering. You're not safe here.'

'I'm not safe anywhere,' she replied. She looked up at me. 'You were the one who taught me that. I thought I believed you, about the Council. But now that I've seen the refuge, I know it's real. They're going to bomb my home. Even if I get there and warn them – what difference will it make? You can't run from the bomb. You can't evacuate a million people.' She closed her eyes for a moment.

'Anyway,' she went on, 'it makes no difference. I'm not leaving.' Her hand rested on top of Zoe's. 'I didn't know what to expect, when I signed on as emissary.' I was surprised when she gave a small smile. There had been little enough to smile about these last days.

'Of all the things that have happened,' she said, looking at Zoe. 'Finding *The Rosalind*. Surviving the storms, and finding another country, where there are still twins. None of it has been more unlikely than her.'

*

Zach avoided the untanked as much as he could. If one of them passed him in the corridor while he was being led through to the kitchen, he flinched and pressed back against the wall. More and more, he stayed in our room, sitting on his bed, refusing to come to the courtyard or kitchen for meals. I didn't complain – I preferred it that way, not having him with me and Elsa at the table.

I found him, one morning, staring through our bedroom window at Rhona. She was sitting on the ground in the courtyard, eating an orange from Elsa's tree, concentrating on it with a single-minded focus. The pips that she found, she put on the gravel in front of her, placing each one with great care in a row. I'd seen her do things like this before: straightening each of the forks on the table, or combing the ashes from the kitchen fire into neat lines. I understood, or thought I did, her attempt to make some kind of order in a world that made so little sense to her.

'Not much use to you, are they?' Zach said. 'I don't exactly see them swelling the ranks of your army.'

'It's not about *use*,' I said. 'That's always been your problem.'

'Look around you,' he said. 'You've killed off half your army to fish out a bunch of half-wits. The General's closing in by the day. I'd say I'm not the only one with problems.'

He turned back to the window, his shoulder blades prominent under his shirt. He'd always been thin, but the angles of his face had taken on a new sharpness. I saw how his hand played at his jawbone. The nails of his two biggest fingers were chipped and blackened. He was afraid – I knew it, because I recognised my own fear in him. Each day, the scouts brought news of more of The General's troops massing outside.

'What does The General want from you?'

I'd asked him that so many times, since The General had come to demand that we hand him over. He'd never given an answer – not to me, nor to The Ringmaster or Piper, when they'd interrogated him. I wondered, now, whether even under torture he'd been as desperate as he'd made it seem. He'd given up nothing but Blackwood, which had gained us nothing and cost us Tash's life.

But with The General's army closing around the town, he had grown more agitated every day. Now, for the first time, when I asked him about The General he didn't ignore me.

'She thought I was disposable,' he said, keeping his back to me as he stared out the window. 'She's had time, since then, to realise she was wrong.'

'Why?' I said. 'You've said it yourself – it was The Confessor who really understood the machines, and found a way to get them working again.' The Confessor was dead – what Kip had started with his leap, I had finished when I'd consigned her body to the waters of the flooded Ark. 'So what does The General want from you?'

He turned to look at me.

'The Confessor might have had the way with the machines, but she worked for me. She was too smart to trust The General. The General's come to understand that now, I think. She's realised that she needs me.' He looked out the window again, towards the east, where her troops were gathering. 'It started with me,' he said. 'And it ends with me.'

He gave a laugh, high and bleak, and none of my threats and rants could persuade him to say anything further. I did not understand what he meant, but I knew he was right about one thing: the end was coming.

CHAPTER 26

I was with Paloma in the stuffy sickroom later that night, when one of Zoe's eyes peeled partly open. I didn't want to hope for too much, at first – we had seen her eyes flicker briefly open before, and it had never meant anything. But this time her mouth opened too, and she gave a low grunt of pain.

Paloma exhaled through a sob. For days she had barely spoken, lips pinched around her silence. Now she bent low over Zoe's face, whispering and crying and kissing her forehead, and I felt that I should look away.

I turned to watch Piper instead, and waited. When he first opened his eyes, he didn't seem to see me.

'Can you hear me?' I asked, as I saw his eyes scanning the ceiling.

He nodded, then winced at the movement, and cleared his throat.

'Did you do it?' His voice was always deep, but now it was croaky with disuse.

'Yes,' I said. It was a lie, only as much as all words are lies, skimming over the surface of things, and leaving out the messiness of truth. There were things Piper would see for himself, eventually: that the thousands we had got out of the tanks were broken, in ways that we might never understand. That hundreds had been lost in the refuge and in the convoys, as well as at the canyon. That the Council's forces from Wyndham were now massing on the plains outside New Hobart.

But for now, for him, I let it be that simple: *Yes.*

*

I tried not to listen when Paloma and Zoe were whispering together, in those first hours after Zoe and Piper had woken. I busied myself with caring for him – spooning into his mouth the broth that Elsa had made him; warning him away when he tried to touch his wound, which still seeped into its bandages; answering his questions about what had happened in the days since I'd left him at the canyon. I sat between his bed and Zoe's, my back to her and Paloma, so that they could have at least the illusion of privacy. But it was a small room, and I heard everything.

Zoe had surfaced more quickly than Piper, and was already trying to sit, and even talking about getting up, despite Paloma's protestations. When Paloma insisted, for the third time, that Zoe lie back, I heard Zoe slump back down on to the pillow.

'It wasn't meant to be like this,' she grumbled. 'You taking care of me.'

'Meant to?' Paloma laughed. 'As if any of this was meant to happen.'

Zoe's voice, though, was serious. 'I used to think I could keep you safe,' she said. 'When you first arrived, I thought I'd be able to protect you, until it was time to send you home. It was as if my life, and my world, were a nightmare that you'd accidentally wandered into.'

There was a pause while Zoe swallowed, her throat still dry. 'But there isn't any waking from this,' she continued. 'I can't keep you safe, let alone Elsewhere—'

Paloma interrupted. 'I wasn't *wandering* anywhere. I chose to join the expedition ships. I chose to come aboard *The Rosalind*, and not to flee once I heard what your Council was capable of. I chose this.' I had my back to them, but in the glass of the water jug that I held, I saw Paloma lean forward and place her hand, slowly and deliberately, in Zoe's. 'All of this.'

*

Zoe recovered quickly – by the second day she was up and about, crossing the courtyard and getting in Elsa's way in the kitchen. But Paloma was never quite the same with Piper. In those next few days, as he continued his halting recovery, I noticed the new reserve in Paloma's interactions with him. She spoke to him just the same as ever, and helped him willingly, in those early days when even sitting up in bed was difficult. But she was aware of him all the time; the first day he managed to shuffle from the bed to the window, she watched his every movement. As he began to move more freely around the holding house, I noticed how she sometimes instinctively shifted herself between him and Zoe, as if her body, standing between them, could block the bond that gave them a shared death.

Paloma had known already what the fatal bond was, but until she saw Zoe fall, she hadn't seen what it really meant. It had been an abstraction, right up until the moment she'd seen Zoe drop from the wagon. Only now, I thought, did she really understand what the twinning was, and what her arrival had meant to us. The power to end the twinning was, in its own way, a power as great as the blast.

Those were long and uneasy days. Summer was drawing closer, and each day by mid-morning it was already so hot that the bars on the window burned my face if I leant my head against them. I still tried, every day, to seek the blast machine, but it evaded me. Most days I could sense nothing at all. The days on which I could sense something were even more frustrating, because the location remained capricious: I felt the fire calling me to the north-east, but days later, I would wake just as certain it was south. I was used to feeling unmoored in time – that was a seer's lot. But now I was coming unmoored in space as well, and this was a new kind of disorientation, a new fear.

Piper and Zoe were recovering, Zoe first and Piper more slowly. The untanked were also learning their lives again. More of them spoke now: just a few words here and there, leavening the silence of their dormitories. Some had remembered their names; others had begun to ask questions: *Where are we? What happened?* Rhona spoke little, but turned immediately when I called her by name. I asked her, once, if she remembered Lewis, and her face split into a smile so wide that it demanded an answering smile from me. For a minute I forgot everything else – forgot the troops massing beyond the town walls. Forgot that Lewis was dead.

What I was learning, with the untanked, was patience. There was progress, but it took such a long time. And it felt increasingly as though it was time itself that we were up against. All the worthwhile things, the good things, took so long: Piper, strong enough now to pick up his sword and do some light sparring with Zoe in the courtyard; the accidental friendships between Alphas and Omegas that had formed in this town; the gradual emergence of Rhona's memories. Destruction could be so fast: a blade; an arrow; the blast.

The General's troops continued to gather east of the town. The approach of summer meant that the Council's fleet would set out in search of Elsewhere. Elsewhere's ships might already be on their way south, seeking us. I didn't know which would happen first, but the result would be same: the total destruction of Elsewhere, and hope for the resistance here.

Piper had said to me, before he rode into the canyon: *There's more to the world than fire and ash*. It was true – I knew it, and it was what I kept fighting for. But the longer I failed to find the blast machine, and the more the blast visions flared in my head, the more I remembered Xander, his blank eyes and churning hands. Each time I surfaced, gasping, from the visions of flame, I understood that even if we did manage to save this world, fire and ash might be all that was left of me.

*

The General's army was encamped now on the eastern plain. Each night we saw the smoke rising from their fires, barely five miles away. We had debated riding out to tackle them, but with our army depleted, it was too great a risk.

'If they're wise,' The Ringmaster said, 'they'll try to besiege us. They know how many of the untanked we have here. They must know we can't feed them forever. If they concentrate on re-taking Wreckers' Pass, they could have us on our knees within two months.'

'They're not wise,' I said. 'They're angry.' I could feel

The General's fury because it matched my own. 'She's impatient for the end now.' I had never believed I would have anything in common with The General, but I understood this. One way or another, I wanted this to be over.

The General sent a messenger that same day. A simple note: *Give us The Reformer and the pale woman from Elsewhere, or we will raze New Hobart.*

'You can all stop glaring at me like that,' The Ringmaster said. Zoe had stepped in front of Paloma and had one hand resting on the dagger at her belt, eyes on The Ringmaster. Beside me, Piper was watching him too, and had moved to put himself between The Ringmaster and the kitchen door, beyond which was the dining room where Zach was shackled.

'I might not be as convinced as you are about the medicine that Elsewhere can offer us,' The Ringmaster said. 'But I know we don't want to see another blast – not anywhere. And if they bomb Elsewhere today, who knows what they'll bomb next.'

He stood. 'Anyway, The General doesn't keep promises. We could hand Zach and Paloma over right now, and still be standing in the town's ashes by tomorrow.'

He rubbed his hand down his face, and took a deep breath as he looked at me.

'The General and your brother are the same: they always want more. Ruling the Council wasn't enough – they had to make the tanks. Finding the Ark wasn't enough – they had to dig up the blast machine. And ruling here wasn't enough – they want to be sure the Elsewhere can never be an alternative.'

'Will you send her an answer?' Paloma said.

'She had my answer months ago,' he said, 'when I first

led my army into battle against hers. In a way, The General knows me better than any of you do. She knows already that I'll see this through.'

*

The next day, at dawn, I sent Crispin running up the hill with a message to The Ringmaster. It was only one word, but enough to turn Crispin pale when I told him: *Tonight.*

When The Ringmaster came, I told him everything my vision had shown me: the signal fire on the eastern road flaring in the half-dark of the early evening. The General's soldiers pressing forward. I saw how our pits and defences worked: her soldiers stumbling, impaled on the spikes. And I saw how they failed: The General driving them forward until the dead made a bridge for the living to clamber over. I had known about The General's ruthlessness, but this was a new parade of horror, my visions showing me the plain choked with the dead. I had woken screaming so loudly that Zach woke with a startled yell. Even when I recounted the dream to The Ringmaster, my breath shortened, my voice rasping.

'Do they breach the wall?' The Ringmaster asked. They were all watching me – not just him, but Piper, Zoe, Paloma, Simon, and Elsa. Waiting for answers from me, when all I had was a head full of scrambled images: blood; blades; fire.

'They reach the wall,' I said. 'After that, nothing was clear.'

We had been readying for attack since our return from the refuge. Nonetheless it felt different now, knowing that it was imminent.

'I won't have you in the fighting on the front line,' The Ringmaster said to me. 'But I need you at the eastern tower, telling me anything you can see.'

I hoped I would have something useful to tell him – something other than what I saw then, as I closed my eyes: the blast, swallowing the world.

*

In the afternoon, as I sharpened my sword, Zach was sitting cross-legged on his bed, the chain trailing from the wall to his wrists.

'Be cautious,' he said. 'Don't get us killed out there.'

I ran the blade along the whetstone again. 'It's a bit late for warnings, don't you think?'

'Listen,' he said, as I was walking to the door. 'This is important.' He moved closer, the chain stretched to its limit. He looked out the window, checking there was nobody nearby.

'I have something they want,' he said, his voice low and fast. 'You know that already.'

I remembered his words a few days earlier, when he'd told me that The General needed him: *It started with me. And it ends with me.*

'If she gets hold of me,' he went on, 'she'll torture me for it. If that happens – if you feel the pain start – make sure they kill you. Get Piper to do it, fast. Or do it yourself. Do you understand? Because they will torture me, and then they'll kill us anyway.'

'What is it?' I said. 'What's to stop me torturing it out of you right now?'

His hand moved, instinctively, to the place on his leg where I had cut myself last time. My leg, his leg; my pain, his pain.

He didn't answer my question. 'Tell nobody else what I've said,' he said. 'Especially The Ringmaster.'

'I'm not keeping secrets for you,' I yelled. 'Tell me what you know.'

'Do you want to stay alive?' he asked. 'If the others find out, they'll kill you straightaway, to be rid of me.'

Later, when I looked back, I wondered if that was where I should have ended it myself. Lifted my sword to my throat, or to his, right then, so that whatever information he had could never be used. But I didn't. That was the trick of our bodies, as I'd learned when mine had scrambled for life in the flooded Ark: hope. The habit of life was hard for our bodies to break. They chose hope, instead, making the choice as instinctively as snatching a finger back from a fire. Hope was the blessing or the curse of being human.

So I scabbarded my sword, and left. There didn't seem to be any point saying goodbye. What did goodbye even mean, when my death lived in him, and his in me? I stepped past Ash, who had already taken his place at the door. Across the courtyard, Violet was left to watch the door of Paloma's room. The dormitory was already empty – Elsa had led the untanked to the market square, where all of them would wait together, along with others, like Elsa, too old or infirm to fight.

We'd debated sending Paloma and Zach to the square with them, but in the end The Ringmaster had shaken his head.

'If the town falls, I want them hidden. Not gathered with all the others, like chickens waiting for the fox.'

In the dying afternoon light, Piper and I walked down to the eastern gate. He was on the mend; on the side of his head, the open wound had healed to a patch of scar tissue. It had its own whorls, like an ear, and was pinkish-white against his brown skin. These last few days he'd been sparring each morning in the courtyard with Zoe, who was already moving and sounding like herself. But Piper was not back to anything like his former strength, and I had begged him not to go to the front lines with Zoe, Simon and The Ringmaster.

'I need you with me,' I said. It was true. Even weakened, there was nobody that I trusted like him, and I wanted him close to me. Not for his sword, or his fighting skills, though I had need enough of those. For his presence alone, which had sustained me through the deadlands, and through the tunnels of the Ark, and through all the months since then. Before we'd attacked the refuge, Zoe had said, *Such courage as there is, we must find in ourselves.* I knew she was right – but I also felt no shame in knowing my courage felt closer to hand when Piper was beside me.

All day the soldiers and townsfolk had been scrambling with the final preparations. Now there was nothing left to do but wait. Our archers were gathered along the walls and in the watchtowers; troughs of water had been hauled to the inside of the walls to quell fires. Piper and I waited atop the eastern tower, looking down at the soldiers assembled below us, within the walls. Many of them still bore the injuries of the canyon and the refuge. We were an army pieced back together, assembled of stitches and scar tissue.

Behind us, to the west, the sun had begun to slump below the horizon.

'There,' said Piper, raising his arm to the east. I followed his pointed finger. When I saw the signal fire on the eastern road flare into light, it was a remembering. I had seen this already in my dreams, just as I had seen it extinguished. They were coming.

*

My vision had been right, and wrong. Right about the attack, and the sheer force of it. Wrong about the speed. In the dream, I'd seen the events as if they were a sequence, happening one after another: The General's army charging across the plain. Their struggles to cross our defences. Fighting at the walls. When these things actually happened, though, they all seemed to happen at once. Their arrows struck the wooden watchtower where Piper and I crouched, and we felt the boards under our feet shake with the impact. Our own archers seemed not to dent their numbers; each time an advancing soldier fell, another rushed in to fill the gap.

We did not ride to meet them; with our numbers diminished, the defences of New Hobart were a safer bet than open battle outside the walls. But The Ringmaster was ready for them, coordinating the defences and the archers. He was directly below me and Piper at the eastern gate, close enough that I could hear his shouted orders.

Even from my vantage point up high, I hadn't noticed the barrels placed in the pits on the town's perimeter, until The Ringmaster shouted, 'Light the arrows,' and I saw how our archers aimed their blazing arrows at the pits. There, just ahead of the front line of the Council's advance, I noticed the wooden vats, at least twenty of them. The first few arrows fell short; then one struck a pit, and a barrel answered with an eruption of flame.

The attacking soldiers who had been negotiating the pits were caught, now, as one by one the barrels ignited, the flame spreading as though it had been poured along the plain.

'It's a kind of oil,' Piper said, watching beside me. 'We found it in the tank room, when we seized the town. It was being used to power the tanks.'

'Was it The Ringmaster's idea?' I asked. 'To put it in the pits?'

'Mine,' said Piper, meeting my gaze without shame.

The fire slowed the attackers' advance, at least on the northern side of the plain. But on the south, the press of bodies had continued, breaking through the wall of fire, and coming hard at the gate. The soldiers at the fore were dragging something. I thought it might be some kind of belfry ladder for scaling the walls, or a battering ram for attacking the door. But they stopped it at least a hundred yards short of the walls, and scrambled to set it up. It was a catapult, a huge version of the toys that Zach and I had rigged as children for hurling acorns at one another across the yard.

First came the stones. One landed close to the wall just east of the gate; the quivering passed along the wall like a wave.

The Ringmaster, below us, was ordering the archers to aim at the soldiers operating the catapult. Within the gate, he was readying a small squadron to ride out and target the machine, which was already feathered with arrows. But the soldiers scurrying around it were still unharmed, and the next time the wooden arm was levered down and released, the object flying towards us left a streak of flame in the night sky. Piper grabbed me and pulled me towards the ladder.

We weren't the only ones to use some kind of fuel. The projectile, boulder-big and cloaked in fire, hit the gate, and then exploded.

The tower was already starting to sway, and now the explosion took out one of the supporting pillars. Piper didn't have to tell me what to do, or drag me over the edge. We leaped together.

I didn't see the tower fall. I only heard it, a tearing sound like a huge tree being uprooted. I was lying on my face, my mouth full of dust and gravel, just trying to breathe, my hands wrapped around my stomach. The air had been knocked from me, and pain radiated from my chest, along with a rising nausea. Piper crouched beside me. He'd managed to land upright, but his face was stretched into a breathless grimace. I turned to see the wreckage. The tower had fallen outwards, half across the ruptured gate. There was a series of groans that might have been the last settling of the fallen tower, or the sound of those trapped beneath it.

The Ringmaster, who had been just behind the gate, had been thrown from his horse, the soldiers around him scattered. Already he was on his feet, shouting orders and waving his soldiers forward to meet the Council's forces who were pressing through the shattered gate. Through the flames and the settling dust I saw Simon just behind him, his axes raised, and Zoe's silhouette.

I couldn't breathe. I thought it was another wave of breathlessness from the fall, and I pushed up to all fours and waited for it to pass. But this didn't end – the tightness in my neck only grew, and then a pain came too, and I threw my hands to my throat.

Piper saw me gasping for breath and clutching my own neck. Hooking his arm around my chest, he dragged me away from the smouldering tower and the fighting at the gate, to the cover of the steel horse trough. He yanked my hands away from my neck, scanning my skin for an injury.

'Zach,' I wheezed, but I had no air to make a sound.

The pain stopped, and I could breathe again. I gulped air, then coughed, my throat and mouth still coated with dust from the explosion.

'Zach,' I said again.

I stood, but Piper pulled me back down behind the metal

trough, just before an arrow scudded overhead. I peered under the base of the trough, and I could see the scramble of bodies and blades where The Ringmaster and his squadron were still holding the gate. A little to the south, on the other side of the burning tower, a few Council soldiers had fought their way through the breach. They'd been blocked by our soldiers, and the fighting was vicious, but some of The General's red tunics were inside the wall, and their archers were giving them cover. Another arrow went overhead; the next two hit the trough behind which Piper and I crouched. The trough was almost empty, and the arrow strikes made it ring like cymbals, painfully loud. Two more shots clanged, and then nothing. Piper hazarded a peek around the side, but jerked back immediately when another volley of arrows came at him, digging up the dirt beside the tank, and sending gravel spraying at us.

It felt like a long time that we were pinned there. All I could think of was Zach, and the crush of fingers I had felt around my neck. His neck. How had the raiders penetrated as far as the holding house already? What would The General do to him, and to me, if he had been taken?

'Pull,' Piper said in my ear. He'd wedged his hand under the base of the trough itself, and began to drag the whole thing, to give us cover as we shuffled on our knees towards the mouth of an alley, fifty yards away. Our progress was slow – even with me pulling too, we could only just drag the trough, the water inside it sloshing with each jerking movement. The archers saw what we were doing; one arrow skidded from the side of the trough barely an inch from where my hand clutched the edge.

We'd almost reached the cover of the alley when the arrows stopped. There was a man's scream. I thought I heard Zoe's voice, and the sound of renewed fighting.

I didn't look back. Piper and I stood up and ran, sprinting together for the alley, and then up the hill for the holding house, the sounds of the battle receding behind us.

The front door to the holding house was open. The Ringmaster had posted a guard there, but there was no sign of him until we stepped inside and saw the man lying face up in the corridor, his tunic black with blood and his eyes stiffly open, unblinking.

We ran through the corridor, the rooms on either side empty and silent. The door to the dining room was open. Inside, the chain at the wall trailed to Zach's shackles, which lay open on his bed, the keys still in them.

Violet lay on her back beneath the window. Blood had spread around her, from a wound on the back of her head. Her jaw was broken or dislocated, so that her mouth was stuck in a lopsided, soundless scream. On her neck, the bruises were deep purple, nearly black. I could see the marks of fingers on her flesh – Zach's fingers – and caught myself looking down at my own hands.

I squatted to pick up the metal bar that lay a few feet from Violet's body. Her blood was caked on the white paint on one end. Certainty settled in me, heavy as the steel bar in my hands. It was a crossbar from the foot of one of the children's beds. At each end were the holes where it had been screwed to the bed frame. I thought of Zach's fingernails, chipped and broken. All the times he been left alone in our room, on his bed. I wondered how many nights it had taken him, with his bare hands, to unscrew it, and how long he'd had it ready, waiting for his chance.

Violet had fought back, even after he'd surprised her with a blow to the head. A mirror on the wall was broken, and two chairs were knocked over. Even when he'd cornered her and strangled her, she'd fought him – I'd felt it myself, the crush of her dying fingers around his neck, and mine.

But he had won. Her belt was twisted where the sword and keys had been wrenched from it. The knife in her knee-strap was gone too.

I thought again about what Zach had said to me just before I'd left. I had nearly pitied him, in that moment, because I knew that the fear in his eyes was real. And it had been real – but it wasn't fear of being captured in the attack on the town. He knew what was coming, because he had planned the whole thing.

'He's stupider than I thought,' Piper said. 'The General will kill him as soon as she has the chance.'

'Not if he's got something to bargain with,' I said.

I was already up, rushing to the door so quickly that I knocked over the remaining chair. Both of us ran.

In Paloma and Zoe's room, there hadn't been a protracted struggle. Zach had been armed, and must have taken Ash by surprise. The room was undisturbed except for Ash's body, fallen from the chair by the door. He had a single wound to the side of his neck. I hoped it had been quick.

Paloma was gone.

As we'd run to her room, I'd pictured the worst: Paloma's body on the floor, her throat slit. Or hanged, as Leonard had been. I'd imagined a hundred different deaths for her, in those few steps across the courtyard. So when she wasn't there, I was momentarily relieved not to find her body next to Ash's.

There were noises behind us in the main house. The door to the courtyard banged, and I heard Zoe's running footsteps.

When she saw Ash's body, she gave a scream that was unlike anything I'd ever heard from her before. It was an animal wail, broken at the edges and bleeding into the night.

On the floor, not far from where Ash lay, was the capsule that Sally had given to Paloma. The leather cord was snapped, and the capsule had rolled away from it.

I didn't know whether Zach, in weeks of quiet watching, had known that she had the capsule, and had torn it from her. Or perhaps he'd only noticed it when she reached for it, when he'd smashed into her room. Or perhaps neither: it might have been torn off by accident. It made no difference: she didn't have it now. I bent and picked up the capsule, rolled it between my fingers for a second before slipping it into my pocket.

And I realised that I hadn't yet imagined the worst. Zach had taken her for a reason. He and The General would break her apart to get the location of Elsewhere. They would do things to her that would make her long for the mercy of the capsule, or of a swift blade to the throat. And, at the end of it, they would take the blast to Elsewhere and unleash it once again. In Zoe's scream I heard it all: Paloma's screams; the roar of flames; the screams of thousands, charred and burnt. It was no wonder the crows had taken flight from the holding house roof, answering Zoe's screams with caws of their own.

*

We ran, stepping over the dead guard in the corridor, and sprinting for the eastern gate. The city was choked with smoke, but down by the fallen tower the shouts of battle had been replaced by different sounds. The wounded were being carried through the breached gate and tended in rows on the street. Already, troughs and planks were being hauled into place to form a hasty barricade where the gate and tower had given way. From beyond the wall the occasional shout still came, but they were the yells of the injured and of patrols calling out to one another, and not the raw cries of battle.

Lit by a torch planted in the debris, Crispin was sifting the wreckage of the burned tower for bodies. He saw us and straightened. 'This gate's down,' he yelled, wiping his hand across his face, leaving a streak of ash. 'And several small breaches on the other side. But they're retreating.' He gave an incredulous shake of his head. 'Not just to their camp, either – The General's squadron's ridden off.'

He looked from me, to Piper, and then back again, wondering why his news wasn't being greeted with relief.

'They're retreating,' Crispin said again.

'No they're not,' I said. 'They've got what they came for.'

CHAPTER 27

Zoe's entire body was shaking. She hunched on a bench in Elsa's kitchen, her hands twisting incessantly in her lap, strangling the air. Beyond the open door, two soldiers walked past, carrying Ash's body. Violet and the other dead sentry had already been carried out. There was no time to grieve for them.

Down at the wall, Piper had shouted orders to Crispin, to saddle horses and muster a small troop. Now, back in the holding house, The Ringmaster was giving his own orders to one of his soldiers. One of The Ringmaster's sleeves was burnt, and the flesh of his arm was blistered, but he ignored it.

'Coordinate the search,' he was saying to the soldier. 'Every building, every alley.'

'Don't bother.' I pressed my lips together. 'He's gone.'

The Ringmaster ignored me. 'Search it,' he said, and the soldier saluted and left.

I knew that searching New Hobart was a waste of time. I remembered how Kip and I had managed to slip out of the island's fort, when it was under attack from the Council's forces. In the chaos of battle, with multiple breaches in the wall, who would have noticed Zach and Paloma slipping out, him with a knife at her back?

'He was the one who came to us,' The Ringmaster said. 'The General wants him dead. Why go back to them now?'

'He came to us because he had no choice,' I said. 'They wanted him dead because they want me dead. But once he knew about Paloma, that changed everything. She's worth even more to them than getting rid of me. She's his ticket back to the Council: he's giving them Elsewhere.'

'They'll take her, and then they'll kill him,' Zoe said. She was wild-eyed now, and if she realised what she'd said, she gave no sign, her eyes not even pausing on me as they darted around the room.

'Probably,' I said, the word snagging in my throat.

Piper put his hand on my arm. 'Zach knows that. He knows The General's ruthlessness better than anyone. He has a plan.'

It was meant to comfort me, but it could not. All Zach's plans ended in fire. If my life depended on his plan succeeding, then I was complicit. Perhaps I already was: I hadn't told them what Zach had said to me only hours before. Paloma was not the only card he held – there was something else he knew, something that The General needed, and the only reason he wasn't being tortured for it as we spoke was because I was his protection. He knew that I would rather kill us both than let him give The General the information that she so valued. But what if he gave it up willingly? Would I kill myself to stop him? And would it be too late?

Zoe was pacing by the door now, backwards and forwards, the way that Xander used to pace sometimes. Her hands moved from her head to her sword and back again.

'Why didn't you know?' she shouted, stopping suddenly

and turning to me. 'What's the point of you, if you can't see something like this coming?'

I thought of Paloma's pale eyes, and her narrow wrists. I thought of what The General would do to her.

'They've headed west,' I said.

Piper looked up at me. 'Not east, back to Wyndham?'

'No,' I said. 'West. I can feel it.'

'You can feel Zach?'

I shook my head. I didn't want to say it out loud, in front of Zoe. It wasn't Zach I could feel: it was Paloma. The raw surge of terror and pain that swelled to me from the west came from her, not Zach.

Zoe didn't need to be told. She grabbed me with both hands.

'Is she alive?'

She was clutching my shirt, pulling me close. I didn't know if she was fighting me, or embracing me. She didn't know either.

'She's alive,' I said. 'For now.'

Horses clattered up the street. Zoe was out the door and mounted, waiting with Crispin and Simon, before I'd even reached the end of the corridor.

Simon was leading horses for me and Piper too. Piper swung himself into the saddle.

'Think for a second,' The Ringmaster said, standing in the holding house door. 'If you rush after them like this, you endanger yourselves. And we have to defend the town. The General might have left, but most of her army's still on the eastern plain. I can't send our army after Paloma.'

My foot was already in the stirrup. I hoisted myself up, swinging my other leg over the saddle. There could be no greater danger for me than what we already faced: Zach in their hands. They could kill us both at any moment.

'I can't win this fight without somebody to rally the Omegas,' The Ringmaster said to me. 'We've already lost Sally. If we lose you, Piper and Zoe, as well as Paloma, we won't come back from it.'

'Come back for what?' I said, turning my horse around. 'This is the end. If they bomb Elsewhere, there isn't anything left to fight for.' I pressed my heels into the horse's flanks, felt its warmth on my calves. 'Send a squadron after us,' I called over my shoulder, as the horse took off. 'Supplies, too.'

We rode up the hill through the town, racing through the narrow roads towards the western gate. When we turned the corner near the Tithe Collector's office, Zoe nearly ran down the figure stumbling down the middle of the road.

It was Elsa. She grabbed my ankle.

'I heard,' she said, reaching up and thrusting a package into my hands. 'This is for when you find her.'

There was no time for any further words – Zoe was already spurring her horse back into motion. I followed her, grateful for Elsa's small show of faith: *when you find her*, not *if*. Then I peered into the parcel, and saw the tiny jars and bottles that I knew so well. I wrapped it hastily, and leant back to stash it in my saddlebag. As I rode off after the others, I ran through the bottles' labels in my mind: poppy tincture, valerian, and henbane for pain. Tea tree oil for wounds. Comfrey salve for burns. Each one was a reminder of what Paloma was going through, and each time the bottles clanked in my saddlebag, I winced.

There were only five of us, riding out in that first pursuit: Crispin, Simon, me, Piper, and Zoe, always at the front, riding with a recklessness I had not seen before. After we passed through the western gate, we had to thread our way through the troughs and pits of the town's outer defences, with only the full moon to light our way, but Zoe barely slowed.

The main attack had been on the eastern wall, but even here, on the western side, our army was still at work, securing the perimeter once again, and fixing the two small breaches in the wall. The Omega soldiers that we passed saluted when they saw Piper. Nobody stopped us, and one glance at Zoe was enough to warn them not to try.

Another mile along the western road, the last sentry post stood. There were arrows lodged in the roof of the watch-tower, a flock of birds that did not take flight as we rode closer. Drawing nearer, I saw a body had fallen on to the wall, the stake beneath it black with blood.

We stayed only long enough to circle the tower. Twice Piper called out; twice he was answered by nothing but the flies, already massing in a black cloud on the bodies. We rode on.

When the ground grew marshy and the horses foundered, Piper shouted ahead to Zoe. 'Slow down,' he called, pushing his horse to match hers.

She ignored him.

'You'll kill your horse,' he said. 'Then what?'

'Then I kill The General, and Zach,' she said, with a jerk of her head to the road ahead of us.

'You won't have a chance, if we can't catch them,' he said, reaching down to pull back on her reins. She shoved his arm away and rode onwards, but she slowed slightly.

It was nearly dawn when we reached the western ridge, a few miles past where we'd found Leonard's body, and saw them. There were forty riders or more, dust cloaking them as they rode. We were gaining on them, but only slowly, and our horses couldn't sustain that pace. On the ridge, where we could keep The General's squadron in sight, we let the horses rest. We gave them an hour, letting them slurp noisily from the spring that ran by the road.

While we waited, hoofbeats sounded behind us. Piper's jaw tightened, his hand on his sword hilt as he looked back to the east. Our horses were spent, and we could not flee. I could see him assessing the area, calculating the advantage of the high ground, and the best spots for an ambush. But he relaxed when they finally came into sight, half a mile below us on the ridge: it was the squadron that The Ringmaster had sent from New Hobart. He had sent us fourteen of his soldiers. Not as many as we needed, but more than I'd feared. There were spare horses, too, to speed our progress, and saddlebags stuffed with food and oats.

We chased Paloma and Zach for three days. We changed horses every few hours, but even so our mounts flagged and tired. After the first day, when we were clear of the swamps, there weren't enough springs, and we were all thirsty, white froth around the horses' mouths, dust on our tongues. When The General's squadron paused, we paused, setting lookouts and taking turns to snatch a few hours' rest. They must have known that we were following them. We were travelling too fast for concealment, and much of the time moving through open country, but they outnumbered us comfortably, and maintained their lead. If, after resting, we set off before them, they quickly countered, the column of dust once more moving away from us to the west.

The third day was dark with clouds, and when the rain came in the afternoon we turned our mouths to the sky, and our horses jerked at their reins and drank from the shallow rivulets of water on the dust road. We lost sight of The General's soldiers in the downpour, but I could feel them still, even though we had long left behind the roads and were travelling across the open plains. I couldn't bring myself to tell Zoe why it was so easy. It was like tracking a wounded animal – Paloma left a trail of terror, like drops of blood, along the ground.

'Where's The General taking them?' Piper asked me.

'To the coast,' I replied. Each night, in the few hours' sleep that we snatched, I saw nothing but fire and water. The two had merged: I was drowning in flames, scorched by waves.

The fourth day, I woke bleary and exhausted from a bare hour's sleep.

'Hurry,' said Zoe, swinging herself into the saddle. 'They're already on the move.'

It was easier to see them this morning – they'd lit lamps, moving in the distance.

'Why the lamps?' I said.

'Maybe they're not bothering to hide,' Simon said. 'They know we're on their trail. They know they haven't been able to shake us yet.'

I nodded, but my eyes still followed.

'They knew that yesterday,' I said. 'And it was darker yesterday, too, with the rainstorm. What's changed?'

'Hurry up,' called Zoe again.

I shook my head. 'Watch the ground,' I said to Piper, as the rest of us followed her.

We came to the place where The General's squadron had passed the night, a clearing in the low scrub. In the heat, the ground had dried quickly from yesterday's downpour, but the trampled ring of grass showed where the horses had been picketed. Nearby, the grass still bore the indentations of sleeping bodies; I wondered where Paloma had lain, and Zach.

Beyond the clearing, the mass of hoofprints continued westwards on the dusty earth. I couldn't count them – there was nothing to be read from the dust except that horses had passed that way. But I thought again of those lamps, lit for the first time, on a clear night. Drawing us on, to follow them.

Zoe was standing in her stirrups, looking back at me impatiently. 'Come on,' she called.

'Wait,' I said.

She ignored me, and started out, following the trail. But Piper drew his horse close to mine. 'What are you looking for?' he said.

'They wanted us to follow them, this morning,' I said.

'Why?'

I gestured to the trail that Zoe had followed. 'They didn't all go that way.'

He looked at me appraisingly. 'Where, then?' he asked.

I surveyed the clearing. To the northern side, a natural barrier of thorn bushes clustered, studded with spikes as long as my forearm.

'Leave her if she won't come,' Zoe shouted to Piper.

But he slipped from his horse.

He found the tracks first. The soldiers had been careful, avoiding the patches of bare dirt where prints would show. But amidst the long grass there were places where the horses had snatched a bite as they passed, leaving grass blades shorn blunt. So many times in these last six months I had yanked on my reins, frustrated by my mount's attempts to crop grass. Now I was so grateful for the infinite greed of horses.

The only other sign we found was half a hoofprint in the narrow passage that traced between the thorn bushes. It wasn't much to go on: a semi-circular indentation in the dirt, and some torn grass. But I knew, with a certainty that rang as loudly as Paloma's pain.

Zoe had stopped a few hundred yards away. Her horse had picked up on her restlessness and was jittering on the spot. She was staring back at us, Simon, Crispin, and the other soldiers waiting behind her.

'Boss?' called Crispin.

'This way,' replied Piper. 'Some of them went this way, peeling off to the north. And they didn't want us to know.'

*

We split up. Ten of The Ringmaster's soldiers were to follow the main squadron, while four of them joined the rest of us heading north. There was, after all, a chance that the small, covert group that had peeled off was a decoy, an elaborate bluff. But I closed my eyes and opened myself to Paloma's pain. When I reached for it, I regretted it instantly – it came like a roar of sound, and my face clenched against it, my breath speeding up.

'They took Paloma that way,' I said, pointing through the thorns to the north.

'You're sure?' Zoe asked, her gaze scouring my face.

I nodded. 'I can feel her,' I said.

'And Zach?' Piper said. But Zoe had already wheeled her horse around and taken off, leaning low over its side to trace the trail.

'Zach?' Piper said again.

'I can't feel him,' I said. 'But I don't care. We need to follow Paloma.'

Those words ran through my mind as we rode after Zoe. *I can't feel him*. He was not being tortured himself – my own body was the proof of that. I had never monitored my own body so intently. Each instant that the pain didn't come was both a relief and a horror. I was part of his plan, and I still didn't know what it was.

Zach had told me to kill myself if the torture started. Without thinking, I put my hand to my neck, where I'd fastened Paloma's capsule, its snapped cord tied double, just to be sure. *Not an easy death*, Sally had said – but easier than torture. If The General valued whatever it was that Zach knew, then I couldn't let her get hold of it. But Zach could no more be trusted than The General herself. His information was already in the wrong hands. And the only way to stop it was to kill myself.

But I was our best chance of finding Paloma. With me gone, Piper and Zoe might never find her.

Once again, I succumbed to the trick of hope. I let myself imagine that I could find Paloma. That she would be alive. That I could somehow find a way to stop Zach, before it was too late.

*

We moved more carefully now – we didn't want them to know that we had tracked their departure from the main squadron. They were a smaller group, and left fewer tracks. It was harder, too, for me to trace them. In the last few hours, Paloma's pain was growing more muted – it was still there, but muffled, exhausted.

Halfway through the first day, when we found some churned mud and prints at the edge of a stream, Piper looked further north.

'They'll be heading to Sulpice – it's the closest garrison

still held by The General. Probably two days' ride north of here.'

'And The General?' I said. I was standing ankle-deep in the stream while my horse drank, and Piper examined the prints.

Piper shook his head. 'She wouldn't travel without her squadron. I'd bet anything on her having stayed with the larger group.'

'Why've they split up?' Crispin asked.

I hesitated, glancing at Zoe, who was slumped on the bank of the creek. She caught my glance and exhaled. 'Don't kid yourself that you're sparing me. There's nothing you can say that's worse than what I've imagined.'

I nodded. 'Paloma's injured. She's probably slowing them down. And they might've got what they need from her.'

'So we ride,' Zoe said, standing. 'We need to attack before they reach the garrison.'

We kept our distance from the Council's riders, and lit no torches to guide us through the dark, and no fire when we stopped for a hurried meal or to rest the horses. At dawn the next day, we found a ring of ashes where they had camped amongst the pines.

'They think they shook us off, when they left the main group,' Piper said. 'They'd never have lit a fire if they thought they were being followed.'

He crossed to the largest tree, not far from the ashes, and knelt to look more closely. At its base, a ring of bark half a foot from the ground had been chafed away. The dirt beneath it was scattered with flakes of bark.

'They're keeping her shackled,' Piper said.

It was the ants that drew my eye to the blood. The drops

had clotted black on the dirt, a border of ants encircling each one.

I stood quickly. 'Let's go,' I said. But Zoe wasn't to be fobbed off. She knelt beside us and examined the ground.

She said nothing about the blood, though I saw her eyes linger on it. When she bent to look more closely at the tree, she gave a grim smile.

'She's still fighting,' she said, pointing to the naked strip of tree, where Paloma's shackles had sawed at the bark. 'Still trying to get free.'

CHAPTER 28

We caught up with them about midnight that night. They'd chosen their safehouse well. The modest hut sat deep in grass, in a clearing amongst the pines. There was no cover around the hut itself, other than one small thicket, halfway between the trees and the building.

We had left the horses tied in the pine forest half a mile back, when we'd first spotted the light from the hut's window. Now, on our elbows and knees in the thick scrub at the clearing's edge, we could get no closer to the hut without leaving cover.

'Better to wait until they're on the move again,' Simon whispered.

'We can't,' Piper said. 'There could be reinforcements heading south from Sulpice to join them.' He nodded at the soldiers' horses, tethered to a stake in the clearing. There were ten of them, grazing unconcerned as we peered from the trees. 'There are no more than ten of them in there,' he said. 'This is as good a chance as we're going to get.'

'There'll be sentries in that thicket,' said Zoe, pointing

to the cluster of shrubs fifty yards from us. She slipped a knife from her belt.

'How do we get closer?' I asked.

'We don't,' said Zoe. 'We burn the sentries out.'

She rooted in her bag for a moment, then quietly sliced three strips from a blanket, and wrapped them, one by one, around the handles of three of her throwing knives. She bit her lip as she forced the cork from a jar of lamp oil, pouring it slowly until each of the rags was soaked.

She took two of the knives; Piper took one. I watched as he balanced the knife in his hand, testing its new weight.

Slicing a fourth strip from the blanket, Zoe soaked it carefully, then stuffed it into the neck of the oil jar itself.

She turned to the others. 'Spread out,' she said to The Ringmaster's four soldiers. 'Cover the other sides, in case they make a break for it.' They saluted, slipping backwards into deep cover before moving to encircle the clearing. Zoe turned back to Simon and Crispin, and pointed to the clearing's eastern edge. 'Be ready to charge the front door, from there,' she told them, 'as soon as I've taken out the sentries.'

Simon gave a quick nod, peeling off to the east, with Crispin following closely.

'You ready?' Zoe said to me and Piper. 'As soon as I strike a flame, we'll be a target. They'll have bows.'

We nodded. She bent over the matches, her back turned to the sentry post to shield the flame. The first time, the match didn't take. There was a spark, but nothing more. The second time, the match kindled. Once she lit the first rag, there was no hiding it. The oil hissed and flared, and even though she held the dagger by the blade, flaming hilt raised, I could smell the hairs on her hand as they singed.

She lit the second dagger from the first; Piper held his blade up to hers, and the flame leaped to his dagger.

A shout came from within the clearing, but already Zoe was hurling the first knife, the flame spinning through the darkness, Piper's crossing beneath it mid-flight.

The sentries responded quickly. There was another shout, and then three arrows came at us, in such quick succession that there must have been more than one archer firing. They hit the earth so close to me that dirt sprayed my face as I huddled, my back pressed against the tree that shielded me.

Before Zoe threw the third dagger, Piper held the oil jar out to her, and she lowered the flame to the rag that trailed from the jar's mouth. The flame hissed up the rag, and Piper lobbed the jar just as Zoe threw the final blade.

The next volley of arrows came before she'd even lowered her arm; one arrow struck the tree behind which she crouched. Then there was a blast in the sentries' thicket, a swelling of light, and flame bursting amid the trees. More shouts, and then a scream. A shape ran from the thicket, all thoughts of concealment gone. His clothes were aflame. He ran towards us, blindly. He was a man made of fire, running from himself. His mouth was open, a dark hole in the flames. I couldn't bear to watch, but couldn't look away.

Piper stepped out of cover as the burning man reeled across the clearing. In two steps Piper had reached him, and swung his sword at his neck. For a moment, fire clung to Piper's blade, a stripe of flame across the night. Then the man fell, dead, and Piper was back beside me, the smell of burnt flesh following him.

By the flames' light we saw another man step from the sentry post. He looked towards the three of us crouching in the trees behind the still-burning body. Then he sprinted toward the hut.

Zoe sent a knife flying after him, but it flew wide.

We ran, all of us, leaving the dead man in his bed of flames.

I had a short sword, and my dagger in my belt. For the first time, I wanted to use them, and not only to stay alive and defend myself. As we sprinted towards that hut, and Paloma, I wanted to kill.

They were ready for us. When the arrows came, Zoe darted forwards, and Piper and I dived to the left. Not fast enough: an arrow skimmed my right arm. I didn't feel my flesh tearing, at first – just a streak of heat. My first thought: *Feel that, Zach? Feel that.*

My sword had dropped from my injured arm. On hands and knees, I groped for it in the grass. In the hut ahead, I could see an archer at the front door reaching for another arrow. Everything seemed to be moving very slowly. His hand, raised to his quiver. My hands, one of them wet now with blood, frantically patting the grass in search of the sword. I found the steel at the same moment that he notched the arrow to the bowstring.

When I grabbed my sword by the blade, it cut the webbing between my finger and thumb; I didn't care. I groped my way to the hilt, but it was too late – he had drawn back the arrow. I was only twenty feet from him – too close to dodge an arrow, and too close for him to miss. Zoe was a little ahead of me, Piper to my right. For that moment there was nobody else in the world but me and the soldier: me crouching, clutching my sword; him in the shelter of the door, arrow cocked.

In the long grass, I hadn't noticed Crispin creeping to the side of the house. He shot up and charged at the door from the side, taking out the archer's legs with an axe blow. The man buckled, his arrow shooting into the top of the doorframe as he fell backwards into the house. He was still alive, and tried to shove the door shut behind him, but his own arrow was jamming it, and Crispin wedged the haft of his axe into the opening as well. When Zoe got there a moment later, and threw her weight against the door, it gave way, and she and Crispin were inside and out of sight.

I ran, Piper just ahead of me. To the right, I glimpsed Simon sprinting to join us. From inside the hut came yells, and then a woman's scream. The way the scream ended was unmistakable: it stopped with the suddenness that only comes from a blade.

I followed Piper through the door. It was totally dark, and the sound of Piper's breathing, just ahead of me, was all that I navigated by as we moved down the corridor. I stumbled over a warm body stretched across the floor – the archer, I guessed, as I stepped over him. There was broken glass on the floor, noisy underfoot. I'd forgotten that I was injured until I had to wipe my sword hand, wet with blood.

The first room had a candle burning on the mantel. I stepped around the chairs that had been knocked over in the fighting, and then over a soldier's body. She was face down, her head turned to the side. Her eyes were open. She still wore Zoe's knife in the side of her neck.

'It's clear,' whispered Simon, from the room on the other side of the corridor. He moved further back.

'How many more of them are there?' I whispered to Piper.

'At least three,' he said.

Glancing down in the half-lit room, he saw the wound on my arm.

'Is it serious?' he asked.

I shook my head and kept my sword raised, the blood pooling in the crease of my elbow.

Piper nodded. 'Stay close.'

At the far end of the corridor, something wooden splintered. There was a shout that could have been Zoe's voice, and the sound of swords. Simon stumbled into sight, staggering backwards through a door to our right, locked in a struggle with a tall soldier. Their weapons were gone, and they were grappling hand to hand, the pair of them ricocheting down the narrow corridor. Piper raised a knife, but Simon and the man were intertwined and moving too fast for Piper to get a clear shot. The pair of them crashed to the ground, the man landing on top of Simon. Simon spat blood from the side of his mouth.

I sent my dagger skidding along the floor towards him, hilt first. The soldier had pinned Simon's arms with both of his, but Simon's third arm grabbed my dagger and thrust upwards.

We were all so close, in that small corridor, and the man's yell seemed to bounce off the walls. His twin's scream, too, was loud in my head, and I could taste her blood and his in the back of my mouth.

On his way past, Piper hooked the dead man with his foot and rolled him off Simon – there was no time to check on him or help him up. I gripped my sword in both hands and stepped over him and the dead man's legs. Behind me, I heard Simon groan as he shifted.

Piper and I reached the door at the end of the corridor, where the sounds of fighting were loudest. There was blood on the floor, and I slipped as I followed Piper, my wounded arm painful against the wall as I caught myself.

Blades had been hard at work in the room that we entered.

A dead soldier lay on his back by the doorway; another was slumped against the wall, her head flopped to the side at an unlikely angle, and a thread of blood trailing from her mouth. Crispin's shirt was soaked in blood, but he stood steadily enough, axe in hand, and I guessed that the blood was not his own.

We were in a kitchen. There was something incongruous about the scene: the cosy familiarity of the cottage kitchen against the drawn swords, the broken glass, and the bodies on the floor. Hoisted above the fireplace was a pulley with copper pots and pans suspended, along with ladles and herbs. The smell of blood mixed with the scent of dried thyme and garlic hanging above us.

By the other door, at the back of the kitchen, Zoe had her sword raised.

'They've got her in there,' she said.

'Is there any way out for them?' Piper asked.

Zoe shook her head. 'It's a storeroom – no window.'

She leaned closer to the door, trying to peer through one of the cracks in the warped wood. I pulled her backwards before I even knew what I was doing – I had felt the blade on the other side, poised like an arrow about to be launched. She turned to me, her face a snarl, just as a sword thrust through the gap, its hilt jarring it to a stop half an inch from her face. She took one breath, then leaned backwards, below the blade, and aimed a kick at the door. It was wrenched open just as her foot hit the wood.

The soldier charged through, and reached Zoe while she was still off balance. He was fast, stocky arms wielding his sword as though it weighed nothing.

Zoe regained her footing and swung her sword, but he dodged it. Her blade swiped the rack of pans that hung above us, setting the whole thing swinging and sending one small copper pot flying against the wall.

She continued to press forward. Piper yanked me back, out of the way, and fought by her side. The soldier blocked a strike from him, grunting as their swords clashed. Without a word being spoken, Zoe and Piper manoeuvred around one another so that she was fighting at his left, covering the side where he had no sword arm. The man fought strongly, but he couldn't hold off Piper and Zoe at once. In a matter of moments they had driven him to the corner, and Zoe had her sword at his throat.

'It's too late to save that little blonde bitch,' the soldier said. I saw the tendons in Zoe's hand tighten around her sword hilt, and I turned my head away. I had seen enough killing for one day.

'Take his sword,' Zoe said.

I looked up.

'And search him for other weapons,' she barked. Her sword was still at his throat, but she just held it there as Piper grabbed the man's weapon and Crispin stepped forward to pat him down.

Zoe and I were nearly back at the storeroom door, swords drawn, when the other soldier burst through.

'I'll kill her,' he shouted, jerking his chin down at Paloma, whom he had dragged through the doorway. It was too dark to get a clear look at Paloma's injuries. Her false leg was missing, and she could hardly stand – the man was holding her up, his arm around her chest, hoisting her under the arms. His wide-bladed dagger, the serrated edge jagged as broken teeth, was pressed to Paloma's neck.

'Stop,' he said again, 'or I'll kill her.' He was blond, only a little darker than Paloma herself, and his eyes scanned the room frantically, spittle flying from his mouth as he spoke.

Paloma couldn't even keep her head upright; it kept lolling to the side, then jerking up again when her cheek pressed against the knife. Her eyes were rolling in her head, like those of a panicked horse. There was no sign that she had even seen us.

Zoe stepped backwards, hands raised above her head.

'Get back, against the wall,' the blond soldier yelled, 'and throw down your weapons.'

'Do what he says,' said Zoe.

I took three steps away, until the kitchen wall nudged my back. I dropped my sword and heard it clatter on the ground. Piper and Crispin obeyed too, releasing the other soldier with a shove, and stepping back. When Piper lowered his sword, the freed soldier bent down to take it.

But I was watching Zoe. The whole time, her eyes never moved from the knife at Paloma's neck. She moved backwards, one slow step after another. Before she lowered her knife she lifted it higher, just for a moment, and then lowered it in a sweeping motion.

It took a second for me to realise what she'd done. Just above her head the rope for raising and lowering the kitchen rack ran, on its way to the cleat on the back wall. She had severed the rope with one slice.

The copper pans dropped on the soldier and Paloma, followed by the heavy rack itself. It wasn't enough to knock him out, but it sent him stumbling, one hand raised to shield his head, loosening his grip on Paloma. That was all Zoe needed. She leaped forwards, knocking both him and Paloma to the ground. By the time I'd reached them, it was already over: the soldier, still under the detritus of the wooden slats and pots, lying with his throat slit, his blood pooling in a copper pan that had settled on its side. On the far side of the room the other soldier, too, was lying dead, Crispin's knife in his back.

Zoe kicked aside the broken rack, and pulled Paloma free.

CHAPTER 29

We fled, Zoe carrying Paloma. We would have moved faster if Piper had helped her, but nobody suggested it, and I don't think Paloma would have tolerated anybody but Zoe touching her.

In the corridor, Simon was staggering to his feet, leaning against the wall, blood still coursing from his nose and mouth. Outside, where The Ringmaster's soldiers had kept their guard around the hut, two of the Council's soldiers who had escaped through a side window now lay dead in the long grass, along with one of our men, an arrow in his stomach, his dead eyes staring at the night sky. We left the bodies where they lay, and ran through the pines to the horses.

Nine of us had ridden there that night, and nine of us rode away, but everything had changed. Zoe held Paloma in front of her; I rode ahead of them, and every time I looked back I saw Paloma's face. Her left eye was nearly swollen shut, the other unfocused. I wasn't sure whether she even knew that she had been rescued.

We rode for miles on the plain, and even as the sky grew lighter there were no signs of pursuit. The grass was bleached grey by the sun; when the winds came, the whole plain seemed to shift and waver.

Zoe made us stop before noon, at the first spring we reached. The sun was hot, and some of Paloma's wounds had started to bleed again, her blood staining the pale neck of Zoe's horse. I brought Zoe a water flask, and offered to help her with washing Paloma's wounds, but Zoe did it all herself.

I couldn't see what they had done to Paloma. Not only because Zoe shielded her so fiercely, but because Paloma's whole body was a mass of wounds, swollen and blood-caked.

By the time Zoe had finished, the cloth she was using was streaked deep brown with blood. She had cut away Paloma's own clothes, burnt and blood-soaked, and wrapped her in a blanket. When I saw Paloma's hands, resting on top of the dark cloth, I felt vomit rise at the back of my throat. Where each of her fingernails should have been, only a crust of blood sat. A row of burns measured out the inside of each wrist, where a hot iron had been pressed onto her flesh at neat intervals. Several of her fingers had been broken, sticking out at strange angles, so that her hands looked as though they'd been drawn by a clumsy artist, or a child. The smallest finger on her left hand had been cut off. The bone, snapped into a sharp point, poked through the opened flesh.

One of her eyes was still barely able to open; with the other, she looked at me.

'I told them,' she said. There was no apology in her eyes, only exhaustion. 'They know where to go.' Her voice scraped; it had been blunted against days of screaming.

'I told them,' she said again.

'I know,' said Zoe.

None of us were surprised. Push a body far enough, and pain will find its own voice. Some might have the chance to choose death first, to stop the tongue's mutiny. But if the torturers were skilful enough to keep their victim alive, there was no secret that wouldn't come out eventually. I looked at Paloma's shattered hands; I didn't delude myself that I would have lasted as long as she had.

Zoe wrung out the cloth as though twisting a neck. The water from it dripped red. 'I'll kill them all,' Zoe said. 'Everyone who did this to you.'

Paloma shook her head. 'I don't want that.' She closed her good eye slowly, then opened it. 'Concentrate on stopping them. Saving my home. My sisters.'

Zoe's nostrils were pinched, the tendons in her neck standing out, and every muscle tensed. Her rage was a wind against which she had to brace herself. But she said nothing more. She didn't touch Paloma's broken fingers, only bent her head to each one, even the missing finger that was just a spur of bone. One finger at a time, Zoe placed her lips an inch above the damaged flesh, and kissed the air.

This was a victory of sorts, I tried to remind myself as I re-saddled my horse. We had found Paloma, and freed her. But it was hard to feel victorious, in the face of Paloma's wounds, the dead we had left behind us in the hut, and their twins. In the face of Elsewhere, condemned to burn.

If I thought about it too much, all I saw was fire. I leaned my head against my horse's flank, and closed my eyes, but there was no darkness, and no rest: only the heat and roar of fire. Flesh burning on the wind. A sea turned to steam; islands turned to rubble.

*

I went to the spring to refill Zoe's water flask. Piper was already there. He was sitting with his back against one of the stones, his knees raised and his head lowered. His mouth was open, and he was crying.

I stopped, scuffing my feet on the stone with deliberate noisiness, looking down to uncork the flask and give him a chance to wipe his face. I'd assumed that he would be embarrassed for me to see him like this. But when I looked up, he hadn't moved, hadn't brushed away the tears that still striped his cheeks. He met my stare.

'She'll be all right,' I said to him. I didn't know if I meant Zoe or Paloma. It didn't matter – we both knew that my words meant nothing, and that neither Paloma nor Zoe would ever be all right. What had happened to Paloma, and what was going to happen to Elsewhere, were forever things. Things that couldn't be put right.

I was staring at him. 'I'm only realising now,' I said, 'that I've never seen you cry.' Not when we had dredged the drowned children from the tanks at New Hobart. Not after Sally's death. Not even after he brought Xander back to New Hobart to bury, the boy's broken body slung across the front of his horse.

'You put on a good act,' I said. 'You've done a good job of convincing me that you were—' I hesitated, sifting the words for the right one, '—hardened.'

'I am,' he said. 'It's not an act. I am everything that you fear I am. I am what I've been forced to become, and to do, including to protect you.' He looked at me without shame. 'But that doesn't mean that's all that I am.'

It felt wrong to be glad of anything, while Paloma lay twenty yards away with her fingernails torn out, and Elsewhere was about to be burned from the world. But it was those things, in the end, that made me clutch this moment even more tightly.

*

I had washed the wound in my arm, and bound it clumsily. Crispin was checking Simon's face; he blenched when Crispin touched his broken nose, but next to Paloma's injuries, none of us complained.

I unwrapped Elsa's parcel of herbs. As I ground and mixed the medicine for Paloma, I was so grateful for those weeks in the kitchen at the holding house, Elsa peering over my shoulder and bossing me as I helped her with the herbs.

'What will this do?' Zoe asked, eyeing the gritty mixture suspiciously when I passed it to her.

'Not enough,' I said. 'But it should numb the pain.'

It took Paloma a long time to tell us what had happened. Some of her teeth had been broken, and she kept pausing to run her tongue over them, her upper lip drawn into a grimace as she tested the new configuration of her mouth. Her false leg was gone – even the metal false bone protruding below her knee had been bent, as though the leg had been wrenched off.

'Once they were finished . . .' She paused for a moment, and I knew that in avoiding the words, she was trying to spare us all, not just herself. 'Once they were finished with me,' she continued, 'they said something about the coast.' She paused for another minute, swallowing slowly.

'They thought I was unconscious,' she said. 'I almost was – I was coming in and out. And I don't think, by that point, they even cared much. They'd finished with me, by then. The more they asked me about home, the more they realised how little I knew. I'm not a doctor, couldn't give them any details about the machines. Once I'd told them the location, the machines and the medicines were all they were asking about. I couldn't tell them any details about that, so they . . .' Again her voice stopped. What words did she have that would describe what they had done to her? When she'd first come to us, I had thought that we would need new maps to understand the scale and distance of Elsewhere. Now, for us to understand what she had suffered, we would need a new language.

Eventually she went on, the words slipping shyly out from between the sharpened remnants of her cracked front teeth. 'The General wanted me killed, at first – she told them to finish me off – but Zach talked her out of it.' I knew better than to think it would be kindness. Paloma confirmed this as she continued: 'He told them about me and Zoe. Said I might be *leverage*.' Her swollen lips struggled to navigate the word. 'He said they could use me to get at you, if bombing Elsewhere wasn't enough to put an end to the resistance. The General agreed to send me back to Wyndham.' She bent over to cough, wrapping her arm around her broken ribs.

Zoe wiped Paloma's face with the rinsed cloth, pressing it gently to her forehead.

'That was when they mentioned the coast,' Paloma said. 'Talked about a launch.'

'Launching what?' Piper asked. 'A boat? A bomb?'

Paloma shook her head. 'I don't know. I told you – I was slipping in and out. I didn't understand half of what they said.'

'It's OK.' Zoe lifted the cloth from Paloma's forehead. 'You need to rest,' she said. 'I'll get another blanket.'

'Did Zach do any of this?' I said quietly to Paloma, when

Zoe had crossed to the heap of saddlebags. In a way, it was irrelevant. Zach was responsible. He had taken her from New Hobart and handed her to The General. He had caused her torture, as surely as if he had held the knife himself. But I wanted to know.

She kept her eyes closed, but shook her head again. 'He was there, with The General. But he never touched me,' she said. Her tongue ran over her broken teeth again. 'And they didn't hurt him either. The General was very clear about that. *I'd kill him myself if I didn't need him*, she said.'

So they needed him yet. There was hope and despair in that: hope, that I might live longer. Despair, that Zach was still caught up in it all. That whatever The General was planning, he was going to be a part of it. We both were. My stomach lurched and the air in my throat felt as thick as tank liquid.

'Was he a prisoner too?' Piper asked.

Paloma shook her head. 'With him, it was more like a negotiation. He'd brought me to them, he kept saying. He was on their side, he said, over and over. And he knew things. He had something they needed.'

'What?' I asked. 'What did they want from him?'

She kept her eyes closed.

'I don't know. They were offering him stuff: said they'd make it easy for him, let him back on the Council. Even said they'd help him to catch you. *Bring her in for good*, they said.'

I knew what that meant: the tanks.

'What did he tell them?'

Her good eye was barely open. 'I don't know. But he told them something. After the second day, it was different. They untied him, talked to him differently. I think they were still watching him – they always made sure the guards were close – but they treated him differently. Like one of them.'

She lapsed back into silence. Zoe returned, and spread a blanket on the ground for Paloma. I tried not to stare at Paloma's reconfigured body. When Zoe helped her to lie down, I saw the places where Paloma's fingernails should have been, and my hands curled instinctively inward to shield themselves.

I reached to my neck, where I had fastened the snakewood capsule that I'd picked up from the floor of her room, and I wondered how something as simple as a leather cord snapping, or being slit, could lead to this: Paloma's broken body; Elsewhere's burning.

'They mentioned a name,' she said. Her voice was a croak, as broken as the rest of her. 'When they talked about the coast. *The bay*, they said, a few times. But once, one of the soldiers called it something else: *Cloven Bay*.'

That was when I really saw it for the first time. My hand on the snakewood capsule, I closed my eyes and saw the Scattered Islands, as if from high above: a collection of rocky isles, flung across the sea like something broken.

Then I saw the blast. It was like a travelling trickster, whipping a rabbit from a hat. It was sleight of hand on a massive scale: in a flash, a mountain was changed into dust, an island turned into the sea.

The flash was a light that nothing could withstand. Bright enough to strip everything down to bones, and bones down to dust. It broke time – everything was impossible except for the light, which had become everything.

When the flames hit, the smaller islands disappeared altogether. The ash made a funnel in the air, then spread, draping itself over the sky.

Winds, too, blowing from the north. Elsewhere would not send an answering bomb. But it would send an answer nonetheless, carried here on the winds: more ash, more poison.

*

That night, when Piper and I rode for Cloven Bay, Zoe stayed with Paloma. Nobody even suggested otherwise. With Simon, Crispin and the three other soldiers, they would ride to Hepburn, the nearest garrison still held by The Ringmaster, half a day to the south. But Paloma's injuries meant they could only travel slowly, and we were still close enough to the safehouse, and The General's garrison at Sulpice, to worry about pursuit. Piper and I took two spare horses, for speed, and left everyone else to guard Paloma.

'Are you sure?' Piper had asked me.

I nodded. 'This isn't about armies any more. It's about me and Zach.'

The blast, so close, had stripped away all the peripheral things. I knew now, with total certainty, that this would come down to the two of us: me and my twin. I would have preferred to go alone, but I knew that I would never win that argument with Piper. But I knew, too, that it would not be a matter of numbers. We weren't going to overthrow The General's army at Cloven Bay, or try to rescue Zach. If Zach needed rescuing, it was only from himself, and the capsule around my neck would achieve that as swiftly as all our soldiers.

Piper helped me to lift Paloma onto the horse. When she was settled, Zoe behind her holding her tightly around the waist, Paloma looked down at me. She spoke slowly. The corners of her lips were still crusted with blood, and her words fumbled, as though some of them fell into the holes where her teeth had been.

'You're not your twin, Cass,' she said.

There was no reproach in her words, but her voice itself, hoarse with screaming, was its own reproach.

Zoe was holding the reins, keeping the horse steady as it shifted, protesting the double load.

'We'll send soldiers from Hepburn to Cloven Bay,' she said to me. She turned to Piper. 'Stop Zach,' she said. 'Whatever it takes.'

She didn't look at me again. I knew what her last words meant. We all did. There would not be any happy endings, for any of us, if Elsewhere burned.

'I'll do it myself,' I said to her, quietly.

I didn't know it was true until I said it. The words sounded strange to me: flat and heavy.

Zoe looked at me for a few seconds. Then she gave a slow nod. There was nothing else to be said – not blame, or apologies, or thanks. We stared at each other: two women who knew that things had come to a point where none of these would make any difference. This was what had to be done. There were no choices left now.

Zoe turned the horse and led the small procession away. Piper and I watched them, for a moment, then headed west. I was going to find my brother and finish what we had started, all those years ago, when we were only children.

CHAPTER 30

The flames, my faithful companions, accompanied me as we rode. The blast was both past and future, balanced, and I was the fulcrum between them, on which the world teetered. I knew what I had to do.

After two nights and two days, we were approaching the Coast. On the last day, we stopped to let the horses drink at a low rivulet, already widening as it drew closer to the sea. I let myself lie back on the bank, my head turned to the side, to stare at the grass, and the spurs of a thistle, half-crushed by my horse's hoof. I wanted to commit it all to memory. Would this be the last thistle I'd see? The last time I'd narrow my eyes against the glare of the noon sun?

We came upon the sea sooner than I had expected. Cloven Bay was an inlet, a fracture set deep in the main coastline, so that while to the north the mountains continued to block the sky, and to the south the sea was still nothing but a haze on the horizon, immediately ahead of us was a deep bay, opening wide before two spurs of land narrowed in the distance, letting in the open sea.

Perhaps at Cloven Bay there had once been shrubs or

trees. Now, for those final miles before the water, there was nothing but stone, layers of shattered slate forming drifts of scree. We left the horses by the rivulet in the last stretches of the plain, before the grass surrendered to stone. We hobbled them, so that they could graze but not wander too far – but it seemed irrelevant to think of finding them again. I couldn't focus on the future, when there seemed no future possible beyond the blast.

To the south of us a dirt road snaked towards the bay; we avoided it, and walked towards the coast over the panes of broken slate, which slipped and scraped underfoot. By day's end we were close enough to the sea that we could hear the gulls, each harsh cry the sound of a knife being sharpened. Piper found a small cave – a fissure where one sheet of slate overhung another. Inside, coughing with the smoke, I crouched over a small fire and made a weak stew with the last shreds of our jerky and some mushrooms.

'You have to eat too,' he said, observing me as we sat outside and watched the sun lowering beyond the neck of the bay.

'I can't,' I said.

He reached for my hand and jerked his head towards the coast, where Zach was waiting.

'We'll find a way,' he said.

'Do you really believe that?' I asked.

'You're the seer,' he said. 'Do you?'

I believed in these things: the strange beauty of the scree below us, the shattered stones slipping away to the sea. Piper's hand, warm and wide, in mine. The cool slate under my crossed legs. These things were real – no more and no less real than the blast. I concentrated on them now.

Piper let go of my hand while he ate. Before the pot was half-empty, his movements seemed to slow. He coughed twice, and I watched as he looked at the spoon he was holding. It was shaking. By the time he'd lowered it back to the pot, sweat had sprung on his upper lip and temples.

I hadn't expected it to work so quickly – I'd thought he would slip into a heavy sleep later on. I'd not known exactly how much of the henbane and poppy tincture to add, when I'd slipped them into the stew. *Two spoons of that stuff*, Sally had said, *with a little henbane thrown in, and you can knock someone out entirely*. But I hadn't forgotten what she'd said next: *A little more, and you can kill them.* I'd tried to factor in Piper's size, and weight, adding a drop at a time as I squatted over the fire in the narrow cave, while he was on lookout.

He tried to say something, but the word didn't form. When he slumped sideways I was ready to catch him, and lower his shoulders to the ground.

It wasn't that I was afraid Piper would kill me. I was afraid that he wouldn't – or that he would try to stop me, if the time came. Once, I'd been afraid of his ruthlessness. Now, I was scared that he might hesitate, even if only for a second, when it came time to do what had to be done. I couldn't take that risk – not now, with the blast so near.

He gave a small groan in his sleep. I hooked my arms around his chest and dragged him into the cave, and made sure he was lying on his side, so he wouldn't choke if he threw up.

Outside, I sharpened my knife one final time, the way Zoe had shown me. Held the blade at the right angle to the whetstone; dragged it again, and again, and again, until the metal was hot to the touch. The snakewood capsule rested in the notch between my collarbones, but I knew the poison it contained was years old. If it failed, I trusted my knife, though I didn't relish the thought of raising the blade to my wrist. Wrist, or throat? I thought of Sally's body on the floor at Elsa's house, and I tried to remember what Zoe had taught me about the best places to stab somebody. If the capsule failed, I would have to do it quickly, and deeply enough that there'd be no surviving. I'd already witnessed my body's stubborn clutching at life. This had to be final: no chances, no escapes. No opportunity to be dredged back to a half-life in the tanks, like Kip and The Confessor.

It was time. I hated leaving Piper undefended and poisoned, so close to The General's squadron. But I had seen the blast. I had a job to do.

*

The cliffs at the water's edge were stark and black, but interrupted at intervals by collapsed sections, where the walls had given way to the sea. I had walked through the night to reach the cliffs with the dawn. There was no huge garrison waiting for me there, or even an encampment. Just a tower, cupped in the bay, and a long jetty on the beach below it. Near the middle of the bay, a ship floated at anchor. It looked nothing like any ship I'd ever seen. It was made of metal, gleaming beetle-black on the water. There was a certain beauty to it: its sharp lines, its sheer size. Like the beauty of a storm, or a sword, or a rockfall that takes with it half a mountainside.

It was so simple, so obvious. The blast machine had been moving the whole time: my wavering sense of its location had not been my mind failing me. It had been this ship, moving up and down the coast with its cargo of death.

I approached the cliff edge, broken slate scraping underfoot. A mile north of the tower, I came to the point where the ground finished, a sheer drop to the sea. I was relieved.

It would be easier that way. No need for the capsule, after all, or for the knife. This would be just a leap. I'd be following Kip, launching myself into air.

Staying close to the cliff edge, I traced it south toward the tower. Along the clifftop there was sand underfoot, and a few small clumps of marram grass, faded by the sun. The tower, several storeys tall, was made of the same grey slate as the rock all around. Grey tower, grey cliffs, grey sea. When the door gaped open at the tower's base, the red tunics were vivid. Six soldiers, riding straight for me.

I stood on the cliff and waited. The wind dragged my clothes against my body, my shirt flapping behind me, wrapping the front of me as tight as a shroud.

I raised my hands, palms toward the riders. It could have looked like a sign of surrender, or an order to stop. When they were within forty yards I took a small step closer to the edge, to make my point clear. I was so close to the edge that sand scuttled over the side when I shifted my feet. I felt the tremors in the ground from the horses' approach.

'Stop,' I shouted. The wind grabbed at my voice, but the tall soldier in front shouted something, and all of them reined in their mounts. The two women on the right were archers. Their arrows were notched, and pointed at me, but the tall man at the front still had one hand raised.

'Stop,' I said again, 'or I jump, and I take The Reformer with me.'

The tall man raised his chin as he appraised me. I didn't wait for him to speak.

'Tell my brother I'm waiting for him,' I said, shouting into the wind.

'I don't take orders from any Omega,' he said. 'Nor will he.'

'He'll come,' I said. I crossed my arms across my chest, and tried to look as confident as I sounded.

Everything depended on Zach now. Paloma had said that he had some sway with The General. He had given them Paloma and the location of Elsewhere, and they needed him for something else as well. Something that had kept him alive, and unharmed, since he'd escaped from New Hobart. *It started with me. And it ends with me* – that was what he'd told me.

I didn't know if he was a prisoner, or a Councillor again. But there had been no torture, and if The General wanted him dead, he'd be dead already.

The lead soldier leaned over and said a few words to the rider closest to him, who turned and galloped back to the tower. The rest of them stayed, a wall of horses in front of me, the cliff behind me. The tall soldier's horse shifted his weight from leg to leg. The red-haired archer lowered her chin slightly, letting her forehead rest against the bowstring, and the foot of the other archer fidgeted in the stirrup. Their arrows were still trained on me. I was poised to jump. If anyone made a move, there were two possible outcomes. Each of them ended in my death, and Zach's.

I heard Zach's horse coming, hoofbeats on the shale, but I didn't dare to move my gaze from the soldiers. Only when they had turned to see him did I turn too.

He had ridden alone. Last time I'd seen him his shirt had been ripped at the elbows and yellowing at the back of the neck, his trousers ragged and stained. Now his shirt was finest white, embroidered at the cuffs, and his boots were polished. He looked every bit the Councillor again, except for the healed brand on his forehead, and the way his chest rose and fell too fast.

'Draw back,' he shouted at the soldiers.

They hesitated. Zach looked from them to me, and back. I risked a glance at the cliff edge, inches from my feet. I felt strangely calm. Everything had been leading us to this point. My branding, and his. Kip's jump, and now mine.

'We have orders from The General to watch you, sir,' the soldier said. 'I can't leave you here with her.'

The archers' bowstrings quivered, pulled even more taut. The red-haired archer narrowed one eye; her other eye was fixed on me.

'The General ordered you to protect me,' Zach shouted. 'You heard what she said: I'm to be protected at all costs.'

The soldiers didn't move.

'Kill her and you kill me. Want to explain that to The General when she comes back? You heard what I said: draw back.'

The tall soldier looked back at his patrol. A slight nod to the archers, and they lowered their bows.

The riders withdrew, fanning out into a semi-circle on one side of us, the cliff on the other. Each of the soldiers was about a hundred yards away. They waited there, still mounted, and unmoving.

Zach took a step closer.

'Keep your distance,' I said.

He raised his hands, stopping where he was, barely four yards from me. His eyes were not on my face, but on my feet. I could see him calculating, measuring the distance from my feet to the edge, from the edge to the rocks and water below.

Behind him, away from the cliffs, the sun was fully risen. It was already hot on my face, and I felt so glad of my body, this warm and living thing. I was sorry I had to turn against it at the end. That the only weapon I had left was my own body, betraying itself.

Zach was still waiting, hands raised.

'I've come to finish it,' I said.

'You've come all this way just to kill us both?' he said. 'Is that really what you want?'

'No,' I said. 'I don't want it. But I'll do it, if that's what it takes. It finishes here.'

He gave a small sigh. 'So here we are again,' he said. I knew that we were both remembering that time, more than half a year ago, when I'd stood on the ramparts above the Keeping Rooms and threatened to jump. 'You keep pulling the same stunts.'

'So do you,' I said.

He acknowledged it with a slight nod. 'Come away from the edge.'

'You know it's too late for that,' I told him.

'It's later than you realise. The General's already leaving. The missile's been armed.' He jerked his head towards the ship. 'You're too late to save Elsewhere.'

I'd thought that I was prepared for this possibility – I'd seen the blast often enough. But hearing Zach's words, my guts lurched, and I felt as though all the air had dropped away from us over the cliff's edge.

'You can't do this,' I said.

'You can't stop us. You slowed us down a bit, along the way. You didn't make it easy for me,' he said. 'We'd got most of the bomb machine out before you came along and flooded the Ark, but that still delayed us, and cost us a few crucial components. But we had the bombs themselves. The people who made the Ark had protected them, at all costs. But the launch equipment and the long-range missile system needed work. Not just because of you. Some of it depended on things that aren't around any more: satellite navigation; the right kind of fuel.'

I understood only a handful of the words he was throwing at me, but they all meant the same thing: fire.

'The General came up with the boat,' he went on, glancing beyond me into the bay. 'She had everything shifted here without telling me, when she'd begun to turn on me. But it was a good idea, making the launch site portable. I'll give her that.'

'You don't have to do this,' I said. 'You can stop it.'

'How many times do I have to tell you? It's already done. We got the coordinates from Paloma – Elsewhere's within range. We're only moving the ship to open sea so that the western ranges won't be in the launch path. And to make sure the launch is out of sight – while the taboo still clings on, we don't need more trouble from our own people.'

I risked a glance behind me. He was right – the ship was moving, rows of oars low by the waterline, like the scuttling legs of a spider. The ship was making a slow turn so that it could head for the narrow mouth of the bay.

'What did you give them?' I said. 'Why hasn't The General killed you?'

'I was never as helpless as they thought,' he said. 'I always knew it was coming – that The General would try to push me out if I got too powerful. I knew I'd be vulnerable if I ever lost The Confessor. So we made sure I had a backup. Something to bargain with.'

'Paloma,' I said.

He shook his head impatiently. 'She was just a bonus. A gesture, to help remind The General of how useful I could be, when I came back to her.'

It sickened me to hear him speak of it in that offhand way. I thought again of the raw pink skin where Paloma's fingernails used to be. Each one with its cuticle of blood.

'We'd have found Elsewhere eventually,' he said, his

words rushing over one another, as though if he could just fill the silence for long enough he could stall my jump. 'It was only a matter of time. And if Paloma had been the only thing I'd brought to them, they'd just have taken her and then killed me. But The General had realised, by then, that she needed me. She had the bombs, but she couldn't use them without me.'

I remembered how The General had come to us, asking us to hand him over. The urgency in her words.

'It was The Confessor,' he said, and pride had sneaked into his voice. 'She did it for me.'

'I should have known,' I said.

He talked over me. 'You,' he said, drawing breath sharply between his teeth. 'You and all your secrets. Hiding who you were all those years. The Confessor wasn't like that. She didn't keep things from me the way you did.'

'What did she do?'

'She was the one who oversaw the rebuilding of the bombs. She understood the machines like nobody else. She put it all together.'

'Stop rambling,' I shouted. 'Tell me what she did.'

'She was too smart to trust The General. She knew that bitch would betray us if she could. We couldn't hide the Ark project from The General – too big, and she had too much power. But The Confessor made it so that only I could arm the bombs. A code – a number – that she gave only to me.'

'And without it?'

'Without it, each bomb's no more than a dangerous lump of metal. It can't be detonated. Only I can do that.' Again, that hint of pride in his voice. 'The Confessor made it like that. You never did anything but lie to me, hide things from me. But she gave me everything.'

What a gift it was. The power to end entire worlds.

'The General might have found a way around it, given enough time. That's why she wanted a seer – somebody who could understand the machines the way The Confessor had. But she had nobody. It might have taken her years to find a way, if ever.'

He swallowed, then went on. 'Even then I wasn't sure, at first, that the code would be enough to save me,' he said. 'When I fled from Wyndham, The General wanted me dead. I wasn't lying about that. I really thought she would do it – she was so angry, after you flooded the Ark. She wanted your uprising finished, no matter the cost. I had to come to you, to protect myself, and to give her a chance to see the bigger picture. To understand what I already knew: that the uprising and Elsewhere were linked, and that when she bombed Elsewhere, it would be the last nail in the coffin of the uprising, too. And that she couldn't do that without me.'

He raised his chin slightly. 'She understands that now,' he said. 'I handed her Paloma. I told her about the code. And I told them that if they tried to torture it out of me, you'd be dead in minutes.' He smiled at me, and it was worse than any threats or insults he could have hurled at me. 'You made this possible. You were useful, for once. You kept me safe.'

I was used to being dirty – in these last months, I had slept in swamps and wrung blood from my clothes. But I had never felt as filthy as I did in that moment.

'Safe for now,' I said. 'Once Elsewhere's destroyed, you think she won't betray you again?'

'She and I want the same thing,' he said. 'And I'm the one who's made it possible.' He gestured to his waist. Clipped to his belt was a metal box. When he'd first approached, I'd thought it was just a decoration: a gaudy belt buckle to match his embroidered cuffs. Now I looked more closely. It was square and steel, barely the size of his palm. On the front of the box, rows of buttons were shielded by a glass panel.

'I didn't tell her the code,' he said. 'I'm not an idiot – I know what I need to do to keep myself safe. There are other warheads on the ship. We're not using the whole arsenal on Elsewhere.'

I tried to imagine the idea of multiple blasts, but my mind couldn't even form the shape.

'As long as she wants to use them, she'll need me,' he continued. 'But I keyed the code in willingly,' he said. 'She and I will rule together.'

'There aren't any guarantees,' I said. 'Not with The General. She's betrayed you once already, when you had to come crawling to us.'

'It doesn't matter,' he said, arms thrown wide. 'I get what I want, because it's the same thing she wants: Elsewhere, gone.'

Once he'd told me that he wanted to change the world. That wasn't what he wanted at all, I realised. He wanted it all to stay the same. Everything frozen in time: the Omegas in our tanks, the Alphas in their perfection. Elsewhere gone, as if it had never been. He would preserve it all, like the old men in the tanks in the Ark.

'There are a million people there, Zach.' I thought of Paloma's parents and sisters, and all the families that I had never met. The knowledge and the medicines and the answers that would all burn. Even the animals, seadogs and trusses and alks, that would be seared from the face of the earth. The end of the world for Elsewhere, and the end of hope for us.

'Stop her,' I said, looking down at the ship. It had completed its turn now, and begun moving out towards where the head of the bay narrowed. On the decks, figures were moving, readying the sails for when they reached the open sea. 'Stop her, or I'll jump.'

'When you escaped from Wyndham, you threatened to jump,' he said. 'It was a bluff. You didn't have the courage then, and you don't have it now.'

He was right that I was afraid: afraid of the unyielding rocks below, and of pain. More than that: afraid to leave it all behind. The feeling of wind on my skin. Everything I had seen and known. I was so afraid that my windpipe clutched painfully at every breath, and my eyes were blurred with tears. But that didn't mean that I wouldn't jump.

'I don't have any choice,' I told him.

It was a relief, in an odd way. It was no longer a matter of choice – the burden of decisions had been lifted from me. It was straightforward now: if he didn't stop, I would kill us both.

'I don't have a choice either,' he said. 'We'll never be safe – not while Elsewhere's out there.'

I looked at him. He was squinting against the wind, and the sand that it threw at us.

'You are so afraid,' I said. I was thinking of the young soldier next to me, before the charge on Refuge 6, standing in his soiled trousers and shaking. Zach's fear was just as palpable. He carried it with him everywhere.

'You haven't come here to kill us,' he said. 'I know you. You'll have a plan.'

I shook my head. I was done with plans. I'd pulled them off so many times already. I'd got out of the Keeping Rooms when he'd locked me up. I'd escaped from the island, destroyed The Confessor and her machine. I'd freed New Hobart, destroyed the Ark, emptied Refuge 6. I had finished with plans now – I had no more left. There were no secret tunnels, no rivers to flood them, no decoys, no armies. Whatever luck I had, it had run out. Now it was just me and Zach, here on the cliffside.

'There's no plan,' I said.

'Then why are you here?' There was a hysterical tinge to his burst of laughter: too high, too quick.

'To make you stop the blast,' I said.

'I can't.'

'Then I jump.'

'Are you deaf?' he shouted. 'You can't stop me. It can't be stopped. It's not even up to me any more. I armed the bomb. She's out there now. When they reach open sea, she can launch it whenever she wants. And you can't stop her.' Again that unhinged laugh, like glass shrieking against glass.

I was too late. Elsewhere would burn, because I hadn't had the courage to end it earlier. I should have done it months ago, when The General had first come to us and asked us to turn him over. I should have known, then, exactly how much she needed Zach.

I turned away from him to face the cliff's edge. The sea below was choppy in the wind, its peaks as sharp as the rocks at the base of the cliff. How far out would my fall carry me? Would I land on the rocks or water, I wondered? It would make no difference.

'You're too late,' he said again. 'So there's nothing to be gained by killing me now.'

I looked back at him, and bent my legs slightly.

'Do you think I could live,' I asked him, 'knowing what will happen? Knowing I could have stopped it?'

What would it matter, one small death, in the face of

the destruction that my cowardice had already unleashed? I raised my head, felt the wind on my face, and listened to my own breath one last time.

'It won't achieve anything,' he screamed. 'And if you kill me, it can't be stopped.'

I froze. My legs were still bent, braced to jump. The sand beneath my feet was trickling over the edge. I could feel its minute shiftings, and the beckoning of the rocks below.

CHAPTER 31

'You said there was no way it could be stopped,' I said.

I eased away from the edge. Not even one complete step – just a few inches. But it was enough for him to release a shuddering breath.

'Talk now,' I said, 'or die.'

His breathing was still loud, and too fast.

'You said it couldn't be stopped, if I killed us both,' I said. 'So there must be a way that you can stop it.'

Still nothing.

'What else did The Confessor give to you?' I knew it would come back to her. When I was readying myself to jump, I had been thinking of Kip. And I knew that Zach was thinking of The Confessor, in what he thought were his final moments. The four of us were still locked together, somehow.

'There are two codes,' he said. His eyes kept darting beyond the cliff's edge, rehearsing our death. 'There's the one that arms the bomb – that's the one I entered, to buy my way back into the Council.'

'But that's not all,' I said.

He hesitated. 'The Confessor gave me an override code,' he said, dragging each word from himself.

I shouted, my voice rising until it split. 'What does that mean?'

'It's a safeguard – in case the bombs ever fell into enemy hands. It was already fitted, when we found the missiles in the Ark. The Confessor worked it all out. And she set the code, and gave it to me. The General doesn't even know about it. It cancels the warhead's activation, remotely, and deploys a localised blast.'

'Stop talking like a machine,' I yelled. 'Talk so I can understand you.'

'It stops the blast. And it triggers an explosion. Not a proper nuclear detonation, like the blast, but enough to damage the warheads, and probably take out the launch system and anything nearby.'

'So The Confessor gave you a choice,' I said. 'And not just the choice to use the bombs. She gave you the ability to do that – but she also gave you the choice to stop it.'

He shook his head. 'She knew what I wanted,' he said. 'She knew, more than anyone, that we couldn't take the risk of letting Elsewhere survive.'

'She gave you the choice,' I said again. 'Maybe she knew you better than you know yourself.'

'And that's what you've always thought, isn't it? That you know me better than I know myself.' He spat. The phlegm hit the sand by my feet.

'I do know you,' I said. It seemed such a small thing – a tiny claim. *I do know you.* Four words to stand against that black ship, the machinery of death moving through the bay below us.

'You don't know me,' he shouted. 'You have an idea of me, and you want to limit me to that. You always have. You think I should have stayed with you. Lived a small life. Never joined the Council, never followed my ambitions.'

'Never killed. Never drowned children in tanks, or sent a bomb off to kill thousands upon thousands.'

'Have you had a vision of me stopping?' he said. 'Is that it? You've seen me change my mind?'

And I realised, then, that he wanted me to say yes. He wanted, more than anything, for me to nod, to tell him that my visions had shown me his redemption.

In the Ark, when the black water was rising around us, and I thought I would give up, my body had ambushed me with hope, and had fought to survive. And in the months since then, I had let myself foster that small thing. I recognised little enough of Zach these days. But I did recognise that clutch in his voice: he wanted me to say that he would change. He didn't believe it, but he did hope for it.

But I wasn't going to lie to him.

'No,' I said. 'In my visions, the blast comes again. Elsewhere burns. Xander saw it too. We both had visions of the blast that you make.'

There was such a mixture of triumph and defeat in his eyes.

'That's it, then,' he said.

'No,' I said again. I saw it all very clearly, for the first time. 'It's not about the visions. It's never been about me being a seer. The visions have never been anything but a distraction. I'm not the only seer. Lucia and Xander had visions too. And The Confessor's visions were as strong as mine – stronger, probably. It's not the visions that are going to make the difference to what happens now. They don't matter.

'The important thing that being a seer gave me was that it allowed me to hold off being split for so long. It meant that I could stay with you. That time, those thirteen years – that's my only gift. It's nothing to do with the visions. Because those years were what allowed me to see things differently.'

'They were the worst years of my life,' he said.

'Perhaps,' I agreed. 'But I know you. Not because of any visions. Because I was there, for all those years. I hate you, more than I would ever have thought it possible to hate somebody. But I know you. I know how you became what you are. And I know that you're capable of being something else.'

I was thinking of Piper's words, when I'd found him crying by the spring: *I am everything that you fear I am. But that doesn't mean that's all that I am.*'

'You can't make me do anything,' Zach said. 'Even if you jump.'

I nodded. 'I know. I haven't seen you stop it. And there's no seer magic in me that can make you stop it, or undo the things you've already done. There's nothing but the choices you make.'

So many choices had already led us here. And we were stuck in a cycle, bigger by far than all of us. The blast, then and now. The tanks in the Ark and now in the refuges. The rooms in the Ark where the mad had been locked away to die, and the Keeping Rooms. It was a cycle, and Zach and I would either continue it or find a way to break it.

I had lied to Zach, when I said there was no magic. There was the only kind of magic I believed in: the same magic that had seen Kip make his jump. The magic that had led Paloma to stay here, and not to flee. It was a messy magic that promised no happy endings. It had not saved Kip's life, or spared Paloma. But it had led Zoe to find her and to carry her away. It had not saved the drowned children of

New Hobart, but it had seen them wrapped, one by one, by Elsa's shaking hands. It was love, and kindness, and hope, and there was little enough of it in our scorched world, but I knew it to be real.

'I made my own choices,' Zach said. 'Nobody forced me.'

'Yes,' I said. 'It wasn't an accident. You chose. And you'll have to live with your choices. You're responsible for them. I saw how you were shaped, but you still made choices.'

'Lecturing me about that isn't going to change anything.'

'You don't get it, do you?' I said. 'It was all your choice. That's something you'll have to bear. But it means that you're free to make a different choice now.' I thought about all the choices that had been made. Kip's leap. Zoe's decision, to step away from the comfort of an Alpha life and to work with Piper and the resistance. Paloma, and her choice to stay here and help us, despite what it had cost her. 'You're not limited by what my visions have shown me,' I said, 'or by what you've done so far. It's your choice.'

Zach was staring at me, his nostrils pinching with each breath, his face rigid.

I looked at him and I saw the boy I grew up with. His face across our childhood bedroom as we passed whispers between our beds. The boy with the thin legs who had learned to swim with me in the river. Sun coming through the willow trees. Water up to our chins. Him watching me, me watching him.

'Don't be afraid,' I whispered. 'It's up to you. Your choice.'

*

I don't know what he saw, or what he thought, in those moments on the cliffside, while the wind threw itself against our faces and the soldiers watched us, shifting at the edges of my vision. But he gave a tiny nod, a slow bowing of the head, and something changed in him. An old fear, slipping away down the cliff like sand under our feet. There was still terror in his face, and there was plenty to be afraid of – the soldiers, the task ahead of us – but something had shifted in him. He had been running from himself for so long that there must have been some element of relief in stopping, at last, to face himself.

'Keep your distance,' he shouted to the soldiers, as he led me further north along the cliff. 'A move from any one of you, and we both go over. You'll swing for it – The General will make sure of it. So keep your distance,' he said again. 'I have this under control.'

I noticed how he slipped back into his authority. A few seconds ago, his voice had been wavering as he'd begged me not to jump. Now he was The Reformer again, and not Zach. He hurled orders at the soldiers, and I watched them juggling their different fears: their fear of disobeying orders; their fear of him; their fear of The General.

If he'd headed back towards the stronghold of the tower, or towards his horse, it might have been too great a provocation, forcing the soldiers to disobey. But he simply walked away along the cliff, with me following close behind. And they did obey him, holding back as the two of us followed the cliff edge north, closer to the mouth of the bay.

A few hundred yards along was a path down to the water. Barely a path, really – steps cut into the stone, and patches where the cliff eased into a slope that we could scramble down. After the first few yards of descent, I could no longer see the soldiers on the clifftop, and they didn't follow – Zach's authority was holding, and the path led to nothing but the water. What could we do, there or anywhere, against that black boat, larger than the tower?

He was below me, and when my feet dislodged stones they dropped onto him and he swore, but didn't slow. When we were close enough that I could hear the individual waves hitting the rocks, I pulled the snakewood capsule from my shirt and pressed it between my lips, pursed over my teeth. I no longer trusted that the fall would kill me, and I had learned better than to trust him.

There, at the northern side of the bay was a small jetty with a handful of fishing boats – abandoned, probably since The General's soldiers had claimed the bay and built the huge jetty below the tower.

Zach stepped into the dinghy first. I didn't waste time untying the rope from the jetty's post – just sliced it with my dagger.

The water was choppy and cold when the low waves sprayed us. We rowed side by side, in silence. I could feel his shoulder close to mine, our bodies moving in time. In the open sea, the ship at sail would leave us far behind. But here in the shelter of the bay, the huge ship lumbering at oar, our dinghy was nimbler, and faster too.

I spat out the capsule, though it still hung around my neck with the weight of a promise. 'How close do you have to be, to stop them?' I asked, looking down at the box on his belt.

'Close,' he said. 'A few hundred yards, at most. It used to work long distance, The Confessor said, but all that went down with the rest of the machines. She was working on a way to fix it. But then—' He fell silent. That story ended the same way as so many stories, these days: a broken body. A tank.

'There'll be an explosion,' he went on, eventually. We

were both panting as we rowed. 'Nothing like the blast itself – the nuclear detonation isn't easy to pull off. It's a careful sequence, initiated only when The General launches the bomb. This blast will be nothing like that – but it'll be big enough to take down her ship.'

I peered over my shoulder again, without stopping rowing, to see the ship. It had looked big from the cliff; now that we were at the water level, and less than two hundred yards away, it was so tall that it seemed to block half the sky. It was its own island. On the clifftop, when Zach had conceded that single nod, I'd wondered if he was doing it just to save his own life. I had my answer now. We both knew that any explosion big enough to take the black ship down would be big enough to take us with it.

'They've seen us,' Zach said.

I looked over my shoulder again; there was new movement on the black deck, and shouts.

Zach reached for the metal box and unclipped it from his belt. Now that we'd stopped rowing, our small boat was knocked about by the waves. When I tried to see the numbers on the buttons, they were blurred by his shaking hands.

An arrow came at us, and now I was grateful for the choppy water that kept us turning and shifting. The arrow's shaft passed over my shoulder and into the waves; I dropped from the seat and crouched on the floor of the dinghy, in the shallow water that sloshed there. Another arrow hit the dinghy's prow and stuck there like a figurehead.

Zach was crouching opposite me, holding the box on the wooden seat between us. He had slid back the glass cover, the numbered buttons exposed, and the outstretched finger of his right hand hovering above them. It came down to such a small thing. Not a war, or even a battle. No heroics, or speeches. Just the two of us together in the boat, and his hand on those buttons.

I took his wrist. I was not trying to comfort him – there was no comfort to be had, even if he had deserved it. I only wanted to still his shaking fingers, so that he wouldn't press the wrong buttons and waste our only chance.

He raised the box slightly, keeping it pointed at the ship even as our boat was jostled by the waves. He pressed a button, and then two more. Another arrow plunged into the water just beyond him. He ignored it, and pressed again, then looked straight at me as he pressed the last button.

For a long moment, nothing happened. *That's it*, I thought. *The end of Elsewhere. The end of everything.*

Then the blast bloomed in the belly of the ship. The whole ship seemed to swell for a moment, fattening and bulging, until the explosion burst from inside, shattering the hull.

And so it did end in fire, after all: the flame bursting from its white centre. The fire opening like an eye. I'd seen that shape in my visions so many times that the explosion felt like coming home. The mast hung for a moment in the air, like a finger pointed at the sky, and then it, too, fell. There were only fragments, now, of the ship. It was black dust, settling in a ring around the flames. From somewhere beneath the surface, another blast came, pushing a plume of water fifty yards in the air. I'd seen that shape in my visions, a spreading spire of fire the size of the sky. But this was smaller, and made of white water. Then it was gone, and the spire of water was collapsing on itself. Beneath the water, a bright circle expanded from where the ship had been.

The hot breath of the first explosion had pushed our boat away, and then almost immediately we were sucked back towards the blast. The dinghy lurched forward, so fast that I felt the very air dragged from my lungs. Then, when the plume shot into the sky, it unleashed a second wave of heat, roiling outwards. Our boat was gone, and we were hurled into the scorching air.

I landed flat on my back, the impact knocking from me any air that the blast had not already snatched. The sea was alive, thrashing and pulling. I opened my eyes underwater, and saw the sea staring back at me. Through the black water, a bloom of light, brighter than the sky.

Then my lungs reminded me, with a jab of pain, that time still existed, and that it had been a long while since I had breathed. Somewhere above me the day waited, but I didn't know which way was up. There was only dark water around me, and the blaze of light in front of me, which allowed for nothing else.

I must have screamed or cried out, because the last shreds of air in my lungs emerged as a scatter of bubbles, glowing orange with the blast's reflected light. My mind had stopped working, but my body, faithful to some old wisdom, followed the bubbles upwards. My legs kicked and my arms thrashed, and I thought that even if it was too late, it was better to go like this, fighting and kicking.

I found the air, bursting into a day that was only a pale mirror of the light burning in the sea's belly. My lungs hurt with air, a good hurting, and I gulped breath after breath. The surface was oddly still, a glassy sheen laid over the churning below. I looked to where the blast had been. Already it had faded, the water returning to its habitual blackness.

Zach was floating nearby, on his back. I hauled myself through the water to where he lay. He turned his head to look at me. His eyes were as glassy as the water.

'Are we alive?' he said.

I still didn't have enough breath to speak. I coughed up water, and when I tried to breathe in again, more sodden coughs came, refusing the air. Behind Zach, I could see debris from the ship floating.

'Are we alive?' he repeated.

I opened my mouth to answer, but I was slipping under, salt water in my mouth and nostrils. Zach was slipping too, and we grabbed at each other as we sank.

It was the same as it had always been. We would either drown each other, or save each other.

CHAPTER 32

Finding the boat was the easy part – it had been thrown clear, and though it was half-filled with water, it was still the right way up, floating lopsidedly barely fifty yards away. Zach and I dragged ourselves there together, pushing through the pieces of debris from The General's ship. Climbing into the dinghy was harder. For a long time we just clung to the side, until my hands began to slip, chilled, from the wooden edge, and I realised that if we didn't stir ourselves from our exhaustion and clamber in, we wouldn't get a second chance. I dragged myself in, scraping my stomach and thighs on the side and was bailing water with my hands by the time Zach followed. Both the oars were gone, so we drifted at first, debris scraping and bumping against the boat's bruised sides. Then we paddled with our hands through the wreckage, until I found a long strip of metal, twisted out of shape, and hauled it in; Zach reached for a plank, scorched at one side, and together we paddled.

I talked to him, as we heaved our makeshift oars for shore. There was a ringing in my ears that I hadn't noticed until

I began to speak and found I could hardly hear my own words. I spoke anyway. It was the final task I had to do.

'When you first came to us for shelter, I told you that you'd done unspeakable things. But they're not unspeakable.' I had let myself, and him, off the hook, by refusing to name them. There would always be a gap between the words and the reality – but I could have spoken them, if I'd dared. I'd had the words, but I hadn't wanted to speak them, to attach them to my twin, and to myself.

And so I spoke them. I had learned a lot about the inadequacies of words, but also about their power. I spoke his crimes, one at a time, as we paddled. I thought of the battles, and the tankings, and I named as many of the victims as I could. *Kip. Rhona. Violet. Tash.* I named each of the children that I had recognised when I'd pulled their bodies from the tanks in New Hobart. *Alex. Louisa. Oliver. Liliana.* I spoke about Leonard, and his torture and death. Xander, and his small, broken body. Paloma, and the rows of scars on her hands, her wrists. For some of his victims, all I had was a name – so I spoke that. For most of his victims, I didn't even have names, but I described the faces and the bodies of those I had seen in the refuge, and everywhere else.

I didn't know if he even heard me. I kept talking anyway, my words keeping time, one stroke for each name. Beside me, he paddled to the same rhythm. My words were not a penance for him, and they could not begin to heal the damage he had done – how could they, when the dead were in their graves, Paloma's wounds still open, the untanked still pale and silent at New Hobart? But I needed to say it: to lay each of those crimes at his feet, and not at my own. To say: *You did this.*

I imagined that our boat was sinking lower and lower as I spoke, filling with the names of the dead and the tanked.

I ran out of water before I ran out of names. A small pebbled beach was in front of us. Piper was waiting there, already wading thigh-high to meet the boat. Behind him, on the shore, I saw the red tunics and black armbands of The Ringmaster's soldiers.

When I let my clumsy paddle drop, Piper towed us to the shallows. I stumbled when I stepped into the water.

'We saw the blast,' he said. 'Is it over?'

His voice barely reached me over the ringing in my ears. I looked back to the boat, and to Zach, slumped on the seat. Beyond, the water had calmed. The sea had once again swallowed its secret. The General and the blast machine were in the depths, and nothing marked where they had gone down but a stain of smoke on the horizon.

'Is it over?' Piper asked again.

I looked up at him.

'Yes,' I said, and until I heard myself say it I had hardly believed that it was true.

Together, we pulled the boat to the shore. Zach still sat, unspeaking. He threw out his arms to steady himself as we wedged the boat up onto the beach. I felt the small pebbles shifting beneath my feet and closed my eyes for a moment.

No blast came. Only the dark of my own eyelids, which had never before seemed so merciful.

'What happens now?' Piper asked.

I opened my eyes, looked at him, and smiled. 'I don't know.'

PART 3

CHAPTER 33

I don't remember much of what happened in those next hours and days. My ears were blocked with water, and by a ringing sound that didn't recede. Piper was there, and more of our soldiers – those who had followed The General's squadron when our party split up, and others, sent by Zoe and Simon from The Ringmaster's garrison at Hepburn. There was no fighting – or if there had been, it was over by the time Piper led me and Zach up to the tower. The General's soldiers had seen her ship go down. Leaderless, disarmed and outnumbered by The Ringmaster's soldiers, they were lined up in front of the tower when we approached. Seeing Zach, some of them saluted him.

He didn't even seem to see them.

In the days and weeks that followed, he did not change. It wasn't an injury from the explosion – neither of us seemed to have sustained any physical damage beyond superficial cuts and bruises, and the ringing in my ears that I could still hear whenever it was quiet. But something in him had changed, or broken. I wondered, sometimes, if it was the blast that had knocked the words from him, or if it was the recitation of his crimes while we were paddling back to shore. Either way, it made no difference. During the journey back to New Hobart, he rode silently, shackled hands slack on the front of his saddle.

Back at New Hobart we kept him shackled and guarded, but there was nothing to guard. He ate, and slept, and even followed instructions – Elsa brought him simple tasks for the kitchen sometimes, and he sat on his bed and shelled peas, or peeled potatoes. He was never allowed out of our room, now. It wasn't that we feared he would escape. It was Paloma: it was enough that she knew he was in the same building, and I had promised myself that she would never have to see him again.

*

During that journey back to New Hobart, I too had mostly ridden in silence. I had spent my life trying to look forward and fathom the future. Now I had a chance to look back, and to think about all the things that we had saved, and all the things that we had been unable to save. It was a reckoning, a sifting through the ash that the blast visions had left in my mind, and through the new visions that the nights still threw at me. It was heavy work, and often, during those quiet weeks that followed the end of the blast, I felt more tired even than I had during the months of running and fighting.

It was a time of dispersal. For so long, everything had seemed to be converging at New Hobart. Now, in the weeks while we waited for Paloma to heal, people were leaving. The General's soldiers had surrendered to The Ringmaster, and there was already talk of who would sit on the new Council. The Council's encampment outside New Hobart had been disbanded, leaving acres of trampled grass. When the wind gusted from the east, it carried with it the fetid odour of the dead, buried in swampy ground that had spat them back out as the late spring days grew hotter.

The ships were waiting on the coast, and the spring northerlies were easing, but the fleet could not leave until Paloma was well enough to travel. The soldiers at New Hobart began to be dispatched back to Wyndham, and to garrisons along the coast. Squadrons rode out to begin liberating the remaining refuges and empty the tanks, while others were sent to build places for the untanked to be housed. This would not be a quick process, and there were no easy solutions. But I remembered what I had thought, weeks before: that destruction can be quick, but worthwhile things take time. And now, for the first time that I could remember, we weren't running out of days.

It took time, too, for Paloma to recover. Back in the holding house, even after her wounds had closed and her broken fingers were straightened and beginning to mend, she didn't want to be touched. If Elsa passed her a bowl of food, she flinched when their hands met on the bowl, and if any of us passed her in the corridor, leaning on her crutch, she flattened her back against the wall. She wouldn't even touch Zoe, though Paloma stayed near her, and was uneasy whenever Zoe left the holding house.

Zoe never complained. On one of the first mornings of summer, I saw her at the log heap stacked against the courtyard wall, picking up each of the large boughs and inspecting it, turning them in her hands and checking them from every angle. She inspected each piece, testing its weight in her hands and peering at it closely. One after another she tossed them aside – the pieces that were riddled with knots, or where the wood grain was too wide – until she finally found a log that suited her. I watched as she peeled the bark from it in long strips. The first shaping she did with her dagger, slicing chunks from the wood, and then shavings, which fell around her feet like snow. Then she sanded it, smoothing the surface until the leg began to take shape.

It took days. I sat by her, one afternoon in Elsa's courtyard, while she sanded the leg. Paloma was sleeping – she slept a lot these days, while her body was still healing.

'It's slow work,' I said to Zoe, gesturing at her coaxing of the leg shape from the wood.

She looked at me and shrugged. 'One thing you learn as a fighter: don't make the same mistake twice.' A pause, as she wrapped the sandpaper more tightly around her hand. 'You fight somebody and cop a strong left jab to the face, you learn to duck fast.'

The rasping of the sandpaper matched the sound of the cicadas on the roof.

'I wasn't patient enough,' she said, 'with Lucia. I won't make that mistake again.'

She couldn't replicate the metal socket of Paloma's old false leg, useless now anyway given the damage to the metal bone; instead, Zoe created a curved nest to fit around Paloma's knee and thigh. I watched how she hollowed the wood where it widened at the top, so that it would fit perfectly over Paloma's knee. She never touched Paloma or measured anything, but I saw her tracing the wood with her hands, remembering exactly how Paloma's stump curved. In the base of the hollow she carved a notch to house the bent metal tip that protruded from Paloma's knee, and spent half a day sanding around it so that no splinters would snag or rub at Paloma's skin.

She didn't attempt to carve a foot; the leg tapered to a

flattened tip which she coated in tar, letting each layer dry before applying the next, until she'd built up a black nub, slightly rounded. She fixed leather straps around the top of the leg. I watched how she trimmed the screws, chopping the ends off so that they wouldn't poke through to the inside, where Paloma's leg would nestle.

Paloma never said anything about the leg, as we all watched it take shape beneath Zoe's hands. She sat, always the same careful distance from Zoe, and waited. When it was finished, Zoe oiled it: three layers, each one turning the wood a shade darker. Zoe's hands, too, took on the oil, which made them darken and gleam, until the wood and her skin were almost the same shade. Then it was finished. She gave it to Paloma, handing it over carefully so that Paloma could take it without touching Zoe's hands. Paloma took it in silence. She didn't try it on in front of the rest of us, or even in front of Zoe. She went on her crutch to their room, and when she came back a few hours later, she was wearing the new leg, strapped tightly over her trousers. She walked slowly on it, still using her crutch at first while she got used to the balance. But she walked towards Zoe, and when she sat she was closer, their elbows nearly touching. The next day, she laid the crutch down, and leaned on Zoe's shoulder as she took her first hesitant steps around the courtyard.

*

The Ringmaster's soldiers had retaken control of Wyndham, meeting no resistance from The General's army, rudderless and unsure about their future under the new Council. Simon accompanied The Ringmaster to Wyndham, and came back full of tales: Omega soldiers walking the streets of Wyndham for the first time. The Council chambers thrown open – half stripped by looters, Alpha and Omega alike.

I asked Simon, quietly, whether they'd found The General's twin.

'There was a room,' he said. 'A cell, really. Directly underneath The General's own chambers. She was the only one with the key, her soldiers said. It took us two days to get the doors down.'

I didn't need to ask what they'd found inside. I'd felt it, in those first moments after The General's ship had exploded. I had felt him, her twin, underwater like me, and dying in the dark.

'We gave him a proper burial,' Simon said, and I nodded. So often, lately, it had felt that laying out the dead was the only amends available to us. We had buried Xander, and burned the dead children, and it had changed nothing, except perhaps making it easier for us to keep breathing. Perhaps that was reason enough.

*

The untanking was happening, but only gradually. Four of the refuges closest to Wyndham had been emptied, but plenty remained. I understood the need for caution – I'd seen for myself, at Refuge 6, those who didn't survive being brought back into the air. And Zach, adrift in his silence, was no help to us now in navigating the tank machines. But some of the Council soldiers who had worked on the tanks were assisting, trading their information, and their advice on the best way to bring out the Omegas safely, for clemency.

'We have to control the narrative,' The Ringmaster said,

when I complained to him about how long the process was taking. 'If we're hasty, it won't be a story about The General and The Reformer's inhumanity and cruelty. It'll be a story about how we killed hundreds, or thousands, and their twins, by dragging them out of the tanks.'

All day, I thought about what he'd said. That night, I found Piper.

'There's something I need you to do for me.'

He raised an eyebrow and waited.

'Gather the bards. As many as you can. Especially Eva, if you can find her. Send them to the remaining refuges, along with the soldiers. Let them see what the Council did there.'

I couldn't order the bards to write a song about it. But I knew that if they saw the tanks, the pristine torture of those half-dark rooms, it would find its way into song and story. It would spread, like the refuge song that Leonard and Eva had written together, so that people would know the truth of what had happened inside those places. So that it would never be allowed to happen again.

But Piper looked grave. 'You saw what they did to Leonard,' he said. I could hardly forget: his neck stretched out of shape as he'd hung from the tree. His broken fingers. 'They travelled together,' Piper went on. 'Sang together. You know that Eva's probably dead.'

'But she might not be.'

I smiled as I said it. Since we had snatched the world back from the blast, every day seemed so unlikely that I could believe almost anything.

'Haven't you learned by now not to underestimate their cruelty?' he said.

'Their cruelty is exactly why I think she might be alive. They hanged Leonard where they knew we'd find him, to send a message to all of us in New Hobart. If they'd caught Eva, they'd have wanted us to know. She'd have been hanging there too.'

He nodded. 'OK. I'll put the word out.' He thought for a moment. 'And not just for Omega bards. The Alphas need to hear the truth too – need it most of all, probably. I'll get The Ringmaster to summon the Alpha bards as well.'

For the rest of the day, I kept thinking of Leonard and his voice, deep and frayed at the edges. I was imagining a new song, spreading.

*

I talked to Piper about who else would sit on the new Council.

'You, and Zoe, obviously,' he said. 'Me, The Ringmaster, Simon. Probably June.' I nodded – the grey-haired Omega had led the residents of New Hobart in their uprising within the walls, when we'd attacked from outside. 'And we'll need another Alpha, too. There's a Councilwoman from the eastern districts who's been a long-time moderate – she's the most likely.'

'Does Simon even want to be on the Council?' I remembered how relieved he'd been to hand control back over to Piper, when Piper had returned from the deadlands.

He shook his head. 'No more than I do. But we need him. The old guard of the Omegas will follow him. There are plenty who don't want to see us ruling with the Alphas at all, now that the truth about the tanks is coming out. They'd rather split entirely – a separate state. And plenty who'd go further, to be honest – who, given the chance, would treat the Alphas like they used to treat us.'

After we'd freed Refuge 6, The Ringmaster had said to

me: *It's easier to start a war than end one.* It wasn't going to be easy, unifying people behind the new Council. It would take time.

'When things have settled down,' Piper went on, 'we'll have to organise elections, work out regional governance, too. But this is all a long way away. For now, I'm not thinking any further than stability. Emptying the refuges, and starting negotiations with the Scattered Islands. It will only be an interim Council, to see us through until things are more stable.'

I thought of the Ark papers, and the *Interim Government* that had been set up there. They had still ruled decades later, when the Ark was falling apart, and they had entombed the mad in locked rooms, and built the tanks for themselves.

'Be careful,' I said.

He laughed. 'I'm not stupid. I know Wyndham's a nest of snakes – we've changed a lot of things, but we're not miracle workers.'

'That wasn't what I meant,' I said. It wasn't assassins or betrayals that I was warning him about, though doubtless there would be plenty of them. It was comfort, and power, and the things that they could do to people.

'I might be on the Council,' he said, 'but I'll still be the same person.'

'You won't be,' I said. 'And that's OK.'

I had learned this, slowly: that we could survive more than I had imagined, but that there was always a price to pay.

*

As the new Council began to take shape, and her body continued to heal, Paloma spent less time resting, and more time in discussions with us, about the shape that a relationship with the Scattered Islands might take. For hours, she wrangled with The Ringmaster, Piper, Simon, and Zoe, over trade, and resources. They debated how and when the Confederacy might distribute the untwinning medicine, and how we might repay them. How to work together to curb the piracy in Elsewhere's outer islands, if a trade route was to be established. Paloma was not authorised to make decisions on such things – only to commence negotiations – but as I sat in the Tithe Collector's office and heard her arguing and cajoling about trade routes and fuel tariffs, I knew that she had found a new role, and it suited her.

The holding house was noisier these days, with the voices of the untanked. Some of them remained silent, but most had begun to talk again. A number of those who had been staying at Elsa's were well enough to move out now and live alone. I would not have said they were fully recovered – perhaps they never would be. But they'd grown strong again, many of them now spending their days working. The wall around the town had to be dismantled, the lumber hauled up through the streets to be used to rebuild some of the burnt houses. During the long days of work, the untanked had begun to remember fragments of their lives, and to discuss them with each other. When Piper and I walked through the town, we could hear snatches of their conversations, their voices quiet amidst the hammer blows. *Abberley? There was a market there, wasn't there? I remember the bards coming through, for market day. I remember.* They were reassembling their pasts along with the houses.

Rhona had not yet left Elsa's, but she spoke now, if haltingly, and remembered a little of her life before the tanks. Of her time in the tanks, she remembered nothing, and I was glad of it.

I wondered whether some of the papers that we had

found in the Kissing Tree, salvaged from the Ark, might be able to help the untanked in their recovery. The papers were largely technical – page after page of numbers and diagrams – from the Ark dwellers' research, including into medicine. It was incomprehensible to us, but I thought that if the doctors came from the Scattered Islands, they might be able to make more sense of it than we could.

'But we'll have to be careful,' I said, when I suggested it to Piper. 'It wasn't only medicine they were working on. There's stuff in there that could be dangerous, in the hands of people with enough knowledge. Things about the bomb, and their experiments—'

Piper cut me off. 'You didn't hear?'

I looked at him blankly.

'There was a fire, in the Tithe Collector's office. It was while we were at the coast, chasing Paloma. The documents all burned.'

I cocked my head at him.

'All of them?'

He nodded. A smile was threatening the edges of his lips, but he held it at bay.

'The funny thing is, the fire was only in the storeroom where the papers were kept. And The Ringmaster said Elsa had been up there that same afternoon, helping with the untanked.'

I never said anything about it to Elsa, nor did she confide anything to me. Her husband had been tortured and killed for those papers. I watched her move about the holding house, and wondered if she moved with a new lightness, or whether I was imagining it. There were things in those papers that I wished had not been lost: the story of Heaton's courage; glimpses of useful medical information amidst the grim details of experiments and tanks and bombs. But I couldn't blame Elsa, and part of me was relieved to know that the papers had been consigned to the flames.

*

The Ringmaster was the first of us to move back to Wyndham for good. He came to see me before he left.

'We can't delay any longer,' he said. 'Now that the fort's secured, people need to see leadership from the new Council.'

'And what of the rest of the old Council?'

He shrugged. 'The General's at the bottom of Cloven Bay. As for him—' He glanced towards our room, where Zach was shackled. 'He's not fit for anything, and if he showed up in public he'd be lynched.'

'And the others?'

'They've mainly slunk off. Our soldiers captured a few of them – The Legislator, and The Senator. The Benefactor handed himself in. There'll be a handful of them who'll claim they were in the dark about what The General and The Reformer were doing. But that won't do them any favours – people will just see them as ineffective, instead of evil. They're finished – they'll never sit on the Council again.'

'Not you, though,' I said.

'Of course not,' he replied. His scar puckered slightly as he smiled. 'I'll still be there.'

I watched him for a moment.

'Like you never left,' I said.

'It won't be the same as before,' he said.

'You'll be more powerful than before, you mean. Not sidelined by Zach and The General. You'll have more power than ever, and the whole army behind you.' I paused. 'You got what you wanted.'

Did it matter? Did it make any difference, if he had done the right things for the wrong reasons?

'And what about your twin?' I said.

'What about her?' He jerked his head to the side, as if shaking off a fly. 'She's got nothing to do with this, or with me.'

'Then free her,' I said.

'She could still be a risk,' he said. 'We've made great progress, Cass – but don't pretend that those of us in power won't still be targets.'

'If you don't free her, you're not fit to be part of this new Council.'

'That's your idealism talking. We have to take small steps. We can't change everything overnight.'

'I'm not asking you to change everything. I'm asking you to take one fundamental step, to show that you understand that it's finished. The time of tankings, and Keeping Rooms, and Alpha rule – that's over.'

He kept his head still, but his eyes followed me as I moved to the door.

'You need me on the Council,' he said. 'An element of stability. The Alpha hero who saw the need for change and started the uprising. Someone the Alpha soldiers will follow.'

'You, starting the uprising?' I shook my head. 'You knew about the tanks for years, before you finally joined us at New Hobart. It was you and your troops who oversaw what was happening, while the resistance were risking their lives to fight back. Your soldiers were amongst those who attacked the island. You didn't even want us to chase after Paloma when they took her.'

'People don't want to hear that story,' he said. 'They want to hear the story about the brave rebel who risked his place on the Council to do the right thing.'

Neither of us had moved, but we were watching each other like fighters before the blades come out.

'It was you, all those months ago, who started that song the Omega bards were singing,' he said. 'You understand the power of stories. It doesn't matter if every word isn't accurate. It's the message that matters. You knew that, even then. You know that stories matter.'

'And what about the truth? Does that matter?'

'People don't need the truth. They sure as hell don't want it. They want a story they can believe in. We're asking them to believe in a whole new world, Cass. They want the stories that will make it palatable. They want leaders they can believe in.'

He held his hands out and shrugged, as though he had nothing to do with this system – as though he were just as bemused by it as I was.

'Let your twin go,' I said. 'Live up to the story that you're telling about yourself. Make it something more than a lie.'

'You have to face facts,' he said. 'I'd be at risk if I released her. What world are you living in?'

'The world we make,' I said.

He was still staring at me as I left.

*

I had a dream that night, of a woman a few years older than me. She had the same curly hair as The Ringmaster, but it was longer – so long that its weight dragged her head back as she sat against the wall of her cell.

They came for her at night. When the soldiers hauled

her to the door, it had been so long since she had been outside that she hesitated at the threshold, as if she didn't know how to walk past.

'Get out,' the guard said. He shoved a bag at her. 'We've had orders. You're to go, and quickly.'

She squinted at the light. I remembered that pain, when I'd seen the light for the first time after my years in the Keeping Rooms. How my eyes had longed for the light, and winced from it.

'Go,' the guard shouted. He gave her a push in the small of her back.

It was raining when she stumbled outside. I felt it on her face, because it was my face too, turned to the sky, letting the rain fall on my eyelids, her eyelids.

'Run,' the guard said. 'Don't stop running. Tell nobody where you've been, or who you are.'

She stepped out. She was me and Kip, all those months ago, stepping out of the cave after we'd escaped from Wyndham. She was Professor Heaton, making the escape from the Ark that he'd never managed. She was all those people in Refuge 6, emerging from the tanks and back into life. All with their chins raised at the same angle, to face the sky. More than any of that: she was herself, hot rain on her face, body starting to remember the world.

*

The northerly winds had changed. Spring was over, the grass on the plains already turning blonde in the sun. Paloma was walking more confidently on her new leg; in the hottest part of the afternoons, she sat in the courtyard with a length of rope and practised tying sailing knots with her nine crooked fingers. It was time for the ships to sail.

Zoe told me, early on, that she would be leaving with Paloma and the fleet.

'We've waited as long as we can. Probably longer than we should have – but with Paloma's knowledge of the northern seas, we should be able to sail swiftly. There's work to be done, in Elsewhere, to coordinate the help that they can offer us. Piper will need somebody to speak for us there – somebody he can trust. Four other advisers from the new Council will be coming too.'

I wasn't surprised that Zoe was going. But I thought of her dreams, pounded by the unforgiving sea, and I remembered when we'd sailed from the Sunken Shore, Zoe clutching the tiller so tightly that her knuckles were sharp in her hands.

'It'll be months at sea,' I said. And we both knew the dangers of the journey: not just the storms and the reefs, but the northern ice sheets, and the pirates in the outer islands of Paloma's home.

'The only thing more frightening to me than the thought of getting on that ship,' she said, 'is the thought of seeing her sail off without me.'

I had never before heard Zoe admit to fear. I thought of Lucia, and how Zoe had watched her leave on a ship and had never seen her again.

I remembered, too, that this would not be the first time that Zoe had left everything behind and started again. She'd done it at only ten years old, stepping out of the comfort of an Alpha life to follow Piper, when he'd been branded and sent away.

We both watched Paloma crossing the courtyard, practising on her new leg. 'She's the bravest person I know,' Zoe said, 'but she still needs my help.'

I stared at Zoe for a few moments. 'The second bravest,' I said.

She smiled, and we stood in silence.

'Have you told Piper yet?' I asked, eventually.

'Yes,' she said. 'But this isn't about him. This is for me.'

*

'You can't put it off forever,' Piper said to me that night, as the two of us sat in the kitchen. 'We need to decide what to do about Zach.'

I looked to the corridor, towards the closed door behind which Zach was shackled, and felt weariness settle on me. At every stage in my life, that had been the refrain: *What about Zach?* Every decision dictated by him.

'You know we can't set him free,' said Piper.

'I don't want him free,' I said. He didn't deserve freedom – he didn't deserve anything.

'They're clamouring for his death,' Piper said. 'Half the local representatives to the new Council. And the people in the streets. There's talk of a public hanging, or a whipping at the very least.'

I thought of the children's drowned bodies, and the faces of the crowd that had gathered on the streets of New Hobart to watch the procession of the untanked, when we'd returned from Refuge 6. I couldn't argue with the rage of those who wanted Zach dead – I'd felt it myself. The General had been sent to her death, under the sea. Did Zach deserve mercy any more than she had? Did I?

'You know I won't let you be killed, or harmed,' Piper said. 'But we can't keep him here forever. We need to be at Wyndham before much longer – I don't want The

Ringmaster to establish himself as the sole voice in the new Council. And we need to keep Zach safe. He has more enemies than you can imagine.'

I had no trouble imagining it. Who could we trust to guard Zach, year after year?

'At Wyndham—' He paused, and looked at me. He knew I wasn't going to like what he said next. 'There are the cells there,' he went on. 'Under the Council chambers. We'd be able to keep him secure there – keep you safe.'

I remembered my own years in the Keeping Room cells.

'Zach will go mad,' I said. It wasn't a complaint – just a statement of fact. Nonetheless, the thought of him in the cells set my own madness stirring, like a hunger.

'More than he has already?' Piper said.

I didn't respond. I was thinking not just of the Keeping Rooms, but also of the Ark. All of them locked down there, passing their madness from one to another. How some of them had been sealed away in Sector F. And I thought of The Ringmaster's twin in her cell, and The General's twin in the buried tank room below her chambers. It was the same old story, passed on through history: the Ark, the tanks, and the Keeping Rooms. It was time for a new story.

'Don't lock him underground in a cell,' I said.

'Would that be any more than he deserves?'

'Who gets what they deserve?' I asked. 'Did Kip? Or Xander?'

'You'd give him freedom, then?' said Piper.

'No.' I turned to him. 'There's one other option.'

CHAPTER 34

Before we left for the coast, to escort Zoe and Paloma to the fleet, I said goodbye to Elsa.

'Will you stay in this house?' I asked her.

'Of course,' she said. I hadn't been so sure – so much horror had gone on in this place. I wondered how many times she would be able to scrub blood from the holding-house floors, how many times she could patch the broken doors and shutters together, before she could bear it no longer.

'I'm needed here,' she said, with a jerk of her head at the courtyard window. I could see Rhona out there, sitting with some of the other untanked.

'You said to me once,' Elsa went on, 'that there weren't going to be any more children.'

I remembered that: I'd spoken in anger, in the trashed kitchen of the holding house, after we'd freed New Hobart. I'd hurled the words, to shatter on the floor like another piece of broken crockery. I'd meant that no more children would be brought to her holding house while we were at war and the town all but under siege.

'You were right,' she said, exhaling. 'There won't be more Omega babies brought here now. But not for the reason you thought.'

If the Scattered Islands brought us their medicines, there would be no more twins born, and no Alphas and Omegas. No unwanted Omega children to be abandoned on Elsa's doorstep.

'But the untanked still need caring for,' she said. 'There will be thousands more to come. And there'll always be children that aren't wanted.'

I nodded. If we ended the twinning, and every child bore a mutation, some parents would be reluctant to face the reality of our new world. I knew that Elsa would not turn those children away.

I took her hand. Her skin was roughened, and her joints were beginning to thicken, as Sally's had.

'I wish I'd met you in different times,' I said. 'Away from all of this.' I waved a hand at the kitchen wall, scorched and repaired, and the courtyard where Rhona and the others sat.

'No,' she said, shaking her head. 'You met me when you needed me. And when I needed you.'

*

We travelled with Paloma and Zoe to the coast. It was a big convoy, laden with supplies. Zach, shackled hand and foot, travelled in a guarded wagon in the centre. The closed wagon, with slatted walls, was meant to protect him, but it was also for Paloma. I didn't want her to have to look at him.

We passed one convoy coming the other way: a squadron of soldiers escorting a group of untanked, recently released from Refuge 12. They were heading for a new encampment built at Merricat, the lead soldier reported to Piper. We paused, and waited for them to pass.

Watching their slow progress, I wondered which of the sights would have seemed the most bizarre to me, just a few years earlier: the row of half-naked people, pale as the inside of a shell, walking in silence; or the soldiers escorting them, a mixture of Alphas and Omegas, riding together.

When we crested the final hills and came within sight of the coast, I saw *The Rosalind*. The two other ships in the fleet were larger and sleeker, lacking her tarred patches – but I smiled at her like an old friend.

In the camp the final night, with Paloma and Zoe sleeping on the other side of the fire, Zoe's dreams once again seeped into mine. It was, I thought, the last time this would happen.

She still dreamed of the sea, but it was a different dream now: a ship in sail, going somewhere.

*

The last things Paloma gave to Piper were the maps – the most detailed charts that she'd been able to draw in these last few weeks, showing the currents, the reefs, and the outer islands most prone to pirate raids.

It wasn't a promise – the sea made no promises. But it was an offering of sorts.

'Do you think your people will want to help us?' I asked Paloma, on that last day.

I couldn't blame the people of the Scattered Islands if they turned from our request in horror. Of the two emissaries who had come aboard *The Rosalind*, one had drowned before even landing here; the second had been tortured.

Paloma didn't ever talk about her torture. She didn't have to – there was no escaping what had been done to her. On her lap rested her broken hands. For all Zoe's careful tending, the fingers were still twisted at the joints, the scars pink and raised. The flesh on the inside of her wrists had healed well, but the precision of that orderly row of scars made them worse, somehow, than the huge scar on Piper's head, where his hair still had not grown back.

'I can't make any guarantees,' Paloma said. 'You know that. The Confederacy is the same as any other group of leaders – they'll want to know what's in it for them. I've seen it, often enough, in the negotiations between the separate islands at home. It'll come down to trade, in the end – power and money, the same as it always does.'

She jerked her head northwards, to the sea, away from the wind-brushed plains that spread out behind us.

'A lot of the islands are rocky,' she said, 'and the winters are harsh. There are things you can grow here, that we can't. Animals that have survived here, that didn't survive at home. And, somewhere, there are still some fuel reservoirs here that escaped the fires – Zach was using them to power the tanks. So there'll be delegations, and endless dull hours of negotiations – meetings between us and the Confederacy, and the doctors, too.' I noted the reverence with which she always spoke of the doctors. 'But it will happen, eventually.'

She looked over at Zoe, and her eyes creased into a smile. 'And Simon and I will keep her in line, during the negotiations, if she gets too fired up.'

Simon was going with them, so that the new Council would have both Alpha and Omega representatives during the negotiations. I was sorry to bid him goodbye, but glad to know that he would be with Zoe and Paloma.

I slipped my hand under my collar, and lifted the leather strap from my neck.

'This belongs to you,' I said, holding it out to Paloma. 'I found it on the floor after they took you.'

She took it, raising it high and letting the capsule swing. 'It's a bit late for that, don't you think?' She looked at it carefully. It was another past, in which things had gone differently. I didn't ask her which one she would have chosen.

She wrapped her crooked fingers around the locket for a moment, then drew back her hand and hurled the capsule over the cliff. We watched it fall, entering the grey water without a splash.

*

They sailed before dawn. By unspoken agreement, Paloma and I left Piper and Zoe alone to say goodbye. We walked ahead of them down the cliff path, and when we finally turned, everything that they had to say had been spoken, and Zoe, her face fierce with tears, was already striding forward to join Paloma.

Hand in hand, Paloma and Zoe waded through the knee-deep water to the dinghy, where Simon waited at the oars. On the horizon *The Rosalind* was waiting between the other ships. The dawn mist sat over the fleet, making it look like something half remembered from a dream.

Zoe held Paloma's arm to steady her as she stepped up into the boat. They sat together at the bow. When Simon began to row, Zoe didn't look back.

Piper stood in the shallows until the dinghy reached *The Rosalind*, and the fleet itself had begun to chase the horizon.

Whether or not the ship ever reached Elsewhere, whether or not they brought us their medicines, I watched Piper and I thought: That was the moment, right there. That was where the untwinning started.

*

We left that night. Just me, Piper, and Zach, slipping away from the camp after dark. We were taking Zach to the island.

If he knew where we were taking him, he showed no sign – just followed Piper silently, shackled hands fastened to the chain that Piper held.

It had been my idea. A prison that needed no jailers, and where there was nobody from whom he would need protection. It was the last gift that Piper could give to me: to keep Zach safe, and to spare me the certainty of his madness.

I'd wondered, at first, whether the island would remain abandoned, whether any of the islanders might want to move back there, eventually, but Piper was sure.

'After what they witnessed?' We were both thinking of the blood on the cobbles of the market square when The Confessor had executed her captives, one by one. 'The survivors aren't going back,' Piper said. 'And what's there for them? The town burned.'

It wasn't only that. The island had been a bolt-hole, a place of concealment. Before the battle of New Hobart, Piper had spoken to our soldiers. He'd said, *There is no place, any more, for Omegas in this world, except the one we begin to build here, tonight.* We had begun to build it, and now it was time for Omegas to claim it, and not to slink back to the island to hide once again.

The island didn't offer an easy life, either. The steep slopes inside the crater had to be coaxed to yield crops, and the winters were merciless. The crossing was dangerous in summer, and impossible in winter: nearly two days and two nights of sailing, ending in the reef, jagged spurs of rock shredding the sea for miles. Even if anyone had wanted to return, only a select few knew the way. The Council's fleet had been able to negotiate the reef only because of The Confessor, and she was dead.

So we sailed, ready once again to trust our secrets to the island.

*

This time the crossing was comfortable. The wind was steady, and the waves stayed low. Piper had arranged a neat little boat, with a covered deck to shield us from the worst of the sun. Zach sat at the prow, staring forward at the always-shifting sea, while Piper moved confidently around, winding the ropes and making the sails do his bidding.

The water sealed over the boat's wake, erasing all trace of us. The sea had always been good at keeping secrets.

There was a song that bards used to sing, about ghosts. I'd heard it when Zach and I were children. Leonard and Eva had sung it, too, the night we met them. In the song, a man had strangled his lover and then been haunted by her ghost. He'd fled across the river to escape her, because ghosts can't travel over water.

As I sat in the prow of the boat, I knew better.

*

Piper knew the reef so well that I didn't have to navigate, and I could sit at the back of the boat and watch the island emerge, its single sharp peak, from the reef-sliced water.

Nobody had been there since the Council's raid. In the hidden harbour on the island's western side, part of the jetty was burnt away, black spars piercing the water. Some of the Council's landing craft still floated there, but they looked less frightening now, painted with seagull droppings and weathered by the winter.

Zach sat on the jetty, staring down at the water, while we unloaded all of his things. Piper had been generous: there was food enough for months, as well as the seeds to plant. The stone tower above the harbour still stood, though the roof had been burnt away, and we stacked the provisions inside and covered them with canvas. We guided Zach up to the entrance to the north tunnel. The doors hung, mangled, from their hinges – one of them fell off altogether when we pushed our way in, to climb the tunnel up through the crater's side to emerge into what was left of the town. Of the dead who had fallen in the tunnel, vermin and time together had carried off any flesh that remained, leaving only bones that snapped cleanly underfoot. It was the same in the courtyard: a winter's worth of rain had scoured the stones of blood, and the carrion birds had picked the skeletons clean.

The fire had claimed most of the town, but the stone fort still stood, looking across the crater at the terraced fields, tangled and overgrown.

'You know I have to destroy the boats,' Piper said, before we began to descend back to the water.

'I know.'

The thought that Zach, lost in his own silence, could ever handle a boat, let alone negotiate the reef and find his way back to the mainland, was outlandish. But I knew we could take no more chances.

Piper checked the caves and the harbour, and together we dragged down two of the children's wherries that had been left behind when the last of the resistance had escaped. Piper poured lamp oil into the boats, and we pushed them away from the jetty and watched them burn, until our boat was the only thing that floated in the harbour.

Zach was shackled in the tower, while Piper and I sat on the jetty and watched the flames rise from the burning boats, sparks launching into the night.

'Do you ever think about it?' he said. 'That if Zoe and Paloma come back, and if they can persuade Elsewhere to help us, we'll be among the last of the twins?'

The way that Paloma described it, in the Scattered Islands the twinning was already the stuff of myth. *The plague of twins.* One day, if we succeeded, it would be the same here. There would probably be a different name, but it would be the same thing: a story told around the fire at night; a song sung by bards. Eventually, people would no longer believe it had really happened.

'They'll be saved,' he said. 'They'll never have to deal with any of this.' He waved his hand vaguely in front of him, but I knew what he meant. The unique helplessness of walking through the world knowing that your death is held in your twin's body. The manipulations and cruelties that the fatal bond permitted.

'But not us,' he went on. 'It's too late for us.'

I looked at him. He was smiling, but it was a grave smile.

'It was never going to be for us,' I said.

A crow took off nearby, its cawing two-note shriek echoing Piper's words: *Too late. Too late.*

*

That night, on the island, Piper and I slept together. Zach was in the tower; the sky was clear, and the two of us lay on a blanket on the pebbled beach.

There was a time when my body was a question, and his body might have been the answer. This was not that time: I was not in need of answers, or of comfort. I wasn't trying to escape Kip's death, or to replace him. There was none of that – just Piper's body, and his face pressed into my shoulder, his stubble on my skin, and the rocks beneath me still warm from the day's heat. The body has its own honesty: there were no words, and no lies. We knew this for what it was – not more and not less. So I took that night for what it was: not a consolation for anything, but a joy. Its own, entirely. He had said to me, a long time ago, back in New Hobart: *I need you*. I didn't need him. But I did want him, which was truer, and more real.

So we slept together, and took pleasure in one another. We were friends, after all, and had travelled a long way together. There were no surprises – we knew each other already, and knew each other's bodies, with a kind of intimacy that many lovers might not have shared. I knew his skin, and its many different colours. The freshly minted pink of his palms; the waxy feel of the patch of scar behind his left ear; the dusky place on the back of his neck where it darkened. I ran my fingers over the matte texture there, like a piece of sea-washed glass.

We had lived through a world where death was often the only gift: everything that Sally had taught Piper and Zoe.

Kip's sacrifice, for me. The capsule around Paloma's neck. It felt good to give a different kind of gift, and to receive it. We shed our distrust and our suspicions, left them on the beach next to our clothes.

There were no revelations, no declarations of love, no promises made. Each of us had enough burdens, enough obligations. Everything that needed to said that night was spoken by our bodies. We lay there in the moon's reluctant light, and looked at one another.

'It's all going to change, isn't it,' Piper said. 'I can feel it.'

'It was changing anyway,' I said. My hand was on his chest, feeling the tides of his breath. 'At least now some of the change will be for good.'

Somewhere to the north, Zoe and Paloma were sailing the dark waves, drawing closer to Elsewhere. In months, or years, the ships might come, with their cargo of medicines and machines. Nothing would ever be the same.

*

At dawn, we refilled the water casket and prepared the boat for us to sail. It was Piper who unlocked Zach's shackles. Zach didn't even respond – just let them fall between his feet, and kept staring up at the hole where the tower roof used to be. The sea was Zach's prison now.

We left him by the tower and walked down the jetty together. When we reached the boat, Piper turned back to me.

'You're not coming with me, are you.'

I smiled. Our bodies had not lied last night. We did know each other well, after all.

'Is there any point me trying to change your mind?' he said.

'No.' I looked up at him. 'I need to do this.'

'How can you forgive him?' asked Piper.

'I can't,' I said. 'It's not up to me, anyway. The only people who could forgive him are the people he killed – and they're not around to make that choice. Even Paloma's gone.' I turned back to where Zach stood, his back to us, looking up at the island's peak.

'I used to think I could save him. I used to want to redeem him, or forgive him. I don't, any more. But he's my twin. I can't change that, or make it right.' I remembered those moments in the holding house dormitory, when I'd tried to torture Zach. I had only been able to do it by turning my knife against myself. There was no freedom to be found that way – only pain and denial.

'All that I can do is own it. Live it,' I said. 'And if I go back, there's always going to be someone trying to get at me, to get at Zach. I can't even blame them for it. But I know I'd always have to be watching my back.'

'I would have kept you safe,' he said.

I squeezed his hand. 'I don't want to be kept,' I said. I had spent long enough being watched over and guarded.

'And this is better?' He waved his arm up at the island, piercing the sky. 'Just because it has a view doesn't mean it's not a prison.'

'It will be my own,' I said. No locked doors, no guards. Just me, Zach and the sea.

'It's better this way,' I went on. 'Tell everyone that we're dead. Tell them that you killed Zach yourself, if you think that will make you seem a stronger leader.' The Ringmaster had taught me well: the stories we tell are important. Sometimes they carry more weight than the truth.

'Even Elsa? Zoe?'

I smiled. 'Elsa will guess. She knows me well enough.

She knows you well enough, too. She won't believe you killed me. And she knows enough, too, to keep her mouth shut. As for Zoe—' I turned, to look over the implacable sea. 'If she comes back, I wish you luck trying to lie to her. But everyone else: tell them we're dead. It's safer for me.'

Months ago, before the attack on the canyon, Piper had worried about his legacy – about how he would be remembered. I wanted nothing more, now, than to be forgotten.

'I'll come back,' he said, 'when I can.'

I shook my head. 'You can't. You have important work to do. And every trip you make out here is a risk. Not just the journey itself, but also the chance that somebody might find out where you're going. That Zach and I are out here.'

'I'll come back,' he said again.

I didn't argue with him. Perhaps he meant it. Perhaps, one day, I would see a ship threading the needle of the harbour's narrow entrance again. I wouldn't live for such a possibility, though, or wait for it. I was waiting for nothing.

I ran a hand over his face, wondered how long I'd remember the feel of it: the ridge of his cheekbone under my palm, his stubble against my wrist.

'There's a whole new world coming,' Piper said. 'Elsewhere, and all the changes it will bring. A new time. And you're not going to see any of it.'

There were stories that were not finished yet. I did wonder about the fleet sailing for Elsewhere, and whether Zoe and Paloma would return. Whether the untwinning would happen. Whether Eva was still alive, and what song she would write about the tanks. How far Rhona and the other untanked Omegas would recover, over time. But I thought of all these things as if from a great distance. I had lived for too long with the flames. These were not my stories any more.

'I'm a seer, Piper. I've had enough of seeing what's to come.'

*

He left while the wind was still low, to get through the reef safely. We didn't hug. All that had passed between us now was too large for any single embrace, or for any farewells that could be contained in words. I stood on the burned planks of the jetty and watched him leave. He guided the boat through the harbour mouth, and was gone.

I turned back, looked up at the island's peak. There, in the rocky nest of the caldera, Zach and I would hide our final secret: that we lived.

CHAPTER 35

Some of the ghosts were waiting for me on the island. Others had followed me there. But I had learned, at last, not to try to outrun them, any more than I could outrun Zach. I made my home on the island with him, and with the unburied dead.

Zach's words came back to him, through that summer, in a piecemeal way. He could talk if he chose to, and sometimes he muttered to himself. But his words didn't fit together, and his sentences were jumbled and unclear. He could not find his place in language any more, and most of the time he chose silence. That suited me well enough.

It would have made a neat ending, if my visions had stopped altogether. Sometimes, when I saw Zach murmuring to himself, I imagined that he might have taken the visions for me. That somehow, in that moment of fire and water, when we destroyed The General's ship and the bomb machine, the visions had passed to him. His burden now, not mine, the same way that Omegas had for centuries carried the burden of the blast. It would have been fitting – a neat story. But our story was never neat, and Zach's madness was his own, as was mine.

My visions of the blast had stopped, but I still had other dreams, and other visions. Often enough I felt myself unstuck in time, as if days and years were beads on a broken necklace that I could not rethread. I saw places I had never seen, and people I had never known, and I knew they were things that had not yet come to pass. But the flames of the blast no longer flared in my mind, and that was a blessing. I felt my mind settling, like the ash after a fire.

With The General dead, and Xander and Lucia too, Zach and I were the only ones who truly knew how close the blast had come to happening again. We lived with that knowledge. We passed it from one to another as we'd once passed each other the treasured finds of our childhood days: the stone with the fossil; the empty oyster shell. We had seen what no one else had seen, and on the island we were each other's punishment and consolation.

*

The island was no idyll. We had bones to clear from the courtyard, and half-burnt spars to clear from the paths. It took us four days just to haul all of our gear up through the tunnel to the fort. We rooted through looted storerooms for whatever dry goods and utensils we could salvage. I did not go to the room that Kip and I had once shared – I didn't want Zach there, and I didn't need to disturb those memories. Instead, I chose for us a modest room on the ground floor, with a window that looked towards the lake at the crater's base. The roof leaked in heavy rain; we caught the drops in a bucket, the drip and spatter keeping us awake all night.

The terraced fields had run to seed, and needed clearing and tending. I liked the work – the honesty of a day's labour with my hands. I was responsible for what I did, and I saw the consequences daily: the weeds uprooted and massed at the field's edge for burning; the corn sown; the beans already threading their way up the poles that we planted.

Zach was more useful than I'd expected. Unaccustomed to this sort of work, his hands were soft, so at first he stopped, often, to pick at his blisters or to stretch his sore back. But he pushed on, copying whatever task I had set myself. It wasn't a penance, and it wasn't a meditation. It was work, and it needed to be done, and so we did it.

Sometimes, at night, he woke screaming. Although we shared the same room, I still saw no glimpse of his dreams. I was happy not to know. We had shared enough, he and I, and I had my own dreams to contend with. I lit a candle against the dark, if he cried, but I never asked him what his sleeping mind had shown him. There was enough horror in his past to fill a million nights, and he deserved all of it.

*

There were places on the island where the dead made more noise than the wind. When they passed me, on the narrow paths on the crater's edge, it was with the sound of arrows tearing air.

Despite these echoes, I felt no trace of Kip, and that comforted me. I had buried him now, with Piper's help, when the river had reclaimed the Ark. If Kip haunted any place, it wasn't this island where we had been happy for a while.

It didn't mean I didn't think of him. When I went down to the harbour, to fish from the rocks, I watched the water and remembered how he and I had found the way to each other, through the reef.

Kip had once said that we should run away together and build a place by the sea. Here I was, now, surrounded by sea on an island full of ghosts. It wasn't what I had wanted, then, but it was what I had. I chose it, and I lived it, finding my joy where I could. In summer, I went barefoot and felt the sun that warmed the flagstones of the fort. In autumn, I climbed to the crater's edge at dawn and watched the mist sprawling over the sea. When winter brought its storms to the island, I wrapped my blanket around me as I sat at our window and listened to what the thunder said.

The animals that the resistance once kept on the island had run wild, roaming the crater and growing fat on the crops that had never been harvested. Zach and I caught some of the goats, and coaxed a flock of chickens into a pen that we built near the courtyard. I found that I was finished with killing, so we didn't use them for meat – but we had eggs, and fresh goats' milk, and I liked to hear the clatter of goat hoofs on the top of the crater, and the sound of the roosters foretelling each dawn. It was the only prophecy I listened to, these days.

One day Zach asked me, 'Where's the river?'

I told him there was no river here – only the lake, and the small streams that sprang out of the stone when there was heavy rain. But he asked, again and again, and I wondered whether he was remembering the river of our childhood.

'It's a long way away,' I said.

It was – miles away, and years away, and there was no going back through either.

One night I dreamed of a bird that might have been a truss. It was bigger even than I had pictured it when Paloma described it. It hung in the air, its outstretched wings mirroring the horizon's curve. I didn't know whether it flew above the Scattered Islands, or whether trusses had made their way across the sea to our own land, perhaps riding the masts of ships. All I saw was the bird, its wings spread wide, holding up the sky.

ACKNOWLEDGMENTS

My extraordinary agent, Juliet Mushens, has been a superb advocate for this trilogy – I will always be grateful for her support before, during, and after publication, and for her friendship throughout. Juliet was ably assisted by Sarah Manning and Nathalie Hallam, and by my US agent, Sasha Raskin.

In the writing and editing process, Clara Haig-White has been a help beyond measure, providing both reassurance and useful criticism. Alan Haig was a thorough, generous, and invaluably pedantic reader. Andrew North was, as always, an indispensable support in matters both grammatical and emotional.

With great affection, I would particularly like to thank Julie Bonaparte, who helped to care for my son while I wrote this book, and without whose work it could not have been written.

Thank you to the entire team at HarperVoyager (UK) and Gallery Books (US) for their support of The Fire Sermon series. I'm grateful for the patience and encouragement of my editors, Natasha Bardon, Emma Coode, and

Lily Cooper (UK) and Adam Wilson (US). Thanks also to my copyeditors for this book, Joy Chamberlain and Janette Currie (UK) and Joal Hetherington (US), and my proofreader Simon Fox (UK). Warm thanks also to my publishers and translators around the world, for taking my books on such wonderful journeys, and reaching such diverse readers.